Deadly
Remains

by

KATHERINE BAYLESS

Printed in the USA

First Printing, October 2010

Second Edition, December 2015

ISBN 978-0-9971055-2-0

www.katherinebayless.com

For my husband Scot, who never let me doubt that writing a book was possible.

CONTENTS

ACKNOWLEDGMENTS

Scot deserves thanks not only for his encouragement but also the hours devoted to reading, editing, and explaining the intricacies of English grammar—sometimes to a grumpy recipient. Trish and Sarina, my trusted first readers, your honest opinions and helpful suggestions were invaluable. Without Agnes and Mina, my French dialog would have been barely accurate web translations. Thank you, Dave, for your last minute, diligent edits. Mom, I know it isn't your typical fare, but thanks for giving it a whirl.

One

Gloves are the mark of a clairvoyant. Of course, if you're over twenty-five, then the true mark is the small tattoo on each of your hands, just above the first thumb knuckle. No, not scarlet—blue. Blue ink. It's the color that fades the least over time, or so I've been told. The government would know. They've had over a hundred years of perfecting the craft—a hundred years and thousands of test subjects. Even if someone tried to get rid of the marks, the scars were an obvious sign. Once they got you, it was for life.

Five years after I was born, the tattooing stopped. I can have mine removed legally now, just a simple procedure and a little pain, but there's not much point. I have to wear gloves if I don't want to go insane, and they mark me anyway, especially when it's the middle of July and 98 degrees outside. Not that there are many 98 degree days here in Seattle, but gloves in the summer, whether it's hot or not, are a giveaway. Some clairvoyants wear flesh-colored cloth to avoid being so obvious, but I've never been the type to hide what I am. I don't flaunt it, but I'm not going to keep to the shadows either. Don't get me wrong, if I could shed the gloves, I would. Wearing them all the time gets really old, trust me. But if I don't want to end up in a clean-room, I have to wear them. The thin stretch of fabric is what keeps me from experiencing all the memories lurking within whatever I happen to touch.

Deadly Remains - Chapter One

At the moment, however, my long, black gloves were lying on a table next to my water bottle in an interrogation room at the Chiliquitham Police Department. I sat across from Vince Vanelli, a hard-faced detective with a body to match, who had a chip on his shoulder large enough to house an entire family of woodchucks.

Detective Vanelli glared at me. "Something funny?"

I decided not to tell him about the woodchucks. Just a guess, but I was betting he wouldn't find that visual particularly amusing.

I shook my head and lied. "Nothing. I was just thinking about a friend of mine. So, are we going to get down to business soon? I have another appointment at eleven." It was an effort to sound polite, since the detective had been nothing but unfriendly ever since we sat down.

He gave me a cold glare and it was probably worth a squirm or two, but I was accustomed to receiving unfriendly stares. It didn't faze me, and since I refused to flinch, I stared back and gave him the once over. The detective's eyes had been continually narrowed from the first moment we met, but I noted they were brown and most likely strikingly large when he wasn't pissed off. The Italian roots his name implied were done proud. Although his skin didn't wander far into the Mediterranean olive tones, it was obvious he was more likely to tan than burn from the sun. He had a strong jaw counterbalanced by slender eyebrows and thick, dark-brown hair cut in a mid-length tousled style. When they weren't pressed together in an expression of annoyance, his lips were full and well defined. If not for the detective's rude demeanor and sourpuss face, I'd have said he was attractive.

"Lieutenant Jensen will be here in a few minutes."

"Okay." I leaned back as best I could in the straight-backed metal chair and placed my hands in my lap. The last thing I wanted to do was touch the interrogation table. It was bound to have some seriously bad vibes that I didn't need floating around in my head. I could put my gloves back on, but I didn't want to waste the effort. I hoped this other officer would show up soon to spare me any more stunning discussion with Ace Detective Vince Vanelli.

After a few more minutes of excruciating silence and blank stares from Vanelli, I surrendered to my curiosity and indulged in some chain yanking. "So, you guys called my agency, but it wasn't your idea, was it?" This wasn't much of a guess. The detective had been about as welcoming as a rattlesnake doormat.

His gaze sharpened. "Why do you say that?"

Because you're acting like a complete jerk. "Oh, nothing paranormal. It's just that you haven't said boo about the case yet. So, it has me thinking you're either really shy, or maybe you don't want to share information about the case with someone like me."

"There's no maybe about it. Asking you here was definitely not my idea." He looked away and muttered, "We don't need any magical mumbo jumbo to help us solve this case. Intellect and shoe leather will get us what we need. And we won't have any worries about whether the evidence is admissible." He glared back at me. "So, you're right. This was not my idea."

Intellect and shoe leather? *Please.*

I took perverse pleasure in revealing the detective's bigotry, although it was hardly surprising. His behavior wasn't anything I hadn't encountered on countless occasions. It was almost entertaining.

My mission accomplished, I gave him a poised, relaxed smile. "I see. Thanks for your candor, Detective. I'm accustomed to working with officers who have opinions like yours. I've dealt with that attitude all my life, so I'm pretty used to it. In fact, I welcome it." I gave him a direct look. "It makes it easier to gloat later when I help you solve the case."

This wasn't an idle boast. I had an excellent track record with several police agencies. My name was fairly well-known, and the FBI had called me in more than once. Okay, so they called only when the case had grown cold, but hey, they had called me two times already. I was on a roll.

Deadly Remains - Chapter One

Detective Vanelli's jaw tightened, but I was spared any further comments by the arrival of a tall, beefy man in a brown suit. He was large, in a linebacker-ish sort of way, with a fair amount of muscle to go with his over-indulgences, but I guessed his days of pursuing a six-minute mile were long gone. His neatly trimmed beard was peppered with gray and it stood in contrast to the wavy, unkempt style of his hair. Although his beard showed some age, his thick head of brown hair did not. Despite the gray, I put his age at thirty-five, maybe forty. His tie was loose and askew, and he gave me an open smile that told me we were going to get along just fine. I was sure this was the person who requested me.

I stood up but folded my arms. I returned his smile with a bright one of my own, so he didn't misinterpret my stance.

"Sorry to keep you waiting, Ms. Devon. Never enough hours in the day." He withdrew his hand when he realized I wasn't going to shake it. "I'm Lieutenant Jensen. Did you meet Detective Sergeant Vanelli?"

I nodded. "Yes, I did. Please, call me Lire." Most people who saw my name on my business card pronounced it wrong. This way they'd hear it correctly from the beginning—*leer*. I wiggled my hands so he could see I wasn't wearing my gloves. "Sorry. I didn't realize someone else was coming. I was all set to handle whatever it is you guys want me to read."

Most clairvoyants made a habit of never shaking hands, even with gloves, but I didn't bother pointing this out. The fact was bound to draw further attention to my 'otherness' and make them more nervous about dealing with me.

"Don't worry about it. Besides, I bet it's nice to take those things off every once in a while, eh?" Lieutenant Jensen rounded the table and took the seat next to Detective Vanelli.

Either Jensen was unusually perceptive or knew someone who had similar problems. "Most people don't think about that. Maybe you know someone who's touch sensitive?"

He nodded and his smile faded. "My sister's kid. It's been tough for them." The pain was apparent on his face. I'd say 'tough' was an understatement. If it was anything like my experience, then they were going through hell.

"Most of us have similar experiences, especially if no one else in the family is a practitioner. Have they hooked up with a support group? Getting with people who have been through it can do wonders." When I glanced at Vanelli, he regarded me with an inquisitive expression but covered it quickly with his cool stare.

"Yeah, they live over in Tacoma. I think they hooked up with the, uh, what's it called?" Jensen narrowed his eyes to slits and poked the side of his head with his finger. "The Paranormal Help Network, I think."

"Oh, that's great. The PHN is a good group. I speak there occasionally. They should help a bunch. Things are so much better than they used to be. When I was growing up, there were pretty much just two options: paranormal boarding school or the reservations. There wasn't any support for the parents who wanted to keep their gifted child at home."

I ended up with the boarding school. Of the two choices that was definitely the better. There was no third choice. My Mom couldn't handle it. To a certain extent, I couldn't blame her too much. I'd learned all of her dark secrets after holding her hand at the park. At three-and-a-half, I had to come to terms with the fact that both of my parents were scared shitless of me. Needless to say, I didn't have a very happy childhood. When I was five, my parents packed me off to a boarding school northeast of Seattle. Actually, I was fortunate my parents had the money to send me to a private school. The paranormal reservations are not the nicest of places to live, much less grow up. All things considered, I was much better off being raised in the confines of Coventry Academy, by teachers who at least had a clue about dealing with children with magical abilities.

"So, Detective Vanelli was just getting ready to tell me about what you guys need me to look at today." Amazingly,

Deadly Remains - Chapter One

I was able to keep a pleasant, professional expression on my face.

"Uh-huh." I don't think Jensen was fooled. "What we've got is a shirt from a murder victim."

In response to Jensen's statement, Vanelli pulled out a package that must have been resting in his lap and then slid it down the table.

"Boy. You guys don't ask for much, do you?" I hadn't expected a serious reading and needed to conserve energy for my upcoming clients.

"If you can't handle it, let's just move on and stop wasting each other's time." Vanelli regarded me with angry, narrowed eyes.

"*Please*. I never said I couldn't do it." I sighed and directed my explanation to Jensen. "Because the appointment was made last minute, it's not a full session. I assumed you guys knew what that meant."

Most people assume clothing is easy to read because it has intimate contact with a person. But, for that very reason, such a psychically charged object can be challenging, especially if the person experienced something emotionally disturbing. It's easy to become overwhelmed by the memories. Only an experienced clairvoyant can control the inputs and separate out the important details. It also requires a lot of physical stamina.

Jensen gave me a puzzled look and Vanelli regarded me with a smug expression.

"More excuses. I think we're finished here." Vanelli stood up to leave.

"Hang on, Vince." Jensen looked tired.

Vanelli stopped, but he didn't retake his seat. He just crossed his arms and made a point of looking down at me with an annoyed expression.

I know it was partially my fault that Vanelli was in my face, but it still pissed me off. Their lack of knowledge made me appear weak, and my professional reputation was important to me. I guessed whoever set up the appointment didn't fax the detectives my background sheet, which specifies what to expect from me and how much time is needed for the different types of readings. When I got back to the office, I was going to have some serious words with Monica—not that it would do any good. We all knew why she remained employed, and it had nothing to do with her dispatching skills.

Jensen leaned forward. "Ms. Devon, time is critical. I appealed to your partner for an emergency appointment because we have a fresh crime scene. I want an opinion from an expert such as yourself before we pack it in."

Okay, Plan B: Monica was off the hook; it was time to rumble with Jack.

"Jack neglected to inform me of the situation, and I guess he didn't fax you my background sheet." I sighed. "Let's go ahead and see what happens. Hopefully I won't pass out."

Jensen looked concerned. "I'm reluctant to delay, but would a later appointment be better?" He glanced over at Vanelli and got an answering 'I told you so' look that I personally wanted to scrape off Vanelli's face with a blowtorch.

I chuckled. "Don't worry. I'm sure it'll be fine. Open the bag and dump the shirt in front of me. Let's see what we've got." I scooted myself toward the table, no small feat considering I had to do it without touching the chair with my hands. Kudos for me, I managed to get comfortable without falling on my face.

Vanelli retook his seat as Jensen poured the shirt from the bag. It landed in a soft, purple heap in front of me. The fabric was silk, or maybe that new synthetic stuff, I forget what they call it, but it looks and feels just like the real thing. It appeared to be a women's blouse. From the color and the size of the pile, I didn't think it belonged to a man. There were several stains on the fabric. I avoided thinking too closely about them.

Apparently, I was taking too long for Vanelli's taste. "Is there a problem?"

Deadly Remains - Chapter One

I shot him a scathing look and wished my magic extended to curses. I would have given anything to send a couple hundred boils his way.

I directed my conversation to Jensen since he was the only supportive person in the room. "Lieutenant Jensen, when I touch the blouse, please keep things as quiet as possible. With fewer distractions, I'll have more focus and won't have to expend as much energy. It'd be nice if I can make it to my next client without keeling over."

I winked at him, and he chuckled before nodding and turning serious. "Will do. And, you can drop the Lieutenant. Jensen's fine. Or Rich."

"Gotcha. Jensen. Thanks," I said with a genuine smile. When I glanced over at Detective Vanelli, he just continued to stare at me icily. I turned away before my smile turned into something less friendly.

I considered the blouse and prepared myself for what I expected to be some serious emotional baggage and, most likely, at least one traumatic, violent experience. I've been asked, more times than I can count, to describe my power and what it feels like. What do I do? How does it work? What do I experience? My ability was frustratingly difficult to put into words; after all, everything happened in my head. So, I usually resorted to clichés to explain it.

I started by closing off areas of my mind to avoid the full impact of the blouse. Most practitioners described this process as building up a psychic shield. When I was ready, I touched the fabric. My magic flared from my core with blinding speed, sucking in the object's essence. As the energy rushed into my mind, I used my shield to push it round and round until it formed a disk; like a music CD. Once everything swirled in my mind, I was free to examine things more closely.

I detected several fouled streams, the most corrupted of which lurked at the outside edge. Those were the most recent memories. A fuzzy tail, at the very end of the disk, told me another psychic had previously read the blouse. If I examined it, I could probably determine which clairvoyant had read the blouse before me. There weren't many of us who worked with the police and most didn't have the power to hide their identities. My shield was strong enough that I rarely left a mark behind.

I stopped procrastinating and lowered myself into the stream just prior to the most fouled section. I wasn't ready for the heavy stuff yet. I decided to keep myself fairly shielded, even though it meant getting a choppy view of things. I could always get more details later.

I'm anxious and depressed. I smell wet leaves, feel mist on my face. I'm walking down a poorly lit street. A forest looms next to the road. Work sucks. Pizza. Justin's Pizza. Anger burns in my chest. Eric said he'd pick me up. It's so dark. And the forest is darker. I shouldn't walk home alone. It's late, and that old farmhouse gives me the creeps. What am I going to do about Eric? I should dump him. He's a jerk, but I don't want to be alone. I probably can't get any better anyway. The other day he called me a whore in front of everyone. Oooh! That made me so mad! Why didn't I break up with him right then? I am such an idiot. What was that? I scream. That jerk! It's Eric. I see him running down the trail, laughing at me.

I didn't bother experiencing the murder. I already knew who the killer was. I also knew the identity of the victim. The blouse slid from my hands, the buttons clacking softly against the tabletop as it landed.

"I guess my credentials weren't enough to convince you I'm legit?" I glared at both detectives and then rubbed my hands over my face. If I wasn't so tired, I might have been more tempted to storm out of the room. I leaned back in my chair instead. Chalk one up to professionalism.

"What do you mean?" Jensen asked. It struck me that Lieutenant Rich Jensen excelled at playing 'good cop.' Vanelli was a definite ringer for 'bad cop.' He didn't even have to act.

"Come on! Give me some credit, *Lieutenant*. This blouse belonged to Jessica Levin and you know it. A couple years ago, her boyfriend Eric Parks murdered her. It was in all the papers for months. Somehow, I don't think this is the case you guys need help with." I crossed my arms, refusing to feel bad about snapping at him.

Jensen cleared his throat. "No. It isn't."

I was all set to rip him a new one when I saw the expression on his face—grim determination and, now, some hope.

He pushed the blouse into the bag with the end of his pencil, careful not to touch it with his bare hands. "It's been suggested that any clairvoyant who can deal with this without a problem might be able to help us. You were one of the practitioners we were told to contact."

"Really." My anger faded, and I didn't try to hold on to it. "And who told you that?"

"Judith Kitchell. Randy Peterson also suggested we give you a call. Judith was the expert we used on the Levin case. After doing what you just did, she was unconscious for an hour. The blouse has become a sort of benchmark, you might say."

"Alright, you've got my attention. Judith and Randy are among the best in the business. Are you telling me they both turned you down for this case?"

There weren't many things that would deter Judith. She owned Which Witch, the talent agency that rivaled mine. Randy ran the psi-ward down at Coventry Hospital. They were both exceptional clairvoyants and tough. I guess you had to be tough, just to survive on the outside. If not, you ended up in a clean-room at a state-run psi-hospital. There weren't many of us willing to work with the public, much less the police. Because of that, Judith and I often referred clients to one another.

"We need your help. So far, you're the only one who has come close." Jensen hadn't answered my question, so I took it as a yes. They both had turned him down.

"Fine. But can we please just get down to it?" Worn-out from my psi-expenditure and tired of the games, I just wanted to cut to the chase.

Jensen sat back in his chair, trying not to look triumphant, and nodded at Vanelli.

Vanelli retrieved a file folder from the empty chair next to him. "Later today, we'd like you to take a look at our newest site. These are the photos of the first crime scene." He had put on his professional voice. It was deep and confident, without a trace of hostility. He waited while I donned my gloves and then handed me the folder.

I wanted to ask, 'What kind of crime scene?' but didn't want to give Vanelli any ammunition. Never show weakness to your enemies. I'm pretty sure it's a rule somewhere. I wasn't sure if Vanelli was the enemy, but I erred on the side of caution.

I prepared myself for the worst and opened the folder. The first photo had been taken from outside a crime scene. Yellow 'DO NOT CROSS' tape encircled the trunks of several large evergreen trees. Since I didn't see any carnage, I slowly let out my held breath and told the butterflies to take five. Although the location looked heavily forested, the photo centered on an area unnaturally devoid of vegetation. A pile of driftwood sat in the center of the clearing. Since this was a photo of a crime scene and there weren't sunbathers or seashells in view, I guessed it wasn't driftwood.

I placed the photo face down on the table. The next one had been taken from within the circle of police tape. From the closer vantage, the objects in the center of the dirt patch became clear. They were human bones. The precariously balanced skull faced obliquely to the camera. For some reason, I found the way it lolled to one side particularly disturbing. Inside the perimeter, I noticed one—no, make that two—circular green spots where the dirt met the lush green surroundings. The small patches were spaced a fair distance apart. It wasn't clear whether these spots continued around the entire circumference because less than half of the large dirt area was visible. I put the photo on top of the earlier one.

In the third photo, the photographer had taken a close-up of one of the green spots. A ruler had been placed through its center, showing it to be nearly four inches in diameter. The circle of flattened grass stood in sharp contrast to the brown powdery looking soil that comprised ground zero. Easy cliché, that. The large dirt area looked as though a blast, centering on the bones, cremated everything around it. Outside of the blast zone, clumps of lush grass, wet leaves, and mossy twigs covered the ground. Inside, there seemed to be nothing except the bones and the small round patches of green at the outer edge. A sense of dread began to percolate in the pit of my stomach.

I flipped through five or six more photos, noticing nothing new, until I came to one showing a circular patch of unaffected vegetation inside the blast zone. Unlike the other grassy spots, which were at the very edge of the barren circle, this one looked like it was larger and further inside. There wasn't a ruler to show the size of the patch, but in the background of the photo, two of the smaller green spots were visible in the distance. I could only guess at the size of this larger circle—perhaps three feet in diameter?

After viewing the rest of the photos, I picked them up, tapped their edges on the table to straighten the stack, and put them back in the file folder. During my study session, the boys had been quiet, interrupting me only once to ask if I wanted coffee. I'd mainline coffee if I could, but the Chiliquitham PD didn't use psi-free beans, so I had to pass.

Jensen took the file folder from me. "What can you tell us? I know it's not the same as being there, but I'd appreciate hearing your opinion anyway."

Both Jensen and Vanelli had retaken their seats. Jensen held a mechanical pencil at the ready, while Vanelli's brushed stainless-steel pen sat on top of his small notebook.

I put both of my glove-encased elbows on the table and folded my arms. "I have a couple of questions first if you don't mind." Jensen nodded, so I asked, "You said these were from the first crime scene. How does the newest crime scene compare with this one?"

Even though my question had nothing to do with assessing the photos, Jensen answered, "Almost identical. Different locations, of course, but the MO is the same."

"And the small green patches around the edge of the blast zone ... are there five of them?" My stomach clenched. The scenario I dreaded hinged on this question.

Jensen's left eyebrow went up. "Yes."

I closed my eyes briefly and sighed. "And the new site has the same configuration—a roughly circular dirt area with the small circles around the perimeter?" I looked first at Jensen and then at Vanelli. They both nodded.

"I didn't see a photo that showed a ruler next to the larger grass circle. How big was it?"

Jensen looked puzzled and leafed through the photos in the folder. "We must be missing a shot. I'll check into it." He glanced at Vanelli for confirmation. "I'd say five feet wide, give or take."

Vanelli nodded in agreement.

Again, not what I wanted to hear. I regarded the two men steadily. If my theory was correct, then I wasn't the only magic user the detectives needed to consult. I had a sinking feeling they weren't going to like hearing it.

"Have you called a witch or warlock to the site yet?"

Vanelli muttered something unintelligible under his breath.

"I assume that translates to no."

Jensen folded his arms. "After investigating the first site, it was ruled an accidental death. Now that we have a second, nearly identical scene, it seemed prudent to call in someone like you."

"So, the original theory was ... what? Spell backfires and nukes the mage?"

"Yes." Jensen looked almost sheepish. "There were only one set of tracks leading toward the scene and none leading out. At the time, it seemed clear cut that a magic user had lost control of a spell and suffered the consequences."

I didn't criticize. In his shoes, with limited knowledge of magic, I might have guessed the same thing. I nodded. "You'll want to have a witch or warlock examine the newest site, preferably one who has knowledge of the dark arts." I figured this would go over about as well as a stripper at a church social, but I plunged ahead anyway. "If you don't have a contact, I can arrange something for you."

Vanelli stared at me like I had thrown up pea soup and my head was doing 360s. "We're not putting any devil worshipers on the payroll."

Jensen said, "I have to agree with Vince. There's not much chance of convincing this department to hire a black magician, even if I wanted to, and I don't. It was an uphill battle bringing *you* in."

I shook my head. "Just because someone is familiar with the dark arts, it doesn't mean they're a devil worshiper." The explanation was useless, but I felt obligated to battle ignorance whenever I came across it. I'm sure my eyes flashed hotly, mostly at Vanelli, but his magi-phobia had rubbed me raw. "You do understand there is a difference, right? The dark arts encompass a field of magic dealing with death and darkness, not the devil. A devil worshiper can be a magic user *or* a normal. The point is anyone can be in the devil's employ. Practicing black magic doesn't automatically make the practitioner a devil worshiper. Just like owning a gun doesn't make you a murderer."

I held up my hand before either of them could respond. "I know. It doesn't change things, but magic stereotyping and hysteria really gets on my nerves. That's the type of thing that led to the Salem witch trials."

Jensen glanced at Vanelli and received a set of raised eyebrows in return. The hired help was getting uppity.

"Why should a witch look at the scene?" Jensen asked.

"Because a witch may be able to sense the type of spell that was used."

"And you can't?"

"No. I'm a psychic, not a spell caster. We all have magic, but it's not used in the same way." I shook my head, waving them off. Getting into a huge discussion about why psychics were different than spell casters would only cause more confusion, so I switched tack. "Look, I can tell you whether I sense magic, but I won't be able to tell you exactly what flavor. In my opinion, this is a case of human sacrifice. What the perpetrator needed the power for, I don't know. A witch might be able to tell you."

"Why do you think this was a human sacrifice?" Vanelli had taken up his pen and jotted a few notes.

"Because I'm pretty sure the large dirt circle was a circle of power. A circle of power is used for one of two reasons: to keep power or magic from escaping, or to prevent magic from entering, or both. Okay, make that three reasons." I smiled and then shrugged. "In the photos, the circle looks large. And it had been delineated by runes, placed in the form of a pentagram. The runes are what protected the smaller patches of grass around the edge. The warlock then placed another circle inside the main one, which he may have used to summon a demon or other magical creature. Or I suppose he may have used it to protect himself."

Vanelli peered at me. "That's what the larger green patch was, another circle of power?"

"Yes."

"Why would he or she summon a demon?" Jensen asked, glancing up from his notepad.

"In this case, I'm not sure. A creature is summoned when the conjurer needs something it can provide—typically power or knowledge or both."

Jensen frowned. "Could the creature have escaped and killed the magician?"

"That's always a risk when a mage summons a demon, but I don't think that's what happened in this case. We know the smaller circle of power was in force when the final spell culminated because the vegetation inside of it wasn't destroyed."

"And someone picked up the runes and carried them away," Vanelli observed. "Although, an accomplice could have waited outside the main circle and remained unaffected?"

I nodded. "Yes. All the magic was confined to the main circle."

Jensen asked, "Do most magicians use runes?"

Deadly Remains - Chapter One

"Magician is a name for someone who does parlor tricks. A *magus* is someone who practices magic." Shrugging, I answered his question, "No, only witches and warlocks use runes. You know the difference between witchcraft and sorcery, right?" I regarded the detectives' confused expressions. "A witch or warlock is a magus who can only employ spoken or chanted magic and they often use runes to power or strengthen their spells." They both nodded, so I continued, "A sorcerer or sorceress, on the other hand, doesn't use spoken words of power to cast a spell. They use gestures. Runes are of no use to them."

Jensen tilted his head, looking thoughtful. "Interesting. So a witch has to use words and a sorceress uses gestures."

Like most people, he had used the terms witch and sorceress interchangeably and assumed they were the same because they both practiced magic.

"Yes. A sorceress is more powerful than a witch in that regard, but they are restricted to a specific field of magic. You've heard of necromancers, haven't you? Well, a necromancer is a sorcerer who has power over the dead but can't practice other forms of magic, say, like conjuring fire or turning a boulder into dust. There are many types of sorcerers—sorcerers with power over light, earth, wind, fire, just about anything you can think of—and most of the time they have skill in just one area of magic."

Vanelli put his left elbow on the table and waved his pen at me. "Let me get this straight. You think a witch or warlock set up this circle of power and the second pentagram, possibly called up a demon, and murdered the victim, all to gain power for a spell that blasted the entire circle flat?"

I nodded. "From only the photos, yeah, that's what I think." I wasn't able to suppress a shudder. "The mage who did this is beyond redemption. They're bad. Bad, bad, bad." I rubbed my hand across my mouth and chin as though the action would wipe away the horror of the act. "This person cares nothing for human life, much less the threefold principle. And to work with a demon in this way ... " I shook my head.

Jensen cocked his head to the side. "The threefold principle?"

"It's a widely held belief among magic users and those close to the magic community. It basically means whatever you do will come back to you threefold. You reap what you sow."

"Back to the crime scene." Vanelli motioned toward the closed manila folder. "If the warlock didn't use the second circle for protection and used it for a demon instead, how did he or she survive the blast? It destroyed every trace of organic matter inside the circle and presumably cleaned the bones like they'd been sitting there for years."

There was a slight chance Vanelli was starting to impress me. Even though he was a bigoted, magi-phobic SOB, he was paying attention and seemed to be treating the case as though there wasn't anything strange about a warlock serial killer who was sacrificing victims for a power boost. In fact, he hadn't said anything inflammatory for five or ten minutes, easy.

I answered him honestly. "I don't know. Quite possibly it has something to do with the type of spell he used."

"You're not a witch, how do you know this is the likely scenario?"

I frowned. "Detective Vanelli, are you familiar with Coventry Academy?" When I received an answering nod, I continued while trying hard not to sound snippy. "That's where I grew up. From the age of five, I spent all of my school years there, all the way through high school. Most of my friends were witches, sorcerers, cursed, or psychically inclined. And, for the past seven years, I have co-owned a paranormal talent agency, where everyone, except my partner and receptionist, has some sort of magical ability."

He raised his eyebrows. "Is that all?"

I was all set to say something scathing when I realized Vanelli was teasing me. Okay, so maybe I didn't have him figured out. I sat with my mouth hanging open and nothing to say came to mind. Somehow I managed to close my mouth before I drooled on my shirt. The day was looking up.

Deadly Remains - Chapter One

I sighed. "I don't know all there is to know about magic— far from it. But, I know quite a bit, and it tells me this is a case of human sacrifice. To get as much information as possible, I strongly recommend you seek the opinion of a witch or warlock."

"Ms. Devon, I know you're not a witch, but you do have a useful gift that might help us. I'd like you to take a look at our new crime scene later today. I realize you have an appointment coming up, but are you available afterward?" Jensen asked.

I knew he was in a difficult position, so I couldn't very well say no. "I'm pretty booked up, but I can probably shift some things around." I retrieved my iPhone from my purse and checked the calendar. "I think I can free up a couple of hours after one o'clock."

"Fair enough. Vince will take you to the scene."

Lucky me. I tried not to sigh out loud.

Before escorting me from the room, Jensen paused to consider me. "If a co-worker goes out on call with you today, I guess they'd have to tag along."

I must have looked puzzled because Jensen gave me a quick wink. If Vanelli disagreed with Jensen's ploy, he covered it with a bored stare.

Now the question was: who could I get to accompany me at such short notice?

Vanelli and I made arrangements for him to meet me at Sotheby's at one o'clock, and I left the station feeling the suspicious stares of everyone I passed press into my back. My instincts screamed at me to draw in my head like a turtle and slink my way out of the building, but I sternly reminded myself that I was not a freak. I was a good person with an unusual gift. Instead of lowering my head in shame, I forced myself to smile pleasantly, make eye contact with everyone nearby, and strut like a runway model out the front door, but it sure wasn't easy.

Once I had folded myself into my car and enveloped myself in black upholstery, tinted windows, and high-tech gadgetry, I slumped down and took what I told myself was a deep cleansing breath, not a sigh of dejection. Before I could revel any further in self-pity, movement from the passenger seat caught my eye. A muffled voice echoed from inside my ridiculously priced designer shoulder bag.

"Why do you persist in dealing with these stake-burners anyway?" The voice was deep—ironic considering its source was a six-inch black teddy bear—and it resonated with an unusual accent and cadence that I always found comforting.

His fuzzy head popped out of my open handbag, followed, with some difficulty, by the rest of his adequately stuffed body. I moved my arm, so he could perch on the center console armrest.

I gave him an exasperated look as I started the car's engine to get some air circulating, and then folded down the sun visor to regard my partial reflection in the small rectangular mirror. There weren't any improvements over my slap dash makeup application from earlier in the morning, but I spied a fine dark-red eyelash that had fallen onto the bridge of my freckled nose. I wiped it away before regarding my green eyes with a sigh.

"Red, do you have to ask me that every time I meet up with a psi-challenged police officer?" After snapping shut the mirror's cover, I turned to look at my companion.

"Of course I do." He sat with his cute teddy bear legs hanging over the edge of the armrest, kicking them back and forth. I tried not to find the action endearing but failed miserably.

"Why?" I glanced around the parking lot. Conversing with Red wasn't extraordinary—he had been my confidant since childhood—but anyone who noticed me talking to a teddy bear was likely to come to a different conclusion.

"Because I have yet to hear a sufficient answer."

I closed my eyes and pressed my head against the seatback. "I know. What can I say? I'm a sucker. I'm a glutton for punishment."

Deadly Remains - Chapter One

When Red didn't immediately respond, I opened my eyes and gazed down at him. "That wasn't a sufficient answer, was it?"

Red regarded me with his black button eyes, head tilted, legs swinging. "No. It wasn't."

I threw my hands down into my lap. "Oh, I don't know. I guess I just want to help people. I want to turn this curse of mine into something positive, besides cash flow. I have more money than I know what to do with, especially with what Dad left me, and it's made things easier, but there's got to be more to life than just being comfortable. Helping the police seems like the right thing to do, and it exposes people to my gift, hopefully showing them it's not something to be feared."

"You realize you called your magic both a curse and a gift in almost the same breath?"

"What can I say? I'm conflicted."

"That much is certain," he told me.

"You're not making me feel any better."

"Easily remedied."

Red slid from the edge of the armrest to the center console, deftly skirting the gearshift, and pressed a button to select a CD from the disk changer. Suddenly we were bathed in a pulsing riot of backbeat and harmony that had my fingers tapping and head bopping all the way to downtown Seattle.

When we were most of the way there, I turned down the volume and asked Red what he thought about the Chiliquitham murder.

"Without viewing the photos, I cannot say. However, from what I overheard, your theory sounds plausible."

"If I take you to the site, can you tell me what spells were used?" I asked.

"Perhaps. It has been a long time since I have been in the presence of high magic."

Before Red became my companion, he lived a human life as an outcast necromancer in seventeenth century America.

The teddy bear was only the latest vessel housing his soul and probably wouldn't be the last.

Although he lost his skills in sorcery when he died, Red could still detect magic. He had also been enchanted with several useful spells when he became my familiar.

On my mental list of experts, Red was the most qualified, and I wasn't likely to get any of the others to accompany me to the crime scene on such short notice.

"You're just being humble. Jake is the only one I could call at the last minute, and he's on vacation this week. Besides, I'd rather owe you a favor than him."

Jake frequently pestered me to read items that belonged to his girlfriend of the week. God knows what he wanted to know. I always refused to do it. That's all I needed, intimate knowledge of Jake and his girlfriend. No thanks.

I considered Red's past. "Do you mind too much? I know you're not terribly enamored of the police."

His hatred may have mellowed since his execution during the Salem witch trials, but Red had little good to say about public servants and the judicial system. It bothered him that I spent time helping them, and I suddenly realized one of the reasons I aided the police was out of spite. Spite for what happened to Red all those years ago. A small part of me wanted nothing more than to rub their noses in my power, to show them I was better because of it, and to make them feel inadequate. However, down deep, I knew this wasn't the key to easing the past, or fixing the present. I had other more noble reasons for aiding the police, and they had nothing to do with personal retribution and everything to do with getting the bad guys.

"I will help you not because I think the police deserve it, but because this warlock must be stopped. A crime like this could set us back three hundred years." He paused before adding, "I am also curious to hear how you intend to explain my expert credentials to Detective Vanelli."

He wasn't the only one.

TWO

We arrived at the Puget Pacific Towers twenty minutes early. After telephoning Monica to adjust my afternoon schedule, I decided to walk over to Peabody's Beans for a cappuccino fix.

My favorite coffee shop was owned and operated by Julie and Steven Peabody, who started their business before anyone else envisioned the popularity of psi-free products. Their coffees, teas, and treats (not to mention the paper cups, stir sticks, sugar, et cetera) were prepared using materials untouched by humans, which meant misfits like me didn't end up with disturbing visions with every bite or sip. Fortunately, psi-free products appealed to more than just the psychically sensitive, since there weren't nearly enough of us to keep a specialty business like Julie's afloat. Untouched products had taken off with the health conscious crowd, too. Even regular folks liked the idea. Julie and Steve managed to get in at the ground floor, just before the psi-free craze took off. Of course, it didn't hurt that their coffee was top notch.

Peabody's Beans was across the street and a block down from Sotheby's, in a brick-fronted building with a hunter-green metal awning. Ten-foot tinted windows ran the length of the first floor, with glass doors splitting the distance in half. On the door marked 'PUSH,' a bright orange sign advised me the store was going to close early on Saturday.

Deadly Remains - Chapter Two

As I pushed my way into the shop, two chattering women on their way out abruptly stopped talking when they noticed me. I did my best to overlook their surprised and somewhat frantic expressions as they skirted to the side, taking the widest detour possible without running into tables. Their behavior was almost comical, but I kept my expression neutral. It used to bother me deeply—all the startled and horrified expressions and the way people tended to treat me like a pariah. I'd learned to ignore it, although, some days I was better at it than others. I reminded myself for the millionth time that clairvoyants were a rare breed and the number of urban legends about us had filled several books. Their behavior was understandable. With so few of us around, most people didn't have any real life experiences to help discredit all the erroneous and farfetched stories. It was no wonder so many people were scared of us. At least, that's what I told myself. Often.

I strode past the startled women, inhaling the rich coffee smell, and looked behind the counter for Julie. Over the years and countless espresso shots, we had grown to know each other and now I considered her to be one of my dearest friends.

The line wasn't too long. Three customers away from the counter, Julie noticed me and waved. Her long, chestnut hair was tied up into a smooth ponytail high on the top of her head. With a section of braid strategically covering the elastic band, the up-do made me think of Barbara Eden from *I Dream Of Jeannie*, the old show from the 1960s, except Julie had brown hair instead of blonde. Although before my time, I could hardly consider the show's premise without shaking my head. Clearly, the person who created the sitcom had never met a djinn in person. The Barbara Eden character was nothing like a true djinn, and I inwardly shuddered at the thought of a human marrying one.

I moved up in line, now only moments away from espresso goodness. Julie and Steven maneuvered behind the bar like partners in a synchronized dance. After years of running the store and pulling countless shots, they moved between the machines, refrigerators, and pastry cases with ease. I couldn't think of a time when I'd ever seen them get in each other's way.

Under her dark green apron, Julie wore a faded gray sleeveless shirt-dress that showed off her toned arms. A vibrant tie-died shawl cinched her narrow waist, which she had coordinated with faded orange Keds. Julie always looked comfortable and hip. I couldn't help but envy her free-spirited nature and eccentric style. She wasn't afraid to try new things and always seemed to maintain a positive attitude about everything.

When I reached the front of the line, Julie made my usual and then gave Steven the signal that he was on his own. Steven waved at me while I stuck my customary payment, which they always refused to accept, into the tip jar. Julie came around the counter and we found a small round table near the front window. I hung my wool coat over the back of the chair before sitting.

"How're things going lately? You on your way to Sotheby's?" Julie asked as we sat down.

"Yep. I'm a little early, so I thought I'd kill some time."

"Uh-huh." We both knew I'd stop by, even if I were running late. Coffee was my vice.

I made a sound of appreciation while savoring a sip from my cup. I smiled. "I'm doing good. What's up with you? I like your hair, by the way. Oh! Did Tom get the job?"

She looked surprised. "Yes! I'm sorry. I forgot to tell you. He found out a couple days ago. He is so happy, and he told me to tell you thank you. He thought your reference really cinched it."

"Nah. It might have helped get him in the door, but they wouldn't have hired him if he weren't the right one for the job. That's great news."

A couple of months ago, Julie's brother had asked me to put in a word for him with the administration at Coventry Academy. I contacted Warren Kilgaran, the Assistant Dean. Of course, I knew him as 'the Shadman' in high school, so named because he was a shadow sorcerer and expert in throwing veils, which came in handy whenever we slipped out after curfew. Shad had been a junior when I was a freshman.

Julie narrowed her eyes. "So you're coming on Saturday, right?"

I swirled the remains of my cappuccino in the cup and studied the tiny bubbles of foamed milk still clinging to the sides. "Maybe."

"Are you kidding? What else you going to do? Give Red a bath?"

"Maybe. He's been looking pretty raggedy lately."

"I heard that," Red quipped from inside my purse.

"What does he do in there, anyway?" Julie feigned peeking inside my purse and then gave me a you-need-to-get-a-life look. "You're going and that's all there is to it."

I groaned. "I don't think I'm up for it, to be honest with you."

"Lire, you need to get out. This is the perfect party, you know more than half the people coming. Who knows, maybe you'll meet someone nice."

"That would be a miracle and you know it." I dropped my head into the palms of my hands. "It's hopeless. In fact, I'm giving up on hope. That way, I can go on with life and not be disappointed. Don't you think?" I peeked at her from between my fingers.

"Not! You're discouraged because of Glen. Girl, don't give him the satisfaction. There are tons of guys out there who will jump at the chance to be with you, I'm telling you! Besides, it will be an excuse to doll up and let word get back to jerk-face about how awesome you look these days. Everyone's going to be so surprised at your new look."

Two weeks ago, after nine months of being obsessed with getting lean and fit, I culminated my achievement by having a total makeover. I'll never forget the look on Julie's face when I walked into the store after taking the plunge. My long, straight hair went from strawberry blonde to dark auburn red, and I swear my stylist did a little jig when I asked him to hack half of it off. I'm proud to say I hardly batted an eye or bit a nail during the process.

There's nothing like getting dumped to motivate a girl to make some serious changes, although, even after two weeks, my reflection still startled me. Actually, the red was natural. I'd been coloring it since the eighth grade. When going through puberty and longing to be Miss Popular, red was not the color of choice. Not if you wanted to fit in. Well, that's how I felt at thirteen. At thirty, I decided it was time to get real.

"If you don't come, I'm giving Theo your telephone number."

Julie knew how to play dirty. Theo was the pock-faced, chain-smoking sleaze who worked at the liquor store down the street. Every time I saw him, he tried to get me to touch him, saying I'd see how good he was.

"Okay, okay! Don't get your undies in a bunch! I'll come." I rolled my eyes and she laughed before I looked down at my watch. "I've got to go. My appointment is at eleven."

Julie walked with me to the door. "So what does Red do in there?" she whispered.

"He plays video games. Sometimes he reads, or listens to his music."

She shook her head in amazement and walked away. "See you on Saturday if not sooner."

I made it up to Sotheby's on time, but froze in my steps when I spotted Detective Vanelli waiting in the lobby. He sat, right leg crossed over left knee, exposing black leather shoes and sleek trouser socks. The suit was silver gray, shirt midnight blue, tie geometric. For a small town cop, Vanelli knew how to put together a halfway decent ensemble. He wasn't bad looking either. Too bad he was such a pill.

I checked in with the receptionist before walking over to stand in front of the detective, my arms folded. "Detective Vanelli. Here a bit early, aren't you?"

He reclined in the chair and bobbed his chin toward me in greeting. "Call me Vince." He tossed the magazine he had been reading to the side and gave me an appraising look.

Deadly Remains - Chapter Two

"I'm not busy right now, so I thought I'd take a look at you in action."

Vince, is it? I couldn't help being suspicious. "I'd have thought your test earlier this morning was enough. You don't strike me as a magic groupie, why the interest?"

He gave me a smug smile. "Sue me, I'm curious."

I felt my right eyebrow go up.

Before I could comment, a door opened to the right of the reception desk. Veronica Michaels stepped through, looking stunning in an impeccable Chanel suit. Tall, slim, and Southern, with a drawl that made me think of mint juleps and Tennessee Williams, she was as elegant as she was genuine. Her skin was the color of dark brown sugar, and she was one of those lucky women who looked thirty-five while pushing fifty. Of course, it might have been the two-carat diamond earrings she always wore. I bet it was easy to look a dozen years younger with rocks like those. The glare alone was enough to distract the eye from any unwanted wrinkles.

She smiled at me. "Good morning, Lire. Lovely to see you." Veronica glanced at Vince, who had risen from his chair to stand near us. Her eyebrows twitched downward, but she continued talking to me. "Are you ready to come on back?"

I nodded and gave her an affectionate smile. "Morning, Veronica. May I introduce Detective Sergeant Vince Vanelli? Vince, this is Veronica Michaels. She's the Acquisitions Director for Sotheby's here in Seattle."

Vince offered Veronica his hand. "Nice to meet you, Ms. Michaels."

"And you, Detective. Please, call me Veronica." She shook his hand.

He returned her smile. "Vince, please."

Veronica laughed. "Fair enough, thank you."

It was irritating how Vince came across so amiable and good-natured when I knew full well he was a big jerk, but I kept my tone neutral. "I'll be working with Vince after our session today. He came by early, hoping to get a preview. He's curious to see what I do for Sotheby's."

"Really. Well, good. We have some interesting pieces today. You're in luck. Come on back."

Veronica and I chatted about this and that on the way to the conference room, while Vince trailed behind like a yo-yo, lagging behind when he spotted something interesting and then catching up again. I'd been known to do the same thing. It was hard not to. The office had been designed around dozens of display cases, strategically arranged along the route to the main conference room, and their contents were utterly distracting.

Inside the conference room, I surveyed the various items scattered around the table. Furniture was kept on a different floor.

"How many are downstairs?" I asked.

"Nothing that can't wait until our next appointment."

I glanced back toward the table. "Any of these getting more than the usual reading?"

Sometimes clients requested a full accounting of an item for sentimental reasons—or because they hoped to get top dollar, but the extra effort didn't always pay off. Sotheby's discouraged sellers from insisting on a full reading unless there was reason to believe the piece had a questionable past. It never ceased to amaze me how a piece of sordid information about an item increased its value threefold, or more. Murder was always the hands down favorite, followed by adultery, theft, and financial ruin.

"Yes. This one." Veronica pointed to a diamond ring. "The owner seems to think it was once owned by Marie Antoinette." So much white showed when she rolled her eyes it almost looked like she was going to pass out.

"Get that all the time, do you?" Vince asked.

"You wouldn't believe it. If it's not Marie Antoinette, then it's Empress Josephine." She shook her head.

I placed my purse and coat on a chair near the door. "Okay, this isn't too bad. The items in here will take forty-five minutes or so, I should think."

Deadly Remains - Chapter Two

When I sat down to examine the ring, Veronica placed a digital voice recorder and notebook on the table across from me. I pulled off my gloves and laid them in my lap. Vince sat comfortably at the end of the table, arms crossed loosely, looking very cool.

The corner of Veronica's mouth twitched upward. "Couldn't resist Marie Antoinette, now, could you?"

I laughed. She knew me too well.

After Veronica pressed record on the small black device and announced the item's description, I began my routine. With the ring clenched between both hands, I closed my eyes and coiled its energy around in my mind. I savored its history like a sip of expensive wine, rolled it around, and gauged its age. It was fairly old. Not the oldest thing I've ever felt, not by a long shot, but it clearly had history. There were dozens upon dozens of flavors, if you will, intertwined in the stream. Many people had touched the ring. Many more had touched the stone. I probed the disk of energy, starting at the center—the beginning—scanning for the high points.

Through the veil of energy ...

I look down at my hands. I have a mallet and sharp tool. My cleave is perfect, exactly where I want it. I need to work quickly, without being careless. The diamonds must be ready soon ...

As usual, I spoke out loud for the voice recorder while probing through the psychic stream. It made it easier, not having to remember all the details and trying to sum up my findings afterward. For extra measure, Veronica liked to scribble notes in her small notebook.

"I found the stone cutter. The stone was transported to Venice from Golconda, where it was discovered. Giovanni Pertramo cut the raw diamond into several stones. By the clothing styles I'd guess mid to late eighteenth century. Oh, I've got it. It's 1770. He is cutting the stones for a French jeweler and needs to get it done by the end of the week."

I stopped talking and concentrated on the stream. Several more people came into it. The gem dealer, for one. I told Veronica the name and kept moving. If I didn't move quickly, I wouldn't make it through all the items on the docket.

I carefully place the diamond into the setting. My masterpiece is nearly complete!

"Here it is. I've found him. The jeweler is French. His name is Charles Bohmer. Oh! He's the royal jeweler. Not only that, he's the royal jeweler for King Louis XV. Wait a minute. The stone is part of a larger piece, not this ring. He didn't make this ring. He's putting the stone into a necklace. God, what a necklace! It's his masterpiece. He's making it for a woman who reveres extravagance. Her name is Madame du Barry. The King will pay. She gets anything she wants and no one questions it. It's worth a fortune."

Veronica gasped, and I had to keep the volume of my voice from increasing along with my excitement. It had been a long time since reading something so historically interesting. I wished for several hours to examine it, instead of only minutes.

Up the stream, not too far, I found an area of strong emotion.

"But, wait ... the King has died, and Bohmer is out. He has been cast out of court, and the necklace wasn't completed in time to be given to Madame du Barry. He's been saddled with its cost and pinned all his hopes on the new Queen purchasing the necklace. But the Queen ... ah! The Queen is Marie Antoinette! The Queen told him to break it up. She doesn't want it."

Unthinkable!

I encountered a new life force in the stream.

I admire the necklace, letting the elaborate rope of diamonds flow over my hands. They are breathtaking. The center diamond is astounding! At least ten carats. I will live like royalty. No one will believe the Queen isn't actually the one with the necklace. Her reputation is soiled, and when I stay in Paris, instead of running away, people will say I am innocent. If I had taken the necklace, surely I wouldn't stay in Paris!

I continued down several other new avenues and finally arrived at the desired location—the ring maker.

Deadly Remains - Chapter Two

I opened my eyes. After replacing the ring into the padded box, I summarized my findings, barely containing my enthusiasm. "This is incredible. I mean, I've read a lot of amazing things, but this ... this you're just not going to believe. Okay, you got the part about this stone being part of a much larger piece, right?" Veronica nodded and my mouth ran full speed ahead. "Okay. That necklace—that incredible symbol of excess—was stolen by an extremely crafty woman named Countess de Lamotte. And how she went about it was audacious. I mean, it's like something out of a master spy novel or something, except it took place like two hundred plus years ago!"

Veronica's eyes gleamed with anticipation. She chortled, "Girl, don't keep me hanging! How did she do it?"

I gushed like a schoolgirl with a tasty piece of gossip. "She lured a prominent Cardinal into being an unwitting accomplice, for one. To accomplish her plan, the Countess seduced this big shot cardinal—Cardinal Rohan—and then convinced him she was also the Queen's lesbian lover. Talk about intrigue. She actually hired a prostitute to impersonate the Queen and then arranged for Rohan to see the two of them together. Can you believe it?

"After that little escapade, the Cardinal was convinced his new lover had the Queen's confidence. So, sometime later, the Countess told Rohan the Queen wanted his help to secretly purchase Bohmer's necklace on her behalf. She told the Cardinal the Queen wanted the necklace, but couldn't come up with all the money at once and would pay him back on the installment plan." I laughed. "Can you just believe that? The installment plan! Anyway, the Cardinal fell for it and purchased the necklace from Bohmer, thinking he was going to make points with the new Queen for this gracious favor. Not to mention get his money back, but things didn't work out too well for the Cardinal as you might imagine.

"Anyway, the Countess then arranged for the Cardinal to give her the necklace, so she could secretly deliver it to the Queen. Hello! Instead, the Countess gave the necklace to her husband, who fenced it in London, where it was broken up.

"The goldsmith, who made this ring, was Edward Niles of London. He made it for a woman named Lady Ann Becket in 1789. He told her the diamond had come from one of Marie Antoinette's necklaces. That's probably where the current owner got the Marie Antoinette connection."

Veronica turned off the recorder and then clasped her hands together. "My goodness. That's almost better than being worn by Antoinette. The owner is going to be very pleased. And I owe her an apology. I encouraged her not to spend the extra money on a full accounting. The Necklace Affair is a famous historical scandal. It's known to have contributed to the French Revolution, not to mention the downfall of King Louis and Marie Antoinette. I'll have to do further research on it. This is the first item I've encountered that relates to the infamous necklace."

When I glanced over at Vince, he regarded me with narrowed eyes, giving him a guarded, suspicious expression.

"What?" I stopped short of adding 'is your problem,' but I think my tone said it anyway. I couldn't help it. Vince's suspicious looks irritated me.

He replied, "I know you have a gift. You proved it with our evidence. It was a verifiable test. But this," he motioned to the ring, "isn't something that can be verified. How does someone know the appraisal isn't ... embellished?"

It was a valid question. Vince had been careful with his tone and choice of words to lessen the chance I'd take offense. Briefly, I considered reevaluating the role in which I had cast the detective, but I set the thought aside. I'd think about it later after spending more time with him.

I looked at Veronica and nodded in her direction.

She replied, "There are several reasons why a buyer can trust our psychic authentications, Detective. First, we are Sotheby's. Our reputation is beyond reproach, and we are most eager to maintain that status. Second, we only use licensed clairvoyants. The licensing process is rigorous and is administered by the Paranormal Regulatory Commission. Third, on a historically important item such as this, we will have a second licensed clairvoyant examine the ring, for further endorsement. And finally, we always perform a non-psychic appraisal on our items, which in this case bolsters Lire's reading. The ring was indeed made in the late eighteenth century. Our antiquities expert also indicated the ring's mounting is English."

She paused and leaned toward Vince. "In addition, Vince, on a more personal level, I've known Lire for close to eight years. She is one of the finest people I know and has never been wrong on any of the readings she's done for me. Never. And there have been literally hundreds."

Vince nodded. "I see."

If Vince was uncomfortable, he didn't look it. If he wasn't, I was. I've never been graceful at taking compliments. When he glanced in my direction, I looked down. I covered my embarrassment by pretending to admire the ring, which wasn't difficult.

I spent the next thirty minutes examining over half of the remaining items on the table. There were no big surprises, but after the sixteenth item, I needed a break. No surprise there either, I guess.

Veronica looked up from taking notes. "Lire, you okay? You look pale."

I rubbed my face with both hands. My brain felt fuzzy, like I had just woken up from an afternoon nap. "Yeah. I'm lagging a bit today for some reason."

"Maybe the blouse this morning taxed you more than you thought." Even though his voice didn't sound accusatory or condescending, Vince's comment rubbed me the wrong way.

"Doubtful. Actually, the blouse wasn't as taxing as it could have been because I didn't experience the worst it had to offer. I don't think it's a factor."

Vince put his hand on the table. "What do you mean?"

I sat up straight and crossed my legs. "I examined the psychic stream just prior to the murder. When I recognized the victim and the murderer, I stopped reading. I avoided experiencing the murder, so I didn't have to expend a bunch of power dealing with the trauma."

His eyes narrowed. "So, the blouse wasn't the test it could have been."

"Are you kidding? You want to grill me about the blouse now?" I shook my head. "We can discuss the merits of the blouse test later, okay? Right now, I'm here on Veronica's dime."

"Lire, how about a coffee break? I can send someone down to Peabody's." Veronica's genial voice diffused any further discussion about the blouse, at least temporarily, but I suspected Vince wasn't going to let it slide completely.

"Thanks. A latte would be nice." I put my gloves back on and stood to retrieve my wallet from my handbag.

Vince got up. "I'll go down. I could use a stretch anyway."

"That's mighty kind of you, Vince." There was something about the genteel twang of Veronica's accent that I found especially appealing. Doubly so when she was being gracious.

I found my own manners. "Thanks. Just tell Julie or Steve the latte is for me. They know how I like it." I thrust my hand toward him, bills dangling from my fingers.

He waved it away and then looked at Veronica. "Can I get you something as well?" When Veronica declined politely, he announced, "Okay. I'll be right back."

Before I could stop myself, I evaluated the view of his backside as he strode from the room. He had taken off the suit jacket, revealing slacks that fell smoothly over his, ah, contours. I might have enjoyed it more if he wasn't such an ass.

Veronica gave me a knowing look. I busied myself with putting away my money, while trying not to feel like I had been caught with my hand in the cookie jar.

"Oooh, girl. Talk about your fringe benefits. Do you think it's too late for a change of vocation?" Veronica's laugh was contagious. In a moment, I was laughing too.

Deadly Remains - Chapter Two

By the time Vince came back with my coffee, our conversation had moved on to more professional subjects, and I had finished examining the remaining items on the table.

Vince set the cup down next to me and then removed several layers of napkins, which had been wrapped around the middle, carefully not touching the cup with his hands.

"Julie's got you trained up, I see."

"Yeah. She was quite specific," he grumbled.

It was terribly schoolgirl of me, but I couldn't wait to hear what Julie thought about Vince.

He motioned toward the table. "Did I miss anything interesting?"

"Not really." I went through the items in my head and picked out the ones I thought were worth mentioning. "Most of the readings just confirmed dates of the appraisals. Oh, there was a manuscript that really was dictated by Robert Louis Stevenson and a beaded purse supposedly owned by Marilyn Monroe but wasn't." I shrugged. "Nothing earth shattering."

"Uh-huh."

I studied his face for a moment, but didn't have any luck reading it, so I turned to Veronica and renewed our discussion about scheduling the next visit. Figuring out Vince was exhausting.

After retrieving my purse and coat, we headed to a bank of cubicles, not far from the lobby. Veronica walked close to my side and looked at me frequently, I'm sure to verify I was truly feeling okay. When we arrived in Peg's cubicle, Veronica observed the color had returned to my face and Peg immediately ordered me to sit down in the guest chair. Peg was blonde and blue eyed, with a face like Kim Basinger— that is, if Kim Basinger was a size twenty-four. Her glossy, shoulder length blonde hair was out of her face, caught up in embellished bobby pins. She looked at me with concern.

I laughed and sat down. "I'm fine. Really."

"Humor us, Lire," Veronica ordered. "This is the first time you've shown any sign of not being a superwoman."

I rolled my eyes at Peg, and she gave me a sympathetic wink. Peg was Veronica's gregarious but efficient administrative assistant, and was on my top ten list of favorite people. She had worked with Veronica for several years before I began my relationship with Sotheby's. I counted her as somewhere between a good acquaintance and a personal friend. We didn't telephone each other regularly, but I attended her wedding last year, and we exchanged small gifts at Christmas time.

I introduced Vince. Peg replied demurely, "It's nice to meet you too, Detective."

Her altered demeanor surprised me, and I smiled to myself when I realized Peg was both flustered and intrigued by Vince's presence. If I hadn't known her as well as I did, I probably wouldn't have noticed, but she wasn't her usual, efficacious self. After much paper shuffling, eye roaming, and flipping of hair (all on Peg's part), I signed off on the day's authentications. We came up with a date for my next visit, and afterward, Veronica led the way back to the lobby. Trailing behind, I glanced over my shoulder. When Peg saw I was looking, she leered large and bit her clenched fist. We both laughed. Clearly, Peg thought Vince was a hottie.

It was ironic that the guy my friends seemed to admire was one I could hardly stand.

Before we left, I was mortified when Veronica charged Vince with taking good care of me. "I'm counting on you, Vince, to keep Lire safe when she's helping you on whatever this case of yours is. She has a generous streak and doesn't always look out for her own best interests." She glanced at me before returning her attention to Vince. "She's a real gem, and I hope you know how much it costs her to help people like us. It's a gift—don't ever forget it."

Vince responded to Veronica, but his gaze settled on me. "Yes. I'm beginning to see that."

When Vince turned to Veronica and extended his hand, I gave her a definitive I-can't-believe-you-just-said-that look, which she acknowledged with an innocent smile.

Vince said, "Don't worry, I'll keep a close eye on her."

She shook his hand. "Thank you, Vince. It was wonderful meeting you."

He nodded. "You too. Thanks for allowing me to indulge my curiosity."

"Any time, Detective." Veronica beamed.

I shook my head and gave her a meaningful smile. "I'll talk to you later."

After we had made our way to the elevator, he commented, "She really cares about you."

I smiled. "Yeah. I know. I'm the daughter she never had, and she's the mother I never knew. It's a good arrangement."

He pressed the down arrow to call the elevator. "Are you up for this?"

Was this concern? Briefly taken aback, I hesitated before answering, "Yes, I think so. Let's just see how it goes, okay?"

We entered the elevator, and Vince pressed the button for the first parking garage level. "We'll take my car to the site. I'll bring you back when we're finished."

I nodded, and then Vince filled the silence of the elevator with a discussion of where he was taking me. I wasn't familiar with the area, so the names of the various back roads didn't ring any bells, but I got the general idea of where we were headed.

Now that we were on our way to the murder site, I worried again about how I was going to explain any information Red might come up with.

THREE

Vince drove an older navy-blue Jeep Cherokee. Its windows were tinted and a black coiled antenna protruded from the roof. He unlocked the doors with his remote. I was relieved he didn't open the passenger door and hold it for me. Maybe it sounded silly, but that would have made me feel like we were headed out on an awkward date, instead of going to a crime scene.

I slid into the tan interior, placed my folded coat on my knees, and looked around. Not a fast food bag, gasoline receipt, or candy wrapper in sight. "This car belong to you?" I asked when he got in.

"Yeah. Why?"

"Wow. It's just ... I don't think I've ever seen such a clean car that wasn't new or a rental. You're not a neat freak, are you?"

Vince just grunted and then started the car. I guess he wasn't going to dignify my question with an answer. What I didn't mention was that I was an unequivocal anal-retentive clutter buster myself.

I settled myself in the seat by way of buckling my safety belt and Vince headed toward the freeway. He drove conservatively, maybe only five over the limit, keeping one hand at the bottom of the steering wheel and the other loose on his thigh.

Deadly Remains - Chapter Three

We drove for nearly five minutes without a word before Vince broke the silence. "So, what kind of name is Lear? Parents obsessed with Shakespeare or something?"

I couldn't help but laugh. "No," I managed to say between chuckles. "It's spelled L-I-R-E, not L-E-A-R. It's a nickname I picked up in school." I added quickly, "And to answer your next question, it means 'to read' in French. My dad was French, so I let the name stick."

"Ah. And, the next obvious question?"

I blinked, thought for a second, and then laughed. "My real name? No. If you want to know that, you can find out for yourself."

"Embarrassed?"

"No," I lied and then laughed again. The main reason I embraced my nickname in high school was because my real first name had subjected me to ceaseless teasing. It was an unusual name and the boys in school somehow likened it to a sexual part of female anatomy. Leave it to teenage boys to twist anything into a sexual innuendo. Vince could figure that one out on his own. "A girl's entitled to a few secrets."

"Like duping Jensen and me with the blouse." He made it a statement, instead of a question.

I was astonished that Vince leveled the accusation of duplicity when he and Jensen set up the phony reading in the first place. "Now that's calling the kettle black. You wanted to know whether I could read such an emotionally potent object, and I can. Experiencing the murder only demonstrates my psychological stamina, not my magical ability."

"You're right. That's exactly what we were after. We need to know you won't miss important clues because you're avoiding something unpleasant. If we can't rely on you to get the whole picture, we need to get someone who can."

For a guy who didn't know me, Vince sure knew how to press my buttons. "I hate to break it to you, but I'm probably all you've got. There are eleven licensed clairvoyants west of the Mississippi and I know of only three who'll work with the police on a regular basis. You've already interviewed the other two. The fact is I've dealt with more psychologically wrenching crap than you and Jensen put together. I've committed countless crimes. I've been a murderer, a thief, a rapist, and I've been scores of victims. I am well and truly psychologically hardened, Detective. All starting from the age of three when I discovered my mother was having an affair with my uncle."

Vince glanced over at me with raised eyebrows and then shook his head as he looked back to the road. "Jesus," he muttered. He didn't call me a freak, but I didn't have to be a mind reader to know he was thinking it.

The tension in the car was palpable, but I refused to smooth things over. I stared angrily out of the passenger window, looking at nothing. Why the hell was I doing this? It wasn't like it paid well, since all police work was done *pro bono*. I toyed with the idea of telling Vince to take me back to the city, but then I remembered Red's earlier comment. Once word got out that a warlock serial killer was on the loose ...

I sighed resignedly.

I continued to simmer as Vince took an exit from the freeway, putting us on a two-lane country road. The scenery was green and delicious, with houses few and far between. Blue sky peeked from behind low misty clouds, the sun breaking through here and there, and I dared to hope the fog might actually burn off soon.

After shifting my legs to ease a cramp, the car careened from side to side. My hands flew to the armrest and dashboard reflexively. I looked to the road for an explanation, but we were alone on the two-lane highway.

"Holy fucking shit!" Vince pressed his body as close as possible to the driver side door, barely managing to keep the car in the appropriate lane. It might have been funny if not for his horrified expression and the fact that the car careened down the road at fifty-five.

I flinched away from the center console, which seemed to be the source of Vince's panic. Expecting something terrifying, I darted my eyes to the area between us.

"Oh my God! Vince! It's okay, it's okay." I reached toward the floor where my purse had fallen over and gathered the spilled items.

Vince regained control of the car if not his composure. He gripped the steering wheel, breathing hard. "Jesus H. Christ! What the fuck was that thing?"

"Jeez. I'm sorry. I was careless." I took a deep breath, trying to calm my fiercely pounding heart. "Don't worry. You're not losing it. It's an aversion spell, a powerful one."

He removed one hand from the steering wheel to run it through his hair. "Christ! How could you touch it?"

"The spell doesn't affect me."

Vince continued to look distressed and his body remained rigid. Considering the power of the spell, the persistence of his reaction wasn't unusual.

I peered at his face, trying to gauge his temper. "If you don't mind telling me, what exactly did you see?"

His knuckles turned white on the steering wheel, and he stared hard at the road. "A swarming, putrid mass of squirming snakes ... and God knows what else. Leeches, maybe. I don't know. It was a slithering pile. Dark and— " He grunted, shaking his head. "I was sure they were deadly." He let out a shaky laugh. "Now that I think about it ... it's stupid. I mean, how likely is it you'd carry something like that in your purse?" He glared at me. "If it's not snakes, then what the fuck is it?"

"I'll show you, but I think you should pull over first."

"Jesus." He checked the rear view mirror and slowed the car before pulling into a small dirt clearing.

"Is this going to freak me out again? I've about had it with this magic shit." His voice was almost normal, albeit a tad on the grumpy side, and there were no more nervous gestures. Too bad, because I almost enjoyed watching him run his fingers through his wavy, dark hair.

"Probably." I added hastily, "But not like before. Don't try to get close, and you'll be fine."

I lowered my hand, palm up, into my purse, and Red hopped on to it. I avoided grabbing him because he was a person, not a stuffed toy—current body not withstanding. If I were trapped inside a stuffed animal body, I think it would really get on my nerves having someone grab me and throw me around all the time. It was already an indignity for him to be carried around in my purse. I tried not to make it worse by treating him like a toy.

I moved my hand to the dashboard, as far away from Vince as possible, and waited for Red to climb off. "Vince, may I introduce my good friend Red. Red, this is Detective Vince Vanelli of the Chiliquitham Police Department."

"Pleased to make your acquaintance, Detective." Red sat down and leaned against the corner strut of the windshield.

Vince stared at him open mouthed for longer than was polite. Finally, he looked at me. "He's black, not red."

"Red is the nickname he acquired when he lived a normal life over three hundred years ago. His full name is John Redborn. Being cast into the body of a black teddy bear is an ironic twist of fate."

"Uh-huh. Three hundred years ago ..."

When Vince didn't say anything else, I glanced over at Red. "Do you think we've done irreparable damage to Vince's psyche? He's not speaking in complete sentences. That's not a good sign."

"It is possible. You should keep a close eye on him." He added, "And you might consider driving too." Red crossed his legs and tapped his foot. He was a fidget, and it made the contrast between toy and human even more unnerving.

Vince rubbed his right hand over the lower part of his face. I faintly heard the scratching sound of his five o'clock shadow. He shook his head slowly, with his hand cupped over his chin and lower lip, and chuckled. "Very funny. Miss Wise-ass." He rested his right arm over the back of his seat and took a deep breath. Vince was clearly trying to remain calm, despite seeing something completely out of the ordinary. He nodded toward Red. "So what's the story? Why is a grown woman carrying an animated, three-hundred-year-old teddy bear in her purse? And why the spell? You know I almost crashed the car back there. You're lucky we're not spread all over the pavement."

"I know. I'm sorry." Vince was understandably upset, but his 'grown woman' comment hit me the wrong way. "And for your information, Red isn't just a stuffed animal I tote around for fun. He's a person and not something I can leave in a basket at home."

Vince glanced at Red and then regarded me with a raised eyebrow.

I sighed and thought of where to begin telling him about Red. "My father got Red for me when I was four-and-a-half, about a year after my ability came to light. Early on, my dad knew my life was destined to be virtually devoid of true companionship. By that time, my mother practically refused to have anything to do with me and kept me inside, away from other children. So, my father searched for something or someone who could be my companion. It took him almost a year to acquire Red."

I glared at Vince. "It makes complete sense that my dad would get his little girl a teddy bear. What else would he choose?" Past ridicule gave me a definite sore spot where toting Red was concerned. I had to work to keep the tone of my voice reasonable. "Of course, when I first got him, being just four, I thought he was a toy brought to life. As I grew up, I learned he was a real person, like me." I glanced at Red. "I don't know how he managed to endure those first few years when I treated him like a cuddly toy. But, eventually, I learned who he was, and we became good friends; in spite, I think, of the binding spell that compels him to protect me."

I motioned toward the floorboards where Red had spilled out from my purse. "The aversion spell is one of several meant to keep anyone from intentionally or unintentionally touching Red. I'm able to touch him without my gloves because he's psychically clean. The spells are meant to keep it that way. There's also a more powerful one that goes into effect if the aversion spell isn't enough to keep someone from touching him."

"I can't imagine that happening." He shuddered. "So, what does that one do—blow you up?"

I gave him a knowing look.

"You're kidding? It blows you up?" His eyes narrowed, and he examined me. I guess he wasn't quite ready to believe anything.

I smiled broadly. "Yeah, I'm kidding. But it'll knock you flat with a nasty shock. Sort of like a stun gun."

"You're enjoying this, aren't you?"

I gave him a puzzled, wide-eyed look in reply and almost kept from smiling.

Vince looked at Red. "What's your story, Red? You've held up well, for being three hundred years old."

He replied, in his slightly accented English, "The benefit of magic, Detective. Over the last three hundred years, I have been in many vessels. This soft body is only the latest. But if you don't mind, I prefer that Lire tell the story."

"Why don't we keep driving, and I'll tell you on the way?" I suggested.

By the time we pulled up to a remote farmhouse, Vince knew as much about Red as most of my good friends. There were several cars parked in the gravel driveway, so Vince drove his Jeep into the overgrown area that was once a front lawn.

"How did your dad find him? This type of thing can't be cheap or easy to come by." He glanced at Red. "Sorry to be so blunt."

"No offense taken, Detective."

I shrugged. "My dad had a lot of contacts. He was a tax attorney and had several witchcraft corporations for clients. I know he traded some big time favors and probably paid a mint, in order to get him."

"I was a guilt gift," Red said.

I gave him a wistful smile. "Yes. You were."

Vince looked puzzled, so I elaborated. "My parents decided to send me away to boarding school as soon as I was old enough to go to kindergarten. That's why my father went to such extremes to get Red. It eased his conscience."

Deadly Remains - Chapter Three

We were starting to get into sensitive territory, so I looked around and asked. "So, where to?"

Vince dipped his head to peer through the windshield and nodded toward the left. "The site's over that hill."

I held my purse open to Red, and he deftly jumped into the inside front pocket while I followed Vince's gaze. A hike wasn't high on my list of priorities, but at least it wasn't raining.

The obligatory faded white farmhouse was tucked between a copse of leafless, thirty-foot maples and a gentle hillside. It was a modest two-story affair, with a large picture window overlooking a now sagging front porch. White lace curtains adorned the downstairs windows, yellowed from the sun and age. Upstairs the windows were a patchwork of different colored draperies—one faded blue, another yellow, and the last that awful seventies burnt orange.

To the left of the house, a dilapidated, white picket fence with matching gate sliced through the lush, vibrant green grass that covered the hillside. Dozens of foot-shaped indentations marched through the gate and up the hill.

With Vince in the lead, we slogged up the slope, adding our own footprints to the trampled greenery. If I had known we'd be trooping through four-inch high, dew-covered grass, I would have chosen a different outfit. I was dressed for meeting with clients. Okay, my ensemble was a little more aggressive than normal. I compensated for my police jitters by wearing a power suit. You know—the hip, black number with my favorite high-heeled boots. These boots were not made for walkin'. Vince seemed to be amused by my struggle to keep the three-inch heels from sinking into the soft ground. I know I caught a smirk at least once.

When we finally reached the weathered, post and wire fence at the top of the hill, my calf muscles burned from the exertion. Over the past year, I had increased my physical stamina, but my workouts didn't entail tiptoeing up a hill for half a mile. Maybe I needed to add a new circuit to my exercise program.

Vince reached the gate first and then waited for me to close the distance, looking comfortable and smug. I tried to ignore the mischievous grin playing on his lips and failed.

"Thank you for telling me all about this wonderful nature hike. I never would have considered changing into the Nikes sitting in the back of my car. It's just so much better having the fun of ruining my boots." I narrowed my eyes. "I won't forget this, *Vince*."

The snub would have been more effective if I'd been able to stalk away. Instead, I had to fumble with figuring out how to get through the gate. It didn't have hinges like the other one. Away from the house, the property had been divided by barbed wire country fencing. The gate consisted of two large posts secured to each other with a loop of heavy rope at the top and a thick wire loop at the bottom. I folded my arms and glared at Vince.

He threw up his hands in supplication and laughed. "I'm sorry. Believe me, I didn't think of it until we started walking. Really."

"Yeah, right. Some detective you are. Didn't even notice my shoes."

I glowered in silence while he opened the gate. After we stepped through and it was re-secured, I demanded, "How much further is it anyway?"

"After we get to the top, it's down about three hundred feet or so."

I followed Vince, grumbling quietly to Red. Once the hill crested, the way was a bit easier. The ground flattened out, was rockier and not as wet, and I could relax and put my heels down. Now, I just had to worry about breaking my neck from tripping over a rock.

On this side of the hill, the land didn't drop off again as I had imagined. Instead, our path took us down a shallow incline toward a large grove of trees. On either side, I could see cows grazing off in the distance. The deciduous and evergreen trees were spaced far apart, with tall, verdant shrubs and weeds growing between them.

From the higher vantage of the hillside, I glimpsed movement behind the greenery. Closer to the grove, I heard voices. The yellow tape delineating the scene stood out against the tawny bark of the maples and glossy leaves of the bushes.

Vince acknowledged the officers waiting nearby and crossed under the tape. On the opposite side of the circle, three men engaged in an animated discussion. At our arrival, however, they quietly observed our entry into the area. A large, blue plastic bin sat on the ground next to them. Vince waited while I picked my way along the rock-strewn path. He held up the tape as I ducked under it.

Even from a distance, I sensed the afterglow of magic emanating from the circle. It rubbed against my body, like a fog or a cat, engulfing me in its soft energy and making the hairs of my arms stand on end. I stood still for several seconds and tasted the magic. Besides the remaining power, something else lingered. Something unpleasant.

One of the men called a greeting across the circle, "Afternoon, Vanelli." He was fiftyish, with receding golden hair and a moderate beer gut protruding from his jacket.

Vince nodded. "Kopeky." His gaze shifted to the next two men in turn. "Andersen. Marshall." Both Marshall and Kopeky had on King County Sheriff's uniforms. A cigarette dangled from Anderson's thin lips and he wore blue unzipped coveralls over a modest brown suit.

"We're ready to wrap it up as soon as she's done," Kopeky said.

Vince nodded again, this time in acknowledgment, and turned to face me. "You're on. How do you work? Do you want me to accompany you, or would you prefer to walk the site alone?"

I glanced at the three men and then focused on Vince. "I'll just work my way around. There's no reason to stay with me. If I have any questions, I'll ask." I felt a little self-conscious but didn't want him thinking I wasn't a big girl. "Just give me the highlights and then you can go talk to your colleagues."

"Other than the location and the victim, the site is virtually identical to the one you saw in the photographs this morning." He turned and gestured toward the center of the circle. "The victim's bones are there. The larger grass circle is on the left side." Vince pointed. "You can just see it from here."

"I take it the plastic bin over there is for transporting the victim's remains?"

Vince looked over at the men, who had resumed their discussion. "Yes. The guy in the coveralls is from the medical examiner's office."

"Okay." I gave him a nod before moving to examine the circle.

A sharp edge delineated the bare earth of the blasted circle from the healthy grass on the outside. I scanned the circumference, looking for a patch of ground that had been protected by one of the warlock's runes. I spotted one a couple of yards away and walked toward it, staying on the outside of the main circle.

I didn't hold out much hope that I'd get a reading from the spot of grass. Even if the warlock had touched the runestone with his flesh before placing it on the ground, inanimate objects don't transfer their psychic energy to other objects. Only living beings could do that. But, on the off chance the perpetrator had touched the grass underneath the rune, I decided to check it out. I removed my gloves and placed them inside my purse.

"You okay, Red?" I asked in a subdued voice.

"Yes. The remnants of the spells are still perceptible. The warlock is a master of darkness, there is no doubt. I will be able to discern more once I am inside." He must have sensed my anxiety because he assured me, "Do not worry, the magic inside the circle will be more apparent, not necessarily stronger. The circle is broken. Much will cling inside, but most of the power behind it has dissipated. "

"Okay. Here we go."

Deadly Remains - Chapter Three

Red was right. The level of residual magic wasn't any stronger on the inside of the circle. Instead, the various essences became more distinct, like shining a light through a prism and seeing its constituent colors. I suspected Red would have no trouble determining the classes of spells used, if not the exact spells themselves.

I bent down and moved the flat of my hand through the flattened blades of grass. As I suspected, the warlock hadn't touched them with his flesh. Even so, I needed to check every patch, for sake of completeness.

I worked my way around the outside of the main circle, squatting down and thoroughly touching each of the five patches. When I drew closer to the two deputies and the medical examiner, their conversation trailed off. They observed me skeptically while probably hoping for theatrics. Unfortunately, they were going to be disappointed and convinced of fakery because my magic isn't showy. It happened all the time. Only verifiable evidence would vindicate me. Until I established my credibility with these men, suspicion was inevitable, no matter what my references said.

I finished my circuit of the small grass patches, finding nothing of interest, and turned my attention to the larger circle at the south side of the blast zone. As soon as I drew close, an overwhelming sense of dread assailed my mind. This, I realized, was the source of my initial feeling of unease when I first approached the site. Now, however, instead of a minor discomfort I could ignore, my inner voice bellowed at me to leave. *Go home! You should not be here! GO NOW OR DIE!*

"Lire?" Red whispered from his hiding place at my side.

Something crashed into my back. I screamed into my hands, which surprised me because I didn't remember covering my mouth beforehand. I whirled around and lashed out against my assailant, while my horrified scream pierced the air. The world moved in slow motion and took on a grainy appearance. My mind felt fuzzy, and I realized too late I had been attacking Vince's chest full bore with my closed fists. Before I could regain my composure, he grabbed both of my arms in an effort to hold me back.

I stared at his hands on my bare skin, gasping in shock, but it was too late. My magic flared out instantly.

"Oh shit!" Vince realized his mistake and pushed my arms away with such force that I stumbled and fell.

Still reeling from the evil emanation, I stayed down and covered my face with my hands. I simply could not take any more input. Only my deep-seated dislike for looking completely pathetic prevented me from rolling over and curling up into a ball, right then and there.

Rarely did I come in contact with someone's bare skin, but it has happened on occasion. Last year, when I'd blocked a woman's path in the supermarket, she tapped me on the shoulder to get my attention. My back had been turned, so she didn't notice my gloves and what they meant. (Most who spied the gloves, kept their distance; as if close proximity allowed me to read their minds.) Unfortunately, I had been wearing a tank top that day, and her fingers touched my skin. With my shield in place, I dealt with the casual touch after only a moment's hesitation. I moved aside, and the woman never noticed her blunder.

I'd learned to keep my psychic shield at a constant low level. It doesn't prevent the psychic energy from entering my body, but I can use it to control the stream and protect myself from being overwhelmed. For a careless touch, it meant the difference between living with another person's life experiences forever, or coiling them up and tossing them back out.

This wasn't always the case. In the beginning, before my power matured and I had learned to control it, accidental contact was much more dangerous. When mistakes happened, I got stuck with every nuance of the person or object's essence. After nearly thirty years, I lived with dozens of other people's memories in my mind. Only time would fade them.

Now, for some unexplained reason, my shield didn't respond. When Vince grabbed me, I had no control. I felt my power blossom and knew I'd be living with him in my head for the rest of my life.

I dropped my hands and stared at him. He paced back and forth, a few yards away. The nervous gestures were back. He alternated between running a hand through his thick hair to rubbing his chin. I think every now and then he muttered expletives under his breath.

Red called out again, "Lire, are you okay?"

My hand covered my mouth. Once again, I didn't remember doing it. I guess it was one of those involuntary gestures people make when they've been shocked silly.

I forced my hand down and muttered, "My God! It's impossible." My hands trembled in my lap.

Vince looked in my direction. He must not have liked my expression because the color drained out of his face and his features hardened. "Think you've got my number now, do you? That's just fucking perfect!"

It took me a few moments for his words to sink in. "Vince— "

His fists clenched at his sides, he closed the distance between us in three large strides and towered above me. "I don't want to hear it." He drew out and bit off each word.

"Vince, it's not what you think."

He turned his back and stalked away. Okay, now I was getting pissed. He had been the one to touch me, not the other way around, and yet it was my fault. But worst of all, he wasn't listening to me. That was a big pet peeve. Nothing made me angrier than someone who deliberately blew me off.

"Dammit, Vanelli!" I struggled to stand up. "If you stopped being such a self-centered bastard for one minute, you'd find out I didn't read anything from you. Thank God. 'Cause the last thing I want in this world is to be stuck with your freaking secrets in my head for the rest of my life."

He froze before turning the upper half of his body toward me. His expression was lanced by uncertainty, his eyes still angry.

"What happened? Are you okay?" Red asked.

I realized he had asked me twice before, but I'd been too distracted to answer.

I looked away from Vince, swallowing my ire, and shifted my purse so I could see Red. "I'm sorry, I was occupied."

"I noticed. What happened back there?" Red motioned toward the circle.

Vince approached and stopped a few feet away from us. Apparently curiosity was winning over his angry embarrassment.

I didn't need to look to know Red had gestured to the larger grass circle. "I … I don't know. I've never experienced anything like it. It's the worst thing I've ever encountered. You know better than anyone just how bad that is."

"Yes. I do. You sensed the psychic imprint left by the summoned demon, although, I did not expect you to be so affected. I'm sorry. If I had known, I would have warned you."

I turned to Vince. "Why did you run into me?" I looked around the circle. "Hey, where did the three other guys go?"

He looked stony. "I sent them up the hill to wait."

I didn't ask him why. It was obvious. He was embarrassed about being touched by a clairvoyant. Wouldn't want the other boys to hear any details, now would we?

He continued, "And I didn't run into you. You ran into me."

"No, I didn't." Even as I said it, I flashed on the memory of screaming into my hands and being surprised they were at my mouth. A twinge of doubt nagged at the back of my mind.

"Yes, you did." He still sounded angry. "How do you think you got all the way over here?"

I looked to my right. The bones rested no more than a few feet away. The grass circle was at least ten yards distant. *Damn.* I must have backed up without realizing it.

"I don't know. I thought we did that when I was fighting you." I glanced away and mumbled, "I'm sorry about that. I didn't hurt you, did I?"

"You got in a couple good shots, but I've had worse." He frowned. "If you didn't read anything from me, why did you look so shocked? Why the freak out?"

"Because I wasn't prepared to deal with your psychic energy. Reading a person is physically and psychically demanding. When you grabbed me, I was far from ready for it." I shook my head. "I don't know why, but my shield is completely shot. That's why I'm amazed I didn't get a reading from you. This has never happened before ... well, not with a normal anyway." I cocked my head at him. "Do you know why I didn't get a reading?"

He looked startled. "Me? How would I know?"

I shrugged. "I don't know. This is new territory for me." I sighed and muttered, "Maybe there's hope for me after all."

"What?"

I waved him away. "Never mind. Let's finish up, so we can get out of here. Red, I don't think I can face the grass circle again. Can you check it out on your own?"

"Sure. Put me down. I'll walk over."

I put my purse near the ground so he could jump down.

After watching Red toddle across the dirt, Vince shook his head. "Watching him walk ... it's disconcerting." He shrugged. "I'm sure you're used to it."

I nodded. "That's why I don't usually expose him to people I don't know, especially normals. Most people are happy to live their lives oblivious to magic. Besides, it makes Red uncomfortable to be so noticed, and I don't want to tempt anyone into trying to touch him. Because of his uniqueness, that's the first thing people want to do, especially kids. And, of course, I worry about theft."

"Would you have shown him to me if he hadn't fallen out of your purse?"

I shrugged. "Most likely. He's my black magic expert, and you probably would have demanded to know how I got my information."

He snorted. "What have you come up with?"

"Not much," I admitted. "I checked the small grassy spots, in case the witch or warlock touched the grass, but they didn't."

"But the suspect touched the runes."

"Yes, but inanimate objects don't transfer psychic energy to other things. Only humans or animals do that."

"Do demons have psychic energy?" he asked.

"I don't know. Maybe. I don't have any direct experience with them, so I can't say for sure."

"And you aren't going to check." I heard the disappointment in his voice, but I let it go. I really didn't want to argue with him. It was tedious.

"I don't think I can." I peered at him. "Have you tried going near it? Even a normal can sense the contamination a demon leaves behind. I think you and everyone else investigating the site have unconsciously avoided it. Or do you think I'm wrong?"

He opened his mouth to say something and then reconsidered, closing his mouth with a slight clack of his teeth. As he turned toward the circle, I could practically see the wheels turning as he considered my question. The muscles surrounding his mouth tightened, which made his square jaw even more pronounced. His eyes narrowed in thought. I could tell by his expression that he had resolved to prove me wrong.

Vince launched himself toward the circle, taking determined strides, but when he got within six feet, his gait faltered. First he slowed and then staggered to a stop about two feet from the circle's leading edge. His hands clenched into tight fists at his sides. I couldn't see his face, but I imagined it wasn't pretty. Slowly, he jerked his feet closer to the edge of the circle, inch by inch. The Frankenstein walk would have been comical if it weren't for his grunts of strain and ragged breathing. I had some idea what he was going through and sympathized. The atmosphere near the circle automatically triggered the flight instinct. Vince struggled to fight instead of flee, and it wasn't easy.

Awkwardly, he went down to one knee and reached toward the defiled grass. Red observed him from about five feet away. Vince's body shook visibly, but he managed to put his left hand on the grass. I heard him grunt, like a bodybuilder lifting some serious weights, before he quickly reversed course. He didn't stop his backward crabwalk until putting several body lengths between himself and the circle. Dirt covered his pants and shoes. I managed to walk to his side, by focusing all my attention on him and gritting my teeth against the repellant ambiance. I squatted beside him, keeping about eighteen inches between us, so he didn't feel crowded.

I peered at his downcast face, but hair shrouded his eyes. "Vince?" When he didn't respond, I tried again. "Vince? Detective Vanelli? You okay?"

"No." His voice came out deep and gravelly.

I had to chuckle. "Right. Stupid question. Can you stand? I think we should back up. The atmosphere's still pretty thick here."

"Yeah, sure." He stood up, pushing one arm down against his thigh for leverage.

Red approached as we made our way back to the pile of bones. "That was about the stupidest thing I have ever seen."

After dusting his hands free of dirt, Vince smoothed his hair out of his face. "I won't argue."

"Then why did you do it?"

"Lire thought we all might have been subconsciously avoiding the area. I wanted to see if she was right."

Red observed, "I believe you got your answer."

I folded my arms and looked at Vince. "Now multiply that by a hundred and you'll know why I can't touch that grass."

"It doesn't matter," Red told us. "I know what was inside the pentagram. The warlock summoned the arch-demon Paimon and compelled its aid. I detected a spell specific to that demon. It is a high level evocation that weakens any magic user's defense and leaves them open to even the most fundamental spells. This is why you are struggling with your shield, Lire. Even the ancillary affects are enough to compromise your defenses to a certain degree."

"How do you know all this?" Vince asked.

"Because in my human life I was a necromancer and a summoner. I believe the going term is black magus, although, that implies devil worship, which is not always the case."

"But you summoned demons. That sure sounds like devil worship to me."

"I summoned many creatures, but they weren't devils. Study your Christian mythology, Detective. You will find that many demons are not wholly evil. True, they are almost always selfish and duplicitous, and one must always be wary, but rarely do they seek your soul as payment for knowledge. Unfortunately, the dark arts have always drawn those looking for the easy path to power. Many of these summoners are evil or eventually turn to evil, so the devil worship appellation has stuck."

Vince folded his arms across his chest. "There are demons that aren't after your soul? That's not what I've been told."

"I didn't say they weren't after your soul. What I said was there are many who don't demand it as payment for their aid. Many demons take pleasure in our world and are willing to work with a summoner in order to enjoy it, even if it is only for a short time."

"Does this ... Paimon have a piece of our warlock?" Vince gestured toward the larger grass circle.

"I do not know. He has either traded his, or someone else's soul, or he knows Paimon's true name. Paimon would not aid a human for any other reason. It is evil through and through."

"Knowing its true name, what does that mean?"

"If you are a summoner and learn a demon's true name—not the common name from mythology, but the name from which the demon draws its magic—then you will have the power to call it at any time and force its aid without any negotiation or agreement." Red added the caveat, "As long as you have the power to keep control and are not tricked into losing it."

"But you're not able to tell which way the demon was called?"

"No."

"Do you know Paimon's true name?" Vince asked.

Red was quick to respond. "No. Anyway, it is immaterial. When I died, my magic abilities died too. I can still sense magic but cannot employ it."

"Okay, can we hire a summoner who knows the true name to compel Paimon to tell us the identity of the warlock?"

Red snapped, "You who think all summoners are devil worshipers—you would ask someone to risk their eternal soul for this information?"

Vince frowned. "No, I wouldn't."

Red continued, "Regardless, the point is moot. Summoners do not brag about knowing such things. A demon's true name is something of great power and a closely guarded secret. No summoner would advertise having such knowledge, especially not of a demon as powerful as Paimon."

"Then this gets us nowhere."

Red shrugged.

Vince turned his attention to me. The early afternoon sun illuminated his dark-brown eyes, making them look the color of milk chocolate. "The identity of the victim. We don't know it yet. We also don't know who the first victim was— the one from the crime scene photos—but you can get that one for us later."

"Okay. Do you have something you know the victim touched?" I asked.

Confusion furrowed his brow. "We have the bones." *Duh*, his voice implied.

I took a step back, aghast. "What? You want me to touch the victim's bones?"

He looked genuinely surprised by my reaction. "Yes."

"Do you know how demanding that is? Even the most powerful clairvoyants avoid them like the plague!"

"What? Now you're telling me you won't read this either?" He jerked his arm toward the pile of bones. "You're not doing us a damn bit of good. Two things that could yield results and you won't touch them. That's just great." He brought his arm down fast and it hit his thigh with a dull slap.

I met his angry gaze with a fierce one of my own.

Dammit! Once again his ignorance about my abilities made me look weak. I'd had just about enough of his you-can't-do-anything-right attitude. It was insulting, and it wasn't like he had done much better on his own. Red and I had already told Vince things he'd never have discovered by normal means. He was a deceptive, small minded, ungrateful jerk, and there was only one way to shut him up. If it put me in the hospital, it would serve him right. I knew it was childish, but I had reached my limit.

"You are so damned clueless!" I practically spat the last word into his face.

I gave him my most lethal, withering glare and, without another word, moved to pick up the nearest bone.

Red bellowed, "Lire! No!"

But it was too late.

My power surged instantaneously, in a blinding, internal glare I'd never felt before. A fluttering feeling ran rampant through the pit of my stomach, and I realized I was airborne a split second before the ground knocked the wind from me. I had just enough time to worry about breathing again before I lost consciousness.

FOUR

When I opened my eyes, I was recumbent on hard ground. The meaty parts of my backside weren't sore, so I didn't think I had been lying there for very long. I blinked several times, waiting for my eyes to adjust to the illumination in the ... room? There was a closed stillness to the atmosphere, but I had a difficult time making out the ceiling. I knew I wasn't looking at the sky, and yet it had a thick, cloudy look to it. I sat up slowly and tried to remember where I was and why I was on the ground. My current surroundings weren't jogging any memories.

I sat in the middle of a semicircular stone dais, partially enclosed by an elegantly turned balustrade the color of creamy alabaster. The railing looked thick and substantial, but somehow managed to retain an ethereal quality. It ran around the circular portion of the platform, leaving the straight face open for the steps. A young man with blonde hair and a slim athletic build sat on the balustrade, where it ended at the stairs. He kicked his dangling heels against the stone. *Thap, thap. Thap, thap. Thap, thap.* He looked at me with a pleasant expression and didn't appear to be distressed in the least about being in such an unusual location. Well, maybe it wasn't so unusual for him.

"Hi."

I tried not to frown. "Uh, hi."

His thin-lipped smile crooked upward at one side, giving him an amused expression, as if he knew something I didn't.

Deadly Remains - Chapter Four

He appeared to be younger than I—early twenties maybe—
with dark blonde hair clipped tight around his ears and neck
but left slightly longer on top. High cheekbones and a prominent brow dominated his features, but large eyes softened
his appearance. Altogether, it was a nice face. It was a face
that belonged next door, one that any young woman might
dream of looking into.

I stood to get a better look at my surroundings. Unfortunately, it didn't provide me with any more information than
I already had. The walls, if you could call them walls, were a
shade or two darker than the ceiling, with the same nebulous aspect, making them seem both near and far away. The
ground surrounding the dais was pale brown but looked too
smooth to be packed dirt. It joined with the walls some in-
determinate distance away. There was nothing else to see.

Maybe the blonde knew something about this place.

I walked over to perch myself on the end of the balustrade directly opposite him. The eight-foot opening for the
steps gaped between us but didn't prevent normal conversation. He continued to regard me with an open, friendly expression.

"How are you feeling?" he asked as I settled myself on the
wide railing. My legs dangled, matching his, and I leaned
back, using my arms to support myself.

"Fine, I guess. I'm just not sure where I am. Do you know
how I got here?" It hadn't occurred to me to be scared or
worried. Here I was in a really strange place, with no
memory of how or why, facing a complete stranger, and yet
I felt completely at ease. I wasn't even concerned by the
thought that I should be more concerned. Weird.

"I'm not sure. I woke up here a little before you did."
Blonde lashes, slightly darker than his hair, framed his blue
eyes. He peered at me. "You're here to help me though."

"Help you? What do you mean? Why do you need help?"

"I'm supposed to go somewhere, but I can't get there
from here. For now, I'm stuck."

I laughed. "What makes you think I'm not stuck too? I
take it you've tried looking for the way out."

"I don't need to look." His eyes shifted in thought. "I just know. I can't leave."

A change in the illumination level made me look out past him toward the distant walls. Had it gotten darker? Shadows seemed to cloak the walls and the ceiling had taken on the color of storm clouds, but maybe I was imagining things.

I shifted my attention back to the blonde. "Does it seem darker to you?"

"You'll be leaving soon."

His knowing eyes and shift in the conversation made me take pause. I frowned. "What are you talking about?"

He nodded toward the horizon, and I followed his gaze. As the walls grew darker, they appeared to close in on us. Shadow encroached the dais, the gradual twilight swallowing the ground's tawny color. Fascinated, I watched the leading edge of darkness creep closer, until the gloom licked the steps. In just moments, the dais had become a small island in the middle of a shadowy ocean.

"Come on!" I jumped down from the railing and tugged his sleeve to get him moving. We hurried to the center of the platform.

I looked at his face and then back at the approaching darkness. "What's happening?" My former calm evaporated. The advancing darkness sucked away my composure, leaving me breathless and afraid.

"Don't worry. You're going back now." He gave me a sad smile. "But you're taking some of me with you."

I examined him. "What? Who are you? What is going on?"

He tilted his head, looking calm and unconcerned about the darkness, and touched my cheek. "I'm Jason. Jason Warner."

With his touch, a warm, feathery essence caressed my mind and soothed my fears, leaving behind a profound joy tempered by a hint of regret. Dumbfounded, I stared into his eyes as the darkness washed over us.

I felt strange and at peace.

I floated in the dark. I heard my name and it sounded tinny, like someone speaking to me through a can and string. I ignored it. The voice came again, this time louder and more insistent. I knew I should recognize the voice, but I couldn't quite place it. Anyway, I didn't want to. My cocoon was warm and comfortable. I tried to disregard the voice, but the darkness receded. I felt the weight of my body, again supine on a hard surface. My hand rested on my cheek, and I remembered, with a jolt of understanding, my strange meeting with Jason.

Unshed tears stung the back of my eyes. I covered my face with both hands and fought for composure. I remembered what led up to my encounter with Jason and realized he was dead. He had been a victim of a crazed warlock and a pent demon, leaving his soul trapped within his bones, unable to reach Heaven. I knew these things because Jason was a part of me. His memories permeated my mind and touched my soul, a lingering psychic embrace.

Vince had been the one calling my name. Now that I was awake, he asked me if I was okay.

I nodded from behind my hands and focused tightly on reigning in my emotions before I lost it. I did not want him or any of the other detectives to see me emotionally compromised.

After a moment, I dropped my hands and sat up, noting we were on the front porch of the abandoned farmhouse. I smoothed my hair and tucked it behind my ears and forced myself to take a deep breath.

When I was brave enough to look up, I found myself staring into Vince's troubled face.

"Lire ..." He was lost for words.

It seemed my magical mumbo jumbo had stumped him yet again. The thought made me smile weakly, and his features loosened into an expression of relief. He reached out, maybe to brush my tangled hair out of my face or give my arm a squeeze, but a voice boomed nearby, "Don't touch her! Are you crazy?"

He withdrew his hand, eyes filled with doubt. I looked down to hide the hurt that was probably raw on my face, but some of it must have shown because his hand wavered midway between his body and mine. I continued to look at my lap, biting back the tears that threatened to return, and jumped when Vince snapped, "Kopeky, go find something constructive to do!"

I heard a condescending snort and turned to see the heavyset deputy standing at the front steps. Kopeky considered me with nervous, wily eyes, but remained quiet. After a few moments under Vince's angry glare, he walked away, shaking his head and muttering to himself.

I looked around the porch. Vince's jacket was folded a few feet away from me, where it must have been placed under my head. "Where's Red?"

"Right there." He pointed toward the wall of the house behind me, and I saw my purse.

I breathed a sigh of relief. "Thank you. But weren't you afraid of getting zapped?"

He gave me a condescending look tempered by a wry smile. "I'm not that stupid. If I thought he'd zap me, I'd have left him down there on his own." He paused. "He told me I was safe from the spells if he stayed concealed inside your purse. And he made sure I wore gloves. He was pretty pissed at me for giving you a hard time. Said you'd never have touched the bone if it weren't for me. He told me why bones are so ... challenging."

It wasn't exactly an apology, but his actions spoke louder than words. He carried me all the way up the hill and put his jacket under my head. Yup—definitely feeling sorry. But I wasn't fooled. If it weren't for the gloves, I'd probably still be down there, lying in the dirt.

"What did Red tell you?"

Vince squirmed a little. I don't think he expected a pop quiz. "He said bones give off more psychic energy than a live person. Something about the soul providing a barrier of some kind when we're alive. After someone dies, you get the full dose of memories because there's no soul to interfere."

I nodded.

"So, I guess I just have a stronger barrier than most normal people." He was obviously still thinking about our close call down at the crime scene.

"Maybe. I don't know. I've never encountered anyone I couldn't read." I amended, "At least, never anyone who wasn't a clairvoyant. And I don't know whether your psychic shield, or whatever it is, will hold up to prolonged exposure or not. Do psychics run in your family?"

"No." The response was a little too quick, but I let it go. It seemed to be a sore spot, and I didn't want to yank his chain. Maybe he wasn't all that bad. He still had psi-phobic issues and I wouldn't choose him as my desert island pal, but I could probably handle working with him.

I glanced in the direction of the murder scene through the rungs of the porch railing. "Thanks for lugging me back up the hill."

He half shrugged, like it was no big deal, and admitted, "I wanted to call an ambulance, but Red talked me out of it. He said if you didn't wake up after we finished wrapping up the site, I should take you to the psi-ward at Swedish. He assured me your life wasn't immediately in danger."

I nodded. As long as I didn't cause myself injury by hitting my head, then the main health risk was not being able to eat or drink. Most psi-induced comas lasted only a day or two, but some had been known to go longer. It all depended upon the psychic trauma inflicted. My longest was three days, back before my powers had totally developed.

I rubbed my head, checking for lumps, but didn't find any. "So how long have I been out?"

He checked his watch. "About twenty minutes."

I leaned over toward the house and grabbed my purse. When I opened it, Red stood in the inside pocket, looking up at me. I smiled at him sheepishly. "Hey. Thanks for helping Vince look after me."

He shrugged. "It was nothing. You woke earlier than I anticipated. I expected a trip to the hospital."

"The day's just been full of surprises. I would have been out longer, but I didn't get a full dose." I pulled out my gloves and slipped them back on.

Red cocked his head to the side. His stuffed animal face didn't promote a wide range of expressions, but he managed to give me a knowing look. "Tell me."

I told them about my strange dream encounter with Jason and belief that Jason's soul was trapped in the bones. Somehow I made it through without crying—not an insignificant feat.

"You knew the bones contained his soul, didn't you?" I asked Red.

"I detected the confinement spell but had no way of knowing where the soul had been trapped. I assumed Paimon had taken it as payment. Apparently Jason's soul was not compromised by evil, which barred the demon from absorbing it. Paimon trapped it in the bones instead, probably out of spite."

"How can we release his soul?" My voice quavered. Jason was right. I was determined to help him, whatever it took.

"A necromancer should be able to free it. When I was alive, I could have done it. It is much easier to release a soul than it is to trap one."

"Why?" Vince asked.

"Because it is almost impossible to trap someone's soul without their express consent. Paimon is able to do so because it is an extremely powerful demon that has the ability to make anyone defenseless to magic. However, Paimon can only absorb the souls that are heavily tainted or those he can trick into becoming enslaved. Apparently Jason couldn't be tricked. Since Paimon couldn't take Jason's soul back to Hell, it trapped it on earth instead."

I sat forward to give Vince a direct look. "When you contact Jason's parents, please let them know about his soul. If they need a reference for a necromancer, I can get them one. This is important to me. And to Jason, for that matter. Have them call me if they want to know about my encounter. It might bring them a measure of peace, and I don't mind speaking with them."

His brows formed a dubious line while he studied me. "I can tell them you had some sort of psychic experience with his remains, but I won't tell them his soul is trapped as though it were fact." He shook his head. "Sorry, but that's way out of my comfort zone."

I closed my eyes and sighed. It was a sad, defeated sound. I hated hearing myself make it. "Fine."

After a moment of silence, he asked, "Did you get anything else from your reading?" He grabbed his jacket from the floor and removed a small notebook and pen from one of the outside pockets.

I suppressed an urge to say something childish about him not believing me anyway, so what was the point. Instead, I nodded, swallowed hard, and took another deep breath. I wasn't up to talking about it yet but knew it was necessary. Until now, I had managed to avoid dwelling on Jason's memories. They waited, just like all recollections, quietly in the recesses of my mind, until I chose to remember them.

I closed my eyes and fully immersed myself in Jason's final moments. I normally liked to keep some sense of my own body when facing traumatic events, since it helped to reduce their emotional impact, but this time, I experienced them full force to glean every possible detail.

"On January the 12th, I went to a lunch meeting with a woman I met in an on-line chat group. Her name is Helen Wilkensen. She's my age and also a telekinetic, so we have something in common. We corresponded for a few weeks before finally deciding to go out. We arranged to meet at the Chili's restaurant in Issaquah because it's the halfway point between our homes. Helen lives in Fall City with her parents, but I know she's hoping to move out on her own soon.

"I got to the Chili's a few minutes early and waited for Helen before getting a table, but she never showed up. After twenty minutes, I finally left my name with the hostess and sat down. I had lunch and then left the restaurant at around two o'clock. After all of our chats and e-mails, I was pretty surprised that Helen stood me up.

"I walked to my car, which was parked two aisles down at the back side of the restaurant. A white van had parked close on the driver's side. It pissed me off because I was worried they had dinged the side of my car. When I turned sideways to move between the cars, the sliding door on the van opened and someone pulled me inside. They put something over my mouth. That's the last thing I remember, until— " My eyes flew open, and I choked back a scream by taking in a long raking gulp of air.

I blurted, "Oh, God," before slapping both hands across my mouth.

Vince looked startled. "You okay?"

I lowered my hands, absently moving them to clutch my purse, which threatened to roll off my lap. Vince had leaned toward me. I didn't want Red to tumble out and zap him by accident. I also wanted Red close to me. I needed his comfort. "Yeah." I pressed my lips together and nodded. "I'm fine."

He sat back, looking doubtful. "Okay."

When Vince moved out of the way, Red jumped out of my purse and scrambled up my arm to perch on my shoulder. My hand hovered under him, in case he slipped, but he didn't. He reached my shoulder, and I pressed him against my face, closing my eyes and breathing deeply. He smelled like home, and his soft, cuddly body gave me some much-needed consolation. Again, Vince's earlier comment about a grown woman having a teddy bear floated into my thoughts, but I refused to feel self-conscious. What Jason went through was horrific. I deserved to be soothed, dammit.

Red's furry arms patted my face in our version of a hug. I murmured a heartfelt thank you before releasing him. He sat down on my shoulder, holding on to my hair for support, legs dangling toward the ground.

"Look, I can see this is upsetting. I certainly don't want to make it worse, but ..." His voice trailed off, and his hands gestured helplessly.

"It's okay. I'll get through it."

After I took a moment to collect myself, I decided to proceed with a little more sense of my own persona. I needed a buffer from Jason's emotional turmoil, but I made sure not to remove myself to the extent that important details escaped my attention.

"Okay. When Jason woke up, he was face down on the ground in an area surrounded by trees and bushes with his hands and feet tied. He heard a woman crying, not too far away. She was also tied up, but unlike him, completely naked." I bit my lip. "And not only that, she was drop dead gorgeous. She was the most beautiful woman Jason had ever seen, and he was captivated."

I frowned and shook my head. "But it was a lie! The beautiful woman ... it was all just a disguise. The woman was the demon." I set my jaw, determined to get through the discussion without falling apart. "That's what many demons do, you know. They're masters of deception and persuasion. But, what they really are is unimaginable. They are every nightmare you've ever had, every terrible thing you've ever witnessed, all the horrors you've heard about—all of that, and none of that. A demon is indescribable because it manifests itself using whatever burdens your soul. The things Jason saw, what he experienced ..." I shook my head. "I'll only say it was hideous and terrifying and just wrong." I shuddered. "It threatened him. Told him all the terrible things it was going to do unless he surrendered to it. Surrendered his soul."

I crossed my arms, rubbing my hands up and down my biceps as though I were cold. Even though I had pulled myself out of Jason's recollections, the indelible memories weighed on my spirit. A fine nervous tremor, which had hardly been noticeable at first, now shook my entire body. My teeth chattered uncontrollably, and I couldn't continue speaking. To keep my clacking teeth from making so much noise, I clenched them together, but the sound of my breath was almost as loud.

I hit my thigh with my fist and grunted. I prided myself on being able to handle any reading. Now, I was an emotional basket case.

Vince got up. "I'll be right back."

He returned with a royal blue wool blanket, which he draped over my shoulders, carefully avoiding Red and my skin. He reclaimed his seat across from me while I pulled the ends of the thick fabric over my arms and tried to calm down. Even though I was privately angry with myself, I resolved to not take it out on Vince. Getting the blanket was a sweet gesture. I felt a little guilty for thinking so poorly of him earlier in the day.

"Thuh-thanks."

He frowned. "I'm sorry this is so difficult."

I tried to smile and told him through clenched teeth, "That's ok-kay. It's my juh-job, remember? Besides, how am I s-suh-posed to gloat later if I don't help you suh-solve this?"

He chuckled. "Right. I wouldn't want you to miss out on that."

I looked down.

"Can I ask you a few questions while you warm up?"

"Shh-sure." I didn't bother to tell him I wasn't cold. I think he probably already knew that.

He reclaimed his notebook and pen from the porch, where he had set them down earlier. "Did Jason see who pulled him into the van?"

I shook my head. "Nuh-no."

"Did he notice the van's license plate, or anything unusual about it?"

I thought back to the van. "He dih-didn't look at the puh-plate. He was more foh-focused on finding duh-door dents on his car. The van was one of the bih-big full size ones—nuh-not a minivan—and it looked new. That's all I cah-can think of—I already told you it was white."

Vince made a few notes on the pad, looking all the part of a determined detective. "This Helen Wilkensen, did he ever speak with her on the telephone?"

I made the effort to relax my body. The chattering grew worse whenever I tensed up. I closed my eyes and recalled Jason's memories. "No. I corresponded with her in chuh-chat groups and on e-mail. We— " I stopped abruptly and opened my eyes. "Sorry. They exchanged photos on-line. She has bruh-brown, straight hair, shoulder length, and brown eyes. Jason thought she was pretty. The photo will be in an e-mail from her on his computer. You'll be able to fuh-find the other e-mails as well, I'd imagine."

Vince regarded me with a strange expression. I'd say he looked spooked, except that wasn't quite it. A little uneasy maybe.

"Do you always do that?" He held his pen poised an inch or two above the small, spiral bound notebook and then lowered it. "You know, like you were doing earlier, talk in the first person as though it really happened to you."

I shrugged. "Yeah, I guess so. Sometimes it's hard not to."

"So you have all his memories now? Like having another person in your head?"

"In a way. I don't have all of his memories, but there are many." I took a shuddering breath. As though my heavy heart wasn't enough of a clue, my body continued to remind me of my recent experience. At least my diaphragm had relaxed, and I no longer sounded like a hypothermia victim.

"Interesting." He shook his head, once again readying his pen. "Do you know why they never spoke on the phone?"

"No. I get the sense he assumed she was being careful."

"You said he was a telekinetic. That's someone who can move objects without touching them, right?"

I tipped my head to the side. "More or less. There are three forms. A type one telekinetic can move only inanimate objects. A type two can move only animate objects, you know, people, animals, bugs, stuff that's alive. A type three can manipulate both animate and inanimate. Jason was a type three. Helen said in one of their chat sessions that she was a type two."

Vince paused to write, muttering something about 'types' under his breath. When he was done, he asked, "Can you tell me Jason's address?"

"That's more difficult. Let me think for a minute." I closed my eyes. "I can't get an exact address; just that he lived in Kirkland, in a condo." Before he could ask why, I opened my eyes and said, "I don't get every stitch of a person's memories, like a computer download or something. I mostly get moments of emotional or physical significance, so when it comes to the more mundane experiences, it's a bit of a crap shoot."

He nodded. "Did Jason have any enemies or shady acquaintances in his life who might be involved in this?"

I looked past his shoulder, eyes unfocused, and thought about it. "No. I don't have any memories of anyone like that. He was a nice guy. He didn't have any enemies."

"Did Jason get a look at the warlock?"

"Yes, but the guy was cloaked and masked. He looked about six feet tall. The cloak covered his body, so I'm not sure about body type."

"What kind of mask? What did it look like?"

I put the warlock in my mind and focused on Jason's impressions. "It was black. The hood of the cloak covered his head and cast a shadow over his face, but I think it was just a black handkerchief or bandana." I shrugged. "The cloak was black too. Honestly, it was pretty theatrical looking, like something you might wear to a costume party."

Vince made some more notes and then asked, "Is there anything else in Jason's memories that might help us?"

I recalled the traumatic events that led to Jason's death. "I can't think of anything. But none of the memories conflict with the theory I outlined earlier. The demon attempted to terrify Jason into surrendering his soul, but its tactics failed. Jason was Catholic, maybe a bit on the liberal side, but he was still a true believer and knew enough to resist the demon's persuasions. He was very brave." I paused to corral my emotions. "The warlock informed Jason that he had made a grave mistake and then chloroformed him. That's it. Jason never woke up again."

"How do you know it was chloroform?"

I stared at him and frowned. "Oh. I guess I just assumed. He forced a cloth over Jason's mouth and nose. Jason struggled against it, but whatever was on the handkerchief worked quickly."

Vince looked grim and nodded, apparently satisfied by my response. He closed his notebook and retrieved a business card from his pocket. "If you think of anything else, let me know." He handed me his card after writing something on it. "My home and cell numbers are on the back. Call me anytime."

"Okay." I shook myself, as if that simple gesture would clear my mind of the distressing memories. I knew it was purely psychological, but it seemed to help. I looked around. "So, can we go now? I had two coffees this morning. I really have to hit a bathroom before I burst."

He laughed. "Yeah. We can go. Kopeky and Marshall are closing up the site. I can talk to the medical examiner later."

Vince was nice enough to stop at the closest gas station, which spared me from complaining about every bump in the road during our return trip. Red reclaimed his position on the dashboard, looking comfortable with his head against the window strut and arms folded across his pudgy tummy.

Once were back on I-90, heading toward downtown, Vince broke the relaxed silence. "Earlier, when you didn't get a reading from me, you said maybe there was hope for you. What did you mean? I'd think not getting a reading would be a bad thing in your business."

I snorted. "Right. If I were in the business of reading people, I guess it would be a bad thing."

Vince frowned. "I don't understand. How is it good?"

I hunched toward the passenger window and stared out at the passing scenery. Vince didn't realize it, but he had lofted a very personal question. It wasn't his fault. Most people had little understanding about what it was like to be a clairvoyant. They'd never considered that the world is full of objects touched by human hands. They never thought about what it would be like to live in a world where practically everything they touch or eat will bring on visions and nightmares. What are you going to wear, eat, brush your teeth with, and sleep on? But the one thing I'd always found most surprising was people didn't think about the most obvious drawback—the social aspect. A clairvoyant can't touch another person with any exposed part of their body, not just their hands. No casual touching, no holding hands, no hugging, no kissing, no … you know.

I shrugged off my discomfort. "That's kind of a loaded question."

"Sorry. I can see that." He glanced at me. "I guess I don't know why."

He wasn't sorry enough to drop it, but at least he was polite about it. I let the silence lengthen before answering. "Let's just say, knowing it's possible for a normal to block my magic gives me hope I might find Prince Charming some day."

I let him reason out my response and turned toward the scenery again. Lake Washington spread out around us, sparkling brightly in the rare winter sun, and I spotted several boats taking advantage of the clement if slightly breezy day. Two aluminum skiffs floated close to the low-lying Lacy V. Murrow Bridge, but we moved too quickly for me to peer down inside them. It seemed to me the vibration from all the cars would drive away the fish, but what did I know? I'd never gone fishing in my life, although, it was one of the only animals I could eat without too many ill effects.

"Why does not reading someone have anything to do with finding your dream guy?"

Drat. My desire to avoid the discussion had only increased his curiosity and focused more attention on the sad state of my love life.

I sighed. "I was trying to be circumspect, but I'll spell it out for you. I can't touch someone—well, a regular someone—without learning a lot about them. And when I mean a lot, I mean everything. When I touch someone, I pick up all they happen to be thinking—about me, about their life, about the weather, whatever is on their mind. And it's generally a bad thing in a relationship to know everything your partner is thinking. For reasons I can't fathom, some people think it sounds romantic. You're so in love, you want to know everything about that person, but in reality it doesn't work. In the real world, everyone needs their privacy, even the ones you love and who love you back."

He glanced at me and then shrugged. "I assumed if you were prepared for it, you could control things and ignore someone's thoughts if you needed to."

I shook my head. "It doesn't work that way. I can't stop the psychic energy from entering my mind. I can control it, and yes, if I'm ready for it, I can push the stream back out without getting stuck with the memories. But that takes a lot of effort and only works for the initial dose. The energy I get from extended touching will breach my shield within a short time." I added, for further clarity, "And it's all touching—not just with my hands. Understand?"

His eyebrows shot up before he nodded. "Got it." He tilted his head. "What about another clairvoyant. You made some comment about not getting a reading from another psychic. Does the magic cancel out?"

"Actually, yes, that works to a degree, but only if the two psychics are of relatively equal power. And our powers can change over time, so ... sometimes that doesn't work out for the long term."

When Vince looked over at me, I had to struggle to keep my expression neutral. Yes, I was well acquainted with that particular theory.

Vince noticed my unhappiness, but didn't have the sense to let it go. "You sound like you're speaking from experience."

"Yeah, well ... life's a bitch."

I stared hard at the road through the windshield, but after a moment my gaze wandered toward Red. He cocked his head. "'Tis better to have loved and lost, than never to have loved at all."

The subject of my social life was not a new one for Red and me, and we frequently traded that verse with each other at some point during our conversations. It had become a joke of sorts between us. My response to this famous phrase was usually something like, 'What bone-head thought that one up?' This time, however, I simply said, "Touché, Red." I guess Jason's memories had left me feeling a bit on the glum side.

Most of the time, I thought Tennyson's verse applied more to Red's past life than to mine. All of his loves were truly lost forever, long since dead. Because he no longer inhabited a human body, Red could reminisce about his past relationships without feeling remorse or regret that he'd never again feel the warmth of a lover's embrace or the thrill of a passionate kiss. He understood my pain but was removed from it at the same time. On occasion, it was something I almost envied.

After several minutes, Vince broke the silence. "So why did you want to know whether psychics run in my family?"

I shot him a look of exasperation. "You just can't give it a rest, can you?"

He shrugged. "No, not when the subject concerns me."

I laughed. "Okay. You have a point. The reason I asked about your family is because magic tends to run in families. Sometimes it skips generations, and it's not uncommon for several members of the same family to exhibit some type of psychic ability. If someone in your family had a talent, then it could possibly explain your resistance to my magic. But since you don't know of any psychic lineage, then I guess it means it's possible for normals to block my power. If that's really true, then it's unprecedented. I've never heard of such a thing." I shook my head. "Of course, most clairvoyants probably haven't gone out of their way to find out, so maybe it's more common than anyone ever thought. I just don't know."

There was another way he could be blocking my magic, but I didn't bring it up because I knew it didn't apply to him. He wasn't a vampire.

"I see. Thanks."

I decided to change the subject, hoping to derail Vince's one-track mind. "So, have you been with the Chiliquitham PD for long?"

He nodded. "Yep. They hired me out of the Academy, about ten years ago now."

"Why Chiliquitham? Did you grow up around here?"

"No. I grew up in Wenatchee, and, no, I didn't grow up on an orchard."

I laughed. "I guess that's the logical question when you're from apple country."

He glanced at me. "What about you. Where did you grow up?"

"Until I was five, I lived with my parents, just south of San Francisco, in a city called Hillsborough. When I was ready for kindergarten, I went to live at Coventry Academy. My parents divorced a few years after, and my father bought a house on Queen Anne Hill. I stayed with him during school holidays and my summer vacations."

"Where do you live now?"

"Downtown, not too far from Sotheby's," I said. "I take it you live in Chiliquitham."

"Yes, but I went to UW." Vince pronounced it 'you-dub,' like a local. "And I lived near Pioneer Square for a while before I went to the Academy."

"Do you miss it? Living in the city, I mean."

"Not too much. I'm a country boy at heart, I guess. When I need my city fix, I have friends who live in town. I usually get down there at least once a week."

I nodded.

"Hey, will you bite my head off if I ask you another personal question?"

I narrowed my eyes at him. "As long as it isn't about my love life, no."

Vince laughed. "Fair enough." He paused for a moment, brows furrowing together while he formulated his question. "Until I met you, I'd never considered what it's like to be a clairvoyant. I assumed you had more control over your magic, or you only had to worry about touching stuff with your hands. It must be tough. How do you survive it? How do you get through the day?" He shrugged and then glanced at me with a quirked smile before adding, "But I'm sure you probably get this question all the time from clueless guys like me."

I cringed and looked down at my hands. "I'm sorry I said you were clueless." I tried not to fidget in my seat and was glad Vince had to keep his eyes mostly on the road. "Unless you knew someone with the gift, there was no way for you to know all my limitations. I should have told you the ground rules ahead of time."

"Nah, I deserved it. I was pushing you." He glanced at me. "So, if it's not too personal, how do you get by? Seems like everything you'd need would be touched somewhere down the line by a human. How do you get around that?"

"There are ways. Back fifteen or twenty years ago, I was mostly out of luck or my parents had to pay a fortune for psychically clean products. Nowadays though, a lot of companies have gotten on the psi-free bandwagon. Believe it or not, there are companies that make psi-free clothing, shampoo, cosmetics, sheets, you name it. If you can think of it, there's probably a way to get it made from psi-free materials."

He nodded. "Right. The psi-free thing. That's for real? I thought it was just a marketing gimmick."

"Nope. It's the real deal." I amended, "Well, most of them are. I still have to be careful and only buy from trustworthy companies."

"What about your home? Can you even get psi-free building materials?" He seemed genuinely interested and almost chatty. For the first time, I felt like I was getting a glimpse of Vince the person, instead of Vanelli the terse detective.

"With a house or building, what you're really talking about are the touchable surfaces—walls, counters, floors, you know. Psi-free products can be easily found for those; of course, they're usually quite a bit more expensive." I leaned my head back and stared out at the road ahead of us. "There really aren't many things I haven't been able to find in a psi-free version." I rolled my head toward Vince and regarded his profile. "As for my place, I live in a loft that I gutted and fitted out with the appropriate products. It's not hard to build psi-free, but it's not cheap either."

He regarded me for a second and then turned back to the road. "What about the people who can't afford it. What do they do?"

"They do the best they can. They can cover their furniture with psi-free fabric, and most day-to-day products aren't prohibitively expensive. They just have to be careful around the other surfaces in their house. It's possible to get by—it's just not as comfortable." I stifled a yawn. "The weaker clairvoyants, the ones who can't shield themselves effectively, usually end up taking refuge in one of the government sponsored clean centers."

"The weakest clairvoyants? I thought the very strongest of you had to live in the clean shelters."

"Nope. But I can understand why you'd think that. The strength of a clairvoyant is measured by how capable they are at maintaining their psychic shield, not by how much information they can pry from a person or object. If you can't even protect yourself from the smallest of psychic incursions, then living on the outside becomes an exercise in torture. Of course, there are always exceptions. Some weaker clairvoyants are able to live on the outside because they can handle the frequent psychic exposures better than others. I guess the reverse is probably true as well. Even a strong clairvoyant, with exceptional shield control, will every now and then suffer a breach. If you don't have the personality to deal with it, then a clean-room is the only option."

I curled my knees toward Vince, turning myself in the seat. The day's trials were weighing heavily on my body.

The sun beating on my legs, the cozy comfort of the interior, and the soothing road vibrations had left my body feeling languid and boneless. I slouched down, so I could rest my cheek against the seat, using my gloved hand as a pillow and psychic buffer. I watched as Vince struggled to unbutton and roll up the sleeves of his dress shirt, revealing nicely muscled forearms sprinkled with a fine layer of straight, dark body hairs. My eyes felt heavy, and I didn't struggle to keep them open.

Vince asked Red about how he managed to stay so clean after sliding his furry feet through the dirt at the crime scene, and Red explained that his body was spelled to be impervious to wear and tear. Even with sleep tugging at my mind, I smiled when Vince made a crack about needing that kind of spell for his dusty trousers.

I dozed on and off for the remaining twenty minutes of our drive back to the city until the car lurched from side to side as it entered the Puget Pacific Building's driveway. Vince eased the car up to the parking ticket dispenser and unrolled his window to grab the protruding ticket. When the gate went up, he drove the car into the waiting shadow of the parking garage. The electric window rolled back up with a hum, sealing us off from the outside air and traffic noises. I unfolded my legs into the passenger footwell and stretched myself while I issued a reluctant groan.

"Have a good nap?"

"Mmuh-huh." I hid a huge yawn behind both hands.

"What level is your car on?" Vince slowed as we approached the entry point to the lower garage levels.

"Level two."

"Are you going to be okay to drive?"

"Yeah."

He gave me a stern look, like he didn't believe me. I laughed. "I'm fine. Besides, you don't want to be my chauffeur today, do you?"

He snorted. "It wouldn't be the worst job I've ever had, but no. I've got to get back to the station. But I can take you back to your place if you're too tired to drive."

I guess he still felt bad about the bone thing. I smiled. "I'm okay, really. There's my car. The black Mercedes, on the right. There." I pointed.

He pulled up and stopped, with the passenger window even with the rear of my car. "It looks more like a tank."

"It's supposed to be a car, but you sure wouldn't know it by the gas mileage." I dug into my purse searching for the keys.

He motioned toward the European stickers on the bumper and the narrow slot for the license plate. "Is it imported?"

"Yeah." I shrugged. "Another gift from my dad—German government surplus. Remember the serial sniper a few years ago who was killing magic users? My dad gave it to me around that time. It's armored." I shook my head. "I don't know why I still drive it. The maintenance is horrific. I'm too sentimental, I guess." I held out my hand to Red, and he jumped down from the dashboard. I moved him toward my body and he hopped onto my shoulder, using my hair for support.

Vince raised his eyebrows. "That's some gift."

I shrugged again. "My dad did his best to take care of me."

The question formed on his face before he opened his mouth to ask it. "Is your dad still around?"

"No. He died two years ago." I headed off any more questions by opening the car door. "See you. Let me know how things go with Jason's parents." I gave him one last look and slid out of the car. "Thanks for driving," I mumbled and closed the door firmly without waiting for a reply.

I walked to my car, resisting the urge to look back at him. He waited until I was halfway into my seat before driving away. The dark comfort of the interior made me relax almost immediately. I locked the doors with a press of a button and then threw my head back against the padded headrest. "What a day."

"Indeed." Red jumped off my shoulder and used my upper arm to slide into my lap. I felt the light pitter-pats of his soft feet across my thighs as he moved to the center console.

I lolled my head to the side, so I could see him. "I so do not want to go back to the office."

"Go home. Surely, Jack will not mind."

"Yeah, right." I rolled my eyes and couldn't suppress a snort. "Jack would have two litters of puppies if I skipped out on my afternoon appointments, and you know it."

Jack was slightly less calm than a squirrel on speed, but in spite of his manic personality, he always managed to acquire new clients and keep current ones happy. If it weren't for the fact that he was such a likeable guy, he'd have driven me crazy years ago.

I sighed and stuck the keys into the ignition. It was going to be a long day.

FIVE

I strode into the Supernatural Talent and Company office at ten after three. That is to say, ten minutes late for my next appointment. I had the foresight to call the office to tell Monica I was on my way. In spite of my precaution, Jack hovered near the lobby, talking to Monica and waiting to pounce on me as soon as I made an entrance. I cut a path straight to my office, doing my best to ignore his anxious expression and eager gesture toward our front conference room. His footsteps echoed softly on the carpet behind me, but I managed to reach my office before he caught up with me.

"Your three o'clock is in the front conference room," he said, as if there was any chance I missed his gyrations in the lobby.

"I know, Jack. I just wanted to put down my stuff and make a pot of coffee." I tried not to sound annoyed.

"Mr. Gibson has been waiting for over ten minutes." His vivid blue eyes danced quickly between me and the direction of the conference room. It was probably all he could do to not jump from foot to foot, like a terrier badly in need of a walk.

"Yes, I realize that, but I haven't even had lunch yet, thanks to my wonderful field trip with the detective. If you don't want me keeling over on our client, I need something to keep me going."

85

Deadly Remains - Chapter Five

I put my purse on the makeshift window seat I'd created with two bookcases and a padded bench from Costco. The sun pierced through the slats in the aluminum blinds, and what I really wanted to do was lie down and take a nap in that enticing golden warmth. Red climbed out of my purse and sat near his tiny basket of books. I spent a small fortune every month, buying books and other leisure items from the *End of the Rainbow* catalog, which specialized in leprechaun and pixie products. In truth, I'd spend a lot more if it meant securing Red's happiness. For that, I'd do almost anything.

"I suggest you listen to her, Jack. She has already fainted once today."

I shot Red a sour look as I hung my coat over the back of my chair.

Jack stared at me. I watched his preoccupied expression transform into a look of puzzlement and concern. "Is that true? What happened?" A look of realization passed over his face, and he paced back and forth in front of my desk. "It was the police, wasn't it? Dammit! I knew I should have said no. I knew it! But that detective was really persuasive, and you've told me several times helping the police is important to you."

I walked closer to Jack and held up my hand. "Look, it's okay. I'm glad you scheduled me with the police. They needed my help. The only thing you could have done differently was to brief them beforehand about my skills and what I'm capable of reading. They didn't realize some items require much more time and energy to read. I had to deal with some significant evidence during the morning appointment. And later on at the crime scene, they wanted me to read the victim's bones."

At this, Jack's eyes widened. I quickly interjected, "I know! I know. I should have said no to the bones, but I was stupid and read them anyway. That wasn't the best decision I've ever made, but I'm glad I did it. We learned a lot from that reading, even though it knocked me for a loop."

"What! Are you out of your mind? You're lucky you didn't end up in a coma ... permanently. What were you thinking?"

"Thought had little to do with it," Red concluded.

Jack had stopped pacing to face me. He thwacked the end of a ballpoint pen over the palm of his left hand and frowned. The pen thing was one of Jack's many nervous habits. It made a dull slapping sound that annoyed me after about three seconds.

I rolled my eyes. "Talk to Red, he'll fill you in. I'll be right back. I'm going to poke my head in with Ben and see if he wants some coffee."

I walked to the conference room and found Ben Gibson reading one of the magazines from our lobby coffee table. He looked down, giving me a view of his slightly receding gray hair. The neat furrows from his comb were frozen in place by whatever hair gel he had used earlier in the morning. Ben pushed sixty, with a face still handsome despite wrinkles and a rugged complexion.

I stood framed in the doorway and leaned my left shoulder against the door jam. "Hi, Ben. Sorry I'm late. If you don't mind, I'm just making a fresh pot of coffee. Would you like a cup?"

He smiled, displaying wide, straight teeth and a set of deep dimples at each side of his mouth. "Hello, Lire. Sure, I'll join you in a cup."

"Okey-doke. I'll be right with you."

When I got back to my office, I overheard Red, "—fortunate the soul was bound to the bones; otherwise, she might have been in the hospital for weeks."

Jack looked up with a grim expression as I entered the room. I grabbed the empty coffee carafe. "Jack, you want any?" I wiggled the glass container at him.

"No." He shook is head and then remembered his manners. "No, thanks."

I left the room again to wash and fill the decanter with water while Jack questioned Red about Jason's bones. When I returned, Jack sat in the straight-backed guest chair across from my desk, chewing on the end of his pen and bopping his heel against the floor. He looked up and watched me as I set up the machine to brew the coffee.

Deadly Remains - Chapter Five

Jack was unusually quiet, although far from still. I don't think he ever stopped fidgeting. His brown hair needed to be cut, his usual generic male haircut had lost to a more messy style, although his bangs hadn't yet obscured his eyebrows. He had one of those faces that would always look youthful, no matter what his age, and it was accented by startling blue eyes surrounded by thick, curled lashes. A small mole on his chin drew attention to his wonderfully full lips. In my book, Jack was very attractive. His muscular build added to the package, although his face was a bit too round and his nose too large to be considered male model perfect. At five-feet-six inches tall, he was one of the few men I knew who I managed to look down on.

Just because I appreciated Jack's good looks, didn't mean I lusted after his body. Quite the contrary. It was one of those mysterious chemistry things, I guess. Not to mention, Jack's constant high energy always left me feeling like I needed to pop a Xanax to settle my nerves. Fortunately, he had never given me the impression he was interested in me, which was a good thing since he was my business partner.

"We should reconsider our policy of working with the police at the drop of a hat and limit how many cases you'll do a year. I'm worried about you burning out, or, worse, landing yourself in a clean-room." Jack's right knee bounced up and down at about a hundred miles an hour as he levered his heel up and down against the floor. His pen was a chewed mess. He absently wiped it off on his pants and started banging it against his bobbing thigh. I had a strong desire to take his pen away and hold him down so he couldn't move, but I resisted the urge and stayed in my chair. Willpower at its best.

"I don't think we need to go to that extreme after one bad day. Today was unusual, you know that. I've been working with the police for how many years now? Four, almost five? And have I ever had a day like today? No, I haven't. The thing that will help prevent this from happening again will be to make sure my clients know my limits and to schedule the

appropriate amount of time for the type of items I'll be reading." I shrugged. "But, I'm ultimately to blame. I shouldn't
have let Vince needle me into reading the bones. I should
have scheduled it for when I'd be totally fresh, without any
other appointments to worry about."

"Or not done it at all." Jack shook his head, looking dubious, but finally sighed in resignation. "All right. Next time I'll
make sure they understand the rules. If I'm not sure, I'll
check with you about how much time to schedule." He
launched himself out of the chair. "I'll pass it on to Monica
since she's the one who usually makes the appointments."
On his way out, Jack leaned back into the room. "Oh, and
don't keep Mr. Gibson waiting. And let me know what happens with the bones and the victim's family." He was gone
before I had time to respond.

I rolled my eyes at Red and then quickly assembled a
serving tray with two coffees, cream, sugar, and some oatmeal cookies. Before heading to the conference room with
the refreshments, I almost forgot to grab my notepad and
camera, which I tucked under my arm and hung from my
wrist, sparing me a return trip.

As soon as I breached the conference room doorway, Ben
jumped up to offer his help getting the tray to the table. I
didn't need it but let him take the tray anyway, out of politeness. He had been born to a generation of men who were
automatically courteous and never dreamed of getting past
any bases on the first date. Whether this last part was true,
I honestly didn't know, but he was always so polite. I closed
the conference room door and took a seat near him at the
table. We indulged in some small talk as we sipped our coffees. After a few minutes, the discussion turned toward the
items he needed authenticated.

Ben owned a small but successful antiques shop near
Queen Anne Hill. Ever since Jack and I began our business,
Ben had been coming in for weekly sessions, but I'd actually
known him for years. I used to frequent his shop in my teens
when I stayed with my dad during school vacations. After

Deadly Remains - Chapter Five

Ben noticed me removing my gloves and deliberately touching items in his store, he asked if I would be interested in helping him appraise some of his merchandise. At first, I think he was simply fascinated by my gift and curious about what information I was able to glean, but soon enough, he realized the monetary benefit of a psychic reading. He started out paying me two dollars per item, which I thought was such a coup at the time, especially since I had already been surreptitiously touching things in his shop just for fun.

It didn't take long for me to realize the implications of my gift and dream of starting the first paranormal business in Seattle. To a certain extent, I owe Ben for my current success and happiness, and I have told him as much on several occasions. He just laughed and said he only gave me a gentle nudge toward my destiny—to keep our history alive. Ben was a hopeless romantic and history buff. It's too bad we were born a generation apart. Or not, considering my togetherness issues.

I stood up and peeked inside the cardboard box he had placed between us on the conference table. It contained several items wrapped in plastic bubble wrap, along with a half dozen smaller boxes perched on top of the pile. A wooden cane with a gold handle, too large to fit inside, rested across the edges of the box.

"Oh boy, more jewelry," I said after noticing the small, hinged boxes.

"Reading a lot of jewelry lately?"

"Not a lot, but I had one earlier at Sotheby's that was a doozy."

"Really? Tell me."

He listened, eyes engaged and studious, while I recounted my reading of the diamond ring, but his expression showed something besides interest. Regret maybe? If it was, the emotion didn't come across in his voice. His tone was warm and enthusiastic. "That must have been something. I wish I'd been there to hear it first hand."

I smiled. "Yeah. It was fun. I had Veronica on the edge of her seat."

"I bet." Ben stood with me and slowly began to remove items from the box. After a moment, he paused to regard me. "I've never told you this, because I know how hard things are for you, but there are times I envy your gift."

"Holy cats! Why?"

He chuckled at me and then shook his head. "When you come up with stories like that one, my God! I want to see what you see. I know it causes you all manner of grief, but for that, ah ... for that, it almost seems worth it."

"You know better than most what I go through, so I know you're not being cavalier." I cocked my head and pressed my lips together. "Still, I don't know if it's worth it exactly, but there are moments. That's for sure."

He put his hands on either side of the box and leaned forward to peer into my face. "If you had the chance to give up your gift and live a normal life, would you do it?"

The question took me aback, but I stopped to consider it. "You know, there are days when I would say yes, without hesitation." I picked up my bright yellow coffee mug, my name emblazoned on the outside to prevent others from touching it, and clutched it between both hands. "But being a clairvoyant is all I've ever known. It's who I am and how I make my living. To be honest, I don't know that I could voluntarily give it up, even though it complicates my life."

"Sort of a love/hate relationship, I gather."

"Yeah. You could say that." I sat down again and asked Ben for his first item. I was tired of thinking deeply about my gift and having conversations that reminded me of the hopeless aspect of my love life. Maybe it was denial, but I preferred cruising through life on autopilot, focusing on the day to day, and avoiding any deep introspection.

I made it through all of Ben's objects without falling over. It helped that he almost never bothered with a full reading on his merchandise—he only wanted to know the original owner or maker and a date, which isn't nearly so taxing. Every once in a while, he'd request additional information if something unusual came up with the basic reading. Today, none of his items called for any extra attention. Of course, my work wasn't done. The documentation process took longer than the readings.

Before Monica began advising new clients about the procedures, I often dealt with 'Type A' personalities getting bent out of shape because their appraisal wasn't ready on the spot. Now, I just had to deal with them being disappointed when the object didn't measure up to their expectations. Two years ago, an antique gun dealer physically attacked me because I didn't confirm his Colt .45 Peacemaker had belonged to Jesse James. Fortunately, his session took place in the presence of the buyer, who helped restrain him. Even with the buyer's help, I still ended up with bruises on my arms where he grabbed and shook me. Thank God I'd been wearing long sleeves on that day because I really didn't need to know what he had been thinking at the same time he assaulted me. I had nightmares enough without that bit of colorful information dancing through my head. Even though it was one of my favorites, I sent the blouse I had been wearing straight to Goodwill.

After Ben's items had been repacked, I walked him to the lobby. The gold-topped cane dangled from the edge of his box by its curved handle. He kept his hand over the top of it, so it wouldn't fall off.

"Thank you, Ben. I'll see you next week, it's my turn to come by the shop."

"Sure enough. I have several large pieces for you to examine. One of them you're going to love." He gave me a conspiratorial wink.

I laughed. "Uh-oh. I know what that means. I guess I better remember my checkbook, huh?"

"Just in case, maybe just in case. Okay, Lire. See you later. You take care now."

After saying goodbye, I walked back toward my office, but Monica caught my eye. She waved me over by curling her manicured fingers back and forth, instead of calling my name, because she had a customer on the telephone.

I waited while Monica answered the customer's questions. Today, instead of her usual cleavage-revealing attire, she wore a skin-tight, lavender turtleneck sweater with a black leather skirt. A rhinestone tension clip held back her professionally highlighted blonde hair, with the exception of two loosely curled locks framing her face. She wasn't exactly beautiful, but she was so expertly made up and revealed her bodily assets with such provocative flair that I was pretty sure most people never noticed.

Monica had worked for ST&C for the past three years. Never once had I seen her wear casual clothes. She always dressed as though she had a hot date right after work. Who knows, maybe she did. I'll be honest, it was hard for me to have much respect for Monica since I knew for a fact the only reason she had been hired was because of her looks. ST&C's employees were heavily skewed toward the young single male persuasion, which definitely swayed the votes when it came time to interview and then select our receptionist candidate. More than once, it had occurred to me I might be a tad jealous, but the fact that Monica went out of her way to dress provocatively, in order to garner as much male attention as possible, bothered me. Don't get me wrong, I didn't dislike Monica, but at the same time she wasn't on my list of favorite people either.

The call ended and Monica looked up at me with her deftly outlined eyes. I suspected she had those semi-permanent false eyelashes—the ones that were professionally adhered one lash at a time.

She smiled. "Thanks for waiting. I have a message from your sister. She sounded anxious to speak with you but didn't want me to interrupt your meeting." Monica handed me the pink message slip with my sister's telephone number on it. "I didn't know you had a sister."

I managed to overcome my initial shock, took the pink slip, and looked at it. "We're not close." Strangers was more like it.

I mumbled a thank you and headed back to my office, avoiding further questions from Monica. What the hell did Giselle want to talk to me about? Before Dad's funeral, we hadn't spoken to or seen each other for just over twenty years, and it had been more than two years since Dad passed away.

When my parents divorced, my mother took custody of Giselle and my father took me. It wasn't a tearful parting. My sister learned early on that my mother preferred her to me and never passed up an opportunity to remind me. She made my life a living hell from the time my gift emerged to the time I was seven when my parents split. My feelings toward Giselle had not changed much over the years. If anything, they'd grown more bitter. It was hard not to feel cheated, especially when I saw a relationship like that between Julie and her pyrokinetic brother Tom.

When my parents separated, it was a relief. A deep resentment had grown within me from the age of three when my gift destroyed any normalcy in my young life. By the time I reached seven, two years of school vacations at home with Giselle and Mother had firmly entrenched my feelings of bitterness and hostility. During that time, the weekends and evenings with my father and having Red for a companion were the only bright spots for me.

Unlike my mother, Dad never openly shied away from me, even at the outset. It hurt him deeply that my mother chose to alienate herself from me, although, at first he had no idea how bad it was. It wasn't until Red came into my life that Dad discovered the magnitude of the problem. After spending just one week as my companion, Red had been outraged. He informed Dad of the agony I experienced on a daily basis.

Giselle blamed me for my parents' divorce. I guess that made us even, because I blamed her too, although she had been just part of the problem. If our mother had been more caring, then our family might have had a chance. But as it was, my mother and sister fed off of each other's fear and jealousy, turning an already difficult situation into an untenable one. My sister despised me because my father lavished me with attention to make up for my mother's rejection. My mother feared and hated me because I knew her dark secret.

After all this time, I'd never revealed the secret of my mother's affair to any of my family and discussed it with very few friends. I don't know what had gotten into me this afternoon when I blurted it out to Vince. In the beginning, I didn't tell anyone because I loved my mother. From holding her hand at the park, I knew she felt overwhelmingly guilty about the brief fling with my uncle. The thought of discovery terrified her. I worshipped my mother. Even at three-and-a-half, I knew revealing her secret would hurt her deeply, which I wouldn't have done for the world. Later, when my secrecy had been rewarded with rejection and thinly-veiled hatred, I didn't expose her secret because I didn't want to hurt my father. Although our family life was dysfunctional to say the least and I was patently miserable, I didn't want to be the one responsible for breaking us up.

Lost in thought, I strayed to the front conference room and retrieved my notes, camera, and coffee tray. When I reached my office, I deposited everything on my desk. Red looked up as I flopped into the window seat next to him.

"What's wrong?"

I gave him a wan smile. "Wrong? What could be wrong? I just got a message from Giselle."

"Good Lord. What could she want?" He considered me. "It must be your mother. Something has happened. Why else would she call?"

I pulled up my knees and rested my chin on them, wrapping my arms around my lower legs to keep them from moving out from under me. "I know. She despises me. That's about the only reason she'd call." I let out the sigh I'd been holding for the past several minutes. It didn't make me feel better.

"Are you going to call her?"

I pressed my lips together and shrugged. "I guess so. Monica thought she sounded anxious. You know me. I'm not so petty that I'd refuse to talk to her, much as I might like to."

"At least have something to eat first. You can't live on coffee and cookies."

Deadly Remains - Chapter Five

I couldn't argue. It wasn't just Giselle's call that had me feeling jittery. I hadn't ingested anything but coffee and two Entenmann's cookies for the past seven hours. My fingers trembled, and Red's voice sounded like it came out of a hollow tube.

I ate leftover pasta salad from yesterday's lunch while contemplating my feelings about Giselle and Mom. It seemed poor payment for the lump it left in the pit of my stomach. I decided my queasiness was due to lack of sugar, so I chased the salad down with a couple more oatmeal cookies. They didn't make me feel any better. Now, I felt sick to my stomach *and* in need of a workout.

Before I could chicken out, I picked up the phone and punched in Giselle's number. It rang three times before a hushed female voice answered, "Hello?"

I couldn't tell if it was Giselle. We hadn't spoken more than four or five words in over twenty years. Even at my father's funeral, we stayed as far apart from each other as the room allowed. "Hi. Uh, may I please speak with Giselle?"

"This is Giselle. Is this Clotilde?"

"It's Lire. I got your message a few minutes ago."

She was silent for a moment, and then I heard muffled sounds of movement. "Just a second." After listening to several counts of her uneven breathing, I heard a faint scrunching noise that sounded like she had settled into a leather couch or chair. "Sorry," she said in a more normal voice. "My son is sleeping, and I needed to get somewhere where I can talk."

"Okay." I didn't know she had a child but kept my mouth shut about it. I just wanted to get to the reason for her call. Besides, she probably didn't want me prying into her business.

"I need to catch my breath for a second. I was all the way upstairs." She paused for a moment and then continued, "So ... the reason I called is because Mom is pretty sick. She's in the hospital, and well," her voice broke, "things aren't good. It's cancer, and the doctors say there's nothing more they can do."

"I had a feeling that's why you called." I didn't know what to say. I was mired in conflicting feelings about my mother and caught off guard by my sister's emotions. "I'm sorry."

She cried softly, but managed to speak without too much difficulty. "Thanks." She took another shuddering breath and blew it out slowly. "The other reason I called is to tell you Mom wants to see you."

This floored me. It had been twenty-three years since I last saw my mother—a woman who typically greeted me by saying, 'Oh, it's you.' It dawned on me that I hadn't come to terms with how I felt about her. I thought I had. I really did. But it was a lie.

For the past several years, I told myself I understood why my mother behaved the way she did. She was terrified by my ability to gaze into her mind and humiliated that I knew her secret. It embarrassed her that magic ran in our family in such a visible way. It was understandable. A lot of people might act the same way, given the circumstances. Wouldn't they? Over the years, I had embraced this excuse, but now, confronted with the possibility of seeing my mother again, I didn't want to let her off the hook so easily.

Boy, this personal introspection stuff was no fun at all.

"Jeez." I couldn't think of what to say. I needed some time to digest this recent news.

Part of me, the angry, spiteful part, wanted to tell Giselle to get lost. I hadn't spoken to Mother for twenty-three years, and the prospect of never speaking with her again would hardly be noticeable. Of course, now that she had asked for me, it was noticeable. I couldn't just ignore it. If I did, I'd always wonder what she wanted and probably regret missing my opportunity to give her a piece of my mind.

"Clo—uh, Lire ... I know what you must be going through, and— "

I cut her off before she could finish. "You couldn't possibly begin to understand."

She was quiet for a moment. "No, I suppose I can't. But if it helps, Mom told me about Uncle Byron. She said you knew and never said anything. She said other things, too, but I think you should hear them for yourself."

Cool silence echoed down the telephone line while I stumbled over that revelation. "She told you. I can't believe it. God! After all of these years ..."

"I know. It wasn't easy for her, but she did eventually get it all out." She paused and then added quietly, "It explains a lot."

I sighed. "Okay, I'll come. Do I have some time, or should I leave as soon as possible?"

"It would be best if you left soon. Yes, tonight if you can manage it. Will you fly?"

"I don't know yet. Probably. What hospital is Mom at?"

"Stanford. If you go to the information desk, they'll tell you what room. Call me when you have your itinerary. I want to tell her when you're coming."

"Okay. I'll call you a little later."

"Thanks, and ... Lire?"

"Yeah?"

"I'm glad you're coming."

Frowning into the receiver, I mumbled, "Uh, sure. Talk to you later."

After hanging up, I slumped back into my chair and pressed the palms of my hands against my closed eyes. "God! The day just can't get any worse."

Red replied, "Yes, it has been ... eventful. So what did Giselle have to say?"

I sighed and swiveled my chair around so I could look at him. "You were right. Mom isn't doing well. She's in the hospital. Giselle says it's cancer. It must be pretty advanced because the doctors can't do anything for her."

He inclined his head. "How do you feel about that?"

I folded my arms over my stomach and shrugged. "Gosh, I don't know, Red. This has happened so suddenly. I thought I had put the past behind me, gotten over my screwed up childhood. Now, well, maybe I'm not as over it as I thought."

"It was never resolved, Lire. That is why you are conflicted."

"Yeah, I've figured that out. It looks like I'm going to get my chance at some type of resolution, though. Giselle said Mom wants to see me. I need to check flights. She says I should come right away."

"What made you decide to go?"

My eyes widened with the knowledge. "Mom told her about the affair. Giselle wouldn't say anything else—said I needed to hear the rest from Mom."

"She was positively conciliatory."

"Yeah, she was. This whole thing is just too weird. It went nothing like I expected. Hell, when Dad died, I got Julie to contact Giselle for me. I had no desire to talk to her if I didn't have to. Of course, I was also pretty much a basket case. I don't know that I could have done it even if I had wanted to."

"Perhaps something your mother said has made a difference to her."

"Maybe. I don't know. I guess we'll see."

I turned to my computer and checked several travel websites before settling on an evening flight. It would put me in San Francisco a little before eleven o'clock. I needed to leave the office soon, so I could pack and allow enough time to get through magic detection. Red was usually good for at least thirty minutes of examination and discussion, and that was with a certificate from the PRC and a special license from the FAA. Let's not even talk about the time spent waiting in line.

Ever since Flight 208 blew up over Los Angeles, anything remotely magical had been treated with intense suspicion by airports around the world. Not without reason, I guess. Over three hundred and fifty people died on that flight and on the ground. The FAA investigation concluded that a terrorist had detonated a magic item enchanted with a powerful inferno spell. Shortly after the cause was announced, public outcry prompted governments to enact magic screening procedures at all airports. Here in the United States, it took almost a year to train and hire all the necessary sensitives to comply.

Deadly Remains - Chapter Five

Now, in addition to the metal detectors, x-ray machines, pat-downs, and bomb-sniffing dogs, all magic items and users were subjected to careful scrutiny by a staff of magic sensitives—individuals who sense and identify different types of magic. In some cases, the screening process took longer than the flight time. Since it was a sixteen-hour drive to the Bay Area, flying would be quicker, although the pain-in-the-ass factor made it really tempting to hop in my car and go.

I arranged with Monica to reschedule my appointments for the next two days and then informed Jack of my trip. They were both sympathetic. I had to assure Monica more than once that I didn't need anyone to drive me home. I was fine. Really.

Red was quiet on the way home. I think he knew I'd had enough emotional discussions for one day. I just wanted to zone out and forget about everything. The afternoon commute traffic had started to crowd the streets, so it was easy to stay distracted on the way home and ignore my inner turmoil. Is it still denial if you are conscious of doing it?

I pulled into the driveway of my building around four-forty-five. I stopped next to the security booth and unrolled my window.

I greeted the familiar guard. "Hi, Chet. How's it going?" Chet had manned the booth almost every day for the past two years.

Chet flashed a friendly smile, but I wasn't fooled. Oh, the smile was genuine, but like many of the building's security guards, Chet was a retired Navy SEAL with enough tough-guy credits to sink a battleship. Anyone fool enough to mess with him after overlooking the 10mm Glock sidearm and 225 pounds of muscle deserved what misery they got.

It occurred to me that Chet must have entered the military at eighteen. He hardly looked older than forty and the military required twenty years of service before retirement. Of course, maybe Chet was older than his well-tended physique led me to believe. He kept his hair cropped short, so any telltale gray hairs wouldn't necessarily be noticeable.

"Doing fine, m'dear." His voice was deep and raspy, which almost seemed at odds with his friendly manner. He checked his watch and then pressed the button to open the gate. "Home a little early tonight, aren'tcha?"

"Yeah. I'm heading to the airport tonight. I'll be gone for a couple of days. A limo should be here around five-thirty or so to pick me up."

"Okay. I call you when it gets here. Have a good trip," he said with a parting smile.

I drove into the parking garage, removing my sunglasses as soon as the shadows enveloped the car, and parked in my assigned parking stall. The elevator ride to my loft was un-interrupted, and in less than a minute, the doors opened onto the entryway to my penthouse apartment. The top-most floor of the building had been split between two 'ter-race' apartments. My front door was to the left. The door to the right belonged to two psychics, Jerome and Peter, two of the nicest, most generous souls I'd ever had the pleasure of knowing. Remember my list of top ten favorite people? Yep, they were on it.

It wasn't a coincidence that my closest neighbors were magically inclined—Jerome was a world famous dowser and Peter was a sensitive. In order to live at Talisman Ter-race, at least one owner had to be magically inclined. The building was the first project of Amanda and Tony Wilks, the sorcerer husband and wife duo who had made it their ambition to create communities of fellow magic users along the west coast. I'd heard their third structure, located in San Francisco, was just months away from completion. Like all of Amanda and Tony's communities, Talisman Terrace was more than just an apartment building. The entire bottom level had been set up for businesses offering magic services or products to the public. The second floor was devoted to resident-only spaces, like the exercise facilities, entertain-ment room, and conference rooms. The remaining upper floors were divided into the loft apartments. We were a close-knit community. We met regularly for cocktail parties,

Sunday afternoon potlucks, and special events. For someone like me, who grew up without the benefit of a close family, the community experience was cathartic.

I walked into the delicious hush of my apartment, relishing the homey smell, and hung my coat on the antique hallway rack next to the front door. Rectangles of afternoon sun
checkered the polished maple floor at the farthest end of the
loft, dappled haphazardly by shadows from the small trees
on the outside patio. I walked through the formal living
spaces to the family room, where the sunlit floor met the
double French doors leading out to the landscaped terrace.
I lingered briefly at the glass paned doors before moving to
flop on the nearby chenille couch.

I reclined, groaning with pleasure, before opening my
purse. Red climbed out on his own while I doubled over to
remove my boots. Each one had dried mud embedded in the
crack between the sole and the faux suede upper, and a thin
layer of caked-on dirt coated both heels. The uppers had
moisture stains, but they weren't too bad. With a good
cleaning, they might not be a total loss. I thought briefly of
sending the cleaning bill to Vince, but I wasn't that petty.

I slumped down into the cushy pillows. "I so don't want
to leave. And I certainly don't want to go through the airport
hassle, jump on a plane, and fly to the Bay Area."

"And see your sister and mother," Red added.

"Those either. Gee, thanks for the reminder." Every time
I thought about seeing Giselle and Mom, my stomach bot-
tomed out.

I grunted with the effort of getting up and then dragged
my feet to the staircase leading upstairs to my bedroom and
office. "I'm going to go pack, you want to come?"

"No. I'm going to sit in the sun for a bit."

I mumbled an acknowledgment and trudged upstairs.
Packing didn't take long. After all, it was just two nights.
Everything fit into my small, rolling bag, including my cosmetics and hairdryer. I'd probably have to do some ironing,
but it was small enough to carry-on the plane instead of

dealing with the baggage check line. Life was full of little victories.

When I returned downstairs, I found Red lying prone, propped up on his elbows, and reading a book. If I tried to do the same thing, I'd have a stiff neck and sore elbows after about two minutes, but Red had the advantage of being boneless, not to mention lacking those pesky pain receptors. He could literally stay in that position for years and not suffer for it. It was one of the benefits of being propelled by magic.

I remembered to telephone Giselle and tell her of my arrival time. We arranged to meet for breakfast (her suggestion) in the hotel restaurant. After I hung up, I pulled out Vince's business card. He probably wasn't at his desk, but I called the station first anyway. I was surprised when the receptionist put me through and I didn't get voicemail.

He answered on the second ring. "Detective Vanelli."

"Hi there, it's Lire."

"Hey. What's up?"

"Not much. I just wanted to let you know I'll be out of town for a couple of days. But, if you need to reach me, you can call my cell. Do you have the number?"

"Is it on your business card?" he asked.

"No. I don't give it out to clients."

"Okay, give it to me."

I gave him the number. "I'll be back on Wednesday."

"Early or late?"

"Late afternoon. My flight comes in at four-something, I think."

"Thanks for letting me know. Where're you off to?" he asked. I should have known that Vince couldn't leave my destination a mystery.

"California. The Bay Area." Because I knew he was bound to ask, I volunteered, "I'm going to see my mother, she's in the hospital."

"I'm sorry to hear that. I hope everything is okay."

"Thanks." I didn't really want to get into a lengthy discussion about my mother's condition, so I drew the conversation to a close. "I might have to turn off my cell while I'm at the hospital, but I'll be sure to check my messages."

We said goodbye, and I hung up, relieved I hadn't needed to do a bunch of explaining about my trip. I checked my watch. Almost five-twenty. If I was lucky, I had ten minutes to eat something before leaving. Airports were probably the worst place to look for psi-free edibles, so I raided the fridge for something to tide me over. I hoped the limo wouldn't be early. I was starved.

Six

When I finally stepped out under the darkened sky in San Francisco, I looked up to see stars instead of the clouded nighttime sky I usually saw in Seattle. It was cool, but not nearly as cold as it was back home. Amazing what several hundred miles would do for the weather.

I picked up my rental car, a white, mid-size Toyota something, and headed toward Palo Alto. I asked Red to get the directions to the hotel out of my purse and help me navigate. I had visited the Bay Area on several occasions, so the freeway system wasn't a complete mystery, but I needed help getting to the on-ramp. Even though it was eleven-thirty on a weeknight, the freeway buzzed with cars. Most people cruised ten to fifteen miles over the speed limit, but I played things conservatively and stayed out of the fast lanes. I was driving a borrowed car on an unfamiliar road with an out-of-state driver's license. I didn't need a speeding ticket to liven up my evening.

With Red's help, we made it to the Stanford Park Hotel without getting lost. Thank God, because I was really beat. I took advantage of valet parking and let the attendant unload my luggage from the trunk, but I drew the line at having it brought to my room. It was hardly more than a handful, so I thanked him and wheeled it into the hotel lobby myself.

The hotel room was tastefully decorated, although, after my trying day followed by six hours of travel, I probably would have appreciated anything short of a wood pallet and scratchy blanket. The suite was split between a well-appointed entertainment section and a sleeping area dominated by a four-poster bed. Crammed into the front part of the suite were a couch, wing chair, small desk, and television armoire, along with a small wet bar. The doorway to the bathroom was to the right of the entry and the marble gleamed from within, despite the near darkness.

I placed my suitcase on the luggage stand and regarded the room. The bed was beautifully made. It seemed a shame to disturb the pillows and muss-up the comforter. That thought lasted about two seconds before the decorative pillows were heaped on the floor and the covers thrown back. The Stanford Park Hotel was one of the few Bay Area hotels that offered psi-free linens. I looked forward to falling into the soft pillow and snuggling under the down comforter without having to put on my protective skin-suit.

Red crawled out of my purse and surveyed the surroundings. "Nice." He jumped up and down on the bed. "You room was not so large the last time we stayed here."

"I know. Last time I made my reservations a month in advance. This time, the less expensive rooms were already booked." I uttered a loud, gushing sigh as I flopped on my stomach in front of Red. "But I'm not complaining. I might as well enjoy what I can while I'm here. The rest of the visit is sure to be less pleasant."

"How do you feel about seeing Giselle?"

I folded my arms in front of me and rested my chin on the back of my overlapped hands, so I could see Red. "A little nervous, I guess. She's been pretty nice on the telephone, so I'm not as tense as I might have been. I'm more freaked out about seeing Mother. Probably because I don't really know what to expect."

"A lot of bitter memories there."

"Mmmm," I agreed.

"Are you willing to put them behind you?"

I closed my eyes briefly and sighed. "I don't know. I thought I had gotten past the bitterness and the anger, but it's still there, down deep. I don't know if I'll ever get over it, but ... I'd like to." My voice broke, and I swallowed hard, blinking back the tears that burned my eyes.

"Being open to it—that is the first step. I know it has not been easy. In some ways, I think you have had a more difficult life than I ever had. It amazes me that you managed to keep your kindness through it all." He paused and cocked his head to the side. "In the end, that is what will save you. Your open-heartedness makes you easier to hurt, but it also means, ultimately, you are more open to healing and forgiveness."

I took a deep breath and smiled at him. "How is it you always know exactly what to say to make me feel better?"

"Amazing perception and a certain amount of skill. Of course, it helps that I have known you all of your life."

I chuckled. "I love you, Red."

"I love you too." And we both knew that was the real reason why he always knew just what to say.

Sleep came for me easily that night. After the blaring lights in the bathroom and the anxiety over the next day's events, I thought for sure I'd be tossing and turning, but I didn't. I fell asleep in what must have been only minutes after snuggling my head on the pillow.

I awoke to muted sunlight streaming through the gauzy curtains and a strange, repetitive sound coming from outside the room. Curious, I threw off the covers and padded slowly to the door while I tried to clear my head. Why wasn't I at home in my own bed? I rubbed my forehead. Maybe what was beyond the door would jog my memory.

I opened the door a crack and peered outside. A draft of clean air wafted over my face, bringing the smells of morning laced with the sweet aromas of the outdoors. I squinted back the brightness and shielded my eyes with my free hand, trying to examine the scene beyond me.

The door opened onto a wide front porch surrounded by a simple farmhouse railing. Past the porch, down a few stairs, was an idyllic country setting, complete with large oak tree and circular driveway. Still not seeing anything familiar, I deliberately opened the door just enough to fit my head and peered toward the offending noise.

Someone swayed on a large bench swing at the other end of the porch. In the shadow of the overhang, the figure was cast in silhouette, but it appeared to be a man with wide shoulders and short hair.

"Hi," said a familiar voice. "Sorry if I woke you."

Since he was aware of my presence, it seemed silly to hide. I stepped out onto the porch to face the figure, belatedly thinking to check myself for decency. Looking down, I admired a long, pale pink nightgown with spaghetti straps and lace-covered bodice. It wasn't something I normally wore. I hesitated, not really sure what to do. Was there a robe inside the room? The temperature was comfortable. I didn't need it for warmth, and the bodice seemed to offer good coverage. While I dallied, looking from my body toward the doorway and back again, a deep chuckle resonated from the other end of the deck. I looked up sharply and tried to peer past the shadows, willing them to reveal the man seated on the swing, but my vision remained frustrated.

"Something amusing?" I asked the figure.

"I'm sorry. Don't worry about a robe. Come sit with me. We need to talk."

Curiosity winning over modesty, I walked toward him. My eyes adjusted to the brightness as I got closer. When I realized who it was, I closed the remaining distance at a quicker pace.

"Jason. What are you doing here?" I paused, realization dawning. "Oh. I'm dreaming."

He nodded and stopped the swing with his feet. I sat down, turning in the seat to face him.

"What's with the country setting?" I asked.

"Hey, it's my dream too. I figured I might as well enjoy the scenery." He quickly wiggled his eyebrows up and down a few times at me, looking playful.

I laughed and shook my head at his exaggerated leer. In life, he would have been too young for me, but I was willing to bet he had been a hit with all the college girls. The line of thought made me wonder about all of his loved ones who were going to be heartbroken when they learned of his death, and then I recalled my earlier discussion with Vince.

"I asked Detective Vanelli to tell your parents about your soul, but I'm not sure he'll go that far. Hopefully he'll at least tell them I had a psychic encounter with your remains. Will they believe him, do you think? Will they call me?"

He thought for a moment. "Yeah, I think so. They're spiritual people, Catholic, but you knew that. Obviously they're well aware magic isn't just a fairy tale. They'll probably be worried enough to at least look into it."

"Good. What did you want to talk about?" I leaned back as Jason rocked the swing to and fro.

He turned serious. "Have you figured out—?"

The telephone jolted me out of sleep and it took a long moment for me to remember why it was on the wrong side of the bed. I rolled over and fumbled with the cloth-covered handset, croaking my greeting before the receiver had made it all the way to my ear. When I finally got it into position, a computerized voice, midway through wishing me a good morning, advised me of my seven o'clock wake up call. I hung up and groaned. My graveled morning voice made it sound particularly pathetic.

"Good morning, Lire." Red had managed to climb up on the desk and turn on the light. He leaned against the lamp, reading one of his paperback books.

I emitted a muffled and somewhat insincere, "Morning," from behind my hands before rubbing my face vigorously and wiping the sleep from my eyes. I retrieved my gloves from the nightstand and slipped them on. Sitting on the edge of the bed with my eyes closed, I hung my head and mourned the loss of additional sleep. *I was having such a nice dream about Jason, too.* After a couple of minutes and some additional grumps and moans, I struggled to my feet and shuffled toward the bathroom. Mornings were not my thing.

Deadly Remains - Chapter Six

Although the hotel linens, toiletries, and furniture slip-covers were psi-free, all the other surfaces and objects in the rooms were not. Consequently, I had to wear my gloves and socks while getting ready, even in the shower. The enclosure had plastic vinyl protectors on the walls, which helped, but I didn't linger in the warm spray like I usually did at home. By the time I had finished getting ready, towels covered the bathroom where I had placed them to prevent bodily contact. My wet gloves and socks hung over the shower door to drip dry.

I gathered the unused towels and placed them in a loosely folded pile on the towel rack. After all, they were still clean and it was expensive to get additional towels. Most hotels charge for extra psi-free towels because they can only be used once before going into the regular linen supply.

My stomach fluttered as I left my room. I checked my watch for the twentieth time to confirm I was now seventeen minutes early. I needed coffee to ward off a morning headache, so I decided to head over the dining room instead of wait for Giselle in the lobby. She had my cell number, so I wasn't too worried about missing her.

I waited for the hostess while she seated a middle-aged, Asian couple at one of the many neatly set tables. The morning sun glowed behind the white louvers of the shutter-clad windows, making the room seem fresh and crisp. The blue, gold, and white striped upholstered chairs stood out against the white table linens.

The young hostess smiled brightly, noticing me as she turned back toward the front of the dining room. Her expression faltered when her eyes glanced down to my elbow length gloves, but she regained her composure quickly. She reached the podium and regarded me with an expectant, amiable expression. "Good morning."

"Morning. I'd like a table for two. I'm meeting my sister at eight."

She nodded. A strand of strawberry blonde hair fell across her cheek, which she promptly tucked behind her right ear. "No problem. Do you want to be seated now?"

"Sure. That would be nice." I waited for her to make some pencil marks on the table chart and pluck two menus from under the podium. I followed her to a table at the back of the dining room. "My name is Lire Devon, in case my sister asks for me. Thanks."

She smiled and walked away. "Enjoy your meal."

I studied the menu, skipping to the bottom, near the kid's and senior's section, and found the psi-free entrees. There were several choices, a nice surprise. My stomach growled and my mouth watered as I savored each one in my mind. I kept an eye out for my waitress while I lingered over the menu, hoping she'd show up with the coffee soon. I tentatively decided on eggs Florentine and placed the closed menu in front of me. Of course, the vegetable omelet sounded good too.

Several times I signaled toward the blonde, heavy-set waitress who seemed to be serving the tables in my section, but we never seemed to connect. After the fourth attempt, I began to suspect she was ignoring me. Maybe the hostess had neglected to assign a waitress to my table. A few minutes later, the blonde walked to the front of the restaurant and had some words with a petite, dark-haired waitress near the podium. I didn't see the hostess. I hoped they were discussing who was supposed to be serving me because I was about to pour my own damn cup of coffee.

The waitresses stayed in their huddle for a minute or so until the blonde shook her head and walked in the direction of the kitchen, plainly displeased with something. Curious, I brought my attention back toward the brunette. As she turned toward the podium, we made eye contact. The expression of hatred on her face startled me. Now, I generally try not to jump to conclusions when people's expressions are concerned, but I suspected the lack of service was not accidental. After years of discrimination, it was difficult not to jump to negative conclusions. I tried to think positive. Maybe the waitresses were annoyed with the hostess for leaving me in the lurch and the brunette was now at the podium to fix things. Right. And maybe I'd never get another request to read something from Marilyn Monroe's death bed either.

I contemplated storming out of the restaurant and waiting for Giselle in the lobby. We could try another restaurant for breakfast. Or, I could raise a fuss with the hotel manager, but doing so usually made for a miserable meal, being served by employees who clearly did not want me there. Before I could decide what to do, I looked up to see Giselle.

It took me more than a moment to realize the pregnant woman walking toward my table was Giselle. She had always been slim, skinny even, and the chubby-cheeked woman moving toward my table was not what I expected.

She wore a maternity outfit that was certainly a designer label because it was stylish. Not a surprise. Even as a child she always dressed impeccably. Her gait was slow and deliberate, with a bit of a waddle. It was no wonder, considering the full load she carried down front. If I had to guess, I'd say she was at least fifty pounds heavier than when I saw her at Dad's funeral and at least eight months pregnant. She smiled tentatively.

"Hi, Lire. Wow, you changed your hair. I like it." She looked at me with a delighted expression.

"Hey, Giselle." I nodded and motioned to the chair. "Take a load off, why don't you?"

With a groan of relief, she settled herself into the seat across from me. "That's better."

"How are you? How's Mom?" Before leaving Seattle, I decided, as long as Giselle continued to be civil, I'd return the favor.

She leaned down to place her purse next to her chair. "As well as can be expected. I spoke with the doctor last night. There's not much more they can do, other than just make her as comfortable as possible. Her kidneys are showing signs of failure. He doesn't expect her to make it past the weekend." Her voice broke, and she apologized after a few shaky breaths. "They moved her to the hospice floor, yesterday. She has the option of going home, but she doesn't want to. I even offered to have her stay with me, but she won't hear of it. She says she's fine where she is. The nurses are just great and they're taking good care of her."

I nodded. "Is she in much pain?"

She pursed her lips and tilted her head from side to side. "A little, I think. She refuses to take the full dose of painkillers because they make her feel fuzzy and sleepy. When I ask her about it, she says she's fine. She doesn't want to hear about trying some different pain killers."

I nodded and then motioned to her stomach. "So how are you? You're looking very pregnant. I like your hair too, by the way." It looked like I wasn't the only one with a recent makeover.

Giselle's naturally curly hair was cut chin length and expertly styled. It suited her narrow face and highlighted her large brown eyes. I was the red sheep in the family, so to speak. Giselle and my parents had the same dark, almost black hair and brown eyes, while I had coloring more consistent with shamrocks and Guinness. Growing up, my sister teased me that I must be adopted because of my red hair. I wasn't. Grandpa Giordano had been a red head like me, but he died before we were born and Mom rarely spoke about him. When Dad caught wind of Giselle's assertion, he gave me a photo of Grandpa that I still keep next to my bed to this day. It made me feel special, and Giselle stopped teasing me about it. Of course, she never lacked for other hurtful things to say.

She touched her hair. "Thanks. Yeah, my due date is in three weeks. It feels like I'm carrying a bowling ball, but other than that, I'm okay." She smiled, but I saw the stress of my mother's illness weighing on her features.

"Do you know what you're having?"

"Yes, another boy. We wanted it to be a surprise, but when Mom got sick, we decided to find out. I wanted her to know." Her eyes filled with tears again, and she dabbed them with a tissue from her purse.

She looked around the room. "So, does anybody work here? I'd like some coffee."

"Yeah. I've been wondering the same thing." I looked at my watch. "I was seated twenty minutes ago, and the waitress has yet to come over."

"Maybe they were waiting for me to show up."

I shrugged. "Maybe. Even so, you'd think they'd have the decency to come by with some coffee."

Giselle tried, with as much success as I had, to flag down a waitress, all the while grumbling about the horrible service and getting increasingly angry.

After another five minutes of being ignored, I suggested, "Maybe we should just grab something at the hospital. I'm sure they'll have something psi-free. Besides, it'll probably be quicker than eating here."

"That won't be necessary. You'll see." Giselle looked at me with an opaque expression.

"Huh? What's going on?" I wasn't much on surprises, and she was clearly up to something.

Before she could answer, a tall, slim gentleman in a double-breasted navy suit stopped at our table. "Ms. Stafford, I must apologize. You were absolutely correct in your assessment." He turned to me with a sincere expression. "Ms. Devon, I'm William Nielson, the hotel manager. Please accept my deepest apology for the rude and inexcusable behavior of two of our restaurant staff. I can assure you that their behavior does not reflect the attitudes of the rest of the staff here at the Stanford Park Hotel. Of course, your breakfast this morning will be complimentary. Here is a gift certificate to be used toward a future meal. I've asked Melinda, our hostess, to serve you personally this morning. If you have any further problems or suggestions, please feel free to speak with me." He handed me his business card and a slim envelope with what I assumed was the gift certificate.

Giselle thanked him curtly. "I appreciate your effort to correct this situation, Mr. Nielson. I know you will ensure that the two staff members in question will not make any more appearances in the restaurant, or anywhere else in the hotel while my sister is a guest here."

"I will see to it personally," he assured us.

Still feeling surprised by the manager's appearance and obsequious speech, I mumbled, "Thank you, Mr. Nielson. I've always enjoyed staying here, and I'd like to feel good about returning in the future."

"Thank you for being so understanding. Please let me know if there's anything else I can do for you." He nodded politely and then walked away.

After he left, I studied Giselle. "You spoke with him before you sat down with me?"

She nodded. "Yes."

"How did you know what was going on?"

Before Giselle could answer, the hostess brought me a wrapped psi-free cup, set down a thermal decanter with psi-free coffee, and then took our order. She apologized and explained she'd been on break, otherwise, she would have done something about the 'shameful' treatment. I assured Melinda we didn't hold it against her. She went away to give our order to the kitchen, looking relieved.

Giselle explained, "I overheard the waitresses talking about you when I first arrived. They didn't notice me, so after I listened to their little discussion, I went to see the hotel manager. I told him who I work for and then pointed out the possibility of legal action."

I must have looked puzzled because she asked, "You know who Stan Worster is, don't you?"

I nodded. Stan Worster was a well-known attorney who prosecuted discrimination lawsuits and didn't draw the line at cases involving magic users. He was practically a legend in the magic community, mostly because of his role in *Gardner v. Templton*. But also because of the hundreds of less historic, but no less important, cases of anti-magic discrimination he's tried and won. His most notable achievement was the role he played in drafting the 1995 Paranormal Rights Act, which extended the 1964 Civil Rights Act to include magic users, psychics, and the cursed.

Giselle continued, barely taking a breath, "I'm a partner at his law firm. I suggested to the manager that he observe the waitresses in action and take whatever action necessary if he saw there was a problem." She considered my expression. "You're surprised."

I shrugged. "A little." To cover my astonishment, I focused on unwrapping my coffee cup.

"I can't blame you for being shocked. I was pretty rotten to you while we were growing up." Giselle looked down nervously at her coffee. "Actually, I've wanted to talk to you about it for a while now. Ever since having my first child, almost two years ago, I couldn't help thinking about our childhood. Being a mother changed me in ways I didn't expect. It made me realize how awful things were for you." She frowned. "It wasn't an easy process. I love Mom very much, and I had to come to terms with the fact that she wasn't a good mother to you." She shook her head. "Knowing how I feel about my own son, I still don't understand how she treated you the way she did. For what it's worth, I'm sorry for making things worse."

I stared at her in stunned silence for several seconds. "Wow. Um … wow." I closed my mouth to stop stammering. I looked down at my coffee and shrugged. "I did my own share of hurtful things too. For a lot of years, I hated you—you and Mom both. But I guess I've realized that we were both kids, acting out the way most kids would probably act with a bigot for a role-model." Giselle flinched, and I sighed. "Anyway, I appreciate your apology, and … I'm sorry too."

Her smile was wistful. "Thanks, Clo—uh! Sorry, it'll take me a while to get used to calling you Lire."

"That's okay."

"So, what about Mom? How are you feeling about her?" She added hastily, "If you don't mind me asking."

I shrugged, careful not to spill my coffee, which was midway between the table and my lips. I considered my response while I took a gulp. "I dunno. Confused. And still pretty bitter. To be honest, I'm not sure it's something I'll get over."

Giselle looked at me sadly. "But you came."

"Yeah." I tipped my head to the side. "I didn't say that I wasn't hoping to get over it. I just don't think it's possible. There are so many bad memories."

Giselle nodded and looked into her cup. I was glad because I didn't know what else to say. My feelings were such a mess that I struggled just to form coherent sentences.

After a moment of silence, she asked, "Do you still have Red?"

I smiled. "Yeah, he still puts up with me."

"Has he ever forgiven me for burying him at the park?" She looked down quickly.

She was embarrassed, and well she should be. Burying Red was one of the most egregious things she did to me during our childhood and probably contributed to the final breach in my parent's marriage.

When I was seven, at home for the summer, Giselle managed to capture and lock Red in a small, play treasure chest and bury him under some bushes in the neighborhood park. She had always been jealous of Red—in her mind he was the symbol of Dad's preference toward me—so she lashed out exactly where she knew it would hurt me most.

It took three days to find him. At first, my parents just assumed I had misplaced him, but as the day wore on, it became clear something more serious had happened. Because of our binding spell, it wasn't possible for Red to run away or resist my call.

It didn't take long for my father to figure out who was responsible for Red's disappearance. At eleven years old, Giselle wasn't an adept liar. Dad grounded her and threatened to take away all of her toys if she didn't fess up. What else could he do? But Giselle was nothing if not stubborn. She figured hurting me was more important than being in Dad's good graces or playing outside with her friends. Of course, as soon as Dad left for work, Mom let Giselle out of her room to play. Giselle was sure she had it made and spent the entire day rubbing it in my face, but her gloating was short lived. When Dad got home and discovered Mom had sabotaged his plan, he was furious. That was one of the few occasions I remember my parents arguing openly. Until that time, they managed to keep their disagreements private, probably because they had mostly to do with me.

After three agonizing days, Dad entered Giselle's room with two big garbage bags and began throwing her toys into them. That was it. She tearfully showed him where Red was buried.

Red later told me Giselle had tricked him into looking into the chest and then pushed him inside with a stick. Once he was locked inside, Giselle used a rope she had tied around the chest to drag it outside to a pre-dug hole. Red's protection spells are powerful, but not completely fool-proof. Ever since that experience, I rarely take my eyes off of him unless I'm very sure about our surroundings, like at work.

I hadn't spoken to Red about that incident for a long time. "I don't know, Giselle. When we have some privacy, you can ask him."

Our breakfast arrived. We chatted about our lives as though we had just met. We talked about where we lived, our jobs, her husband, and my lack of a husband—every day things sisters were supposed to know about each other. We also discussed the past, things that had happened after the divorce that weren't passed on by my dad.

Although I hadn't seen my mother since I was seven, my sister visited Dad occasionally when I was away at school. Because they maintained a loving if distant relationship, Dad always made sure to drop information about each of us in conversation whenever he could. I guess it was his way of keeping us aware of each other. I know he hoped we'd find a way to reconcile, although he knew better than to say anything directly to either of us.

When we were done eating and Giselle had sent the bill away with her credit card (she insisted on paying), I made the observation that if Dad watched us from above, he'd surely be smiling down at us. She looked down thoughtfully and when she met my eyes a moment later, there were silent tears streaming down her face. The sudden display of emotion shocked me, and pretty soon we were both crying, and laughing at ourselves in the process. For the first time in my life, I felt the heaviness in my heart lift that I had spent twenty-seven years convincing myself wasn't there.

As we headed outside, I asked Giselle for directions to the hospital. She had assumed we were going to drive over together, but politely gave me an opportunity to decline the invitation. "Don't worry about being stuck there. As soon as you want to leave, I'll bring you back. It'll give me an excuse to get some air. It's pretty stressful to stay there for long. The longest I've managed in one stretch is a couple of hours."

I didn't have the heart to tell her that two hours was probably one hundred and fifteen minutes longer than I wanted to stay. But, no sooner had the thought entered my mind than a wave of guilt followed it. My own mother lay in pain, dying, and my first thoughts were, 'How long will I have to stay?'

Privately ashamed, I acquiesced, and we walked purposefully to what was Giselle's universally accepted symbol of motherhood—a minivan.

It may have been ugly, but I'll give her vehicle credit for being roomy and comfortable inside. Not surprisingly, hers was chock full of kid debris, though most of it was corralled behind the front seats. A few stray toys were stranded in the footwell, and I spotted a pile of clean diapers under the center console. The passenger seat appeared to be clear of obstacles, so I made myself comfortable. After I settled in and fastened my seatbelt, I opened my purse and asked Red if he wanted to say hi. He agreed, and I brought him out to sit on my lap.

"Hi, Red." Giselle looked uncertain. "How are you?"

"Hello, Giselle. I am faring well. It is nice to see you again."

She hesitated and looked at her lap. "So, Red, before we head over to the hospital, I want you to know I'm really sorry about, you know, burying you when I was little. Do you still think of it? Can you forgive me?"

Red cocked his head. "I haven't thought of it in some time. Certainly, I forgive you. You were a child in difficult circumstances, without clear moral guidance and support. Your behavior was understandable, but I thank you for your apology nonetheless."

Giselle gazed at Red with a mix of relief, wonder, and sadness. She closed her eyes, sighing heavily. "You know, even now I can't help but feel a twinge of jealousy, just seeing you and speaking with you again. If after all of these years, I still feel it—can you imagine what it was like for me as a child? That jealousy was nearly blinding." She took a gulp of air and opened her eyes to gaze at Red again. "Even with children and a husband of my own, I am still envious of Clotilde for having a friend like you. I don't begrudge her—I know her life would have been intolerable without you—but the feeling is still there."

"Boy. Did we have an effed up childhood, or what?" I blurted.

Giselle burst out laughing and shook her head. "You still have a way with words, little sis."

On the way to the hospital, which was only a fifteen-minute drive (mostly due to traffic lights), we spoke about Mom and the disease's progression. I fidgeted while trying to imagine how the disease might have affected her body.

Although we didn't have any semblance of a mother-daughter relationship, I had no desire to torment Mom by reflecting the horror of her disease with my facial expressions. I was bitter and angry, but not cruel. When I told Giselle how I felt, she tried to prepare me the best she could. She told me about Mom's condition and how she looked, and I readied myself for the worst.

I don't know anything could have prepared me for seeing Mom. After all, I hadn't set eyes on her for over twenty years. The difference in age was bound to be startling, but her advanced years combined with the ravages of the disease made her appearance almost unbearably shocking.

When I last saw my mother, she had been in her late thirties with not a gray hair to be found in her thick, dark hair, nor a wrinkle on her clear, pale skin. She had been elegant and beautiful. I once overheard someone say my mother was the most exotically striking woman they'd ever met. 'Exotically striking'—yep, those were the words. For years, those two words rang in my ears. I spent many a tearful night wishing I were 'exotically striking,' instead of Irish barmaid material. Whatever the adjectives, her features were unforgettable—high arching brows, slender nose, prominent cheekbones, and distinct jaw-line. But her crowning glory was her thick, jet-black hair, which she wore loose to hang below her shoulders or twisted into a complicated style at the back of her neck. During my childhood, how I lamented the combination of genes that produced my dreadful Raggedy Ann red locks and yet gave Giselle hair more closely approximating my mother's.

Mom's day nurse, a large-boned blonde with broad features and an easy smile, came out from behind the front counter. She spoke in hushed tones as we walked from the nurse's station toward Mom's bed, telling us about her morning and what she knew about the previous night. Apparently, Mom had mentioned we were coming to visit this morning and was worried about missing us during one of her catnaps. I'm sure the nurse made a point of telling us this, so we weren't tempted to let Mom continue sleeping for politeness' sake, which is probably what we would have done. She said Mom was sleeping much of the time now because her body was in decline. When Giselle stopped walking and asked her whether she 'thought it would be soon,' the nurse nodded gravely and squeezed Giselle's hand.

Fortunately, Mom was asleep when we approached, so I had a moment to recover my composure after the initial shock of seeing her for the first time. It wasn't just the fact that she looked sickly. What I found most disturbing was I actually failed to recognize her. Until Giselle approached the bed, I didn't know the person lying there was my mother. That realization hit me harder than I expected.

I stood awkwardly at the end of the bed as Giselle rubbed Mom's shoulder and whispered her name. After several gentle nudges, Mom's eyes opened and focused on Giselle. She smiled wearily. Her voice was hardly above a whisper, but I heard her say, "Hello, dear. How are you today?"

"I'm doing okay. Mom, how are you doing? Can I get you anything?"

"No, thank you dear. I'm fine."

As she shook her head, her gaze drifted away from Giselle and found me at the foot of the bed. Recognition spread across her features.

"Oh, it's you."

But instead of being laced with disdain, the greeting I hadn't heard since childhood echoed with relief.

My breakfast turned into butterflies. "Hi, Mom."

With the press of a button, she raised the back of her bed. The sound pierced the quiet room. Finally comfortable, she said, "Thank you for coming. I hoped you would come, but I didn't expect you to. I'm glad you did. Let me look at you. Come over here and sit, so I can talk to you. Here."

She pointed weakly at the chair closest to her bed, which was to my right, and I sat down after scooting it to face her. Giselle sat in the chair to my left.

She examined me. "You stopped coloring your hair. I approve." I must have looked surprised because she informed me, "I kept in regular contact with your father until the day he died. I always knew what you were up to. Your father even sent me photos. Does that surprise you?"

"Yes, a little. I knew you kept in touch when Giselle was young to arrange her visits while I was at school, but I didn't know it continued."

She nodded as much as the bed would allow and waved her hand vaguely at my head. "That hair. Just like my father." She sighed, but continued to speak, even though every word seemed to be an effort. "You got more than just his coloring, you know. Did your father ever tell you? Grandpa Giordano had magic too. I've never liked speaking of it—those were dark times for me—but I thought you should know. Your Grandpa communed with the dead. For some reason, his ability got stronger later in life, maybe because he had started drinking, I don't know. By the time I was twelve, he frequently became possessed by spirits of the dead and scared us so badly one night that Momma—your grand-mother—finally left him. In the middle of the night we slipped out and never went back. We lived with Aunt Heidi for several years until Momma remarried. Grandpa Giordano eventually drank himself to death." Talking so much seemed to sap her strength. Mom closed her eyes, breathing heavily, as though she had just run up several flights of stairs.

I glanced at Giselle significantly, and she nodded in ac-knowledgment. She whispered in my ear. "She told me a couple of days ago. I think because she was worried she might not get a chance to tell you herself."

When I looked back at Mom, she breathed easier. After a moment, she opened her eyes. "Sorry. So tired." She sighed. "I have so much to tell you."

"It's okay, Mom. I'm not in a hurry. You should take your time." As soon as I said it, I wanted to smack myself upside the head. She didn't exactly have much time left.

Mom grimaced as a hoarse sound escaped her lips. I star-tled to the edge of my seat, ready to jump up for the nurse, when I realized she was laughing. I glanced at Giselle and she gave me a sympathetic smile. With embarrassment warming my cheeks, I settled back into my chair and tried to relax.

"Sorry," I muttered.

Mom waived away my apology with her hand. "Are you still running your paranormal business?"

"Yes. It's going well."

"Good. I'm glad you were able to find something positive to do with your magic." She hesitated slightly on the word 'magic,' probably substituting it for 'disability,' which was her usual reference. "Your father and I worried you might end up living your life away from people and their things. It pleases me that you were able to overcome those difficul-ties. I know it must be hard for you to believe I care one jot about you, much less love you, but it's the truth. I've always loved you, even if I didn't show it." She stopped to take several shuddering breaths and closed her eyes. When she opened them, tears had formed at their outer corners.

"Before I go, there's one thing I'd like to know." She toiled at each word now, clearly forcing out each one. I leaned forward, hoping she'd take the cue to speak softer. Mom nodded and continued, her voice barely above a whisper. "All those years, you knew my secret, my guilty secret, and yet you never told Giselle or your father. Why?"

"Because of the way you treated me, you want to know why I didn't say something? Why I didn't turn around and seek revenge?" I felt it necessary to voice the part of the question she still couldn't bring herself to say. She was dying, but certain things could not remain unsaid. There were too many bad memories to shove them all under the carpet.

"Yes."

I looked down at my hands and clasped them together when I noticed they were shaking. "At first, I didn't understand what I saw, but when you reacted so angrily, I knew it wasn't something to talk about. I never forgot the horror in your eyes when you realized my discovery and the nature of my ... ability." I sighed and forced myself to look into her eyes. "When I read you, I not only discovered your secret, but also your overwhelming guilt and self-hatred for what happened with Uncle Byron. Your greatest fear was that Dad would find out. I loved you. I didn't want to hurt you, so I resolved to keep quiet and never mention it again, to you or anyone." I paused, struggling to keep my voice even. "Later, when you had distanced yourself from me, I didn't tell Dad because I loved him and didn't want to hurt him. Besides, as unhappy as I was, I had no desire to see you divorce. For all I knew, Dad would have left me as well as you and then I'd have had no support at all."

Mom closed her eyes and turned away with her hand covering her mouth. Tears flowed freely down her face, and she tried unsuccessfully to choke back her sobs. I had managed to keep my emotions in check, but seeing her cry tipped me over. The stress of holding back twenty-three years of tears was too much. Giselle and I wept along with her. Eventually our tears subsided, and Mom drifted off to sleep. Giselle and I sat sniffling, too stunned and emotionally wrecked to do much of anything but watch Mom sleep.

Eventually, we went down to the cafeteria for some coffee, stopping at the restroom first for a bathroom break and to check our makeup. After such a large breakfast, neither of us felt especially hungry, even though it was getting close to the lunch hour.

We didn't say much. I was engrossed with childhood memories and speculation about whether Mom would have told me all this if she hadn't gotten sick. Giselle was obviously grief stricken and stressed about Mom's condition. For a moment of reconciliation, it wasn't particularly happy.

When we got back to Mom's bedside, she was telling the nurse she wasn't hungry for lunch. Instead of just bringing the lunch trays automatically, I guess they checked with the patients first. Hunger and digestion probably tended to take a backseat when someone was dying.

That thought brought me up short. What was I thinking? It didn't matter whether or not Mom's illness had encouraged her to reconcile. The fact that she loved me enough to invite me to her deathbed was what mattered. My past memories were not likely to be forgotten, but it was time for me to stop dwelling on them and forgive.

For both our sakes.

When the nurse left to query the next patient, Giselle and I reclaimed our seats. Now that I had turned aside my resentments, I could give Mom a smile that came from my heart for the first time since I was a small child. She seemed to look a bit perkier and responded with a smile of her own, albeit a dim echo of its former brilliance, but it warmed me nonetheless.

"Clotilde ..." Mom's eyes welled up with tears again, and she blinked them away. "I was scared of you, you know. I spent the better part of my young life being terrified of magic because of my father, and here I was with a psychic for a daughter. That you knew my secret only compounded the problem." She gasped and worked to get the words out. "I'm not offering excuses, just telling you how it was with me. Now I can look back and wish I had been stronger, but back then ..." She shook her head. "Back then my emotions took over. I let my fear guide my actions, destroying everything I cherished most." She peered at me and whispered through her tears, "I'm sorry I wasn't stronger."

I could only look at her and nod, knowing I'd break down if I tried to speak. I pulled several tissues from the box on her bedside table and handed one to Mom and Giselle, mopping my own eyes with one I reserved for myself.

I choked out, "Mom, I forgive you." As I said it, I knew it was true.

She closed her eyes, crying silently. I placed my hand gently on her shoulder. Giselle leaned in and kissed her on the cheek.

With a trembling sigh of relief, Mom opened her eyes and looked at Giselle. "I love you dear. Don't worry about me. All my prayers have been answered now. I'll be watching over you and your family. You're a good mother, much better than I was." She smiled weakly. "You're going to have a beautiful baby boy."

At that, Giselle broke down completely.

Mom rolled her head toward me and labored to continue. "Clotilde, my beautiful baby girl. I'm sorry I didn't tell you sooner ... I love you." She closed her eyes and mumbled, "Tired now."

I whispered in her ear that I loved her too. And I know she heard me because she smiled.

Without waking again, Mom died at 3:48 that afternoon while Giselle and I sat at her bedside. When the end finally came, more tears were shared between us, and I told Giselle I was grateful she had called me. My unspoken regret was that it hadn't happened sooner.

Giselle asked me to stay to help with the arrangements, deal with some estate issues, and attend the funeral, so I changed my flight and hotel reservations. At Mom's service,

Giselle dispelled my feelings of insecurity by telling every-one about our tearful reconciliation the afternoon Mom passed away. The day was filled with many tears, a few laughs, and more people than I could count wanting to ex-press their sadness and sympathy.

By the time I left for the airport late Saturday morning, Giselle's little boy cried at my departure. We promised to keep in touch, and I tentatively accepted her offer to spend Thanksgiving with them. Even the lingering depression of Mom's death, the long lines at the airport, and the annoying bureaucracy associated with traveling with Red couldn't dispel the feeling that all was right with the world.

SEVEN

Seattle greeted me with overcast skies and a thin drizzle that kept getting into my eyes, even when I looked down and used my hand as a shield. It was hard not to miss the warmer, drier weather of California, but it felt great to be home. I even looked forward to doing laundry and housekeeping. Pathetic, I know, but sometimes the mundane things were the most comforting.

When I got home, I cut a path toward the kitchen to make a pot of coffee, stopping only to leave my suitcase next to the stairs and purse on the couch. The light on my answering machine blinked furiously. After I had the coffee brewing, I plopped down in the chair at my kitchen desk and punched the play button. The machine beeped and informed me I had eight messages. Three were hang-ups. The fourth was my friend Claude (how's it going). The fifth was from Jack (so sorry to hear about your mom). Number six was Veronica (I heard about your mother from Jack—let me know if there's anything I can do). Vince claimed number seven (Jason's parents are going to have a necromancer examine the remains—call me when you get back), and the last was Julie (don't forget the party tonight).

I smacked my head with the heel of my hand. I had forgotten about the party. I didn't blame myself too much, especially with what had happened over the past week. I considered the party. Did I really want to go? Unexpectedly, yes. I didn't want to sit home alone, and a party sounded like fun. I checked my watch. It was four-thirty. I had plenty of time to do a few loads of laundry, work out, and make my-self presentable, but first I needed to call Julie.

Julie was suitably shocked to hear about my mom and wanted to know how I was feeling. I ended up telling her everything, and her kindness reminded me how lucky I was to have a friend like her. When I mentioned I still planned to come to the party, much to her delighted surprise, she pointed out that Glen might show up and gushed that she couldn't wait to see his reaction to my new look. I smiled at the subtle way she directed me. The last thing she wanted was for me to show up in sweats, only to be embarrassed when my ex walked in. Julie was looking out for me as any sensible best friend would, and I appreciated it.

My workout was half-hearted, just fifteen minutes on the treadmill, but I also e-mailed Jack, Veronica, and Claude with a quick update; folded two loads of laundry; and emp-tied the dishwasher. By the time I started to get ready for the party, I felt quite virtuous. (I elected to put off the final chore of telephoning Vince until the next day, but I didn't let that interfere with my feeling of accomplishment.) Before heading to the shower, I briefly considered asking my charming and heartbreakingly handsome friend Claude to go with me to Julie's party. I decided he'd end up flirting with every woman in attendance, instead of giving Glen something to chew on, so I nixed the idea. I know. I know! Glen was old news, but rejection isn't easy to get over. It was petty and vindictive, but I wanted to make Glen regret dumping me, more than anything.

After a long shower, a deep conditioning treatment, and fifteen minutes wielding my hair dryer, I was happy with the way my hair turned out. Puffed up by my success, I headed toward the closet to pick out a supreme party outfit worthy of *InStyle Magazine*. Sadly, my confidence evapo-rated as I tried on and modeled at least seven potential out-fits in the bathroom mirror. Seven? I don't know, maybe it was more. It seemed like more. The red dress was a tiny bit too tight. When did that happen? Didn't I just wear that a few weeks ago? Maybe it shrunk at the cleaners. The black skirt did nothing but accentuate my hips. Good grief. What was I thinking when I bought those cropped, green pants? I didn't have any shoes to go with the DKNY pantsuit. The brown knit slacks showed my underwear lines, and I didn't feel like dealing with the joys of thong panties, which meant the pink skirt was out of the running too. I think I came close to plucking out individual eyelashes in frustration.

On the seventh trip to the mirror, I was feeling downright depressed and ready to start throwing things at my reflection. I paused hopefully in front of the mirror before turning to consider every angle. Finally, I hit pay dirt. The dark wash designer jeans and deep purple cashmere sweater looked okay. I sighed and reminded myself for the umpteenth time that, although I might not be super-model material, I still looked pretty damn good. I recalled that the sales woman in the Nordstrom psi-free department seemed envious when she told me the formfitting twinset showed off my narrow waist. I hoped she hadn't said it just to get the sale.

After rechecking my makeup for the third time, I made myself go downstairs. If Red hadn't complimented me on my appearance, I might have resigned myself to a bowl of popcorn and a pay-per-view movie, but he told me I looked lovely. Not only that, but Red went on to express his certainty that Glen would be overwhelmed with regret at seeing me. Although Red's lexicon had evolved over the past three hundred years, he occasionally slipped into 17th century speech patterns, which I always found endearing.

"Doubt not that every man in the room will be stunned speechless at your arrival."

"I don't know about that," I replied, but it was a pleasant thought.

Red dutifully climbed into my purse. I regretted the necessity of having to carry the large satchel at the party instead of just tucking my driver's license and some cash into my pocket, but I never left Red home alone. On the way out, I grabbed my long wool coat from the rack by the door. I detested driving while confined in the thick, restrictive fabric, so I draped it over my arm to carry down to the car. I'd just have to freeze until the heater kicked in. Truthfully, I took the coat just in case I broke down on the side of the road, not because I intended to wear it.

It was almost 8:45 when I approached Peabody's Beans. At this hour, it was easy to find street parking. I enjoyed hearing the solid clacking of my high-heeled ankle boots on the sidewalk as I walked the short distance to the lit storefront. The closed placard was up in the window and an additional 'PRIVATE PARTY' sign hung on the door. Inside, things were going full swing. It officially started at eight, and the boisterous atmosphere welcomed me when I opened the heavy glass door.

Several heads turned, and I made an effort to ignore the surprised expressions and sidelong glances all around me.

I hung my coat on the rack by the door, using the small task to distract me from the (somewhat) unwanted attention, and tried to keep the embarrassed grin from my face. Just then, Julie ran up, along with two other friends, Laura and Trinny, and saved me from feeling awkward. They gushed at my new look while I struggled to smother the inane grin all over again.

While we huddled together, Julie said, "Don't look now, but when you came in, Glen's chin just about hit the floor." We all giggled. "He's mostly recovered now, but he keeps glancing over, trying to get a better look."

I gave Julie a satisfied smile. "I only wish I could have seen it myself." I straightened up and dismissed the subject with a pushing gesture. "Okay. That's enough of that subject. He is such old news anyway." I gave them my best haughty expression before letting my face fall back into geniality.

"That's my girl!" Julie beamed. "Come on, girlfriend, let's get you a drink."

Trinny and I trailed behind Julie and Laura into the store. On the way, I received several hoots of approval and a wolf-whistle that must have come from Jimmy Dubane. Still smiling ear to ear, I shook my head and mouthed 'thank you' to

Julie's brother, who told me I looked positively delicious. I looked forward to things settling down a bit. My cheeks were sore from smiling so much.

Julie and Steve knew how to put on a spread. The back counter and an additional nearby table were laden with several platters of hors d'oeuvres, chips and salsa, pretzels, a cheese ball, and a vegetable tray. A large galvanized tub brimming with beer and various sodas sat on the floor near the wall. At the end of the counter, a striking octagonal glass decanter contained Julie's delicious spiked punch. The jar stood on a decorative metal stand and had a pretty filigree lid and metal spigot. Very clever. Julie must have acquired the beverage server recently because this was the first time I'd seen it. The near disaster of last year must have been on her mind. Steve's friend, Owen, had used his bare hands to put ice into the open punch bowl. Fortunately, Julie noticed it before I had time to ladle myself a cup. I'm sure she was hoping the lid on this one would prevent inadvertent touching.

While I chatted with Trinny, I opened the spigot and let the pink-tinged punch pour into my cup. It had been several months since I had seen her, so we got caught up. Trinny was one of Julie's college friends, an extremely thin woman with stick-straight brown hair, clear skin, and plain features. She wore a long, Asian style tunic over slim, tan trousers and looked incredibly stylish. Trinny was in advertising. Her firm had done some exceptional work for Jack and me, and we discussed her current client, Lyrics, a music store downtown.

When Trinny wandered off to the ladies room, Glen approached me. I had already resolved to be amiable; after all, I was totally over him, right? If I acted all bitchy, like part of me wanted, he'd only end up with an inflated view of himself. So, when Glen walked up, I smiled and said hello, though not too brightly—I did *not* want him to think I was still pining for him.

No, my new look didn't cause him to throw himself on my shoes and beg me to take him back. He did compliment my appearance, and I think there was a small part of him that hoped to indulge in more than just conversation. Okay, that last part was probably wishful thinking, but getting dumped had hurt big-time. I think I was entitled to a little ego boosting.

Midway through my third cup of punch, I started to feel downright cozy. Julie gave me a sharp nudge with her cup and inclined her head toward the front of the store. Puzzled, I looked through the crowd to find the tall, well-built figure of Vince Vanelli moving toward me. His presence was so unexpected that I simply stood and stared at him, probably looking completely dumbfounded.

Julie whispered in my ear, "Close your mouth. He's going to think you're already shit-faced."

I recovered my composure and shot her a withering look before giving Vince a welcoming if not somewhat puzzled smile.

"Hey, Vince. What brings you here?" I asked, but I was pretty sure I already knew.

"Hi, Lire." He nodded toward Julie. "Julie invited me when I came down to get your coffee the other day."

"Oh, did she?" I looked sideways at her with a cocked eyebrow.

"Detective, nice to see you. Help yourself to a beer or something. Wait." Julie grabbed some napkins and wrapped my nearly empty cup, so he could touch it. "Here, get Lire more punch while you're at it. The refreshments are over there." She jerked her thumb past the group of people to her right.

He nodded. "Okay. Thanks. Be right back." He called over his shoulder, "And call me Vince."

I watched his back disappear beyond the gathering partygoers before fiercely whispering to Julie, "I can't believe you invited him. What were you thinking?"

"I was thinking he's gorgeous. And why wouldn't I invite him. You're working with him, aren't you?"

I took a steadying breath. "Yes, but he's also totally phobic. I can't imagine why he decided to come."

Julie looked at me as though I must have been dropped on my head as a child. "He came because he's interested in you." How she could be so confident, given my track record, I had no idea. She added, "Besides, he sure doesn't act phobic."

"Yeah, well ... the only reason is because we figured out I'm not able to get a reading from him. So he knows he's safe." I frowned with disapproval and glanced to see whether Vince was heading back in our direction.

When I turned my attention back to Julie, she looked incredulous.

I frowned. "What?"

"What? Are you kidding? He's a normal and you can't read him, and on top of that he's gorgeous—and you didn't tell me?"

Oh. Put that way it did sound pretty amazing, but Julie hadn't spent hours getting turned off by his phobic antics and bullying. "Julie, first of all, I don't know if he'll remain a closed book after extended contact, and ... and he called my magic 'mumbo jumbo' for God's sake."

Julie gave me a look generally reserved for naughty children and husbands justifying their recent electronics purchase. She nodded toward the drink table, and I turned to see Vince parting the crowd, drinks in hand. She quickly mumbled under her breath, "Get over it, he is hot," and then in a warm voice said, "Hey, Vince, I'm so glad you decided to stop by. Make yourself at home, okay? I'm going to tend to the drinks and check up on hubby-dearest. Talk to you in a bit." Julie waved and disappeared into the fray, but not before shooting me an encouraging look.

Vince smiled and handed me my cup. "How was your trip?"

"Oh. Uh, not so good. It was a family emergency trip, like I told you, and, well ... my mother passed away, actually. I just got in this afternoon."

He looked sympathetic. "I'm sorry to hear that. Was it sudden?"

"For me it was. I didn't find out she was sick until the day I left. That was when I called you—Monday, I guess." Truthfully, it seemed like ages ago, not just five days.

"That must have been rough. Was it cancer or something?" A grieved expression crossed his face. He held up his hand before I could speak. "Sorry. You don't have to answer that. Sometimes I forget I'm off duty."

I smiled. "It's all right. I'm feeling okay about it, I guess. Yeah, it was cancer. My mom and I weren't close; in fact, we hadn't spoken with each other since I was a kid. We had a chance to reconcile though, which was nice."

I drank my punch and tried to scoot my feet around in my too-high heels. "Do you mind if we sit? I've been standing for a while and my feet are killing me."

"Sure."

I led him toward a table away from the crowd.

Several other couples and a few larger groups were dispersed throughout the seating area, but I found an empty table for two in the middle of the shop, near the 360° gas fireplace. I noticed Glen and a small group of his friends were gathered around a large table, several tables away, and took childish pleasure in knowing he was sure to notice me with Vince. Even if I wasn't interested in him romantically, Vince made a great foil. Not that I cared what Glen thought, but it was still fun.

Now that I was sitting, I disengaged my purse from my shoulder and placed it next to my chair. I definitely felt warm and loose, sore feet notwithstanding. Julie's famous punch wasn't strong enough to worry me about getting too far gone, but I resolved to switch to soda after this cup. After all my effort trying to rub Glen's face in how great I looked, I didn't want to ruin it by making a drunken fool out of myself.

Feeling awkward at facing Vince in what was obviously a purely social situation, I took the coward's way out and brought up work. "I got your message. I guess you spoke with Jason's parents?"

He nodded over his beer. "Jensen and I went to their house."

"That must have been rough. I mean ... they knew he was missing, right?"

"Yes. They filed a missing person's report a couple days after his disappearance. It wasn't a complete surprise to them, but it was still a pretty bad scene." His face constricted into the grim expression of someone remembering something unpleasant. "Jensen did most of the talking. He's better at handling that type of situation than I am."

"What did they have to say when you told them about my encounter with Jason? Oh!" I sucked air when I remembered my dream.

He examined me. "What is it?"

I shook my head. "No big deal. I just remembered a dream I had about Jason." I reddened when I recalled what I was wearing in the dream and hoped Vince didn't notice. I took another gulp of the punch.

"Ah." He returned my wow-that-sure-is-weird look and then continued to answer my question. "Hearing about your encounter gave them a shock, but they want to know details. I told them they could meet with you and gave them your number. Like I said in my message, they asked whether you might know of a trustworthy necromancer to examine his bones."

"Yeah, Jake Milovavich. He's supposed to be back from vacation, on Monday. And we're going to waive our fee. Just so you know."

Vince nodded, but before he could comment, Julie breezed up to our table with an expectant expression. I knew that look—she was eager to gossip. She squatted down, carelessly flopped both arms on the table, and peered up at me with an expression of excited anticipation. I could tell she was a wee bit tipsy. "Lire! Steve just told me Glen's feeling more than a little sorry he broke it off with you—the schmuck." She accentuated the word 'schmuck' with as much disgust as she could muster. It came out sounding decidedly slushy.

I bit my lip to keep the smug smile from my face, and we giggled together, our foreheads almost touching. After a moment, she straightened up. "Sorry, Vince. Important girl talk you know. All right, go about your business." She made a 'get on with it' motion with her fingers and then walked away toward the more lively part of the room. I heard her yell something about playing a game of quarters before she disappeared beyond the crush of bodies surrounding the counter.

I turned my attention back to Vince.

His left eyebrow twitched upward. "Who's Glen?"

"My ex-schmuck." I cracked up into a fit of giggles before I could help myself. I covered my mouth with my hand.

Vince just smiled. "Aha."

I ignored him and took another sip of my drink. Julie was such a stinker. She had done this on purpose.

"So where is this ... schmuck?" Vince asked.

My eyes slid toward Glen's table. He stood, talking to one of his friends, Mike Kilborn, with his back to us. No one was looking. "He's over there." I nodded toward the table in question. "He's the one with his back to us—dark hair, navy shirt."

Vince discreetly glanced at Glen while I drank my punch and tried to look elsewhere.

"Why did you guys break up?" Vince's eyebrows screwed down. "Sorry. Don't answer that. None of my business."

"That's okay." I waved away any thought of an offense with my hand. "He was tired of dealing with all the necessary precautions of my magic." I tried to make my voice sound matter of fact, but I don't think it worked because he looked at me askance.

"Necessary precautions?"

Oh, right. Most of the time, it wasn't apparent who was magically inclined and who wasn't, by just looking. Only clairvoyants had the disadvantage of needing gloves.

I shook my head and Vince's face blurred. "Sorry. Duh. You don't know these people. Glen is a normal."

Somehow we always seemed to end up talking about my love life, but, oddly, it didn't bother me tonight. After all, Julie was the one who lobbed the conversation into our laps, so it wasn't exactly an inappropriate topic.

Realization dawned on his face. "So Glen must be like me. He can resist your magic."

"Uh, no. That was the problem." Was I slurring my words?

Vince looked confused. After a moment, he leaned forward and asked, "If he was normal, then, uh, how does that work, exactly? You can't touch him, right? Or am I missing something?"

Normally, this conversation was reserved for guys who were either interested in dating me, having sex with me, or just plain drunk. Unfortunately, more often than not, it seemed to be the last reason. It wasn't clear why Vince was asking, so I chalked it up to his insatiable curiosity.

"There are ways. That's what Glen meant by necessary precautions." When I took another swig from my cup, I realized it was almost empty. Probably a good thing. My lips felt numb.

The look on Vince's face told me he was wondering about the 'necessary precautions,' but was unsure how to ask for details without making me mad. I stared at him, silently daring him to ask the question or move on to another subject. He opened his mouth, thought better of it, and closed it, face pasted with curiosity. Then he tipped back his beer and went through the whole ritual again.

I got so annoyed with his vacillation that I leaned forward and blurted in a loud whisper, "For Pete's sake. One of us has to wear a skin suit, okay? And the guy has to wear a condom. No direct skin-to-skin contact. Understand?"

He looked startled, and I realized with sudden clarity that I must be pretty buzzed if I was saying something like that to a guy I had just met and professionally to boot. But instead of being mortified, I started giggling at the look on Vince's face.

Deadly Remains - Chapter Seven

When I settled down, Vince regarded me with an amused expression. "I wasn't sure how to ask without pissing you off. You weren't eager to answer stuff like this earlier in the week."

"Earlier in the week I wasn't drrrunk." I raised my glass proudly with the slurred cheer before furrowing my brows at the cup. "I don't know how I could be drunk though. Julie's punch isn't usually that strong."

Evidently, Vince wasn't interested in solving the mystery of the intoxicated clairvoyant. "So, you mentioned dating another clairvoyant who was able to block your power. Was that before you dated the schmuck?"

It amused me that he continued referring to Glen as 'the schmuck.' I smiled. "Before. A while before. Um, ten years ago, I guess."

"Ah. How did you guys meet?"

"We were in college together. He transferred in, during my junior year. The psychic community is pretty small and close knit, so it didn't take long for us to hook up." I tried to enunciate each word. I think I was successful.

"He was another clairvoyant?"

I nodded. "Yep. His name's Nick."

"I think you said you guys broke it off because one of you became more powerful."

I probably should have been wary of Vince's interest in my personal life, but his attention pleased me. "Yeah. We didn't know it at the time, but my powers hadn't fully developed. After about a year, we shl—uh, we slowly began picking up bits and pieces from each other. We tried to make it work, but ... well, it was just impossible."

My heart still felt a twinge whenever I thought about the day I first realized our powers were no longer equal. The depression I felt after Nick and I were forced to call it quits hit me incredibly hard and didn't abate for months. It was the first and only time I had truly contemplated chucking it all in and signing myself into a clean-room. It also caused me to lose almost fifteen pounds, which might have been considered a good thing, except I was already thin at the time. Anyway, it wasn't a weight loss method I wanted to repeat, even though I continued to remain one frustrating dress size away from my college weight.

"You guys keep in contact at all?"

"Mmmm." I nodded, bringing my attention back to the conversation. "We talk to each other every month or so. He lives near Coventry and works at the hospital doing psychic research. We're good friends."

Before he could ask me anything more personal, I shifted the conversation to his own love life. "So, what about you? You have any serious relationships that crashed and burned that you want to share with me?"

He chuckled. "I suppose I deserve that. Sorry."

"No, no. Tit for tat. I told you my sob story, now you." My pronunciation might have been messy, but my demand was firm. I curled my fingers back and forth at him in a give-it-to-me-now gesture.

He looked down and shook his head in a combination of amusement and embarrassment. "Okay, okay." He paused for a moment in thought. "I guess I've had a couple messy breakups." He shrugged and the gesture accentuated his well-muscled shoulders.

"Messy, huh? Like Lorena Bobbitt messy?" I eyed him slyly, although, as drunk as I was, it's possible I just leered. "You missing any vital parts, Vince?"

He laughed. "Not the last time I checked." I noticed for the first time that he had a small dimple at the left side of his mouth. It softened his masculine face and gave him a slightly boyish grin that I decided was quite sexy.

When he didn't offer further details, I prompted, "So, emotionally messy."

He shrugged and gave me a stiff nod. "Yeah. Possessive types just seem to gravitate to me, for some reason."

"Really." I regarded him doubtfully. "Like *Fatal Attraction*-possessive types, or what?" Outrageous breakup stories seemed to be on my mind.

He snorted. "No. Nothing that dramatic, or violent."

Even though I was dying to know more, my politeness kicked in. I guess I wasn't plastered enough to completely discard common courtesy. "Uh huh." I shook my head and made a mental note not to do it again; my brains felt like they were sloshing around in there. "So, you dating anyone now?"

"Nope."

My eyebrows went up when he didn't elaborate. Mr. Conversation. When I stubbornly continued to stare at him, he shrugged. "I've been working a lot lately, so I haven't had much time to spare for socializing."

"This party, the notable exception, of course." I waved extravagantly at the room.

"Of course." He smiled and saluted me with the tapered end of the beer bottle.

I placed my elbows on the table, leaned forward, and wagged my finger at him. "But I don't entirely believe you're here just for my charming personality, no matter what Julie thinks. So why did you really come?" I asked, with more directness than sobriety normally allowed me.

Vince's eyebrows popped up. "I think you—"

"Lire." Julie looked desperate as she swooped in from the crowd gathered at the back of the store. "Best watch yourself with my punch. Party animal John Lauten decided to spike it with some one hundred ninety proof Everclear, so it packs a bigger punch than usual."

"Bigger punch. Ha! The punch packs a punch," I slurred and then giggled.

Julie leaned closer and examined me. "Crap. I'm too late, aren't I?"

What? Was I weaving? Or maybe it was the goofy grin permanently affixed to my mouth. "Much, much too late. Yup."

"Shit." Julie looked around the room and then motioned for Vince to come closer. They stood next to me and Julie leaned toward Vince's ear for a more private conversation. I made the attempt to listen to her whispers but only heard bits and pieces. "Vince ... help ... she'll ... If ... does ... embarrassing. God! ... magic ... amok ... In high school ... drunk ... Ended up ... hospital ..." She shook her head.

I laughed at the comical look of distress on Julie's face that oddly seemed to increase as she looked over at me. "Oh, Julie, Julie. Such a worry wart." I laughed heartily. This time Julie didn't join me in merriment, so I wound down after a bit.

Julie had turned her attention back to Vince. " ... touch anything, okay? Thanks." She finished the discussion with a nod of her head and then turned toward me. "Lire? Did you park on the street tonight? Give me your keys, hon. I'll take care of moving your car to our private lot. Is Red in your purse? You'll have to get the keys for me then."

After I gave her the keys (Red handed them to me), Julie pulled off the car key and handed the rest to Vince. "Lire, Vince is going to take you home now. I'll call you tomorrow okay?" She stared at me intently, and I had to stifle a bout of the giggles before she walked away.

I stared after her, looking very confused, I'm sure. Vince tapped me gently on my arm to get my attention. I smiled at him broadly. Gosh, he was handsome.

"Lire. I think the ex is watching. Try to keep it together. Got a hold of your purse? Stand up. Let's go."

Vince guided me to the door before I remembered my coat. "My coat," I mumbled. With his help, I detoured to the coat rack to pull out the correct garment, which Vince kindly draped over my shoulders.

Before I knew it, we were out on the sidewalk, walking arm in arm down the street. I leaned into his body, the alcohol making me languorous, and inhaled his scent. He smelled warm and clean, and I detected something spicy, probably his cologne or deodorant. "Mmmm, you smell yummy."

"We're almost there."

True to his word, I soon waited for him to unlock and open the door to his Jeep. I probably less than gracefully fell into his car, but I'm pretty sure I caught him eyeing the view as I struggled to pull my coat out from under me. I hoped it wasn't because I looked ridiculous.

"What are you doing?"

"I hate ... having my ... coat on in the ... car. Uh!" Finally, it came free. I buckled myself in and pulled the coat over me before Vince closed the car door. I wasn't so drunk that I didn't remember to keep my neck from touching the head-rest though. My skin was sufficiently covered by my sweater and my hair. I didn't have to worry as long as I didn't wiggle around too much. While Vince settled in the driver's seat and started the car, I snuggled under my coat for warmth.

I looked over at him and attempted to say my words clearly, but I think I only succeeded in speaking slower. "Thanks for getting me out, uh, without any ... difficulty."

"Any time." He smiled. I caught a glimpse of that dimple and had to restrain myself from touching it with my finger. Instead, I contented myself with staring at his profile. When my eyes began roaming lower (and enjoying the view), my inner voice told me to behave myself or ... or what? Whoa, my brain was fuzzy. There was a perfectly good reason, I was sure. Wasn't there?

We pulled into the driveway of my apartment building, with only a few minor course corrections from me. Fortunately Vince was familiar with the area and acquainted with the building if only by reputation, so my undivided attention wasn't required; otherwise, it probably would have taken much longer to get there.

After several attempts to open the security gate, I remembered my pass code, and Vince drove us into the garage. He parked in my empty parking space and walked around the car to help me out. That would have normally bothered me, but I couldn't think why. Before I had a chance to argue, Vince picked up my coat, deftly unbuckled my seat belt, and pulled me out of the car. Off balance, I stumbled into him. Slowly, I realized I had been embracing him for several moments as I got my feet under me. I backed up awkwardly and must have mumbled, "Sorry," because he gave me another one of his amused smiles and said, "Any time," again.

My little voice continued to send warning messages, which really irritated me, and I felt like swatting them away with my hands. I covered my face and moaned instead. I think I mumbled something incoherent about wanting to kill John Lauten for his cursed Everclear. This was definitely all his fault.

Vince placed his arm around me and guided me toward the elevator. Once again, I relished the smell of him and tried not to have X-rated visions involving the two of us in various stages of undress. Yikes! I attempted to pull away, but Vince must have thought I was stumbling because he only held me closer. Oh well, when in Rome …

As luck would have it, we ran into one of the building's many armed security guards while I wavered in front of the security panel for the elevator. Five minutes later, after Vince produced his badge and a lengthy explanation of our activities for the guard, I miraculously entered my pass code with no mistakes.

In the elevator, I leaned my body into his warmth and rested my cheek on the firm expanse of his chest, automatically letting my hair fall in between as a buffer. I listened to his heart beat, with my eyes closed to slits, and had to stop myself from running my hands over his upper body, although, I couldn't seem to keep myself from wrapping my free arm around his waist. My body wanted what my body wanted, consequences be damned, and since my head was temporarily out of order, my body was finding ways to push the envelope.

The quiet *bing* of the elevator brought me out of my reverie, and I successfully pulled away from Vince's embrace. See, I could walk on my own, thank you.

I started fumbling at my purse when the familiar key jingling sounds brought my attention to Vince. Oh yeah, Julie had given him my keys. I murmured a thank you and received his amused smile again. Yum. No, no, no. Something wasn't right. I was forgetting something.

Vince pushed open the door and held it for me before stepping into my apartment.

"Wait," I said, swaying in front of him. "Can you come in?"

Vince looked slightly perplexed. "I don't know. Can I?"

"Oh!" I shook my head emphatically, almost losing my balance. "What I mean is ... I can't let people in without protection. They can't be touching everything. You know, this is where I live, uh, where I take off my gloves and stuff." I slapped my hand to my forehead. "Uh! Am I making any sense at all?"

Vince backed up into the doorway, looking confused. "Sure."

"But what I'm wondering is whether you need it or not. You seem to be different." I tried to think and probably weaved in place. "Okay, okay. First I need to do a test. Come in, but don't touch anything."

On unsteady legs, I beckoned him inside and then closed the door and locked it. I snatched my coat from his grasp and threw it, along with my purse, to the floor before quickly removing my gloves. "Okay, here we go. If I pass out, try not to touch anything and put me on the couch. Red can call Julie if I'm not fine by morning."

"What?" He looked alarmed.

"Don't worry. I just want to test a theory. If I can touch you while I'm drunk, then your resistance, or whatever, is good enough to let you in my apartment without wrapping you up like a mummy." I giggled at the image of Vince wrapped up in nothing but strips of cloth.

He backed up when I reached for him. "What did you mean about passing out?"

I guess my slurred explanation and bout of giggles didn't inspire confidence. Go figure.

I cocked my head to the side. "Hmmm. I think I won't, but I guess it's possible. Like I said, just put me on the couch and lock up behind you. Red knows what to do to take care of me."

Vince didn't look reassured, but I pounced on him and lost my balance in the process, so he didn't have much choice but to catch me. When I got my feet under me, I reached up to touch his face with both of my bare hands. My magic flared, and I had no shield to speak of because of my inebriated state. However, like the previous occasion, there was no inflow of psychic information. Good news, but I wanted to see if extended touching was possible. If I could touch him for more than a few minutes without any psychic effects, then he could go into my apartment and touch whatever he wanted. This would be a first. I'd never let anyone into my apartment without wrapping them in a full body suit, so you can imagine how often that happened.

"Don't move," I ordered. After a moment of staring into his chocolate browns, I leaned the side of my head against my arm, so I didn't have to make such intimate eye contact with him, although, my little voice failed to separate my body from his. Part of me was more than happy to take advantage of the situation, and I fully enjoyed the line of warmth that played down my body where we were in such close contact. I made myself focus on my magic, instead of how much I missed having uninhibited contact with a man. My inner voice finally broke through my drunken state to sternly remind myself that, even if this worked, Vince was a magi-phobe and a business associate, therefore wasn't a good romantic choice. But (so far) this test proved that Mr. Right was out there somewhere and might possibly be a normal like Vince.

My body didn't care what my little voice said.

I was startled out of my inner dialog by Vince's warm hands. One gently gripped my waist and the other had moved to stroke my upper arm. My hands were still on his face.

He asked, "You're not passing out on me, are you?"

Oops. I had closed my eyes for a bit, I think. I removed my hands and straightened up. "Sorry."

He chuckled. "Did I pass muster?"

"Yeah, like I thought. You're safe. Come on in." I waved expansively.

As I tottered toward the living area, hitting lights where necessary, I noticed Red was already in his favorite spot next to the couch. He must have crawled out of my purse after I threw it on the floor. Normally, I'd have felt incredibly guilty about throwing Red in a corner without a thought, but I was obviously not in my right mind. Instead, I fell into the cushions next to him and pulled off my boots.

"Ooooh." I rubbed my sore feet.

While I bent over and massaged, I watched Vince through the veil of hair that had fallen over my eyes. He strolled through the rooms, examining the many antiques I had collected over the years. It was difficult not to acquire them after working in the industry for so long, especially when many of them were such a treat to touch and read. I suppose that's what Ben Gibson envied, the fact that I could enjoy another world through my third sense. Of course, many times the visions weren't pleasant.

Vince inspected the items in my eighteenth century display cabinet. I sat up slowly and took the time to admire him. He wore faded jeans and a charcoal gray sweater with the sleeves pushed up. A black tee shirt poked out above the v-neck collar of his sweater. I appreciated the snug fit of his jeans over his nicely muscled, uh, derriere. Mmmm. The little voice was back, but I told it to shut up; after all, I was just looking. What harm could come from looking?

"The rolling pin is from my grandmother." It was a beautiful cherry wood rolling pin with black painted handles, and I absolutely cherished it. Whenever I touched it, I got wonderful memories of my grandmother making pies for Dad and the family.

After peeking into my kitchen, he wandered over to the couch and made himself comfortable. He sat not quite a full cushion away from me—not far enough to be considered unfriendly but not close enough to be presumptuous.

"So what was the test at the door about?" he asked.

I curled sideways on the couch to face him and focused intently on the words coming from my mouth. "Since I didn't get a reading after touching you for so long, I know you're not going to leave any psychic reshi—uh, residue in my apartment either. So, I knew it was safe to let you come in."

"What do you do for someone who doesn't pass the test?"

"It's never come up."

He raised an eyebrow.

"You're the first persh—uh, person I've ever had over without a skin suit."

Both of his dark eyebrows shot up. "How long have you lived here?"

"Uh, five years I guess."

"And you've never had anyone over?"

"I've had a few visitors—they just can't come in without wearing a full body suit. Julie's been here once or twice. My dad shortly after I moved in. And my neighbors next door. Maybe a workman or two." I sighed and attempted to smooth my hair behind my ears with hands that felt somewhat unresponsive. "I don't usually invite anyone up—it's just too much of a pain. Most people don't want to be shwa—uh, swaddled up from head to toe."

Vince shook his head. If he hadn't realized just how special it was that I could touch him at all, psychic or not, he surely realized it by now.

After a brief pause, he grinned and asked, "So how are you feeling?"

"Ohhhh, just fine. Thanks for asking." I giggled while touching my face. "My lips aren't feeling so numb, so maybe that's a good sign. Hmmm, well, I guess I'm pretty drunk. I'm sure you've noticed."

Vince laughed. "You know the trick to avoiding a hangover, don't you?"

I didn't, but I was all for trying it out. "Uh, no. I guess I don't."

"Don't go to bed drunk."

"Don't go to bed drunk," I repeated. This made absolutely no sense to me whatsoever.

"Sure. My theory is that one of the reasons you feel so bad in the morning is because your blood doesn't circulate as well when you're sleeping. I think it keeps the alcohol in your system longer. But if you stay awake and burn off the alcohol before going to bed, you won't feel as bad the next day."

It sounded lame, but figured anything was worth trying to avoid feeling like road kill in the morning. I twirled my hand in the air. "Then sober me up quick because I'm really lagging."

All I could think about was how I wanted to throw everything off and climb into my cozy bed. I'll admit Vince's body and kissable mouth figured in there somewhere too, but mostly I was just thinking about going to sleep. Maybe that was a sign my inner voice had gotten more of a foothold in my oversexed, addled brain. Either that or I was too shit-faced drunk to stay on one track or the other.

"How about some coffee?" Vince suggested.

"I guess that means I should get up." I stuck out my lower lip.

"You want a hangover or not?"

"Oh, all right." I moved to put my back against the couch cushions and then held my arms straight out. "Help me up."

"Lazy," Vince scolded, but he got up and moved in front of me.

Vince pulled on my outstretched hands, but instead of sitting up, I just gave him a devious smile and giggled. He looked exasperated.

"Come on." He sounded like he was talking to a small child.

"You know, you're very cute when you're annoyed." Will the drunken idiot please stand up? I giggled and sat up.

Vince heaved unexpectedly, and I ended up falling into him for the second time that night. Or was it the third? This time, however, I was pretty sure he had done it deliberately.

I clutched at his terrific chest and fumbled with pushing myself upright. "You did that on purpose."

He just chuckled. "Would I do that?"

"Yes, you would." I walked more or less straight toward the kitchen as Vince laughed behind me.

It probably took twice as long as usual, but I brewed a fresh carafe of coffee with no interference from Vince. I sent him on a sightseeing tour of the rest of my apartment, so I didn't have to feel scrutinized. He got back as I plucked two coffee cups from the wrought iron stand. The cream and sugar were already on the kitchen table, although, I left the half-and-half in its cardboard carton, instead of pouring some into a decorative server. The perfect hostess in me lamented my drunkenness. I had a cream decanter in the shape of a cow. When you poured from it, the cream came out of its mouth. I had it stored on a high shelf but didn't dare attempt to get it down. I don't know what possessed me to buy it—it wasn't like I got many visitors for coffee.

"I like your place. A lot of the lofts I've seen are too industrial for my taste, but this is nice."

"Thanks." I put the cups next to the coffee maker. "Here. You pour."

The sound of spoons clinking against ceramic echoed through the kitchen as we sat at my weathered pine farmer's table and fixed our coffees the way we liked them. I took cream and two sugars. Vince, I noticed, drank his with just a splash of cream.

"When was the last time you saw your ex-boyfriend Nick?"

Him again? I thought about it for a few seconds. "I don't know. Almost a year ago, maybe." I narrowed my eyes at him. "Why the fashi—uh, why the fascination with Nick?"

He shrugged. "Just curious. It seems like he was a pretty significant person in your life, that's all."

"Uh huh." I wasn't quite convinced. "The last time I saw him, he was in town for a seminar or something. We met for lunch." I inspected him. "You know, we're just friends now."

Part of me was happy to believe Vince had a romantic interest. Why else would he be asking about my previous flames? But the other, more suspicious part, the part with the little voice, was not so naive. Something about his demeanor wasn't quite right. I suspected (maybe even hoped) he found me attractive, but I didn't think he was the type to care one jot about my previous relationships, especially ones that ended in a break-up ten years ago. I must have sobered up a little if I had enough sense to be skeptical.

"But I don't think that's why you're asking about Nick. Is it?"

The same question kept running through my mind like an annoying song. *Why is he so interested in Nick?*

Realization finally dawned on me. "You bastard. You think Nick is the murderer. That's why you're so interested in him. And you figured you'd get together with me while I was sure to be having some drinks and ... and letting my hair down, and ... pump me for information!" I stood up. "And to think I actually thought you were interested in me. God! I am such an idiot." I careened around the room and slapped the palm of my hand on my forehead. "If it wasn't for that pea-brain John and his freaking Everclear, I'd have figured it out sooner."

I looked over at Vince, ready to yell at him to get the hell out of my house, but the expression on his face stopped me short. It wasn't the look of guilt and resolve that I expected. Instead, his face showed a disturbing mixture of sadness, pity, and sympathy.

With my tirade over, Vince stood up and explained, "I've been trying to find a way to tell you." He looked down at the table. Something bad was coming, and I knew it was worse than knowing the police suspected my friend and former lover of murder.

"Lire, I'm sorry. We just connected a murder in Coventry County to our investigation. Your friend Nick ... I'm afraid he's— "

I guess with the stress of my mother's death, my experience with Jason earlier in the week and the lingering effects of the alcohol—my brain decided to take a brief hiatus. The room spiraled, and I barely registered the fact my knees collapsed underneath me. To make matters worse, on the way down, I managed to smack the side of my face against the kitchen island.

"Owie." My voice sounded pitiful, but the pain of my face didn't matter. All I could think about was the fact that one of my dearest friends was dead.

Although we were no longer lovers, Nick and I shared a bond that was never broken, even after our relationship ended in heartbreak. Because of our mutual gift, we had many things in common—our early experiences were very similar, and, of course, we endured the same daily challenges. Nick and I regularly commiserated about the more personal problems associated with being a clairvoyant, which kept our relationship intimate, even though we were no longer romantically involved.

We had jokingly agreed, a year or two after our breakup, if we reached retirement age without finding our skin-to-skin soul mate, we'd get married and live in joint halves of a refurbished duplex. I can't tell you how many of our conversations started with one of us saying in disgust, 'Remind me again. Just *when* are we buying that duplex?' Although we continued to joke about the duplex, over the years it had become less jest and maybe a little more serious. When my romantic prospects were particularly bleak or I was feeling lonely, it was comforting to know Nick was there for me. And I knew he felt exactly the same way about me.

I sat on the cold floor and grieved, not only for the loss of my friend and confidant, but also for the future that was no longer a possibility. Although, it wasn't the ideal outcome either of us wanted, I felt cheated nonetheless. In my sorrow, I built up our future in my mind—made it into something more than just a joke. I was determined to feel wretched. I felt more than entitled.

The more I thought about Nick and our relationship, the angrier I became. Slowly, my sorrow turned to rage and my heart grew cold as I resolved to make the murderer pay for the misery he had sown. There was no doubt—the murderer was going to pay. Not only for Nick's life, but for Jason's life as well. I was going to see to his downfall, no matter what the consequences.

When Vince sat to put his arm around my shoulders, I pulled away and narrowed my eyes at him. My pitiful sobs had subsided, but I continued to hitch. "Tell me what you know."

He appraised my face. "I will, but first let's get some ice on your cheek. You'll be sorry later if we don't."

The immediate flood of grief had masked the pain, but now that I was in control of myself, the injury began to hurt. I touched the area below my eye and felt a large bump, directly over my cheekbone, covered with tears. It throbbed painfully. I probably looked a sight—bloodshot eyes, mascara tear tracks, and a blossoming bruise—but I hardly cared. My angry determination eclipsed all other concerns. Anyway, Vince's interest in me was purely pretense. He had gone to the party just to get information from me about Nick. Now, it was his turn.

After giving him a stiff nod, Vince helped me back into my kitchen chair before making an ice pack. In response to his query, I pointed at the drawer containing the plastic sandwich bags. While he rustled around in the ice tray and filled the plastic bag, I grabbed the tissues from the kitchen desk and used one to wipe away the tears, along with a fair amount of running mascara, and blow my nose. I resisted the urge to go to the bathroom and check on my face because it was bound to upset me and make me even more self-conscious.

When Vince handed me the towel-covered bag of ice, I nodded my thanks and carefully nestled it against my right cheek. It took a moment, but eventually the towel felt cold and began to numb the pain.

Before Vince had reached his seat across from me, I said, "Tell me. How did Nick die? Was it the same as the others?"

He sat down and regarded me thoughtfully. "Yes. As far as we can tell, it's the same MO."

"Where was he found?"

"I haven't been to the location, but from what I gather, not too far from his house, up in the hills. Unincorporated county land."

"Anything different at his scene? Anything that stood out in the report?" A hint of desperation leaked into my voice.

Vince shook his head. "No. I read them thoroughly. They have no leads."

I sagged forward and put my left elbow on the table while I kept the ice pack on my face. "How did they confirm it was him?"

"His coworkers reported him missing. The county matched the dental records."

I closed my eyes, but I didn't cry. I would not cry, dammit. From here on out, my focus was set firmly on the drive to seek justice ... by any means.

"I'm sorry, Lire. I wanted to tell you sooner, but ..." He sighed. "I told you, I'm not good at this type of thing."

I opened my eyes and studied him. "Somehow I knew you weren't at the party just to see me. All those questions about Nick ..." I shook my head. "I want to be mad at you, but I don't have it in me right now. I just need to sleep." I swayed as I stood up. "It's late. Red can show you where things are if you want to stay over. There isn't a guest room, for obvious reasons, but the couch is pretty comfortable."

Vince's eyes softened and he seemed to think it over. "Thanks. I'd like to take you up on that if you don't mind. There are things I need to do in the city tomorrow. It'll be nice to not have to drive back home tonight."

"That's fine." Before I shambled toward the stairs, I waved at the closed door near the refrigerator. "I'm pretty sure there's an extra pillow in the utility room. Up on the top shelf. If one blanket isn't enough, there's another one up there too."

I thought about offering him a tube of toothpaste, but I wanted to be done with this whole encounter. I continued up to my room, instead. If Vince said anything else, I didn't pay attention. All I wanted was to crawl into bed and find oblivion, at least until the morning.

EIGHT

I woke up feeling chewed up and spat out. The lump on my cheek felt like a softball-sized tumor when I ran my fingers over it, and my right shoulder ached deeply. My head throbbed, but so far, the headache wasn't debilitating. It was morning and the only good thing about it was the lack of a horrible hangover. After ten minutes of growing accustomed to being awake, I sat up, brought my knees to my chest and rested my chin on them. I recalled the previous evening and sighed, stifling the tears. I resigned myself to the fact that the tears would probably be hovering just below the surface for the foreseeable future. My life had gone through some unexpected turns in the last week—that was for sure.

Normally, I would have gone downstairs to make myself some coffee and breakfast. Since I didn't know whether Vince would be there to see me in my sleep tossed, abused state, I decided to take a shower and get ready first. With the Lump That Ate New York on my face, I was going to need all the help I could get.

Not that I care what Vince thinks, I thought. *The sneak.*

I approached the mirror warily as though someone might be hiding inside, waiting to pounce. "Oh, no!" I cried out loud when I finally peeked at my reflection.

I gently fingered the lump that used to be my cheekbone. A huge red bruise with blue highlights ran from below my temple all the way to my cheekbone, and I could hardly wait to see it turn a more brilliant shade of purple as the day wore on. The outside of my upper arm had taken on a decidedly blue hue mixed with splotches of red. No wonder my shoulder hurt. I looked like a shoe-in for a domestic abuse victim.

I can't wait to see the kind of looks Vince gets when we're out together. Not that we'd be hanging out in public any time soon, of course, but the thought had significant amusement value nonetheless.

I got ready in record time, but listened for voices or sounds from downstairs before leaving my room. After not hearing a peep, I crept down the stairs. I smelled the distinct aroma of fresh coffee, and my stomach lurched suddenly at the prospect of seeing Vince—here in my house ... the morning after last night.

The kitchen was empty of Vince and so was the rest of the downstairs as far as I could tell. I found Red sitting in his usual spot, reading a book.

"Good morning, Lire. How are you feeling?"

"Not the greatest I've ever felt, that's for sure. Did Vince stay over last night or not?"

"Yes. He left about an hour ago. There's a note on the table for you." Red motioned toward the kitchen.

Before reading the note, I poured myself a cup of coffee and fixed it the way I preferred. I wished for donuts and resigned myself to having a bowl of cereal instead, but it was a disappointing substitute. When I finally sat down at the table, I read the note. It was neatly printed in all capital letters on a piece of paper from my ST&C notepad.

Lire,

Thanks for the use of your couch. If you need a lift later this afternoon to get your car, call me.

V.

He had left his business card, with cell number scribbled on the back, alongside the note.

Red climbed up his step stool to the top of the kitchen table. "Eating, I see. You must not have much of a hangover."

I shrugged and pushed the bowl away after another miserable bite. "A bit of a headache, and, of course, my cheek hurts every time I chew or talk and my shoulder hurts when I move. God, my life sucks." My voice broke as I shifted subjects, "I'm going to miss him so much, Red."

"I know you will, dearest. Nick was a good man, and I know he was a big source of support and comfort to you. We will get through this. You have had a difficult week, to be sure, but we will make it through." Red walked closer and patted my right arm. It was my first cry of the day. Sadly, I knew it wouldn't be my last.

"Damn." I hitched. "I told myself, last night, I wasn't going to cry anymore. At least, not until I personally find the murderer and grind him into the pavement." I wiped my eyes, careful not to jostle my sore cheek, and sighed. "So much for that wild hope."

"You are not weakened by having strong emotions." Red handed me my napkin, and it came in handy as a hankie. "You honor Nick with every tear."

I smiled feebly at my beloved companion. "I love you, Red. Truly, I don't know what I'd do without you. If it weren't for you, I know I'd be in a clean-room by now."

"Knowing I have made a difference in your life makes being a stuffed bear almost worthwhile."

I lowered the napkin to the table, my tears forgotten. "I think that's the first time you've ever said anything remotely critical of your situation."

"I have no desire to change the way things are, but there are times when I remember what it was like to be human and I miss it."

This revelation took me by surprise. Red had always been closed lipped about his past and had never intoned in any way that he wasn't perfectly happy with his current situation.

When I reached my teens and had a better understanding of life and morality, I began to wonder whether Red's servitude was something he truly wanted or just a unique form of forced slavery. But when I asked him if he wanted me to release his soul, he couldn't answer my question. He was unable to say or do anything that interfered with protecting and serving me. Since he cannot tell me whether he wants to continue his immortal life or be released, I've had to resign myself to providing him with autonomy in my will.

When I die, Red will be released from the binding spells and able to decide for himself whether to continue living in his current state or seek a necromancer to release his soul. My will provided him with the money to live independently, should he choose to do so, with Julie's help. Julie, who I named as executor, understands my wishes, so I know she'll see that my will is followed to the letter and Red has what he needs, whatever he decides.

I realized my will would need to be updated. I had named Nick as a secondary beneficiary and caretaker for Red. Now that I was on better terms with my sister, maybe I'd make her the second beneficiary.

My thoughts jerked from the details of my will back to the conversation at hand. "If there was a way to make you human again without committing a mortal sin, you know I'd do it in an instant."

He touched me with his paw. "I know."

I leaned my face down to the table and hugged him against my uninjured cheek. It was times like these that I had to restrain myself from hugging the stuffing out of him. He was so dear to me. It was incredibly reassuring to know Red would always be a part of my life.

After I released Red from my urgent hug and rinsed out my bowl of cereal, I sat down at the small kitchen desk to telephone Julie. Through the pain of my increasingly sore jaw, I filled her in on my unfortunate evening.

"Oh no! Poor Nick. My God! And what an amazing coincidence that you happened to be working on the same murder investigation. Wow. What are the odds on that?"

I thought about it.

" ... are you there? Lire?"

"He knew," I blurted.

"What? Who knew?"

"Vince. The bastard! I am so stupid. Dumb, dumb, dumb."
I punctuated each pronouncement with a bang on my head
with the heel of my hand. I stopped after the second bang—
my headache wasn't improving.

"I don't understand. What did Vince know? What are you
talking about?" Julie asked.

I slammed my hand on the desk. "Me being on the case!
It's no coincidence. They knew about Nick this whole time.
That's why they contacted me for help with the case. Their
excuse that nobody else wanted to take the case was a
bunch of crap. Oh yeah, and trusting ol' Lire swallowed it
hook, line, and sinker."

"But why go to all that trouble? Why not just talk to you
about it? I mean it's not like you'd hold anything back." She
paused and then gasped, "You don't think ... ?"

"They've tagged me as a suspect. They must have—otherwise, you're right, they would have just come and talked
to me and asked me some questions. Well, you know what?
They can just kiss my help goodbye. The jerks."

Julie was quiet for a moment. "That would serve them
right, but you're not going to do that, and you know it."

"Oh yeah? And why not?"

"Because you need to help find Nick's killer—to prove
your innocence and because it's the right thing to do."

I breathed a heavy sigh into the telephone. "I know. Dammit."

"This is terrible. I wish there was something I could do."

"No, it's okay Julie. It'll be all right."

"What are you going to do?"

I paused. "I don't know. Play along, I guess. Play dumb
and keep helping them. Even though what I'd really like to
do is wring Vince's neck."

"That schmuck! I'm sorry I encouraged you to go for
him."

"That's okay. Thank God, nothing happened. We came
back to my place, and it wasn't long before the truth came
out." I thought about the whole business of hitting my face
and cringed. "Oh, and in my drunken state, I did a nosedive

in my kitchen when he told me about Nick. Smacked my head real good."

"What? No! You did? Are you okay?" Julie squeaked.

"Yeah. I'll live."

"I thought your voice sounded funny, but I thought it was from being hung over."

"I wish. The side of my face is so sore; I can hardly open my mouth to talk."

"That totally sucks. I'm so sorry. It's all my fault! I should have kept more of an eye on the punch bowl. I could kill John right now."

I laughed. "It's not your fault. And don't tell John, okay? I don't want him to feel bad."

Julie didn't say anything for a beat and then grudgingly agreed. "Fine. I won't yell at John." In a perkier voice, she said, "Oh, I almost forgot. How are you going to get your car? You can leave it as long as you want, but I assume you'll need it for work on Monday."

"Oh yeah, my car." I snorted. "Vince left a note saying I should call him if I needed a ride to pick it up."

"Hmmm. I guess if you're playing dumb, you should probably take him up on the offer."

I sighed. "Yeah, I know. I don't really want to though. Every time I think about him, I feel sick to my stomach."

"Then don't do it. Give yourself some time. I'll bring your car later today, and you can drive me back home, okay?"

"Let me think about it, huh? I'll give you a call later and let you know what I want to do."

After saying goodbye, I flopped on the couch next to Red's small recliner, where he was reading.

I butterflied my elbows on the arm of the couch and perched my chin on top of my hands. I looked down at Red and smiled. I'm sure my expression looked unnaturally lopsided.

Red gazed up at me. "You should call Duran and ask her for a healing. Your face must be quite painful."

"It is. I was thinking the same thing, and she still owes me a favor from when I appraised her mother's antiques last year."

Red tilted his head to the side. "Before you go ... I overheard your conversation with Julie and believe you are only partially correct about Vince's motives."

"Oh?"

"I spoke with him at some length last night before he turned in." Red marked his place in the book he was reading and laid it in his lap. "He was intent on asking me what I knew about Nick, your past history together, and the nature of your recent relationship, however, I do not think Vince considers you a suspect. I believe his superiors were the ones to request your involvement in the case, in order to attain unsolicited information. If Vince initially thought you were a suspect, I am not convinced he believes it now. In fact, he seemed quite uncomfortable with his duplicity, last evening in particular."

"Good. He should be ashamed of himself. If I had any choice, I'd tell him, and all the rest, to sit and spin!" I sat back and pounded my fist on the cushion. "But Julie's right. Helping them find the murderer is more important than having the satisfaction of telling all the magic repressed, scheming assholes down at the Chiliquitham PD to go stuff it." I gritted my teeth. "If it's the last thing I do, the warlock is going to pay for what he did."

"You say warlock, but the murderer could just as easily be a witch."

I chewed on the idea for a bit and looked down at him. "I don't know, Red. Jason's impressions were that it was a man."

"Why?"

"Even though the magic user was wrapped in a heavy cloak and masked, the person's stature seemed too large to be a woman. Also, what Jason heard of the perpetrator's voice didn't sound female, but I'll admit, it was dark and Jason's focus was mostly on the demon." I shivered.

"So, it's something to keep in mind, yes?"

"Yes. I will. Thanks." I got up from the couch and stretched. "Okay, time to give Duran a call. God, I hope she's home."

NINE

When Duran opened her door and saw my injured face, she gasped. We said our hellos as she hurried me into the living room, where she had laid out all of her healing witch-eries.

Duran was everything you expected to see in a Glindar-ian Witch if all you had for reference was the good witch from *The Wizard of Oz*. Duran was a dark blonde beauty with flawless skin, blue eyes, and a trim figure. However, in-stead of a puffball gossamer gown, tiara, and sparkly wand, her attire was decidedly modern and so was her apartment. I remembered my shock when I first stepped into her ultra-modern loft last year. I had expected an apartment crammed with traditional furnishings all in pale tones and sumptuous fabrics. Ha! Can you say stereotype? Although most Glindarians were good and some were possibly blonde bombshells, I was willing to bet they didn't all live in tradi-tionally furnished castles.

Duran's loft looked much the same as it did the last time I visited. If she had added any new pieces or rearranged fur-nishings, I didn't notice the changes. On the way to the living room, I again marveled at the striking color scheme, count-ing three, no, four different wall colors. The effect was star-tling, but not off-putting; in fact, the hues managed to look good together. It wasn't my style of décor, but I rather liked it.

Deadly Remains - Chapter Nine

The living room was a contrast of metal, leather, and fur, done in black and shades of gray, all of which stood out dramatically against purple walls. The couch protested with the familiar scrunching sounds of leather rubbing on leather when I sat down to make myself comfortable.

Duran perched in the chair adjacent to the couch. "I won't grill you right now. I'm sure it's painful to move your jaw. After the healing, I'll make some tea and we can talk."

I nodded with relief.

For convenience, Duran placed a small leather ottoman next to me, between the couch and the coffee table. She sat and then held both hands a few inches from either side of my body. I felt the prickle of magic as she muttered a spell under her breath. After ten seconds or so, she lowered her hands, regarding me with a business-like expression. What little makeup she wore was focused around her eyes, which made them appear even more vibrant.

"You have contusions on your face and upper arm, and minor muscle injury to your shoulder and neck. Have I missed anything?"

She asked out of politeness. I knew her magic was strong enough to find any injury, probably down to a paper cut.

"No," I said through my ever-stiffening jaw. "That about sums it up."

She nodded. "Lie back. I'll see what I can do."

Before I reclined on the couch, I pulled a square panel of psi-free fabric from my pocket and placed it over the fur-covered pillow. The couch was more comfortable than I expected, considering its sparse, modern design. I settled down and waited.

Duran selected her herbs and powders from the array of small glass canisters on the table. The round containers lined a black lacquer tray, each lid placed behind their corresponding canister. The ingredients went into a diminutive gray pot, which sat on a metal stand over a lit can of Sterno. The pungent smell of the various herbs swirled around us— strong but not unpleasant. As she brewed, Duran chanted something in one of the numerous witch dialects.

I felt the tingling of magic emanating from her machinations. As she stirred the contents of the pot, her chanting became louder, melodious, and incredibly soothing. Her voice was a beautiful soprano, making me think of fresh snowmelt trickling over the rocks of a streambed. As my body grew distant, my consciousness transformed into a clear drop of water, trembling at the edge of the snow-bank, hanging precariously over the cold, clear water of that harmonious stream. I longed to be free—to join the rest of my kin in the roiling water. As the sun warmed me, my clear capsule grew large and heavy. Abruptly the last bit of me melted. I fell toward the stream, fervent in my quest to join the collective, triumphant in my independence.

As I joined the stream and churned over the time-smoothed rocks, I reveled in my increasing awareness and sense of power. I felt each new drop of snowmelt, every bump and swirl along the stream-bed, the rubbing of my sides along the shores, and the immense expanse as I joined other waterways and became larger, wider and traveled faster toward the beckoning of the great ocean.

After sliding over countless rocks, moving through numerous eddies and meandering currents, and spiraling down dozens of white water rapids, I heard the rhythmic pull of the ocean. It called to me, beckoning me to merge with the regular churning of its tide. It called my name, over and over, louder and louder.

My name?

"Lire?" the voice called again. "Wake up."

I grew back into my body, disconcerted by the sudden loss of freedom, and felt my shoulders given a firm nudge. It took a few seconds of blinking back the light before I reconciled my location. I was greeted with Duran's clear blue stare, which wore a mixed expression of relief and surprise.

"Wow. What was that?" I struggled to a sitting position.

"A vision spell. The accelerated healing is painful, so I distracted your mind. You went a bit deeper though. Normally, it doesn't take much to break it." She cocked her head to the side. "You didn't get a good night's sleep last night, did you?"

"Actually, no."

She moved to sit in an adjacent chair and checked the strength of the tea inside a pretty raku teapot. A wooden tray with two disposable coffee cups, plastic teaspoons, a plate of cookies, and a container of packaged sweeteners had usurped the former position of the witchcraft items. She had also removed the leather ottoman.

"Take it easy today. Stay in bed and sleep. I supplemented only a little with my power, so your own body provided most of the energy for the healing."

I realized I no longer ached. With my fingers, I searched for the bruised lump on my cheek and found only the usual contours of my face.

I smiled, and it didn't hurt. "Oh! That is so much better."

Just as I wondered if there was any bruising left, Duran gestured at the table in front of me. "There's a hand mirror. Feel free to check yourself out."

I picked up the mirror and examined my reflection. My green eyes stared back, and I was startled by how white the whites were. I almost laughed out loud. The healing even soothed my bloodshot eyes. Wow. Aside from looking a bit sallow from lack of sleep and no makeup, I looked my usual self. I couldn't have been more delighted.

"Thank you. Going through the normal healing process would have been awful. Now I don't have to explain through clenched teeth what happened to everyone I meet."

"Except me," she teased. "Unless you don't want to talk about it."

I smiled. "No, that's okay. It's a little traumatic, but I don't mind telling you."

Duran handed me the insulated paper cup. I noticed she was thoughtful enough to wear gloves. "Please, have some cookies too. Everything is psi-free."

I took a tentative sip of my tea before putting down my cup to take a cookie from the plate. I savored my selection for a minute and then gave her the annotated version of my story. I was pretty sure Vince and Jensen didn't want me blabbing information about their investigation to all my friends, so I focused on Nick and our past history together. I had to stop a few times to hold back the tears, but I made it through the conversation without any major waterworks.

"Do the police have any leads?" she asked.

"A few. They think magic was involved. I've seen some of the crime scene photos, and I agree."

"They showed you photos? Was this before or after you fell and hit your face?"

I laughed at her incredulous tone. "Several days before, actually. They called me in to help them with another murder case. Only last night, I learned Nick's death was connected to the same case. It's a long story."

"Magic, huh? That's not good. Do they know what spells were used?"

"No. I probably shouldn't say too much. I don't know how much of what I saw is sensitive information."

"They don't have a SCU? I guess we're not talking about Seattle then."

"Uh, no. No supernatural crime unit in this town. Any mention of witchcraft and they assume black magic. You know the type." I rolled my eyes.

"I'm afraid I do." She peered at me. "I can see you're wearing thin. Time to get you back upstairs. You'll be extremely tired today, but don't worry. You'll be back to normal in the morning, provided you get to bed and sleep."

When Duran asked if I needed help getting home, I told her no and thanked her again for the healing and the tea. I encountered a few of my neighbors in the elevator and was grateful I didn't need to explain my tenderized face. Trading favors with a Glindarian witch had its merits.

The accelerated healing left me feeling lethargic, just as Duran had warned. So it was with more than a little foot dragging that I made my way from the elevator to my apartment. I leaned the crown of my head against the door while I fumbled with my keys. My mind wandered to memories of Nick. I thought about some of the things he used to do when we were dating—things that irritated me at the time. I wasn't sure why, but somehow I knew I'd end up missing those quirks almost more than anything else.

When the deadbolt finally cleared the doorjamb, I snapped out of my daydream and stumbled inside. Now, even simple movements were arduous. My arm felt impossibly heavy as I raised it to secure the security chain on my door. As I struggled with locking up, all I could think about was how much I wanted to fall into bed and snuggle down under the soft comforter. Of course, that was if I made it up the stairs. After a longing look up toward my bedroom, I reconsidered the climb and decided the couch would suffice.

I mumbled something to Red that might have resembled a greeting and collapsed onto the couch with a sound of pure exhaustion. I heard muffled sounds of movement and opened my eyes to see Red peering at me from the coffee table.

"You look great, but you must be tired."

"Mmmm."

I curled my legs onto the couch and made preparations to cozy-up under my chenille throw. The telephone rang, foiling my plan to pass out as soon as my head hit the pillow. I debated for two rings, blanket clutched in my hands, before I resigned myself to getting up. It was probably Julie or Vince wondering when I wanted to pick up my car. Just in case it wasn't, I needed to put the cordless handset within easy reach. I said as much to Red as I struggled to my feet and staggered to grab the receiver.

Like an idiot, I didn't check caller ID before pressing the 'talk' button.

"Hello?" My voice sounded like I had just woken up.

"Yes, hello. May I please speak with Ms. Devon?" a man on the other end asked in a professional 'I-don't-know-you' voice.

"This is she."

"Ms. Devon, my name is Jerry Kinkaid. I'm a reporter from *The Seattle Times*. I am doing an article on the Chiliquitham Circle Murders. I'd like to ask you a few questions."

Since when did the media know about the murders? I wondered. "Uh, okay. But, to be honest, there's not much I can tell you. How did you get my name and number, by the way?"

"A confidential source at the department told me you were called in for questioning ..." The sound of rustling paper came through the receiver. "Last Monday. Is this true, and can you tell me what you discussed?"

"We discussed a crime that had taken place recently. I'm sorry, but I haven't been given permission to talk about the specifics of the meeting. You should really be speaking with the Chiliquitham Police, not me."

"Did they tell you not to say anything?"

"Uh, no. No they didn't." I didn't want to make the reporter think there was a conspiracy to shut out the media.

"Then you should be able to tell me whatever you wish."

"Mister, uh, Kinkaid, was it? If I go blabbing everything I learned at our meeting, then they and other police agencies won't be so eager to work with me in the future. I'm sorry, but I can't help you."

"Work with you? Work with you how exactly?"

I so wanted this conversation to be over. My body felt like it was saddled with twenty-five fully lined leather coats. Too tired to stand any longer, I took the telephone back toward the couch.

"I'm a clairvoyant. I own Supernatural Talent and Company. I guess your confidential source forgot to mention that." It came out sounding a tad snotty, but I was achingly tired, what did he expect?

I attempted to sit down without making any distressed noises to Kinkaid. It wasn't easy, but I felt ten times better not having to rely on my muscles to hold myself upright.

"No, they didn't. My source said you were a person of interest. So you're saying the police did not contact you because of a more personal connection to this case?"

I hesitated to answer for a beat. Technically Vince hadn't mentioned the personal connection until last night, so their original purpose for contacting me was not personal. That was skirting the truth a little too close for comfort. I didn't want to be labeled a liar later. "Mr. Kinkaid, I'm sorry, I'm not going to answer any more questions, not until I clear it with the Chiliquitham Police. Until then, you'll need to consult with them. Goodbye."

I hung up without listening for any response.

"Oh, man." I lolled my head against the back of the couch. "This morning I asked myself how my life could get any worse. God, I wish I hadn't."

"You mentioned something about a confidential source. Was it a reporter?"

"Yeah. He's calling them the Circle Murders. Catchy, huh?"

Red paced back and forth on the coffee table. "Yes, very. It is sure to cause a media sensation. Lire, you must do everything in your power to help the police. I do not need to tell you this warlock has the potential to turn public sentiment against us. Normals only barely tolerate the magic community as it is. Remember what happened after Flight 208? This could be worse."

"I know, I know." I sighed loudly. "But it's not like I'm a detective or anything. I can only work with what they give me. Hopefully they still want my help or will at least continue pretending to want it. God! This is so frustrating!"

I gritted my teeth. "And guess who's being called a person of interest? The jerks up in Chiliquitham can't even tell the truth about using me as a consultant. And at the same time they're saying 'we don't need any magical mumbo jumbo to solve crimes.'" I pitched my voice high and whiny for the last bit. Sometimes it felt really good to act like a third grader.

Red stopped pacing and looked at me. "Either they are embarrassed to admit to hiring a clairvoyant, or you were perhaps correct that the police contacted you only because of your connection to Nick."

"Yeah, or possibly both. Hopefully both! If it's not both, just what do you think will happen when I come up with more verifiable clues?" I didn't wait for him to answer. "I'll tell you what—they'll think they have further confirmation that I'm the murderer—that's what! After all, magic is 'mumbo jumbo,' remember?"

Red was silent for a tick and then agreed. "Talk to Vince. I am certain he believes in your ability. See what he says and then decide what to do. At the very least, someone needs to get the word out that you are a consultant and not a suspect. If the police refuse, maybe you should give that reporter the story he wants."

I thought about it for a moment. "I don't know. Whenever I read or see an interview on TV with a suspect who proclaims his or her innocence to the media, they always seem all the more guilty."

"The lady doth protest too much?"

I nodded. "Exactly."

The telephone rang, startling us both. Apparently my fatigued condition hadn't completely addled my brain because this time I remembered to check caller ID before answering the call. It was one of the guards downstairs, so I answered it.

"Ms. Devon, a Detective Vanelli is here to see you. May I send him up?" I recognized Darren's voice. The tall, densely-muscled, black security guard was well known for his practical jokes and gregarious nature. At the moment, however, there was no humor in his voice. Acting professional for the detective, I guessed.

"Right." I sighed into the telephone. "Thanks, Darren. Send him up."

I hung up. "It's the detective. Boy, the day just gets better and better."

"You needed to talk to him anyway."

"Yeah, but I'd hoped to be a bit more alert when I did it." I turned my head into the soft couch cushion. "I feel like a train wreck. Make sure I don't say anything completely stupid, okay?"

"I will do my best."

I tried to ignore the fact that Red answered as though it would be the most difficult task I'd ever asked him to perform.

When the doorbell buzzed a few minutes later, I hated to haul myself up from the comfy spot on the couch. I grumbled all the way to the front door—it was a long, slow trip in my weakened state, so I got in quite a bit of bitching.

The doorbell rang again when I was a little more than halfway there. I gave the door a nasty look and yelled, "I'm coming."

Struggling to lift my arms, I unchained and unlocked the door, wishing as I did so that I had enough energy to throw it open in a huff. Instead, I dragged it past me while leaning heavily against the doorjamb.

Vince's body came into view as the door crept open. He stood with his hands in the pockets of his jean jacket, looking perplexed. I guess he didn't encounter many doors opening at a snail's pace. I'm sure he was thinking 'weird' was the norm whenever I was around.

"What do you want?" I groused in my sweetest, dulcet just-woke-up-after-taking-a-beating voice.

"I was in the neighborhood, so I decided to check in and see ..." His eyes widened. "Your face ... how did— "

Not being in a particularly polite mood and still angry about his duplicity, I cut him off. "How nice. Do persons of interest always get such special treatment from the Chiliquitham Police Department, or am I just especially lucky?"

Between Nick's death, my healing, the reporter's telephone call, and Vince's surprise appearance, I was emotionally and physically beat. I sagged against the doorframe. If I weren't careful, I'd be heading for another nosedive at Vince's feet. Yeah, just what I needed. The thought was enough to trigger a rush of adrenaline. It helped me stand a bit taller but wouldn't last long.

Vince frowned. "Person of interest? What are you talking about?"

"*Please*. Cut the crap. I just got off the phone with a reporter from *The Seattle Times*. He wanted information from the so called 'person of interest' in the Circle Murder case."

"Shit," he said with a sigh. "Lire— "

"Oh, save it. You better come in. I can't stand up much longer, and I absolutely refuse to let you carry me again."

I turned away and began my slow trek back toward the family room couch, stopping here and there to lean on objects for support. I heard the door close and lock behind me as I shuffled from a living room chair to a console table several feet away.

Vince moved quickly to my side and put his arm around my waist for support. I briefly considered shoving him away, but I knew it would be a childish gesture. I reluctantly leaned into him as we made our way toward the couch. The sooner I got there the better.

"What happened to you? Your face looks great, but you can hardly lift your own feet."

I grunted between steps. "It's a ... little ... involved. I'll, uh, tell ... you ... in a ... second."

When I had settled on the couch with my blanket tucked around me, I told Vince why I was so fatigued.

"Wow. I guess you're out of commission until, when? Tomorrow maybe?" He sounded hopeful. Clearly, he was unperturbed by my surliness.

"Why do you care? Need to drag me downtown for questioning? Yeah, tomorrow should be fine."

Vince sat back and looked at me like I was an unruly child.

I snuggled into my cushion, closed my eyes, and somehow restrained myself from sticking my tongue out at him.

He said, "Look, I'm sorry about that reporter. But the media was bound to find out about the murders eventually."

I opened my eyes to narrow slits. "Yeah, about the murders, fine. But my name has been linked to them as a possible suspect, no thanks to you and the rest of the department. Don't think for a moment I haven't figured out just why you guys contacted me in the first place. A big thank you for that one. And when my name runs in the papers as a, quote, person of interest, unquote, I'm as good as roasted. If I had a ground floor apartment, I'd be investing in an alarm system and fire extinguishers right about now."

After the walk to and from the door, combined with my energetic rant, I was completely worn out. But I still had enough energy to slump back and glower.

"Detective, if I may interrupt." Red made a polite gesture with his paw from his vantage on the coffee table. "Unless someone in authority down at your department vouches for Lire's status as a consultant, I agree with her assessment that things could go badly. Please, remember what happened to the relatives of the sorcerer responsible for the Flight 208 tragedy."

Vince nodded. "I remember. They went into witness protection."

"Yes, but not until after they were burned out of their home and nearly beaten to death. All of which, I might add, happened prior to their son's indictment. I believe he was called a 'person of interest' for a while too."

I struggled to a more upright sitting position. "Tell me, just what am I to you guys? A consultant? A suspect? Because if I'm only a suspect, then anything I come up with from my readings will just make everyone think I'm guilty."

He shook his head. "You haven't been named a suspect. I can see why you're upset, but Jensen and I are on your side. Jensen carries a lot of weight at the department and we both know what you do is for real. Chief Watson knows it too, but he's having to do the political dance."

I rolled my eyes. "Gee, that makes me feel so much better." I pinched the bridge of my nose and shook my head before glaring at him. "Fine. Then what are you going to do about the newspapers?"

"Tell them to contact Jensen. He'll set them straight."

"Not good enough. Before they run their story, someone needs to call *The Seattle Times* and tell them I'm a consultant."

Vince nodded. "Not a problem. I'll talk to Jensen."

"Thank you. If I remember correctly, the reporter's name is Jerry something. Kinkaid, I think." I folded my arms. "But you're still not off the hook for misleading me earlier—and for not telling me about Nick. You know, I'd tell you and Jensen to go pound sand if it weren't for him and Jason. Oh, hell … and the fact that the murderer seems to be targeting paranormals." I wagged my finger at him. "But if it weren't for those things, I'd tell you guys to go jump in a lake."

Vince gave me a tight-lipped smile and tipped his chin. "I guess I can't blame you for that." He hesitated and then asked, "What about it? You up for some work tomorrow?"

"Probably. If you help me upstairs, I can sleep until tomorrow morning and be fresh for more abuse by eight." I gave him a stern look. "What did you have in mind?"

"A big job, actually. We still don't know the identity of the first victim. The one we found in late January. All we have are the remains."

I had given them an inch, and now they wanted a light year. I never should have touched Jason's remains. All the stories I grew up with hearing, about touching the dead, were dire. I had gotten lucky with Jason. There was no guarantee the other remains had a soul to soften the blow. Touching them would probably put me in the hospital, or worse.

"You guys just don't get it." I threw up my hands and slapped them down on the couch. "That's not a big job. It's freaking monumental. I never should have touched Jason's remains in the first place. Clearly you don't realize how risky it is for a clairvoyant to do that type of reading. You know, there's a *reason* why every police department doesn't have a clairvoyant solving every murder case whenever there's a body to be had."

When Vince tried to interject, I stopped him with a hand gesture. "Hold on. I'm not finished." I folded my arms tightly. "Since I swore to myself I'd do everything possible to make this guy pay for what he's done, I'm going to help you, but I want something in return. I want you to let ST&C's necromancer take a look at Nick's remains. If his soul is trapped in the bones like Jason's, I want him released and put to rest."

Vince considered me for a moment and then nodded. "I'll contact the Coventry County Sheriff. This is a joint investigation now, so I should be able to get access to the remains. We'll have to drive up there though."

I knew that was as good as I was going to get, so I didn't press him on whether we'd be allowed to perform the ceremony to release Nick's soul. We'd cross that bridge later.

Vince helped me upstairs without speaking. I was relieved. I didn't have any more energy for conversation. Sleep was at the top of my list of priorities. At the first landing, I had to stop or risk falling. Much to my dismay, he started to pick me up.

"Don't you dare!"

Vince ignored my objection and swept me up anyway. I grumbled, but resigned myself to the indignity. I reluctantly wrapped my arms around his taut neck. Thankfully, he hardly seemed taxed by my burden, no grunts or strained breathing, and I wondered whether he was deliberately playing it cool, for my benefit. After all, I might have been small compared to him, but I was hardly a waif.

Vince sat me gently down on the edge of the bed, and I gave him an irritated look. It was difficult to ignore the forced intimacy of him carrying me to the bed. He must have felt it too because he released me quickly and backed away.

"Thanks for coming by to check on me. I probably would have been stuck sleeping on the couch if you hadn't." I wasn't happy with him but tried not to sound bitchy.

"No problem. I'll talk to you tomorrow. I'm usually in the office by seven. Call me when you wake up. We can set up a time for you to come in then."

I nodded. "Will do. Lock the front door behind you on your way out. Red can climb up the coat rack to do the deadbolt and the chain."

After Vince said goodbye, I slowly unfastened the waistband of my pants while listening intently for sounds of his departure. When I heard the front door click shut, I felt safe to strip down to my tee shirt and panties. I turned off the ringer on the telephone and crawled under the sheets. They felt pleasantly cool against my bare skin, and the hairs of my goose-bumpy legs prickled against the tight weave of the fabric. It was pleasantly quiet. I heard Red turn the deadbolt and fasten the chain.

Satisfied I was secure and alone, I snuggled onto my right side and fell asleep in moments.

TEN

Normally, I wake up in the morning with some sense of my sleep the night before. I'll remember dreaming or waking up briefly to change position. Something. But the previous day and night's sleep was different. My unconsciousness was an impenetrable blackness for over eighteen hours. I woke up just before 7:00 a.m. with not a single memory of the afternoon or night's passing. I don't think I'd ever felt so totally rested in my life.

Since Jack insisted I take some time off after my mom's passing, my calendar was completely clear. I called Vince around seven-fifteen while my coffee brewed. He seemed surprised when I told him I could meet him at the station by ten.

"How were you planning on getting here?" he asked.

"Crap. That's right. I'll have to pick up my car from Julie's. If she can't come get me, I'll just take a taxi to her shop. I can still make ten."

"You haven't looked outside yet, have you?"

"No, I haven't." Realization dawned on me. "Oh. It snowed, didn't it?"

"Yup."

I got up to open the shutters. They turned to reveal a wintery skyline. Even the streets, which were usually bustling with cars at this time, were covered in white. Only a few tire tracks attested to the fact that this was supposed to be a workday.

I laughed. "I guess I won't be meeting you this morning after all."

When Seattle got more than just a dusting, everything ground to a halt. Snow wasn't rare, but it wasn't a common occurrence either. Driving in the snow scared me. Many Seattleites had no idea how to drive in the snow. Myself included. There was no way I'd drive the pass to Chiliquitham on my own.

"Don't be too hasty—not all of us drive snow challenged vehicles. I'll come get you. I can probably be there by nine-thirty or so."

"I don't know. Over the pass? Don't you want to wait until it clears up a bit? It might not be so bad later this afternoon."

"Nah. It's not a problem. I'll call you when I'm out front."

"Okay. If you're sure."

He reassured me again, and we said goodbye.

I turned to face Red at the kitchen table. "Up for another car trip with the detective?"

"He is coming to get you, I take it."

"Yeah. Mr. Four-Wheel Drive. He'll be here around nine-thirty."

"I suggest you pack a change of clothes, in case the roads become impassable while we are there."

I cringed. "Oh, God. Please don't say that. That's all I need—getting stuck over in Chiliquitham with the detective."

Given the way things were going lately, I decided to pack an overnight bag and maybe throw in two changes of clothes instead of just one. With my luck, I'd get snowed in by the worst storm in Washington state history.

By the time Vince arrived, just shy of two hours later, I had prepared and eaten breakfast, put in thirty minutes on the treadmill, showered, packed my small overnight bag, and clipped several recipes from the latest *Vegetarian Times Magazine*. It felt good to do something mundane and normal for a change.

I met the detective at his car in the guest parking area and threw my bag into the backseat before climbing in the front. The seat felt cozy. Vince had turned on the passenger seat warmer for me.

He nodded toward the back. "What's with the extra luggage?"

I put on my seatbelt. "The way my luck has been running lately, I thought it might be smart to plan for the worst."

"And does the worst include winding up unconscious in the hospital, or just getting snowed-in?" He was joking, so I didn't mention the hospital scenario was the more likely of the two. Anyway, I was trying to stay positive.

I snorted. "Given those choices, I'll take the last one."

Vince chuckled. "Me too."

I opened my purse and asked Red where he wanted to ride. He greeted Vince and then told me he wanted to read. I lowered him to the back seat where I figured he'd be most comfortable.

"How was the road over here?" I asked.

"Fine. The freeway isn't bad. The plows are out. Just the side roads are covered."

"If I'd known you were going to be here this morning, I would have offered the couch to you again yesterday. This drive must be getting old for you." After a thought, I added, "Of course, the couch probably isn't the greatest."

Vince laughed. "The couch was fine, but I'm used to the drive. I'm in the city at least once or twice a week. It's no big deal." He checked over his shoulder for traffic as we changed lanes. Well, as we changed into what was probably a lane—the snow obscured most of the street markings. "Anyway, I enjoy the drive. It gives me time to think about things."

We drove in silence for several minutes, and I stared outside at the winter wonderland going by at a (thankfully) relatively slow pace. The rumbling sound of the studded snow tires vibrated up my legs, which reassured me but didn't totally relieve my white-knuckle grasp on the door's armrest.

Snow driving made me nervous. All I seemed to think about was the car slipping off the road at every curve.

Vince glanced at me. "Can I ask you something?"

"Uh-oh. When someone asks permission to ask a question, it usually means it's going to be offensive or personal. Which is this?"

He chuckled, and I hate to admit I enjoyed the deep, throaty sound.

"It's neither, really." He paused to reconsider. "I suppose it could be construed as being personal."

"All right, but I don't guarantee an answer."

The detective chuckled again, this time sounding a bit more nervous. "Okay. I've heard it's possible for a clairvoyant to have a fully consummated relationship with a vampire. Is that true?"

"Whoa. Where'd you hear that?" Jeez, what was with this guy? The conversations always seemed to turn to sex and how freakish it is for someone in my situation. Most people don't think about that particular disadvantage and if they do, tactfully avoid the subject. Vince was almost pathologically forthright.

He glanced at me and then turned his attention back to the road. "Jensen mentioned it. He's been talking to me about his niece, lately. I guess his sister heard it from someone down at that help group you guys talked about. Jensen's pretty freaked out about it. So's his sister."

"No wonder." I shook my head and blew air over my teeth. "Yeah. It's a fact many of us don't like talking about. I've never tested the theory *personally*, but I hear they're unreadable. It has something to do with the vampire curse and, well, they're dead. Sorta." I shivered. "I have a friend who works for a clutch. She migrates with them too. You know about that right? To take advantage of the long nights? Half the year in Iceland and the other half in Patagonia. Personally, I can't imagine living like that, but she seems happy."

Diedra and I stayed in touch through e-mail and Christmas cards. I don't know how she endured the constant winter and so little daylight. Anti-depressants must practically be a requirement for that type of lifestyle. She'd been trying to get me to visit, but I wasn't overly enthusiastic about the vampire thing. Although, I'd be lying if I said I wasn't curious.

"Is the same thing true for werewolves? They're cursed too, aren't they?"

"Yeah, but they're not undead. I know from experience that shifters are readable in their human form." I tilted my head, considering. "When they're in animal form, I can only guess they'd read like an animal. But I don't know. I've never gone out of my way to test it out."

He glanced in my direction, his surprise clearly visible. "Wait a minute. You can read animals?"

"Yeah, sort of. That's why I'm a vegetarian and never wear leather."

"Oh." Vince flicked the switch for his seat warmer, turning it off, and advised me I should do the same if I got too hot. Resuming the conversation, he asked, "So what happens when you touch an animal? What kind of things do you read from them?"

"It depends on the animal and their current mood. Animals don't have much of a memory, per se, so their life streams aren't particularly deep. Mostly, I just get feelings of contentment or discomfort, that kind of thing."

I squirmed a little in my seat. The conversation always seemed to turn toward my gift and its idiosyncrasies. I was dangerously close to feeling like a sideshow freak.

The detective stayed thoughtful for a moment. "So where did you know a werewolf?"

"Don't miss a thing, do you?"

He laughed. "Not something as weir—uh, unusual as that."

I sighed. "Yeah, I guess my world is pretty weird compared to yours."

"And mine is pretty boring compared to yours."

I snorted. "Believe me, there are times when I wish I had a life of vanilla ice cream, instead of ... I don't know, freaky surprise sundae."

"At least you get chocolate sauce on yours."

I frowned. "You know, you've really changed your tune since I first met you."

"Yeah? How so?"

"I've got three words for you—magic mumbo jumbo. And now you're comparing my magic to chocolate sauce. Don't you think that's quite a change?"

He laughed and then rubbed his chin. "When you put it that way, I suppose you're right."

"If you don't mind me asking, why the change?"

He shook his head. "I guess partly because of meeting you, seeing you in action. You know? And Jensen—he's been talking to me about his niece. I guess it's given me a lot to think about." He glanced at me and sighed. "I know it won't surprise to you to learn my parents are what you'd probably call magi-phobic and about as conservatively Christian as you can get. When I was growing up, magic was either a 'bunch of hooey' or the 'work of the devil,' that sort of thing."

"My mom would have had a lot in common with them," I mumbled, but felt immediately guilty. "Okay, that's not really fair. My mother was mostly just terrified of me. She never thought I was in league with the devil."

"In my experience, hate walks hand in hand with fear."

Considering Vince's initial reaction to me, only two weeks ago, his assessment surprised me. I covered my astonishment and nodded. "Unfortunately, that's been my experience too."

In spite of myself, I couldn't help wondering whether his change of heart was mainly due to his immunity to my magic. Vince had nothing to fear from my powers, so there was no reason to keep me at a distance, either physically or personally. I wanted to believe he had truly changed, but decided to reserve my judgment. I'd wait to see how he behaved around other magic users.

We rode for several minutes without talking, just the sound of the studded tires crunching down the freeway and the cold wind sluicing past the side windows. The sky grew darker the further east we drove. I hoped the ominous clouds didn't have 'snowbound' written all over them and chided myself for not checking the weather forecast before I agreed to the meeting. The State Patrol often closed down parts of the interstate when the roads got bad. Only a few years ago, a severe storm shut down the entire length of I-90, between Seattle and Ellensburg, for two days.

Vince broke the silence. "So, you were saying you knew some werewolves?"

I nodded. "I knew several lycanthropes when I went to Coventry Academy. They're one of a few schools in the country that has a special facility for shifters."

"Really?" He frowned. "I never took werewolves seriously until they were covered in one of my academy classes. It shocked me. I can't imagine actually being around one. They didn't scare you?"

"No. I started at Coventry in kindergarten. When you're only five and already feeling like a freak, nothing much fazes you. Besides, the staff isn't stupid. Several days before full moon, most of the shifters go to a separate, high security facility way out in the boondocks, and the school goes into a kind of lockdown. They take it seriously."

"What were they like—the ones you knew? Did you ever see them change? Do they look exactly like a wolf, or is it obvious they're part human?"

I looked out the passenger window as we passed a slow moving eighteen-wheeler. Now that we were at a higher elevation, the snow came down more steadily and had piled thickly along the shoulders. For the moment, the lanes remained clear of snow, but I figured it was only a matter of time for that to change. At the last turnout, several hearty souls had stopped to put on chains. Clearly, they expected the worst.

"I never saw any of them transform. It's very personal and, until they gain control over the change, dangerous to witness. For the large predators, anyway. I like my innards where they are, thank you very much. That's why Coventry takes them to a separate facility."

I peered at him. "And you keep saying werewolves. You do know there are other shifters out there, right? 'Therianthropy' is the accurate name of the curse, but most people tend to use the term 'lycanthropy' or 'were' to describe any human to animal transformation. Technically, 'lycanthropy' is the term specific to wolf transformation." I shrugged. "Anyway, when I was at Coventry, there were several werewolves, but there were also kids cursed by tiger and bear transformations. One of my good friends was a wereserpent."

"What? Snakes? You're kidding." Vince glanced at me to check my expression. "I've heard about werebears, but I didn't know there were snakes." He rubbed his chin. "What's with the predator theme? Does the curse only involve predators?"

"Nope. The curse can be linked with any animal. Predators are most common though. I mean, think about it. Since therianthropy is spread only by directly compromising the blood stream, the carnivores are always going to dominate. You're a lot more likely to be mauled by a wolf than a duck."

He chuckled, and I briefly admired his profile before continuing with a smile of my own. "As far as my friends, they were normal people for most of the month, just like you. You can't tell whether someone is affected by a transformation curse by just looking at them. Most of the time, they don't act any differently."

Vince nodded. "You said they learn to control the change? What can they learn to control? Can they just choose not to?"

"No, it's definitely not a choice. It's a curse, remember? The bad with the good—that's the nature of all curses. The moon dictates the transformation. But after an intensive training program, shifters can learn to retain something of their human consciousness while in their animal form."

"What? You mean they keep their human intelligence? They didn't teach us that at the academy. I was told they lose their humanity and the animal takes over."

"I guess I'm just a wealth of supernatural information."

Vince snorted.

"Seriously though, if you guys had a SCU like the big cities or at least an in-house supernatural consultant, you wouldn't be in the dark about stuff like that."

He shrugged. "There's been talk of hiring someone, but we're a small town. Budget issues. And we don't see a whole lot of supernatural cases. Anyway, that's why you're here."

"But I can only do so much. Take the spells at the most recent crime scene. A witch or warlock may have been able to discern them if they had been called to the scene right away. We still don't know why this warlock is performing ritual sacrifice. He's harnessing power, we think, but for what reason? I'm telling you how to get more factual information, but your department's ..." I wanted to say bigotry, "*conservatism* is getting in the way. It's incredibly frustrating."

"I hear you. I'll speak with Jensen, okay? And God forbid, if there *is* another murder, I'll do whatever it takes to make sure we call in the appropriate expert. That's the one good thing that will come out of any media attention. It'll put pressure on the brass to get results. If that means calling in a witch, then so be it."

Vince sounded determined, and I didn't have much choice but to take him at his word. I sighed inwardly and settled back in the seat. It wasn't long before I was worrying about the weather again.

Twenty minutes later, we pulled up to the Chiliquitham Police Department, a wood-clad single level expanse that looked more like a strip mall than an official government building. The tires scrunched over at least three inches of fresh snow that covered the small parking lot. Vince had been right, the main roads were mostly clear and only the last few side streets had been completely covered, broken only by the occasional random tire tracks. It continued to snow, just a smattering of small, wet flakes, but I couldn't say whether the storm was clearing or getting ready to dump a mountain-full.

On this outing, being at least somewhat prepared, I hopped out of the Jeep wearing the well-insulated, imitation fur snow boots I had owned since college. I looked like a Sherpa reject, but my traction was secure and I walked toward the front door without falling on my ass. Emerging from the snow with my dignity (and ass) intact outweighed my need to be a *fashionista*. Of course, there was no reason to go overboard. I carried my chocolate brown loafers under my arm and had every intention of changing into them after I reached the refuge of the police station. Safety over fashion goes only so far.

We had almost reached the wood steps leading to the front door when a man I hadn't noticed stepped in front of me and shoved a microphone into my face. I guess I was too busy making sure I didn't break my neck to pay attention to my surroundings.

"Ms. Devon, is it true you knew the most recent Circle Murder victim?"

Vince must have been more observant. He immediately moved to my side before I had even registered the fact that I'd been asked a question.

"No comment," Vince said as he forced himself between my body and the microphone. I barely had time to register the presence of a TV camera before Vince guided me up the stairs and into the station, one hand gripped firmly under my right elbow.

I waited until we were through the reception area and completely out of view before removing my boots. I didn't want to be a subject for that cameraman, even through the front windows. When we reached his desk, Vince told me to throw the 'Chewbacca' snow boots under his extra chair.

I stuck my chin out. "Very funny. But I'll be damned if I crack my head open and give you another reason to carry me. Besides, if I hit my head again, I'll start running out of brain cells."

His deep laugh was infectious, and the officers at nearby desks looked up and smiled. A couple expressions faltered into something less friendly when they got a glimpse of my gloves, but I was used to it and ignored them. Laughing made me feel better after the business with the reporter. I'd been interviewed once, but that was a planned event. This was different. I couldn't imagine being followed by photographers who jumped out at me like paparazzi stalking a celebrity.

Our laughter had only just trailed off when Jensen emerged from a back hallway, returning our smiles and probably wondering what was so funny.

"Good to see you again, Ms. Devon." Jensen wore a similar, if not the same, brown suit that I remembered from our last meeting, although the tie was neatly knotted and his hair looked a bit more under control. His eyes focused on mine expectantly, and I was close enough to see they were a beautiful combination of greens and browns. He held out his hand and then quickly withdrew it. "I forgot. No hands. I'm learning about these things from my sister."

I nodded and smiled. "It's good to see you too. The paranormal world has its idiosyncrasies, doesn't it? But you'll be a pro in no time."

Jensen tilted his head to the side and peered at me. "What do you think? You up for this?"

I shrugged. "Gonna give it a whirl. Hopefully, I'll come up with something you don't already know." I tried to sound optimistic, instead of nervous.

"That would be good news for a change. Damned reporters are driving me crazy, and it's only just starting. We're holding a press conference in about an hour. It would be nice to say we have some leads when they descend."

Aha. That explained why Vince went out of his way to pick me up.

Vince and I followed Jensen through the doorway at the rear corner of the squad room. We continued down the hallway, past a jog to the left, until we reached a flimsy looking door with a 'DO NOT DISTURB' sign taped at eye level. Un-like the interrogation rooms, this door wasn't made of metal. It looked like something you'd see in a cheap tract house, not a door you'd find in a police department building.

Vince opened it to reveal a wood paneled room with one small window, which was obscured behind old, white metal blinds. A white refrigerator stood awkwardly to the left of the window, looking stranded without any cabinets around it. A circular laminate table, six chairs, and a brown couch took up the rest of the available floor space. On the left wall, a large bulletin board covered with photos, flyers, and no-tices hung above the relatively new but nondescript couch. To the right, a short expanse of kitchen cabinets with a counter, microwave, and stainless-steel sink rounded out the break room. The décor was something out of the 80s, but the room looked comfortable and clean.

A blue plastic container with a yellow 'EVIDENCE' sticker had been placed on the table. I pulled out a chair to sit and watched Jensen lift the lid from the bin and set it down on the table. When I craned my neck, I could see the smooth shape of at least one bone. The silence felt almost reverent, and I was reluctant to break it.

Vince sat ninety degrees from me around the table, to my right, and I held his eyes briefly. Maybe he sensed my apprehension because he gave me a nod of encouragement.

"Ms. Devon, is there anything I can get you before you begin?" Jensen asked.

"No, thank you. I'm fine. And it's Lire. Remember?"

"Lire. Of course." Jensen sat across from me.

I removed my gloves and placed them on the table. My insides roiled with anxiety, but I kept my voice calm. "Vince, will you please place the bone on the table in front of me?"

"Sure." After first slipping his right hand into a surgical glove, Vince reached inside the box, removed the bone from its resting place, and set it down where I asked.

It was approximately twelve inches in length. I didn't know enough about anatomy to say whether it was a leg bone or an arm bone. However, since they had the whole skeleton, it occurred to me the boys knew for certain whether the victim was male or female. I couldn't remember either detective mentioning it explicitly or using a gender pronoun. The lack of information was deliberate, I was sure. Another way of testing me.

After readying myself, I took a deep breath and mumbled, "Okay, here goes."

I took hold of the bone.

Although my shield was as ready and strong as I could make it, nothing could have prepared me for the power that exploded through my body. The magical forces contained in the bone blasted my mind, shattered my carefully prepared defenses, and left me completely powerless. For an excruciating moment, my body arched uncontrollably as all my muscles contracted and burned with a torrential power not my own. Liquid fire poured through my veins. Pain ripped through my core and poured out of my mouth, transformed into ragged, agonizing screams.

I burned from the inside out. At the same time, my mind was raped by the memories and images of a woman who was a slave to fire. The memories devoured me. Mercifully, I lost consciousness—but not before falling to the floor and vomiting fire.

I don't know how long the blackness persisted. When I opened my eyes, I knew I was dreaming. Once again, I found myself lying in the center of the stone dais with an unusual sky overhead. Unlike my previous blackout, however, a blazing wall of fire surrounded the platform. Alarmed, I rolled from my back into a low crouch and surveyed the landscape. The fire, shimmering orange and red with menacing blue highlights, replaced the delicately turned balustrade from my earlier dream. A hot wind, generated by the inferno, whipped my hair in all directions, plastering much of it to my sweat-covered face.

I stood up and wiped the strands of hair away from my eyes while searching for a way out of the encircled dais. I spun around but saw no break in the wall of fire. The inferno tightened around me, gradually drawing closer.

Wake up! I knew, without a doubt, if the flames reached me, I wouldn't wake up at all and it wouldn't be pleasant.

My breath came in ragged gulps, and I struggled to stay calm. Sweat encased my body, dripped from the tip of my nose, and snaked down my back and sides. I continued to turn slowly in place, as if I'd suddenly find an exit through the impenetrable fire. I tried to remember what I had learned on my last visit, anything that might help me. But nothing came to mind except the tender memory of meeting Jason for the first time.

As if summoned by my very thoughts, I felt Jason's cool presence behind me, just before he whispered into my ear, "You have to control the fire. Don't let it consume you."

Jason's cool breath hit my neck and the back of my ears, immediately forcing a shiver that had all of my body hairs standing at attention. He rubbed his icy hands over the length of my arms. I gasped, and my teeth clacked shut. When he moved his hands to grip my shoulders, they felt like two ice packs. Again, I shivered violently.

"You can do it. I know you can." His cold breath drifted past my face.

"I don't know how! Help me!"

Jason wrapped his arms around my waist. The intense cold of his body pressed into my back. I was all flame on one side and frost on the other.

He pressed his icy cheek against mine. "I can do nothing about the flames. You must control them. You have the power."

Through clenched teeth, I uttered, "What power? This is a dream! I know it's a dream, like last time. I've tried to wake up, but I can't. Make it go away. Please! Bring us back to the porch swing. Anything but this."

My muscles gave out. I was so tired, so hot, despite Jason's frosty intervention, and my body slipped through his icy grip. There was no power available to me that could stop the mad combustion around us. I collapsed to my side, almost past the point of caring. Before I could close my eyes to drift away, Jason shoved me to my back, and prostrated himself on top of me. I shuddered as deep cold swallowed my body from head to toe. Shocked, I stared into Jason's concerned eyes. They were a stunning, unfathomable blue, like the color of a backlit sapphire.

"Lire. They're trying to cool your body from the outside, but it's *here*," he tapped his icy finger against my temple, "that you must deal with the fire. I cannot help. The power lies within you. She will show you if you open up to it."

"No!" I struggled to sit up, and Jason immediately moved to kneel at my side. "She's evil. Jason, the things she did ... the things she enjoyed ... you don't understand. I can't live that life. I can't let it be a part of me. I can't!"

He frowned and shook his head. "Then nothing good can come from her life, and you will die here, without accomplishing your task. Evil will win." His eyes, still an unsettling shade of blue, blazed with an intensity that made me take pause.

I knew he was right. The woman known as Patty Schaeffer, whose deeds were so repugnant I was almost willing to die before reliving them, had the skills necessary to bank the fire, which now burned not ten feet away in every direction. Jason's icy touch was a distant memory, and my core body temperature had vaulted dangerously high.

I cried out in despair and dropped my shield. Patty's memories flooded to the fore—nothing like the initial dose, which had been propelled by the remains of the warlock's spell, but still overwhelming. In my mind, I recoiled from each memory, hundreds of horrible deeds that ranged from leaving flaming dog shit on someone's doorstep to setting fire to animals and watching them die in agony. And with each new atrocity, I mourned the ruination of her soul and the ever-increasing loss of my own innocence.

Unlike my experience with Jason's remains, Patty's soul was not trapped within her bones. Because there was no interference to slow the flow of psychic energy, all of Patty's life experiences became my own almost instantaneously. I grappled with the huge influx of experiences while suppressing my intense feelings of revulsion. On the one hand,

I reveled in the sheer pleasure of playing with fire, watching it burn, and feeding it whatever came to hand, but on the other hand, I cringed at the horrific deeds that derived such pleasure. It was Patty on the one side, Lire on the other.

"Lire!"

I came to my senses to find Jason holding me upright and the fire so close it was no longer possible to sit without getting singed. The hot, dry wind swirled around us, tossing my hair and lashing the flames even closer to where we stood.

Absolute calm filled my mind. This was my element. I was no longer afraid—it was wonderful—but I also knew my body couldn't withstand much more heat.

I took my weight back onto my own feet and wrapped my arms around Jason, pressing my sweat-soaked torso against him. He pulled back to peer into my eyes, his expression a mix of surprise and terror. A small part of me basked in his discomfort. I put my cheek next to his and fought my desire to push him into the fire, to watch his fear unfold completely.

"No!" I stepped back.

Fed by my anger and despair, a new power surged from my core and poured out of me in a torrent, but I easily took control of its potential. As the power danced between my fingertips, I marveled at its beauty. I caressed it, folded it this way and that, before lifting my hands skyward and slamming it down in an immense thunderclap that crushed the fire and depleted all of its fuel.

The darkness that followed was instantaneous and complete.

Katherine Bayless

(E)LEVEN

My eyes opened reluctantly and a little painfully. When I could finally keep them open for longer than a few seconds, I realized I was in a hospital bed. From the partial view visible through a nearby window, probably at Swedish Medical Center, in Seattle.

This wasn't the first time I'd woken up at Swedish, but I'd never been in a room quite like this one. On my previous surprise visits, when I was careless enough to misjudge my skill and power levels, I had been assigned a private room in the portion of the hospital reserved for psi-sensitive patients. It had been years since my last visit. This time, my bed was one of several. Maybe they had increased the size of their psi-ward. I closed my eyes on that thought. I was completely wiped out, and my head felt like it had been split open and stapled back together.

When I next opened my eyes, I noticed an IV bag dripping clear fluid down a tube feeding into my right arm. Countless layers of white gauze obscured my right hand. I tentatively wiggled my fingers and received severe, burning pain in return. The bandages engulfed my entire hand without any delineation that might have represented fingers. I fought down the unfounded fear that some, or all, of my fingers were charred husks. I remembered dreaming about fire and pictured my hand black and skeletal.

Before I panicked completely, a stocky, bronze-skinned nurse appeared at my bedside. Her name, she informed me, was Lupe. She was one of the step-down nurses at the hospital. After she raised the head of my bed, checked my vitals, and asked me several memory recall questions, she bustled away to call for the on-staff doctor. I realized, only after she had walked away, I still knew nothing about what had happened to me.

My eyes wanted to sag shut again, but I resisted and tried to get my mind working. Apparently, my brain wasn't running on all cylinders. I couldn't remember much of anything. Since my body felt like it had gone nine rounds in a UFC cage match and my head pounded faster than the Blue Man Group, I guessed my injured hand wasn't solely responsible for my hospital stay.

What was the last thing I remembered?

My mom's death ... Julie's party ... learning about Nick. My breath caught. *Dear Nick.* More recently, I remembered driving with Vince—he had driven me somewhere in the snow. He had reached into a plastic bin for me.

Oh, God! The bone.

And that's all it took. Like a trip wire, just that one image of Patty Schaeffer's bone triggered the rush of memories that had been lying in wait for my mind to dredge up. Stuck in a hospital bed, with no distractions, I had little to do but dwell on them. The more I tried to put them out of my mind, the more they claimed my attention. Finally, one thought surfaced that shoved all the others aside. Where was Red?

I fought down a new wave of panic and considered the most likely scenarios. Jensen and Vince must have been pretty freaked by my reaction—I remembered falling to the floor and screaming in pain—but I hoped Vince had the presence of mind to take my purse and put it away for safe keeping. He would have remembered Red was in there, right? I know Vince had watched me gather Red and my shoes before we got out of the Jeep. Good God! What if somebody else had gotten a hold of it? If someone else had picked up my purse and attempted to reach inside ... I couldn't bear thinking about it. If it happened at the police station and someone got zapped, what would they do? Shoot to kill? Call the bomb squad?

No, no. I told myself to calm down. If anything like that had happened with my purse, they'd have called Vince. There was no need to freak. Besides, any cop would know better than to rummage around in someone's purse without permission. Especially a purse with bright yellow warning labels on the inside. Wouldn't they?

I couldn't stand not knowing about Red, but before I had a chance to call over a nurse, a tall, impressively thin man appeared at my bedside. He wore a white medical jacket over dark trousers and a stethoscope draped around his neck. His hair was straight and black, streaked slightly with gray, and he had small, narrowly set blue eyes that contrasted against his black eyelashes. His voice was surprisingly deep. When he spoke, I noticed a prominent gap between his front teeth. He introduced himself as Doctor Williams and opened up my medical chart, which hung from a pocket at the foot of my bed.

He asked the usual questions in a serious, slightly detached manner, beginning with the all important, "How are you feeling?" and ending with queries obviously intended to test my memory.

After we established my name, birth date, address, and the current month and year, he asked me, "Do you know why you're here?"

"No. The nurse didn't say much, but I only just woke up about ten minutes ago, I think." With the fuzziness factor going on in my head, I wasn't completely sure of anything.

He flipped back a page or two in my chart. "You came into emergency two days ago, unconscious and exhibiting a dangerously high fever—well over 106—and convulsions." His eyes focused on mine. "I don't know if you know anything about body temperature, but a temperature of 107.6 for more than an hour can cause brain damage and eventually death. The ER put you into a full body ice bath to bring down your fever, but the results weren't encouraging. Your temp hovered just under 106 for a short time before spiking again. Your blood tests showed no sign of bacterial or viral infection, so there was nothing more to do, other than cool your body from the outside. Then, for whatever reason, your fever vanished. You stayed in intensive care until it was clear your body was recovering from the effects of the fever."

I lifted my bandaged hand. "What happened to my hand?"

"Your hand was burned. Not too badly, second degree burns on the palm and the inside of several of your fingers."

I studied him. "So, other than feeling really crappy, am I okay?"

His straight face was disrupted by a smile that disappeared almost as quickly as a box of chocolates in my kitchen. "You had signs of renal failure, but your recent blood test results were good. Your kidney function appears to be back to normal. Brain damage is also a concern with a prolonged high fever, but from initial observation, you appear to be fine. We'll keep an eye on you though and see how things go." He checked his watch. "You'll be transferring down to the psi-ward in an hour or two. They'll remove your catheter and get you moving around soon after, I'd imagine."

That was great news, but I couldn't relax completely until I had some news about Red. "Do you know whether I came in with anything—my purse for example? For that matter, do you know how I got here?"

"You arrived by airlift." He flipped pages in my chart. "Just shoes and socks in your inventory, no mention of a purse. Your clothes, of course, were cut off in emergency." More paper rustling. "A Detective Vincent Vanelli checked you in. A note here says he wants to be notified as soon as you're awake. We can place the call for you if you'd like."

"Yes, please. And will you ask after my friend, Red?"

He nodded his head and closed my chart.

"Thank you, doctor."

After he walked away, I leaned my head back to rest. Now that I had made some effort to locate Red, I didn't fight to keep my eyes open. I fell asleep in moments.

The sensation of rocking woke me, but even before I opened my eyes, I knew it was a dream. There are supposed to be people who can control their dreams, but until recently, I'd never personally experienced such a thing.

I was curled up on the familiar porch swing, using Jason's thigh as a pillow for the back of my head. I smiled up at him. The startling blue of his eyes cut through the shadows of the covered porch. I admired his boy-next-door, clean-cut good looks. He was way too young for me, but I could see how a girl could get used to having nightly dreams about Jason. Daily dreams too, for that matter.

He smiled that same quirky, lopsided smile I'd seen previously. His left eyebrow arched upward. "A guy could get used to this too."

The shock on my face must have been obvious because he laughed richly. I jumped up like a cat evading a spa treatment and narrowed my eyes at him. "You know what I'm thinking!"

He stifled his laughter and looked at me with an expression of both mirth and sympathy. "I'm part of you, remember? Of course I know what you're thinking."

"You what?" I looked at him, dumbfounded. "Well ... that just doesn't seem fair." I threw up my hands.

He laughed. "Sit down. Don't worry. I know you don't think of me that way."

I frowned, but his warm, friendly smile put me at ease. I sat down and studied him. "Are you my subconscious, or what? I have to tell you, this is really weird, even for me."

He smiled. "You're not talking to yourself. And, no, you're not going crazy."

"That wasn't even on my mind, thank you very much, until you piped up with that *I-know-what-you're-thinking* business." Jason chuckled before I asked, "So, what's up with this? Why is this happening? Why are you here, in my head, in my dreams? Not that I mind, exactly."

Jason shook his head. "Beats me. You have my memories, so your guess is as good as mine. It's possible this is what happens whenever someone like you touches another paranormal's remains."

I considered it. "I guess, but don't you think I would have heard of such a thing? I mean, at some point in history, this must have come up." I shook my head. "This is something other clairvoyants would have passed on—talked about. You know? But I've never heard it mentioned as a possible risk. There's just been the talk of being overwhelmed by so many memories, more like what I experienced with Patty's remains. I've never heard anything about having ... what? What are you? I know you're not just a memory. You're more than that. I can feel it. It's like I have a piece of your soul or something." I couldn't suppress a shiver.

He shrugged and then looked thoughtful. "I don't know. Maybe it has something to do with the spell the warlock used for his ritual."

I sighed and bit my lower lip. "I wish we knew more about it. Do you have any idea?" I could have examined the memories myself but didn't. I hated dwelling on his encounter with the demon.

Jason shrugged. "No. I wasn't conscious for that part."

I nodded, feeling drowsy. I regarded him fondly—high cheekbones, straight nose, square jaw with the tiniest hint of stubble—and wished I had known him in life. My eyelids grew heavy. At Jason's urging, I curled up and put my head back on his lap. While he rocked the swing, I closed my eyes and mused about how strange it was to be falling asleep in a dream.

Just before I drifted off, I heard him whisper, "I wish I'd known you too."

Someone jostled my shoulder and called my name. My eyes were slow to focus, but after a moment, I was surprised to see Vince standing next to my bed. I smiled weakly and did my best to blink the sleep away. It occurred to me that waking up to Vince's concerned expression wasn't the worst thing in the world, although, I'd have enjoyed it more if not for the setting.

"Hey," I croaked while trying to brush away a few strands of hair tickling my cheek. My bandaged hand and IV drip line hampered my efforts. I switched to using my left, awkwardly managing to smooth my limp, unwashed hair behind my head.

Vince gave my left shoulder a squeeze and then sat back in a nearby chair.

I looked around. This wasn't the step down unit. I was in a private room, probably in the psi-ward. I must have really been out of it when they moved me. I didn't remember a thing.

"Hey. How're you feeling?" The concern hadn't left Vince's face. He leaned forward, putting his right hand on the bed. I got the impression he wanted to touch me, but didn't want to overstep his bounds.

I patted Vince's hand with my uninjured one and was rewarded with a tight-lipped smile. "I've been better, to be honest." I remembered Red and grasped Vince's wrist. "Red! Where is he?"

I tried to raise myself up but was too exhausted to get far. Vince rose to put a hand on my shoulder and ease me back into bed. "It's okay. I have him here with me. I brought your purse. Let me close the door."

After ensuring our privacy, Vince reached down next to the bed and brought up my satchel, which he placed on my thighs. The outside of the purse bubbled with movement. When I lifted the top of the bag to create a larger opening, Red pushed his head out, climbed to his feet, and pattered a few steps before I hugged him close. His stuffing stayed put and his eyes didn't pop out, but I'm sure it was a close thing considering the tight hug I gave him. When I finally released him, he sat down on my stomach with his back against my purse.

"Thank God! You have no idea how I've let my imagination run wild about what happened to you." I snuggled back into the discomfort of the hospital bed, feeling much more at ease.

"I am sorry it caused you distress. Visitors are allowed very little access to the ICU, and we did not know when you would become conscious. I asked Vince to keep me in his safekeeping until you were released. It seemed the prudent choice at the time," Red explained.

"I'd hoped that's what happened, but I wasn't sure." I looked at Vince. "Thanks."

"It was the least I could do."

I gave him a weary smile. "I seem to spend more time at your feet than I do standing up." When this only yielded a small smile and his expression of worry remained, I reassured him, "Vince, I'm okay. Really."

He gave me a stiff nod but remained silent. He obviously had something on his mind, but I was too worn out to tease it out of him gently. I looked at Red, "Something's wrong. What is it?"

Red tilted his head. "Do you have any idea what happened to you?"

"Yeah, I got my ass kicked by the leftover magic in Patty Schaeffer's remains and about a zillion really unpleasant memories. But I already spoke with the doctor when I was in the step down unit. He said I came through okay."

I stopped and looked back and forth between Vince and Red. "Do you guys know something I don't?"

Red patted my leg. "Actually, there is quite a bit you do not know, but not in the way you think. I am certain the doctor is correct that you are going to recover, but it was a close thing. We nearly watched you die. Ah ... I can see by your frown that you know nothing of what happened before you arrived at the hospital. You are correct that the residual magic overpowered you. It was so powerful, in fact, that it stopped your heart. Vince gave you CPR for several minutes until the paramedics arrived. They were able to restart your heart with a defibrillator; however, almost immediately your temperature began to rise. By the time you reached the emergency room, you were having frequent convulsions.

We then waited as the emergency staff tried to bring down your fever. The attending physician came out and told us the full body ice bath had not worked. They wanted to notify your next of kin and know whether you wanted Last Rites."

"God! I ... I don't know what to say. I had no idea. No wonder you're both upset." I looked over at Vince and reached toward him with my free hand. "Vince, thank you. You saved my life."

He leaned forward to take my extended hand, holding it loosely on the edge of the bed. He shook his head. "I might have helped, but I didn't save your life. The paramedics did that, and then the ER team." He sighed heavily. "No, I set you up for this. I asked you to give a reading when I knew it was a difficult job for you. You have nothing to thank me for."

"This isn't your fault. If you hadn't asked me to do the reading, Jensen would have. And if anyone's to blame, it's the bastard who's running around blasting psychics." I gave his hand an emphatic squeeze. "I knew the risks. I'll do anything to find Jason and Nick's killer. *Anything*."

Vince nodded and then released my hand. I'm not sure he was convinced, but he didn't argue.

I thought about my sister. "Did someone call Giselle?"

Red answered, "No. Vince and I agreed it was best to wait. After all, your mother just died and she is eight months pregnant. Even if Giselle had been called, she could do nothing, other than worry. It seemed to be the right thing to do."

I nodded. "Okay. Thanks. You're right. The last thing I want is for her to be worried about me right now."

Vince said, "Red asked me to call Julie, and we've been keeping her updated. She visited you earlier, but you were asleep, I think. She wants you to call her as soon as you feel up to it."

"And what about Jack, did you call him too?"

"We called him after we knew you were okay." Vince hesitated before adding, "He says you should take as much time off as you need."

"Somehow I don't think that's all he said. Is it?" Jack was probably wound tighter than a balloon caught in a ceiling fan.

"No, it wasn't." Vince shrugged. "He's concerned about you, not without reason. Helping us seems to be bad for your health."

I arched my right eyebrow. "What can I say? I like to live dangerously."

He shook his head and smiled. For the first time since he arrived, I felt the tension in the room ease.

"So, that was quite a day down at the Chiliquitham P.D., huh? Just a guess, but I'm sure clairvoyants don't keel over in your break room every day, do they?" I gasped. "Oh crap. That news guy in the parking lot. And the press conference! Please tell me that reporters weren't out front when all this went down."

"Of course they were. Whatever can go wrong." Vince smirked. "You're living proof of Murphy's Law."

"Only when you're around." I stuck my tongue out at him.

He grinned. "True enough." He shook his head. "Seriously though, we're going to have to sneak you out of here. The media attention has exploded." He glanced at Red and then added, "A couple of photographers managed to get past the staff when you were in the step down unit. I'm afraid they managed to snap a few shots before they were thrown out. The hospital has a security guard posted in the corridor now."

All I could think about was how terrible I must look in those photos before realizing their true impact. "Oh! What about Giselle? Maybe she's seen them. I've got to call her."

Vince nodded. "It started out as just another local story, but Fox picked it up last night."

With Vince's help finding the number in my purse and then dialing it, I was able to leave a message on Giselle's answering machine telling her briefly what was going on and that I was fine. I only had about fifty other things to worry about, but it made me feel better knowing she wouldn't be worried by the news reports. I made a mental note to call her again as soon as I got home.

A knock on the door interrupted any further discussion. I hastily slipped Red back into my purse with a quick apology. I called, "Come in."

The nurse who entered was tall and slender with dark blonde hair pulled into a smooth ponytail. She wore typical psi-ward attire—blue, long sleeve orderlies and latex gloves—with navy blue Crocs. Although she'd probably dealt with dozens of other patients during the course of her shift, her smile appeared genuine and her greeting was cheerful. When she saw Vince, she seemed a little nonplussed, possibly thinking she had interrupted something private. With his head down, pecking away on his cell phone, Vince was oblivious.

She introduced herself and then proceeded to check my vitals. Even though she paid attention to me, asked all the requisite questions, and engaged in typical nurse-like behavior, I could tell she was distracted. After a minute, I realized Vince was the source. She wasn't drooling on his shoes or anything, but every so often she glanced at him and then ducked her head quickly. It was so subtle, I doubt Vince even noticed.

Before she left the room, I told her I wanted to ask the doctor about my progress to get an idea when I might be released. She nodded and politely closed the door behind her, but not before risking another surreptitious look at Vince.

As soon as she left, I opened my purse for Red. Vince helped me get comfortable with the arrangement of hard, lumpy pillows behind my back.

With weariness descending on me, I said, "Get your notebook out. I don't know how much longer I'll be coherent, and there are a few things you should know before you leave." I made an effort to keep my voice loud enough for normal conversation. "I've figured out a few things that may or may not be significant."

His eyebrows went up as he fished around in his coat pocket. When he had his pen and pad ready, he said, "Okay, shoot."

"Like I said earlier, the victim's name was Patty Schaeffer. She was a pyrokinetic who just moved to the area late last year from Ohio. She was ... well, let's just say we never would have been friends."

Vince examined me. "Criminal?"

I nodded. "She has a record, although, she wasn't caught for the worst offenses." I waved my left hand weakly. "I'll tell you about that later. The important thing is she knew Nick. In late November, she participated in a study that Nick helped organize at Coventry City Hospital. She even pursued him romantically after the study was over." I pressed my lips together. "He let her down gently—told her he had a girlfriend."

His expression didn't give much away, but Vince seemed pleased. "Where did she live?"

"Federal Way. She worked at the Home Depot there."

I closed my eyes and took a breath. I was so tired. I felt something soft stroke my cheek. When I opened my eyes, Red stood on my chest gazing at me.

"We're going to let you sleep now, but I was loath to leave without saying goodbye." He gave me one last pat on the cheek before backing away.

"Okay." It took me a moment to get my bearings. I must have drifted off when I closed my eyes earlier, but something nagged at me. There was something important I needed to tell Vince. What was it?

"Vince. Wait. One last thing." He stood at the end of my bed. I had to struggle to raise my voice. "Patty was killed on January 20th. That means she wasn't the first victim. She was murdered after Jason."

Whether this came as a surprise, I couldn't tell. Vince looked thoughtful as he jotted this newest piece of information in his notebook. He looked up, putting away his pad and pen. "I have more questions for you, but we'll go over them later. I left your overnight bag on the chair, so you'll have some clothes. Get some rest."

He waited for Red to climb back into my purse and then placed it into a black duffel bag. Of course, Vince didn't want to be seen carrying a woman's purse. I smiled at his camouflage before drifting back to sleep. I don't remember hearing the sound of the door when he left.

The nurse returned to poke another hole in my arm, shortly after Vince and Red departed, and I was thankful her earlier distraction was gone. The blood draw was understandable, but it seemed like someone was always waking me up once an hour to check my vitals or adjust my IV or serve me a meal or something. It was frustrating and maddening. By the time the doctor arrived, later that evening, I demanded to be released the following morning. I was sick of the constant prodding and questioning and restless sleep. The pillows were hard and the blankets were thin. I couldn't get comfortable no matter how I tried. My own bed was calling my name, and I wanted nothing more than to snuggle down under my own comforter and sleep uninterrupted for a long time.

It took another full day to extract my release from the on-staff doctor, but pacing the hallway in front of the nursing station every hour probably helped.

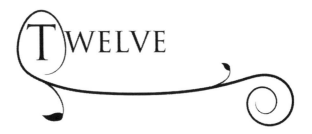

TWELVE

Julie drove my car to pick me up, and I laughed when she darted dramatically into my hospital room. She pressed her back against the wall and peered outside the door as though trying to evade some unfriendly foe. She was a study in black—black shoes, black running tights, black pullover, black wraparound sunglasses, black leather backpack, all topped off with a black baseball hat.

"What are you doing?" I asked, laughing. "You look like an emo Ninja."

She mugged at me and executed a crouching run from the doorway to my bedside chair, ending in laughter. When she caught her breath, she said, "Vince told me about the reporters, so I decided to dress for stealth."

"Uh huh. Everyone knows black equals stealthy, and if anyone tries to snap your picture, you are practically invisible under that hat." The hat looked like it was two sizes too big. It was probably one of Steven's.

"You know it, girlfriend." She huffed onto her nails and then buffed them on her chest.

"You're quite the drama queen today, aren't you?"

A security guard looked inside my room with a perplexed expression, and I waved him away with a smile.

Julie, oblivious to the guard, shrugged at me. "It's so surreal—you in the papers and all. I couldn't help myself."

We giggled. Like Red, Julie had her own way of making me feel better whenever I was down. It usually involved some crazy stunt, but she never failed to make me laugh.

She pulled off the backpack. "The press must have gotten word you're going home today. TV crews and a swarm of reporters are down in the lobby. I swear, every day there's been an update on your condition. It's crazy. If you don't want to be on CNN tonight, we should find out if there's a direct route to the parking garage to avoid the lobby."

"Good plan. Would you mind checking with the nurse's station? I have to wait here for the release nurse."

Unfortunately, there wasn't a way to avoid the lobby. We had to rely on four hospital security guards and three nurses to keep the press at bay when we made our way to the parking garage elevators. We did our best to ignore their questions and the lights of the cameras, but it wasn't easy. After taking the elevator to the second basement level, Julie and I breathed a sigh of relief when we found no one lurking in the shadows. The security guards and just one of the nurses waited with me while Julie fetched the car. I decided to let her drive since I still felt rocky.

If anyone followed us to my apartment building, they'd have to deal with Chet's intimidating presence or the guards in the building's lobby. My homeowner's dues were obscenely high, but I appreciated the security. With trained armed guards, magic wards up the wazoo, and two house djinn, unauthorized entry into the building's residential floors was impossible. I felt a surge of relief when we drove up to the parking garage's security gate and gave Chet a heads up.

After pulling into the garage, Julie turned to me with a broad smile. "I think we just made his day. Did you see the spark in his eyes when you told him unwanted guests might be calling? He looked thrilled." She shook her head. "I pity anyone who tries to get past him without permission."

I giggled. "I know. It almost makes me want to hang around and wait, just to see if anything happens."

Vince and Red waited in my apartment for Julie and I to arrive. Before leaving the hospital, I had called my building's reception desk to tell them Vince was allowed access to my apartment and to turn away any reporters.

Considering I'd only had two or three visitors in the entire time I owned the loft, ringing my doorbell and having Vince answer the door was disconcerting.

I gave him what was probably an awkward, "Hey," and then said goodbye to Julie.

She had decided to wait down in the lobby for Steven, instead of donning a skin suit. I gave her a careful hug, thanked her for picking me up, and promised to call her later.

Vince had brewed a pot of coffee, the darling. He delivered a cup (fixed just how I like it) to me at my perch on the couch. I could have kissed him. Call me crazy, but I just thanked him instead. The psi-free coffee at the hospital had been mediocre at best. The smell of my own Sumatran, brewing in my own kitchen, served in my own coffee mug while sitting on my own couch was enough to make me swoon. I relished the hot drink and delighted in the comfort of the soft cushions. Right then, I think I might have forgiven Vince any transgression.

When we first met, I never would have pegged him for thoughtful and considerate. I wondered if he would ever stop surprising me.

He sat next to me with his own cup of coffee and Red found a spot on the coffee table.

I smirked. "Make yourself right at home Vince."

"Aaaah," he crooned, putting his socked feet on the coffee table and slumping into a comfortable position. "Don't mind if I do."

I rolled my eyes and tried to smother my smile. The blisters were tender on my right hand, so I had to acquaint myself with holding the cup in my left. Awkward, but I managed not to spill.

"I brought my laundry over too. Hope you don't mind." He said this with such a poker face, at first, I wasn't sure if he was joking. After a moment, his eyes slid to the side to check out my reaction, and I realized he was teasing.

I chuckled and shook my head. "I must be more tired than I thought; you totally got me with that one."

He laughed. "How was your departure? Am I gonna see you on the six o'clock news tonight?"

I snorted. "Probably, but if they managed to get a clear shot of me, I'd be surprised. I was surrounded by security guards and riding in a wheel chair. Since I didn't see any cameramen on stilts, I think I'm relatively safe. It was ridiculous though. It must be a pretty dry news day if my exit from the hospital is the most exciting story around."

Vince sipped his coffee. "Conservatives are talking about the Magic User Registration Bill again. It makes for a sensational story. You landed right in the middle of it. Sorry about that."

I shrugged. "No need to apologize. It was my decision to help you, and I'd do it all over again. The whole press thing was probably inevitable. Magic is nothing if not sensational. As long as everyone knows I'm helping with the case and not a prime suspect, I'll be okay."

"I almost forgot. Your neighbors stopped by to check on you. The two guys from next door, Peter and ..." he snapped his fingers while he tried to remember the other name.

"Jerome."

"Right. They wanted to let you know they're back from their trip. If you need anything, they said to call or stop by."

I nodded. "Thanks. Was that today?"

"Yes. They must have heard me come in. They were pretty surprised to see me. Red had to assure them you were okay with me being here, you know, without being covered up." He nodded toward the kitchen. "You also have a lot of messages on your answering machine. I don't know if you noticed."

I sighed. "No, I didn't. I'll check them later. I don't feel like dealing with them right now." I shifted my body on the couch to face him more directly. "Did you verify the information about Patty Schaeffer?"

"Yes. Her coworkers at Home Depot all confirmed the last time she showed up for work was in mid-January. Her boss told me her last day was the eighteenth. No one was surprised when she quit work without notice. Every employee I interviewed told me Patty complained almost continually that she wasn't happy here and intended to move back home."

I nodded. "She was hoping to. She just didn't have the money. Actually, that's what got her tangled up with the murderer. She was hooked by a deal to set fires. Insurance scam. The money was going to be enough to get her back home and then some. She was supposed to meet the contact at the east parking lot of Sammamish State Park, late on the twentieth. It never occurred to her to be wary about meeting a stranger at a potentially deserted location. She had a built-in weapon, you know? Not too many people around who aren't afraid of fire."

"How'd she hear about this job?" Vince had put down his coffee in favor of his dog-eared notepad and ballpoint pen. He licked his finger and flipped to a fresh page.

"Another firestarter from Nick's study. A guy named Keith Deckard. Keith told me ... I mean, Keith told Patty that he met the contact in an on-line chat group and eventually talked with him off-line about the scam. The deal was for five thousand per job. Keith wasn't interested, but he thought Patty could use the extra money, so he passed the tip along to her. Patty wasn't so sure about it though. She figured the guy might be an undercover cop or something— so she decided to just go and meet him, but not agree to anything or take any money until she had a chance to do some checking around. She was so busy worrying the guy was an undercover cop that his attack came as a complete surprise."

"Did she get a look at him?"

"No. He wore a scarf around his face, sunglasses, and a dark hat. He's good. I'm sure he knows a clairvoyant can get that type of information from the remains."

"Or he's just being cautious, in case his quarry gets away."

I tilted my head. "Could be. And she'd have been a bad one to let loose. Does 'burned to a crisp' mean anything to you?"

He chuckled. "How'd he manage to avoid getting fricasseed?"

"Same as Jason. Chloroform maybe? He hit me— " I shook my head. "I mean her—hard and then he put something over her mouth and nose. It was a smart move. She was so stunned there was no way to call her power before she blacked out. She woke up inside the circle with the demon restraining her magic." I inhaled deeply but was unable to stifle a shiver. The memories of her ordeal were horrific, but I think what disturbed me most was that a not so small part of me felt she got what she deserved.

"Anything else? What about the car?"

I closed my eyes and delved into Patty's memories. "The car was a black sedan. She didn't notice the license-plate because she was too busy checking out the guy leaning against the car door." I opened my eyes and shrugged. "It might have been a BMW. Maybe. It had tinted windows and a glass sunroof. Sorry. She really wasn't paying much attention to the car."

I placed my nearly empty mug on a coaster and rearranged my limbs on the couch so I could face him a little more. "One thing I've remembered since I spoke with you last is Jason also participated in Nick's study."

Vince looked up from his notepad and regarded me with a piercing gaze.

I sighed. "I probably would have come up with that sooner, but with all of my various emotional stresses lately, it didn't occur to me until yesterday. Sorry about that. Jason didn't actually meet Nick directly, though. His test was administered by Nick's colleague."

"Did Jason know Patty?" he asked.

"No. They were tested individually."

"What exactly was Nick studying?"

"He was working in conjunction with a neuroscientist to observe a psychic's brainwaves before, during, and after a psychic discharge. Each subject was wired up and then asked to do various tests, sometimes using their power and sometimes not. Jason and Patty don't have any knowledge of what they were hoping to discover. I hadn't spoken with Nick about it, so I don't know either."

Before he could ask, I said, "Dr. Ford was Nick's research associate at Coventry Hospital. I think his first name is Edwin."

While I watched Vince jot the information in his notebook, I reminded him, "Don't forget, I'd like to come with you to Coventry, so I can have Jake examine Nick's remains. If the demon did the same thing to Nick, I want his soul released."

He looked up from his writing. "Technically, we need the approval of his next of kin."

I shook my head. "Nick's family abandoned him when his powers surfaced. They put him in a reservation and signed over guardianship to the government. To say that he was bitter would be an understatement." I smacked my head with the palm of my hand. "You don't think the police contacted his parents, do you? He'd have hated that, and I know Nick left a will. We talked a lot about our screwed up backgrounds. In college, he told me even though he didn't have much in the way of money, he had a will drawn up just to cut his family out of it. The police will search his house for it, right? Or will they just assume it's okay to let his parents inside without supervision? Man! That would really piss Nick off."

Vince held up his empty hand in a stopping gesture. "Settle down. Nick's death is part of a murder investigation. It's safe to assume the police up there won't be letting anyone into his place until they've thoroughly searched for evidence. They'll be looking for legal documents, safety deposit box keys—things of that nature. Don't forget, one of the main motives for murder is money." Vince looked at me askance. "You know, it's possible Nick worked things out with his parents. Don't assume they're out of the picture. After all, didn't you just patch things up with your sister?"

I sank into the couch, abashed, and looked down at my lap. It didn't seem likely, but Vince was right, Nick may have reconciled with his parents. I didn't see how it was possible, since as far as I knew, he had no idea where his parents lived or, for that matter, whether they were still alive. I said as much to Vince, but acknowledged anything was possible. Two weeks ago, I never dreamed of my own reconciliation with Mom and Giselle, and look what happened.

"So, how do we go about getting in to examine Nick's remains?" I asked.

"The examination isn't the problem."

Vince traded his pen and notepad for his coffee cup. Leaning back with his mug, he replaced his socked feet on the table. Suddenly, I realized this was … nice. Vince on my couch, socked feet and all, just hanging out—it was so very normal. And I liked it. I tried hard not to think about how it was going to feel when the case was solved and this small bit of normalcy disappeared.

Vince continued, "It's the soul freeing thing. They're not going to want you tampering with the evidence, not until someone's behind bars." He held his hand up, silencing me. "But before we get ahead of ourselves, let's just take things one step at a time. I'll try to get access to the remains for you and, hopefully, your necromancer. But you have to promise there will be no soul freeing—not until we get it cleared first. I don't want you charged with evidence tampering, okay? We've got enough to worry about." He sighed. "I have to tell you though, without the next of kin demanding the release of his remains, like Jason's parents have done, the soul releasing thing for Nick will probably have to wait until the investigation is closed."

I leaned my head on the couch cushion and sulked. "I suppose that's better than never."

Vince's expression softened. "How are you feeling? You doing okay?"

I gave him a small smile. "Yeah, I guess. A little tired." My smile faltered as various memories of the past couple weeks came to mind. Discussing Nick's remains hadn't helped. "It's better if I don't think too much, but sometimes it's a losing battle."

Even though I had kept my emotions under control for the most part, I felt a tear squeeze out from the corner of my left eye. It rolled down my cheek and disappeared into the softness of the couch fabric.

"I'm sorry, Lire." His look of concern did wonderful things to his eyes.

He tricked me, remember? He pretended to like me at the party.

I sat up straight to clear my head. "It's not your fault but thanks. And thank you for watching out for Red and meeting me here today. I have to say, it's been a new experience having you inside without any protection."

Too late, I realized the double entendre and then laughed like an idiot as my cheeks flushed. My mind seemed to be skirting the edges of the gutter lately.

Vince laughed too and cleared his throat. "Ahem. Yes. Well, it was no problem. Red and I had fun hanging out."

Once again, I was struck by the unexpected consequences of Vince's unusual nature. Red had never shared time with anyone else without me being, at the very least, in the general proximity. Now, I was faced with the knowledge that Vince and Red had a boy's night out together—two nights, actually. The sudden awareness was unsettling.

Vince frowned. "Is something wrong?"

I shook my head and tried not to look as overwhelmed as I felt. "I'm sorry, it's not you. Actually, that's not true." I made an exasperated sound and blurted, "This is just so weird. I'm sure this all seems very normal to you, but this ..." I paused to search for an appropriate word and flailed my good hand in the air, "situation is so not normal for me. Before two weeks ago, I'd never had anyone in my home without a skin suit, much less greet me at my own door, and Red has never been away from me or talked to anyone without me at least being nearby."

"And, to think, I could have given you the full experience by bringing over my dirty clothes." Vince grinned before regarding me thoughtfully. "Seriously though, I can go now. I should have thought about how all this would make you feel. Anyway, you probably want to get some rest." He took his legs down from the coffee table and started to lean forward.

"No. No." I moved in to grab his arm before he got up. I let my hand linger for a moment. "Please don't. This might be strange for me, but it's also been nice. You don't have to go. Well, not unless you want to." I withdrew my hand before my words seemed too much like a come-on and leaned back tentatively into the cushions.

"Are you sure?"

I nodded, but to my dismay, unshed tears pricked my eyes. I looked away while I fought them back.

Vince asked, "You sure you're okay?"

Again, I nodded wordlessly, covering my mouth, for fear of bursting into tears. After a moment of silently berating myself, I removed my hand. "God! I'm a disaster. You must think I'm such a baby."

"Are you kidding? Considering what you've been through, I'm impressed with how well you're holding up. Hell, if I'd been knocked around as much as you have, I'd be a mess."

I snorted and gave him a stiff nod as I ripped a tissue from the box sitting next to the couch. I dabbed my eyes. "I don't know how, but you always manage to see me at my absolute worst."

He reclined back into the couch, apparently satisfied I wasn't going to get hysterical. "Hardly. I've seen worse."

I glanced his way. "Yeah?"

"Sure. I'm a cop, remember?" He shook his head. "Trust me. You don't even come close to being the worst I've ever seen."

I pushed some loose strands of hair behind my ear and thought about my newly acquired memories. "I bet what I've got up here comes close." I poked a finger at the side of my head. "I know it's the worst I've ever seen, and this time I've got the whole show, not just bits and pieces." I took a shuddering deep breath, which I let out slowly.

Vince looked puzzled, but Red understood. "With no soul trapped within the remains, you acquired all of Patty's memories. However, that is not what affected you so profoundly, is it?"

I looked at Red. His pudgy legs hung over the edge of the coffee table. I shook my head.

Red nodded. "Her soul was missing for a reason."

I blinked long and bit my lip. "Yeah. She was evil."

Vince rested his right ankle over left knee and regarded me. "You mentioned something about this at the hospital, so I looked up her record. I would have done it anyway, but your comments made me particularly curious. Her record wasn't exactly clean. Misdemeanors mostly. One case of shoplifting. Nothing too extreme, but then, you said she didn't get caught for the worst of it."

I nodded. I was afraid to open my mouth—afraid if I did, I'd start crying in earnest and not be able to stop. At the same time, I knew I needed to talk to someone about the memories.

"Can you talk about it?" Vince asked.

I was silent while I struggled with the ironclad door I had slammed against Patty's memories. It couldn't possibly be maintained indefinitely. Not if I wanted to function otherwise. With the amount of energy I expended keeping her horrors locked away, there was no way I could maintain my shield effectively. I simply didn't have enough energy to do both.

"I know I'll have to face Patty soon, but I'm not ready. I don't want to think about her. Vince, she was horrible! Truly horrible. And I've seen my share of horrible shit. Believe me. It's taking all my strength just to keep her locked away. But,

I can't do that indefinitely, not if I want to leave my apartment." My voice cracked from emotion. "I wish I had never touched her. I wish I had the strength to keep her out of my head. I wish ..." I swiped at my nose with the tissue and grunted. "I guess I wish a lot of things. But, as my dad used to say, nothing comes from just wishing."

Vince sat forward and braced his arms on his thighs, so he could look into my face. I tried to resist the urge to hide from his gaze, but I looked down at the floor anyway. Talk about vain! Even with all my psychological and emotional turmoil, I worried about Vince seeing me with bloodshot eyes, no makeup, and limp hair.

As I stared at the carpet, lamenting my ugly state, Vince put his arm around my shoulder and pulled me toward him. Startled, I risked a glance into his eyes before resting my head stiffly against his shoulder. Red jumped down from the coffee table and walked in the direction of the kitchen, giving us some privacy.

Vince rubbed my arm. "I know there's not much I can do, but I've seen a lot of bad shit too and I can be a good listener."

I nodded and inhaled his aftershave. It was spicy and not too sweet. Vince sat back, pulling me with him, and I tried to find a comfortable position, in spite of my convoluted feelings about him. I placed my right hand on his chest. Since it was bandaged, it wasn't like I could feel anything with it. Well, that's what I told myself.

After ten years of mostly abstinence and certainly no skin contact, my reaction to Vince's spontaneous closeness was more than a little complicated.

Vince kept his arm around me, and I relaxed as much as possible, which wasn't easy. I was sitting on a ticking memory time bomb and lying against a guy who I was trying not to find irresistibly sexy. My excuse that Vince wasn't my type was wearing thin, and I couldn't help but wonder about his feelings toward me. Was I just a fellow colleague in need? Did he feel sorry for me? Or was he doing this because he was attracted to me? Even if he was attracted to me, I wondered whether it was a mistake to get involved with him. His comments about possessive girlfriends and messy breakups sprang to mind. Was he just unlucky or had he behaved in ways that prompted possessive behavior from his girlfriends? Maybe he wasn't one for commitment.

Just a casual relationship wasn't going to work for me. But, that issue aside, did I really want to be involved with him? I did not want to go through another heartbreaking experience, like the one with Nick. But I guess that was the risk with *any* romantic relationship. Except, for someone like me, the pain of loss was magnified by the rarity of finding a skin-mate. In over thirty years, I'd only met one other person who I could touch without incident. Maybe it was better to stay out of the pool. At least, that way it wasn't possible to drown.

And then there was the business of his deception and not coming clean about Nick's death. Granted, it was possible the decision to mislead me was mainly driven by his superiors.

I sighed. My feelings about Vince were confusing. Pondering them while laying my head against his muscular body probably wasn't going to yield the most objective evaluation.

It occurred to me that I was dwelling on Vince to avoid facing Patty's horrendous life, but I had good reason, dammit. Besides, snuggling up with Vince felt freaking awesome. It was almost impossible not to think romantic, even lustful, thoughts. And Vince stroking my hair and right arm wasn't helping either.

Whoa. My temperature had increased, and I was almost one hundred percent sure the loft's heating system hadn't kicked in.

I blurted, "Patty was an enforcer for a gang leader in Cleveland. She left the area when the police investigating a brutal murder began sniffing around her boss. He gave her money and a ticket to Seattle. She hoped he'd call her back after things cooled down."

I left a world of things unsaid, but it was a start.

Vince's hand, which froze at my outburst, gave my arm a gentle squeeze. "Was she guilty of the murder there?"

"Yes."

"She used her powers?"

I sighed. "Yes."

"Was it the only murder?"

"No."

"How many others?"

I thought for a moment. The fact that I had to stop to think about it was definitely a bad sign. "I'm not sure. It's not that I can't access the memories. She didn't know for sure. At least a dozen, maybe more."

"And the police never caught on after all those deaths?"

"She was careful to first start the fire in a place where it could be explained, like in electrical wiring."

"Ah."

I pressed my lips together. "Yeah. She was brutal. She enjoyed it. She especially liked to see the victims suffer. She toyed with them. She ... it was ... it was ..."

My stomach roiled. I jumped up and ran for the nearest safe location to vomit. I made it just inside the guest bathroom's threshold before losing it. On the second heave, I made it to the toilet. Somehow I managed not to slip on the now-slick tile floor. On my knees, I retched a few more times and then flushed the toilet. I heard Vince's footsteps stop just outside the open door.

"I'm sorry, Lire. Anything I can do?"

"Yes." I wanted him elsewhere. Without turning to look at him, I asked, "Will you please get me the mop and bucket? And the roll of paper towels in the kitchen. Red can show you where I keep the mop. Just leave them at the door. I'll be done in a minute."

"All right, I'll be right back."

As his footsteps echoed away toward the kitchen, I got up and closed the door. When I glanced in the mirror, I couldn't suppress a whimper. I looked a wreck-and-a-half. My nose was red and my eyes were bloodshot from heaving. Since it wasn't likely to get much worse, I dropped all my barriers against Patty's memories and allowed them to flow freely. With the initial shock over, I could dwell on the worst offenses without becoming sick. It wasn't easy, but I forced myself to relive every ghastly detail, especially the most atrocious acts, so they no longer held any terror for me. A few tears certainly weren't going to make Vince think any worse of me, but I choked them back anyway.

After a moment of standing with my back against the door, I moved to the sink to splash some cold water on my face and rinse out my mouth. It was awkward only being able to use my left hand, but not impossible.

Over the sound of the running water, I heard the *clank* of the bucket's metal handle and then Vince's muffled voice telling me everything was ready. When I opened the bathroom door, Vince stood a few feet away, looking concerned. The bucket and mop were near the door, and he held the paper towel roll. Wisps of steam rose from the surface of the soapy water in the bucket. Vince really was a doll.

He stepped forward. "Go sit down. Let me help."

"God, no!" I didn't want him to think I wasn't grateful, so I added, "You've already helped by bringing me this stuff." I held out my hand for the roll of paper towels and he handed it to me.

I didn't want him watching while I got down on my knees to clean the disgusting mess. "I guess I'll need a garbage bag. Would you mind?" I risked a quick glimpse into his eyes. He looked sympathetic and nodded.

By the time Vince returned with the garbage bag, I had finished wiping up. I thanked him for his help and then told him to go sit down. The bathroom wasn't large, so I finished mopping in minutes, although, with just one functional hand, the job took longer than usual. When Vince saw me carrying the bucket toward the laundry room, he jumped up from the couch and took it from my grasp.

Vince headed for the deep-well sink at the far wall. I followed him into the room and leaned my back against the industrial rack shelving opposite the sink. As he emptied the bucket, I wondered again about his motivation. This was hardly a pleasant undertaking.

"Why are you doing this?" It came out a little louder and more accusatory than I intended.

He turned around with a puzzled look. "Doing what?"

"You know, investing all this time in taking care of me." I frowned. "If you're doing it because you feel responsible in some way, you can just stop right now. *Seriously*. It's liable to give me the wrong idea. And because of your unique nature, I'd rather avoid any misunderstandings along those lines, thank you very much."

Vince put the bucket in its place under the sink. "Unique nature?"

My cheeks were burning, which annoyed me, so I got a little testy. "Dammit. Don't play dumb. The fact that I can touch you. If you're just doing this because you feel somehow responsible for my recent injury ... I think ... if that's the case, you *really* need to go."

Vince considered me for several seconds and finally nodded. "Fair enough."

He walked past me, back toward the kitchen. I figured he was on his way out. At the threshold, he turned to me, revealing a nonchalant smile. "So, are you feeling hungry for lunch? Julie dropped off a lasagna earlier, or I can get some takeout if you want." He continued into the kitchen, leaving me behind.

I stood stunned, blinking like an idiot, before following him out into the kitchen. When I finally emerged, he waited, leaning back against the kitchen island with a sly smile.

I rolled my eyes and told him, "You exhaust my brain. I need to sit."

That cracked him up. I heard him chuckling behind me all the way to the family room couch. Meanwhile, my thoughts bounced around like a laser beam in a mirror factory.

When I had curled up, Vince asked whether I wanted any more coffee. His expression was decidedly mischievous, so I scolded him, "Good Lord. Just sit down would you?"

Looking amused, he sat down with his arm draped across the back cushion. Of course, all I could seem to think about was how sexy he looked and how rumpled and disgusting I looked, not to mention having vomit breath.

I jumped up. "Uh, well, I don't have an appetite right now. But, you're welcome to have some lasagna if you're hungry. Um, if you don't mind, I could use a shower. Here's the remote. Feel free to watch TV. The DVDs are in those drawers if you'd rather watch a movie." I gestured toward the entertainment center and then fled upstairs before I could embarrass myself any further.

My legs itched to take the stairs two at a time, but I forced myself to take each tread normally. I knew Vince could see me until I reached the first landing. As soon as the stairs took me out of his sight, I jogged quietly the rest of the way up while my mind wheeled.

By the time I strode into my bedroom, my heart pounded wildly and it wasn't because of the stairs. Did what I think happen just happen? Did Vince acknowledge his attraction to me? Pacing back and forth, I considered our conversation in the laundry room. I had told him to leave if he didn't want me to get the wrong idea. Did he understand what I meant? How could he not? I replayed his response in my mind over and over. *Fair enough.* And there was no mistaking the look on his face when I followed him out of the laundry room. He must have gotten my meaning. What else explained the sly, I-just-put-itch-powder-in-your-bed look on his face? If he weren't interested in me, he would have left as soon as possible. Right?

I fretted for a few more seconds and then gathered some clean clothes from my closet before heading for the shower. Normally, I would have left my bathroom door wide open, but with Vince in the house, I closed it down to a crack. I debated for a moment about closing it all the way, but if Red needed me for any reason, I had to leave it unlatched. Besides, did I really think in my wildest dreams Vince would come striding into the bathroom to ravish me while I was showering?

As I began stripping off my clothes, it dawned on me that I couldn't take a shower with the bandages on my hand. I'd have to settle for a not so quick bath. And washing my hair was going to be tricky. *Damn.*

In spite of my careful efforts, the bottom third of my bandage was soaked by the time I let the water out of the tub. But, on the plus side, my hair was clean, my barfing episode was a distant memory, and I actually felt pretty good. When I looked in the mirror, I was pleased to see my eyes were no longer bloodshot and my face had recovered its normal pallor. I'd have half a chance at looking presentable after all, which was a relief since I'd finally admitted to myself that I was attracted to Vince. I hoped it wasn't a huge mistake to lower my guard. After all, this was the guy I wanted to slap silly only two weeks ago.

"Excuse me, Lire?" Red's voice startled me.

"Yeah?"

"Vince needs to talk to you. Are you presentable?"

"Uh." I wrapped my towel around myself and quickly checked for coverage. "Well, sort of."

I opened the door to ask Red what Vince wanted and found myself face to face with Vince instead. I think I squealed with shock and clutched at the towel to keep it from slipping. My cheeks grew hot as I tried to hide behind the door.

Vince's eyes opened wide with momentary surprise and then focused on me in a way I didn't expect, especially since he could see I wore nothing but a small towel. His expression was serious and all business.

I studied him. "What's wrong? What's happened?"

"I just heard from Jensen. There's been another one." He paused to consider me. "And there's more. This time the murderer left you a calling card."

I blinked. "Come again?"

"They found a note with your name on it. Jensen says it was weighted down by a rock. We need to get down there. Now. Are you up to it?"

My stomach clenched. "No, but I'll go anyway."

"Hurry and get dressed. I'll let Jensen know." Vince walked to my bedroom door and then turned on his way out. "Nice towel by the way." He didn't wait for a response.

I looked down and was relieved to find my towel had stayed in place and nothing private was on display. I gave Red a dirty look. "I didn't expect him to come in here with you. You're lucky I didn't come out totally naked. Jeez."

"I'm sorry. I thought he was going to wait on the landing."

"That's okay. Nothing seems to go according to plan whenever Vince is around."

I tilted my head and sighed. *So much for flirting on the couch.* Of course, maybe that was a good thing.

I blow-dried, dressed, and cosmeticized in record time, and I think things turned out all right. At least nobody would guess I had almost died three days ago. That was something.

THIRTEEN

When I got downstairs, Vince was pacing by the front door. He looked up as I came down to the first landing, and I was pretty sure his expression softened when he saw me. I told myself not to get carried away, but I hoped it meant he liked what he saw.

"Did you turn off the coffee maker?" I asked.

"No I didn't. Sorry."

"No problem. I'll be right back." All the way to the kitchen, I marveled at the fact that I had just asked, casually no less, whether someone other than Red had left the coffee pot turned on. Such a little thing, but it was amazing to me.

As I approached Vince, this time from the direction of the kitchen, I noticed how scrumptious he looked, dressed in his faded blue jeans, button down oxford shirt, and brown leather jacket draped over his arm. He leaned against the front door, looking impatient. I had the absurd urge to walk straight up to him and plant a kiss on his delicious lips, just to see his reaction. I thought of a few other things too.

Hello! Was it possible for me to get my head out of the gutter for more than a few seconds? Here we were, ready to leave for a murder scene, and I was busy thinking about pushing Vince up against the wall. Boy, given the chance at some skin contact with a good-looking guy, I'd suddenly developed a one-track mind. If I didn't get myself under control, I'd end up doing something really embarrassing.

I occupied myself with settling Red inside my purse while I tried to subdue the lascivious thoughts.

When I looked up, Vince stood over me looking smug. "What were you thinking about just now?"

"What? When?" *Uh, oops.* Apparently, my expression had betrayed my earlier impulse. I almost cringed, but kept my face neutral.

He made a motion toward the kitchen. "You know, when you were walking toward me, just now."

Vince's smile was downright roguish, and I wanted to kick myself. Hadn't I just scolded myself about doing something embarrassing if I wasn't careful? *Gah.* Too late.

I felt the blood rushing to my cheeks but ignored it. "Wouldn't you like to know?"

I gave him a provocative look and walked out the door before he could say anything. Of course, I had to wait outside to lock it behind him. Vince strolled out, that same crooked grin dominating his face. He continued over to the elevator while I closed and locked my front door. He didn't say a word the entire trip down in the elevator. He just leaned against the wall with his arms folded and a cat-ate-the-canary expression. I returned his gaze with one of utter boredom, but what I really wanted to do was give his ear a hard flick. Followed by some other things too shocking to mention.

When the elevator doors opened, Vince leaned over to my ear and whispered, "You can tell me later," and then took the lead without waiting for a reply.

I hate to admit it, but my stomach dropped down to my knees, in a very pleasurable way, mind you, and it took me a moment to regain my senses. Fortunately, Vince had his back to me, so I was spared any further embarrassment. God! Could I be anymore pathetic? Maybe this was what flirting was all about, but somehow this recent exchange just made me feel desperate and insecure.

Vince must have been expecting some kind of reply because his gate slowed and he peered at me from under his dark brows. He looked thoughtful, but turned and continued walking without comment. I followed close behind.

He unlocked the passenger door. "Cat got your tongue?"

I looked up at him and fibbed. "Sorry. Just wondering about this message or whatever it is from the murderer. It's really creeping me out."

"Yeah."

I was stern with myself. *Detective Vanelli. With a capital 'D.' Detective. Vanelli.* I chanted his title over and over, in my head. I really needed to get my thoughts under control. *Business associates, remember?* I gave myself another mental scolding.

We settled into the car, which once again lead to the struggle with my coat. I had just pulled it up to my chin like a blanket when Vince began driving.

He shook his head. "You know, it'd be a lot easier if you remembered to take the coat off *before* you got into the car."

I shrugged.

The roads were slick with recent rain—the snow had melted while I was in the hospital—and Vince ran the wipers on their lowest setting to keep the misty drizzle from obscuring our view.

"Where's the scene?" I hoped it didn't involve any backwoods hiking in the rain.

"It's out in Monroe."

"Out in the country, or what?"

"No, behind a Safeway, actually." Vince glanced at me. "The murderer wanted this one found quickly."

My stomach lurched and the ever-present butterflies did their little dance, but this time it wasn't Vince's sex appeal. The murderer wanted the remains found right away, probably because of the note he left for me. What was that all about? Why would the murderer leave me a note? The thought was frightening.

"Did Jensen say what was in the note?"

When Vince didn't answer, I turned to see whether he had heard me. His expression was grim, which made my stomach do another loop-de-loop.

He replied, "He hasn't been allowed to see it. The Feds have stepped in and a joint task force is being formed. The case has been classified a hate crime. Jensen was told to get you down there. That was it." Vince's tone was brusque, more so than usual.

Uh-oh. He seemed annoyed by the FBI's involvement, but I didn't have a grasp of what it meant, in terms of our participation or how it would affect me personally. Jensen and Vince didn't think of me as a suspect, but the FBI might not come to the same conclusion.

"How is that going to affect us? Are we all going to be shut out?" I asked.

Vince remained silent for a beat. "I don't know. If it's a task force, then we'll have some involvement, but it's not our case anymore."

"Okay. Anything else I should know about?"

He sighed, and the sound wasn't reassuring. He replied, "Be prepared for the agents in charge to question you about what you know. They're real curious about why the murderer left you a message."

I mumbled, "Yeah, they're not the only ones."

Vince glanced in my direction. "You know, Jensen thinks the rock wasn't there just to prevent the note from blowing away."

"Oh?" I said, even though I knew what he meant.

"He's pretty sure the murderer left you the rock to touch, but the Feds aren't talking."

I sighed. "That just sucks." I looked out the window. Vince had elected to head east on I-90 and then pick up 405 North toward Monroe. It was a reasonable choice. I guessed it would take at least forty-five minutes to get there, maybe more if we hit traffic.

Now that it had warmed up in the car, I rolled up my coat and used it as a pillow against the passenger window. I really didn't feel like talking, and some extra sleep was probably a good idea. Although, with all the anxious thoughts running through my head, I wasn't sure I'd have much success falling asleep. I closed my eyes and focused on the sound of the tires while attempting to clear my mind. After probably ten or fifteen minutes, I drifted off into a light doze.

Sometime later, I was jostled out of sleep by the turn signal and a change in the sound of the tires. I sat up and blinked my eyes several times.

Vince smiled. "Hello, Sleeping Beauty. Have a nice nap?"

"Sleeping Beauty wasn't woken up by a turn signal. Get your fairy tales straight, Vanelli."

He laughed, and I peered through the windshield at the scenery. The drizzle had tapered off, but the gray clouds were still looming. Vince drove on a two-lane highway that was edged by thick, moist grass and dense woods. Every now and then, the trees tapered off to reveal cultivated acreage and the occasional modest farmhouse.

"Where are we?" I asked.

"I just peeled off onto State Highway 522. We'll be there soon."

My stomach capsized when I thought about meeting the FBI. Going to a crime scene was bad enough, but going there to be interviewed by the FBI was quite another. Worse, the murderer had made things personal. I sat quietly and picked at my fingernails. Vince glanced over occasionally, but remained silent.

We stopped for gas on the edge of town. While Vince pumped and spoke to Jensen on his cell phone, I left the warmth of the car to visit the restroom. Using a public toilet was always a perilous endeavor. All the hoops I had to jump through to avoid accidental psi-exposure took forever. The stupid bandage on my right hand only added to the misery.

By the time I returned, Vince waited inside the car.

"Any update from Jensen?" I settled into my seat and struggled to close the door with my left hand. I straightened out my coat and folded it across my lap.

"Nah. He'll be waiting for us in the parking lot."

The ride turned out to be a short one. The Safeway was a half-mile down the highway, on the left. Vince took us behind the store, our destination marked by several police vehicles, a medical examiners van, and five or six unmarked cars parked beyond an expanse of yellow 'DO NOT CROSS' tape. Three news vehicles had parked haphazardly at the edge of the cordoned off area, along with more cars and dozens of people.

Vince stopped his car in front of the yellow tape, well away from the news crews. "You ready for this?"

I looked into my lap and started to say, "Yes," but shook my head instead. I met his eyes. "I'm nervous ... and scared if you want to know the truth."

He looked sympathetic and reached over to give my arm a squeeze. "Don't worry. If you need a breather at any time, just let me know. I can be a bulldog when I have to, as you know."

I gave him a weak smile and nodded. "Okay."

I noticed Jensen walking toward the car. He lifted the stretch of tape, allowing Vince to drive inside the protected area.

I removed my seatbelt, clutched my coat, and leaned over the back seat to talk to Red. "I'll feel better if you wait for me in the car. There's going to be way too many people to bring you out. If anything happens like last time, I'd rather know you're somewhere safe."

"All right. Just make sure you do not take any unnecessary risks. Vince, I will hold you accountable. Do not allow her take on more than she can handle."

"You have my word," Vince said, putting the car in park and setting the brake.

After Vince got out and closed the door, I said, "I'll do my best to be careful, but I don't see how it could be worse than Patty's remains."

"Maybe so, but I know you, Lire. Consequences tend to be an afterthought. Try to think before you act."

"I'll try."

"Be sure of it." Red sounded stern.

I looked up through the back window and saw reporters had noticed our arrival. "Great. The vultures are about to descend. I'm glad we're inside the taped off area." I looked back down at Red. "I'll see you in a bit. Maybe you should get down on the floor, in case someone looks into the car. I love you."

"I love you too. Be safe."

I got out and made sure Vince locked the car before evaluating the scene around me. A small crowd of individuals had made their way toward our location, held thirty feet away by the yellow tape, shouting questions about the murder and the current crime scene. To my disgust, my name was yelled more than a few times. Both video and still cameras were aimed at us, and I heard the distinct sound of many shutters clicking away.

Following the two detectives, I crossed the parking lot and reassured myself that Red was safe inside the locked car. Even with police in close proximity, I remained anxious. I hated leaving him behind.

Away from the maelstrom of questions, Jensen stopped to talk. "It's a relief to see you up and around. How're you feeling?"

"I'm okay. A little tired." I paused and then added, "Honestly, I'm mostly just nervous."

It was cold enough to need my coat, so I struggled with putting it on. Vince noticed and held it by the collar, so I could get my bandaged hand through the sleeve easier.

Jensen replied, "They'll probably have lots of questions for you, but the Special Agent in Charge, Agent Cunningham, seems decent. And I've made it clear how much you've already sacrificed. You'll be fine. If you need a rest, be sure to let Vince or me know. We don't want you taking any unnecessary risks."

I smiled. "Thanks. That makes me feel better."

He nodded and then directed us toward the back of the parking lot, where the pavement met the landscape. The area was cultivated professionally for the first six feet or so—only what was visible from the lot. Past that point the foliage had been left in its natural state. The mature, densely growing trees were interspersed with overgrown bushes and weeds, which made for a twisted path toward the crime scene.

The scene itself was only fifteen yards away but not visible from the parking lot. I asked how it had been discovered. Apparently two employees had gone outside, presumably for a smoke, when they stumbled upon the pile of bones. I knew from Jensen's rakishly raised eyebrows he suspected the couple had been looking for a place to fool around.

I blurted, "That sure put a crimp in their mojo, I bet."

I think Vince almost choked, he laughed so suddenly. Even Jensen chuckled. It didn't seem right to be laughing near a murder scene, but I couldn't help myself.

Several groups of people surrounded the site, some in uniform and others in suits, and most of them turned to observe our arrival. Magic tickled my senses as we drew closer, and I felt my smile fade down to a thin, nervous grin.

Jensen ignored the people standing at the periphery and strode toward the center of the scene.

Without looking down, I sensed the moment we entered the circle. The magic vibrated at a fever pitch and then lessened slightly when we crossed over the boundary. The residual magic was much stronger than what I encountered at Jason's murder scene—a clear indication this one had happened recently. I found it difficult to think. My gait slowed, and I eventually stopped altogether while I tried to get myself under control.

Vince stopped at my side. "Lire, you okay?"

Jensen turned to look at me.

I waved my left hand in front of my face in a fanning motion, as though the action would help clear the air. "The residual magic. It's thick. Gimme a sec."

I looked up at Vince and would have smiled, except things looked fuzzy around the edges of my vision.

No! I won't faint, I scolded myself. I concentrated on taking deep breaths and rubbed my forehead to help me regain some composure. When I leaned forward, Vince must have thought I was going to pass out again because he grabbed my arm. As soon as he touched me, I felt better. The magic was still there, beating against my skin like a swarm of static charged gnats, but it wasn't overwhelming and I could think clearly again.

When I smiled, Vince released my arm.

I mumbled, "Thanks. I think I'm okay now."

He looked relieved.

I might have stopped to consider his ameliorative touch but didn't have time. Jensen walked up, accompanied by a man in a single-breasted gray suit covered by an open, black trench coat. Although his suit jacket was also unbuttoned, his conservative print tie remained knotted neatly at his neck. If this was Agent Cunningham, he was more ethnic looking than I expected. He was dark of hair and eye with blunt facial features and olive skin. His teenage years must not have been kind because he had a pitted complexion that gave him a rugged appearance.

"Lire, you okay?" Jensen asked.

"Yeah. But for a second or two, I wasn't so sure."

"What happened?" The man spoke with a tone demanding a prompt response. He was taller than me, maybe five-foot-ten, with an average build, but his voice sounded like it should have come from a much larger individual. It was deep and authoritative.

"Lire, this is Special Agent Cunningham," Jensen interjected.

"Nice to meet you, Agent Cunningham." I belatedly hoped it was okay to shorten his title. "The residual magic overwhelmed me for a moment, that's all."

He nodded at me. "I understand you were released from the hospital this morning."

I nodded and shrugged.

He regarded me closely. "Did you have this same reaction at the other crime scene?"

"Not to this degree—probably because that one was older."

Cunningham folded his arms across his chest. "Uh-huh. Can you tell us what spells were used here?"

I tried not to show my surprise. He was a highly placed agent. He had to know I wasn't capable of sensing that type of detail, but I answered anyway. "No. I can sense several different spells but not what they were. A skilled witch or warlock should be able to tell you, if not the specific spells, at least the class of spells that were used."

He nodded. "We've already contacted our magic expert. He should be here in the next few hours." He looked at Vince and extended his hand. "You must be Detective Vanelli."

Vince gave him a stiff nod and shook his hand. "Yes. Good to meet you."

Cunningham glanced at his watch before giving me another considering look. "Ms. Devon, are you aware of the reason for your presence here today?"

"I assumed to continue providing relevant leads on the case."

"Yes, I'm aware of your contribution, Ms. Devon, and hope you continue to provide us with useful information. Specifically, we hope you'll enlighten us as to why the murderer chose to leave you a message."

I shivered. "I really have no idea. And, to be honest, I almost don't want to know."

His expression remained impassive. "Nevertheless, the murderer chose to include you personally. Come with me."

He walked toward the bones piled in the center of the dirt circle. When he reached the far side, he turned, and I followed his gaze. On the ground next to the bones was a white piece of paper inside a sealed plastic bag. A dark oval rock, approximately two-inches long, had been placed on top of the bag. Through the clear plastic, I could see black writing on the paper. The rock itself looked to be nothing more than a polished river stone, but knowing it had been left by the murderer made it seem sinister to the extreme.

I asked, "What does the note say?"

"See for yourself. Don't take the page out of the plastic. You can read it without removing it. I replaced the note and the rock in its original location, so you could see how the murderer left it for you."

That brought me up short, and I probably glared at him before crouching down to inspect the items. I wondered why Cunningham thought it was important for me to see their original placement, but decided if he hadn't, I probably would have asked about it later. There didn't seem to be anything significant about how the rock was positioned nor did I sense any additional magic around the note. With my hand protected by my glove, I knew there wasn't a risk examining it, but I couldn't help feeling tentative. If someone had sneezed when I reached for it, I probably would have jumped a mile, but I managed to pick it up without any major hysterics.

I turned it over in my hand. It was just an ordinary river rock, worn so smooth I almost wanted to rub it with my bare fingers. I placed it in the palm of my bandaged hand, freeing me to pick up the bagged note. Through the plastic, a white piece of letter-sized paper had been unfolded to lay flat inside the bag. Rain had rippled the page, but my name was starkly visible, written in neat, block lettering. The black ink had not blurred from moisture, so I surmised it had been written with permanent pen.

I stood up, being careful to keep my bandaged hand level so the stone didn't tumble off. Rotating the bag, I read the contents of the note, just one line. 'A little something for you to read.'

I wanted to smack the person who had leaked my name to the media. I wouldn't be here, reading a letter from my newest psychotic pen pal, if it weren't for whoever had gone out of their way to blab my name to that *Seattle Times* reporter.

"Not tough to figure out the murderer wants me to touch the rock." I addressed myself to Cunningham since he seemed to be running the show now.

He nodded. "A reasonable assumption."

"Has someone already read it?" I tried to keep my voice from sounding hopeful.

"No. Our primary consultant is busy with another case and won't be available for at least forty-eight hours. We hoped you could take a look at the stone right away to give us a head start." Cunningham's unwavering gaze was so direct that his request seemed more like a command.

I wanted to turn around and go back home. Instead, I mumbled an unhappy acknowledgment and, after a moment's hesitation, gave him a stiff nod.

Jensen asked, "Are you sure you're up for it?"

I looked down at the unassuming rock and bit my lower lip. "Yeah, I can do it. But I need to be well outside the circle. The residual magic here is really distracting."

Cunningham admitted, "I'm afraid we're roughing it out here. The Safeway manager has offered us the use of his back office if you prefer to be indoors."

I didn't want to come off as high maintenance, so I resigned myself to the outdoors. "That's okay. Out here is fine, unless it starts raining. I'd just like a blanket or something to sit on. The ground is a bit damp."

"Certainly."

When Cunningham walked away, Vince turned to me. "Are you sure you're okay with this?"

I was comforted by the fact that he and Jensen were concerned about me. I smiled at him. "Yeah. I'll be fine as long as I'm out of the circle. The residual magic is wreaking havoc with my shield, just like last time."

I looked down at the rock and noticed black smudges on my white bandages where it had shifted in my hand. "What's that? It doesn't look like dirt."

Vince and Jensen both looked down at my extended hand. "Dusting powder." They answered nearly simultaneously.

"Did they find prints?"

"From what I understand, yes," Jensen answered.

"I'm surprised. I wouldn't have thought you could get prints from a porous surface like that."

"Porous items can be difficult but not impossible," Vince said. "The pebble is smooth. It probably wasn't much of a challenge."

As we waited for Cunningham to return, my eyes gravitated toward Vince's strong jaw and warm eyes, bringing on a distinct spike in hormones. I distracted myself by surreptitiously observing the people standing around the edge of the crime scene.

Three groups of loosely gathered men, and a few women, stood around the south side of the site, all of them outside the circle. Considering the relative difficulty of finding a clear space to stand within the foliage, it was interesting that, out of nearly a dozen people, only three of us stood inside the circle. I wondered if the others sensed the magic unconsciously, or whether just the thought of what had happened made it distasteful.

While I mused, Cunningham returned to the site and spoke with another suit. During their exchange, the four men nearby looked over in our direction, none of their expressions friendly. I tried not to jump to conclusions, but it appeared not everyone in the FBI was enthusiastic about clairvoyants. One of the men, a beefy blonde, folded his arms tightly across his chest and glowered at me. I returned his gaze with an utterly angelic expression, deliberately holding his eyes. He looked away first.

Vince must have noticed the exchange because I heard him chuckle. I cocked my head to give him a sideways glance. He turned his back toward the blonde and attempted to smother a smile.

"What?" I maintained my virtuous expression.

Vince shook his head and laughed. "Miss Devon, I like your style."

Jensen laughed as well, and I looked back and forth between the two detectives with a sly grin on my face. Before I could respond, Cunningham approached holding a small package that he slapped against his thigh.

He extended the package to me and asked, "How far do you need to go? There's a small clearing about ten yards that way." He gestured over my shoulder.

My hands were full, so I traded him the bagged note from the murderer and stuck the rock in my coat pocket. The package was a Mylar blanket that he probably got from the ambulance out in the parking lot. Gone were the days of bulky, orange wool blankets, but at least this one had the advantage of being waterproof and psi-free.

Cunningham led the way through the woods. We followed him single file along a skinny, well-defined path through the densely growing bushes. *Whistle While You Work* from *Snow White* came to mind, but I suppressed the urge to hum it out loud. We arrived at the open area between the trees without accompaniment. The clearing wasn't huge—maybe just twenty feet in diameter—but was free of rocks and provided more than enough room for the unfolded foil blanket and several bystanders. After unfolding the blanket, Jensen helped me lay it on the ground.

Sitting cross-legged beneath them, I felt like a fish in a bowl with the three men looming over me. I wished Cunningham had thought to get another blanket or two for themselves. It wouldn't be easy to ignore their scrutiny, and I could have done without feeling so self-conscious. At least I couldn't sense the magic from the circle anymore.

I dug into my coat pocket for the rock and placed it on the blanket in front of me.

"If anything should go wrong, please don't put me in an ambulance. Detective Vanelli can take me home. If I'm not recovered by the time we hit Seattle, he can detour to Swedish." No matter what I said, they'd probably hand me over to the paramedics anyway, but it was worth a try.

Jensen looked uneasy and Vince didn't appear to be much happier. Cunningham was the only one who seemed unperturbed—probably because he hadn't been on hand when I almost fried myself.

I couldn't help but laugh at Jensen's expression. "Don't worry, Lieutenant. This is a non-organic object, a straightforward reading. It won't be like what happened earlier. The only wrinkle is I haven't had much to eat today, so I'm feeling a little shaky."

"Sorry," said Vince. "I should have thought to stop for something on the way here."

I dismissed his apology with a wave of my hand. "It's okay. I wasn't hungry. I'm still not, so don't worry about it."

They regarded each other, looking uncertain, but I ignored it. First the murderer's note and now the prospect of reading the stone had left me with a nervous stomach. There was no way I was going to force myself to eat something, even if I did need the energy.

Removing my glove presented a challenge. Only my thumb was free on my bandaged hand and the blisters were already burning from the process of laying out the blanket. I used my teeth without letting the fabric touch my lips. It wasn't easy, but the glove finally came off.

With nothing left to do, I nodded at the boys and picked up the rock.

Magic flared from my core. I struggled to hang on to my shield, but after a few tense seconds, managed to get it under control. In spite of my jitters, I manipulated the stream and coaxed it into a beautiful, shining disk. I always found it ironic that the stream could look so spectacular in my mind's eye while harboring horrible, corrosive memories at the same time.

Since a scumbag murderer had left the rock, it was no surprise the entire flow was tinged by strong emotion. I coasted back to the center of the disk and plunged into the stream at the beginning ...

Fear envelops me like an ill-fitting skin suit and it is so overwhelming that my stomach churns.

Oh Jesus! How did this happen? Why is this happening to me? Why can't I use my magic? God, if I could just use my power! I'd shove a spike up his ass so far, he'd get brain freeze. But the demon. Dear God ... the demon! It's in a circle, but what if he lets it out? Please don't let the demon get me! Shit! He told me to listen. If I do everything right, maybe he'll let me go like he says.

I focus upon a figure, clad head to toe in black. It's dark outside, but I can see he's wearing a hood and mask. His hands are gesticulating wildly. Every now and then, something glints on his left hand. I'm disturbed by a memory of someone grabbing me from behind, forcing something over my mouth and nose. A wave of unmitigated fear threatens to overtake me.

" ... are you listening? Answer me now, or face the consequences. Are you listening?" the cloaked figure demands.

I scream in a combination of anger and terror, "Yes!"

He rubs his hands together. "Good. Good. Hello, my dear Lire. I hope you're in there, sharing, experiencing, listening. Oh, yes. Lire, listen well. This message is for you."

What the hell? What's this crazy-ass psycho talking about? Who is Lire? Please, God! Maybe he'll show up. God, let this Lire help me! Don't let me die! How can this be happening? What did he just say? Damn! I missed it.

" ... working with the police. I know you want to find me. You want to avenge your dearest Nick. But you won't, you know. I'm much too powerful, and, anyway, they won't let you." He laughs a grating bray of a laugh, and I think about smashing his face with a brick. "It's rather amusing, really. My enemy is your enemy. We're practically on the same side!"

I struggle at the bonds encircling my wrists. There is little play in the rope and both my wrists and ankles are staked to the ground. Who is this enemy he's babbling about? I wonder. I remember hearing about a murder. Fuck! He's talking again. Pay attention, Trinity!

"Here's a piece of friendly advice—stop looking for me. Because, sooner or later they'll come calling, and, believe me, you're no match for them. They don't want the police to catch me, you see. They'll work their deceptions, their subtle magic, and then catching me suddenly won't seem so important."

The cloaked figure pauses and steps forward. "If you're lucky, that's all that will happen. But if you're stubborn ... let's just say you won't be in your right mind for long."

He sighs. "Ah. But I know you, Lire. You won't stop, will you? No. You're much too stubborn for that. How do I know? I already told you. I know you. Shall I prove it? Hmm, yes, let's do that. Let's see. It all started when you asked your mother why she had been naked with Uncle Byron, didn't it? You were holding her hand at the park that day and saw everything.

She never touched you again, did she? And it wasn't long before you were packed off to boarding school. Not too surprising, I guess. Oh, and how is Red doing? Yes, I know about him too. The guilt gift your father gave you, so he didn't have to feel so bad about sending you away. A smart gift, I'd say. Red talked you out of suicide when you were thirteen. You're certain if he hadn't interfered, you would have followed through. And then there's your dearest Nick. Your first love. Your first kiss. Your first fuck. How tragic it was when your powers deviated. Is that enough? Have I convinced you?"

The robes swirl around his feet as he pulls on a pair of black gloves. "Since, I know you will continue helping the ridiculously inept police and eventually the FBI, who are certain to be called in at some point very soon, and because it serves my purpose, I will share something with you. But I won't make it easy. No. I think you know what you're going to have to touch next, and it won't be nearly as pleasant as this."

He strides forward and grabs the stone from my hand.

Although the tall trees blocked much of the ambient light, the sudden brightness shocked me. I squinted, blinking wildly, and shielded my eyes with my now empty left hand. I felt the rock, not quite forgotten, on my thigh where I dropped it. Like waking from a nightmare, I fought to calm my quickened breathing and rapid heart rate. I took steady breaths and grappled with the mix of emotions threatening to break out. I wanted to scream. I wanted to cry. But most of all, I wanted to get my hands on the murderer and beat him into bloody pulp. I closed my eyes and imagined flames engulfing his black robes, burning his skin, and the sickening sweet smell of burning flesh. My mind wheeled with the foreign thoughts, Patty's thoughts. Once again, I fought not to vomit. I whimpered instead.

"Lire?" Vince's voice cut through my turmoil. When I opened my eyes, he was crouched in front of me. "You okay?"

"Not really." I clenched my hand into a fist. "I'd love to hit something, I think."

I took a shuddering, deep breath, and made a point of relaxing. When I glanced up at Jensen and Cunningham, they were both frowning.

"I'd rather not stand in for that job." Vince smiled. "Anything else we can do?"

I shook my head. "No. Thanks. I'm better now."

He gave me an encouraging nod before moving to stand beside Jensen.

"What did you come up with, Ms. Devon?" Cunningham asked.

"Plenty. But can you guys sit down here with me? I'm getting a kink in my neck just looking up at you," I replied, unable to keep the weariness out of my voice.

Cunningham smiled and gave me a stiff nod. "That can be arranged." He didn't sound put out, thankfully.

"Much as I want to stay and hear this, can I get you something to eat?" Jensen asked.

"I'm not very hungry, but I should probably eat something. Yeah, that would be nice. Thank you. I'll need all the energy I can get if I'm going to touch the remains."

Vince's eyes flashed at me. "Are you crazy? That's what put you in the hospital. It nearly killed you."

"Jesus, Lire," Jensen echoed.

I held up my hand. "You'll understand after you hear what the murderer told me. Trust me. If we want to know what the murderer is up to, I have to do it." I sat up straight. "And more importantly, I want to do it."

Vince shook his head and Jensen looked doubtful. I turned my attention to Agent Cunningham. He studied me, arms folded tightly across his chest.

"Let's take this one step at a time. Lieutenant Jensen can pick up something for you to eat while you brief us. Then we can decide how best to proceed." He used the term 'we,' but I knew he meant 'I.' I tried not to think about how I'd feel if Cunningham didn't allow me to touch the remains.

"What do you want?" Jensen asked.

It took me a half-second, but I realized he was asking about food, not what I wanted to do about the remains. I thought it over. I needed something that wouldn't upset my already queasy stomach. "Something from Safeway is fine. There are usually prepackaged psi-free items in the deli case. A cheese sandwich. Or, tuna salad would be okay. Whichever. And a Diet Pepsi, please. Maybe some potato chips? I'll pay you back later."

He told me not to worry about it and walked out of the clearing toward the parking lot.

Cunningham said, "If you don't mind, Lire, I'd like to videotape your recollection."

I wasn't excited about the prospect of having the more personal information of the reading caught on video for anyone to hear. The murderer had revealed private details about my life, and I wasn't looking forward to throwing them out there for anyone but my closest friends to discuss.

I nodded reluctantly. "Fine."

Once Cunningham left, Vince crouched across from me again.

"What's going on?" he asked quietly. "Why are you talking about putting yourself at risk with the remains?"

I stared at him. "Vince, he *knows* me. I've been racking my brain, trying to figure out who he might be. I must know him, but I can't place his voice." I clenched both hands into fists, but the blisters on my right reminded me to stop. "He wants me to touch the remains. He wants to taunt me further with what he's up to. I'm hoping the more I see and hear, the better my chance to figure out who he is."

"Why do you think he knows you?"

"He mentioned several things about my private life—things very few people know. And before you ask, they aren't the type of people who would blab my secrets all over the place. I can count on one hand the number of people I've confided in. You're one of them."

He looked at me in surprise.

I shook my head. "I don't know how he learned these things. Maybe he overheard me talking to Red. He's not somebody close to me but could be an acquaintance. I don't know. All I know is that I have to hear what else he has to say. I might pick up on something another clairvoyant might miss—something personal to me. Anyway, I have to try ... for Nick."

"But you could die. Is it really worth that?"

Was this just normal concern, or something more? I tried to look reassuring. "Don't worry. I have a lot of things to live for these days. I don't plan on dying any time soon. Besides, we don't know the remains are as dangerous as Patty's. Get my purse from your car. Have Red climb inside and then take him through the circle on the way back here. Try to walk as close to the bones as possible, so Red can get a sense of whether an entrapment spell was used."

Vince nodded.

"I'll tell you what, though. I sure wish we were back at my place, pigging out on lasagna, instead of doing this."

"Me too." He squeezed my arm and then got up and walked out the way Jensen had gone.

It wasn't long before Cunningham tromped back to the clearing with two other men trailing behind. The first of them carried a small case that probably held the video camera. In the other hand, he grasped a folded tripod. My stomach sank when I realized the second man was the agent I had stared down earlier. He brought a folded metal chair.

"Where's Detective Vanelli?" Cunningham asked when he saw I was alone. He held several Mylar blankets.

"I asked him to go back to the car for my purse."

He nodded and then introduced the two agents. Agent Tormino was the slim, brown haired one with the video equipment, and Agent Miller was the stocky blonde with the dour face. I said the polite things you're supposed to say and then did my best to ignore them while Tormino set up the video equipment. I filled the time by donning my glove—a relatively frustrating experience without the help of my right hand. Again, I resorted to using my teeth. To my relief, Agent Miller only stayed as long as was necessary to set down the folding chair for Tormino.

Jensen was the next to return. He arrived just as Tormino finished mounting the camera on the tripod. Although

Jensen didn't say anything, I figured he was pleased he hadn't missed anything. I opened up the plastic grocery bag he handed me and found a plastic encased smoked Gouda sandwich, bottled diet Pepsi, small bag of potato chips, and a chocolate chip cookie. A straw and a utensil pack were on the bottom. I verified that everything was psi-free.

I waved the cookie and beamed at him. "You sure know the way to a woman's heart. Thank you."

He smiled. "Don't mention it."

"Aww, did you bring any for me? I have a heart too you know." Tormino batted his eyes at Jensen.

"Yeah, but you're not nearly so nice to look at, Tormino."

He laughed. "Can't argue with that."

I shook my head and giggled as I took out the sandwich. Thankfully, the men stayed busy with various private discussions until I had mostly finished my lunch, so I didn't feel rushed. Vince showed up three bites into the second half of my sandwich and handed me my purse without comment.

Our eyes met, and I had to simply say, "Thank you," instead of asking him what Red discovered near the remains. There were too many people around for me to talk openly about Red, much less open my purse and ask him myself. I had to resign myself to wait, but I wasn't happy about it.

Agent Cunningham handed out the additional blankets to Jensen and Vince. I hoped Miller wouldn't be returning. I didn't see Cunningham hoarding any more packages, so maybe Tormino was the only addition to the group. I loathed the idea of revealing anything remotely personal with Agent Miller around. Agent Tormino, who seemed like a nice guy, sat on the metal chair across from me and adjusted the video camera for a better angle. He appeared to be ready. Immediately the butterflies in my stomach started playing do-si-do with my lunch. I hoped eating it wasn't a mistake.

After one last sip of my drink, I looked at Agent Cunningham. "I'll do another reading for the camera, and describe everything that happens. Is that what you had in mind?"

"Yes. Will it be possible to question you while you're ... working?"

"Yeah, shouldn't be too much of a problem." I capped off the bottle and pushed it, along with my purse and grocery bag, to the side, hoping the items wouldn't be in view of the video camera. "Okay. Let me know when you're ready."

Once everyone had settled, Cunningham gave Tormino the go ahead.

The red light turned green on the camera, and the agent gave me a wink. "Action."

I smiled at him before looking around at the observers in an attempt to ignore the camera. "Uh, first of all, let me start by telling you what this is all about." I picked up the rock and displayed it. "The murderer left me a message by having his victim hold this while he delivered a monologue. The victim was instructed to keep hold of the rock and pay close attention to everything he said. He threatened her with violence if she interrupted him or failed to focus on his every word."

I looked at the rock, turning it in my hand, and then brought my attention back to Cunningham. "If the woman who held this is the murder victim, then her name is Trinity Wilson. She was a cryokinetic. For those who don't know, a cryokinetic is a psychic who has the ability to dissipate ambient heat. They're often called 'icemakers' because, instead of generating heat like a pyrokinetic, they take it away. They can freeze almost anything, instantly."

I removed my glove and dropped it into my lap. Soon, I'd be a one-handed pro. "Okay. That's it. Do you have any questions before I continue with the reading?"

"Yes. What else can you tell us about the victim? Where was she from? How and where was she captured?" Cunningham asked.

"I'm fairly certain she was taken from behind and chloroformed, but because she's so focused on the murderer, I received few of those memories. I'll have to touch her remains to give you more details."

"For this thing with the rock, were they here at the murder scene?" Vince asked.

I cocked my eyes to the side and thought about it. "It was dark, but trees were in the background. It's possible. I can't tell you for sure though."

"Did she see any more of the murderer than the other victims?" Jensen asked.

"No. If anything, she saw less. Like I said, it was dark, and he wore a hooded cloak with a mask. He was dressed all in black. Every part of his body." I stopped. "Wait. Now that I think about it, he was wearing a ring. On his left hand, I think. Yes. I remember something glittering as he moved his hands."

Cunningham looked pleased. "Good. Anything else? How tall is he?"

I considered the victim's viewpoint. "Hard to tell. The victim was sitting down, but ..." I evaluated the group of men, still standing in spite of my previous request that they sit. "Detective Vanelli is too tall. I'd say the murderer is a couple inches shorter, at least. Maybe closer to your height, Agent Cunningham."

Vince evaluated him. "Maybe five-eleven?"

Cunningham corrected, "Five-ten, more like."

I shrugged. "It's a good guess, anyway."

"From any of your other readings, did you get an impression of his hair color?" Cunningham asked.

Jason's experience had been at night, like Trinity's. So I closed my eyes and thought about Patty's recollections. Patty was the only one to see him, during the day. Of course, he had been wearing a hat and scarf that covered almost everything.

I replied, "No. I can't say for sure. It's more of a feeling, really. I think he probably has brown hair. Patty couldn't see much of his face, but he didn't appear to have the coloring that would fit with someone really fair."

Cunningham nodded. "Okay, Ms. Devon. Please proceed with the reading. If we have any other questions, we'll let you know."

Deadly Remains - Chapter Thirteen

"Okey doke."

I mentally prepared myself for another run at the rock. The second or subsequent reading was always easier because there was no shock value to worry about. Once I had the stream spinning, I started at the beginning, describing everything I experienced with as much detail as possible.

Almost immediately, Cunningham wanted me to do a freeze-frame on the murderer. I'm sure he hoped I'd uncover some distinguishing mark or feature if I examined the perpetrator closely.

I paused the reading to explain, "People's memories don't work like a film reel. I can't just freeze on a slice of time and inspect every detail with perfect clarity. I probably get about as much detail as someone under hypnosis, although, some memories will be clearer than others. Most people easily recall faces of close friends and family, those closest to them. For example, I can picture my father's face with almost photo-like clarity, but tomorrow, I'll only vaguely be able to recall Agent Tormino's face." I shot him a lopsided smile. "Sorry to break it to you, Tormino."

He laughed.

My limitations explained, I continued my recital without further interruption, repeating the murderer's message as Trinity had heard it. I decided against asking Tormino to switch off the camera before relating the murderer's knowledge of my personal life. It would just draw more attention to the intimate nature of the secrets. Instead, I recounted the murderer's statements dispassionately, as though they were about someone else.

After I finished the reading, I went back and focused all of my attention on the murderer's appearance. The extra effort didn't reveal much—just that the ring was on his left middle finger and he wore white athletic shoes under the robe.

Too late, I realized I had pushed myself right to the limit. I withdrew from the stream and dropped the rock, but I knew I'd be lucky just to make it back to the car on my own two feet. The world looked grainy when I opened my eyes. I lowered my head to avoid passing out.

"I'm afraid that's it for me today, guys." My voice wavered like an old phonograph record.

"That's fine. Thank you, Ms. Devon," Cunningham said.

Dammit! Now, I was in no condition to read the remains. They'd have to wait. But with the FBI's own clairvoyant showing up soon, it was possible I wouldn't be given the opportunity to read them at all.

After taking a few minutes to recover, I stood up without passing out. I made a fateful decision and asked Vince to take me back to his car. I agreed to visit the FBI field office in Seattle the following morning. Cunningham, in an effort to make me feel at ease, told me no readings would be involved. He just wanted to interview me about my previous readings of Jason and Patty. This reassurance did nothing but make me feel worse. I simply had to read Trinity's remains.

Vince aimed toward the parking lot, but I suggested we go back the way we came, in order to give Red additional time inside the circle. It was a longer walk, and I hoped I'd make it.

When we were safely away from the others, I opened my purse. "Did you detect the spell?"

Red looked up at me, black plastic eyes glinting from the darkness of the interior. "Yes. Although there is no guarantee a soul is confined to the remains. It could have just as easily been confined to something the warlock removed from the site."

"If I take you near the bones, can you tell for sure?" I desperately hoped he could; otherwise, reading them would be extremely risky, even on a good day.

After some hesitation, he replied, "Given enough time. Perhaps."

By the time we reached the circle, I found it difficult to walk without an outward display of weakness. If Vince knew how exhausted I was, he'd have ordered me to the car. I gritted my teeth and strode toward the remains. Only a few stragglers remained. They stood, talking, at the other end of the circle. Vince followed close behind me. He had already asked me twice whether I was okay. I think he resolved not to ask again, especially after I snapped that I was a big girl and could take care of myself. To soften my retort, I promised to let him know if I needed to be carried and gave him a wink.

Standing in front of the bones, I asked God to protect me from what was probably a major blunder.

Vince must have suspected something. He stepped forward and called my name, but before he could intervene, I dropped to my knees, let go of my purse and glove, which I had purposely left off, and grabbed the closest bone.

My magic flared. I had time to utter, "I have to know," before searing cold exploded into my mind. The unstoppable force coursed through my body, sending shards of icy power through every cell. As I collapsed, I marveled at the crystallized breath pouring from my mouth, but my last thought was: *Red's going to be so pissed at me*.

Icy black swallowed me whole.

I woke up face down and shivering on a frozen floor. Half of my face and the entire length of my body were numb from cold. I rolled to a sitting position and rubbed my arms vigorously in a vain attempt to warm myself. Frosty clouds bellowed from my mouth with every breath and my teeth chattered.

This is a little better than being surrounded by a burning inferno, but not by much, I thought to myself. Actually, a nice warm fire sounded downright appealing.

I had lost feeling in my backside, so I stood up, making an effort not to slip, and looked around. I wobbled in the middle of an ice rink, albeit a bizarre one. The unblemished surface was impossibly white and surrounded by a carved stone balustrade, like the one from my first dream with Jason.

From behind, I heard a slicing sound and turned to see Jason skating in my direction with the ease of an ice hockey veteran. He flicked his heels to the side and made a perfect stop next to me.

"Shuh-show off," I scolded from between my chattering teeth.

"You should talk—taking the bone in your hand when you were so weak. What were you thinking?"

More skating sounds came from down the rink where a diminutive woman dressed in a leotard and tights spun on one leg. She stopped with a flourish and then continued to move around the rink gracefully, now and then executing a difficult looking maneuver. After landing a complicated spinning jump, she laughed and then skated toward Jason and me.

The first thing I noticed was her size. She was tiny. Not the size of a pixie or anything—she was just darn petite for a human woman. Her flatiron-straight black hair fell below her shoulders, restrained by a silver headband. As the woman skated closer, I saw she had fairly ordinary features; small, almond-shaped brown eyes, a straight nose, and thin lips. She appeared to be in her mid to late twenties. I'd say she was more cute than beautiful, and her size only helped to accentuate that appearance.

"Not too shabby." Jason twirled his finger in the air to emphasize his point. He turned back to me. "Lire, this is Trinity."

"Nuh-nice to muh-meet you."

"Jason tells me you're going to help us."

I looked at Jason and tried to smile, but I mostly just chattered. "You cah-can beh-bet on it."

Trinity looked perplexed. "You're not going to be much help if you can't even control your own temperature."

I must not have given her a look of confidence because she raised her hands to my temples and said, "Here."

At her touch, a cold essence spiraled through my consciousness, bringing knowledge of power so vast it quite literally brought me to my knees. Breathless, I gazed up at her. Here was someone with ultimate power, one capable of complete destruction, yet she never abused it. She was the antithesis of Patty, whose corruption seemingly had no bounds.

"Th-thank Guh-God. You'll bah-balance her out nuh-nicely."

Trinity gave me a sympathetic smile and nodded.

Pain radiated from the center of my body. I gasped and doubled over, hugging my abdomen.

If Jason hadn't crouched down to steady me, I would have fallen over. "Use Trinity's knowledge to stabilize your temperature, like you did when you put out the fire."

I tried to think, tried to remember, but my thoughts wandered, my mind numb. "Suh-so cuh-cold."

Jason pulled me into his lap and hugged me. "Snap out of it. Think! You can do it."

Trinity leaned down and whispered something into Jason's ear, but I zoned out. All I wanted to do was sleep. Anything else was too much work.

Jason's warm cheek on the side of my neck startled me awake. "Lire. Come back to me."

As Jason levitated us upward, my insides fluttered. My legs dangled uselessly, toes pointed toward the ice. He turned me around to face him and rubbed my arms roughly. "You can do it."

My mind opened, and I thought about Trinity. Her magic was akin to Patty's but foreign to my own. I concentrated on her memories and, since I didn't have any negative recollections associated with her magic, easily recalled the process.

At my bidding, her power sprung from my pores. I took control of it, sending invisible tendrils upward to search the air far above the ice, and found enough heat to warm myself. I could have stolen it from Jason or Trinity. Such a small depletion wouldn't have adversely affected them, but it was wrong to take energy from a being without their permission. Trinity's moral fortitude was refreshing, given what I had experienced of late.

Jason whispered in my ear, "Atta girl," before my dream faded into darkness.

Sound returned first. Initially, just indistinct rumblings, but after some time floating in the dark, I recognized Vince's voice.

"—ank God. Her color's getting better."

I felt myself being jostled.

Vince was at my ear. "Lire. Come on. Wake up. Talk to me."

I groaned and turned my head to the side, hoping to shield my eyes from the incessant brightness seeping through my closed lids.

"Hey. Say something. You awake?"

I grumbled, "Turn the light off, would you?" My frozen lips made me sound drunk.

I opened my eyes, blinked furiously, and confronted a blurry version of Vince leaning over me. As my vision cleared, I saw we were still at the murder scene, just outside the circle. Several figures moved some distance behind him, silhouetted against the brightness, and an EMT worked to secure me to an ambulance gurney. Jensen and Cunningham stood with Tormino a few yards away. They watched with serious expressions.

Vince glared at me. "Goddammit. What the hell were you thinking?"

"I wasn't as usual."

He made a sound of exasperation. "Jesus. You scared the hell out of us. You fucking turned blue. You know that? Frost came out of your mouth and you turned blue, for Christ's sake."

I struggled out of the blanket cocoon, interfering with the strapping the attendant attempted to secure at my waist. It was fine with me because I had no intention of going to the hospital again. I told the medic to take five. At first, I thought he might give me an argument, but he stepped away, although, I noticed he didn't go far.

Struggling to sit up, I peered at Vince. Absently, I realized someone had taken the time to put the glove back on my left hand. "I'm sorry. I was so obsessed with learning more, I didn't stop to consider the consequences. Please, forgive me." The thought of him staying angry bothered me more than I expected. I cursed myself for being so impulsive.

He ran his fingers through his hair, his expression a combination of anger and relief. He scowled at me. "Please, do us all a favor, don't do anything like that again."

"I won't. I promise."

He sighed loudly and shook his head. "God, you're high maintenance."

I kept my voice low. "Yeah, but I'm worth it."

The paramedic, who had been joined by his female partner, sensing that our discussion had come to an end, stepped up and told me to lie down again. Before he could resume tightening the straps, however, I pushed off the blankets and pulled my legs completely out of the bottom strap.

"Nope, nope, nope. I appreciate your attention, really. But I'm fine. I'm not going to the hospital again. Thanks but no thanks."

The paramedic tried to speak, but Vince overrode him. "Dammit, Lire. Your temperature went haywire again. You need medical attention."

The few people around the crime scene had stopped milling about to watch me with rapt attention. Cunningham approached to voice his concerns, echoing Vince, although, he wasn't as emphatic.

I rotated my legs to hang over the edge of the gurney. "Guys, think about it. My temperature went haywire as you put it because both Patty and Trinity are energy manipulators. It was their magic that caused my temperature fluctuations, not some deadly medical condition."

The male paramedic, who was middle-aged and small of stature, made the mistake of grabbing my arm to dissuade me from scooting off the gurney. He wore gloves, but that wasn't the main reason I was annoyed. It ticked me off when someone ignored my words, and he had taken it a step further by making it physical.

Oblivious to his misstep, the paramedic said, "Miss, please, the gentlemen are right. Your temperature plunged to a dangerous level. It could affect your body in ways you don't immediately feel. Let us take you to Swedish. If you check out okay in ER, you'll be free to go in no time. It's for your own safety."

I glared at his hand. He let go, but he wasn't happy. At the foot of the gurney, his female counterpart watched me with a cool eye.

I regarded the male paramedic. "Look. I can see you mean well, but I know what I'm talking about. My temperature fluctuation was the result of a psychic discharge. It was not medically induced. It will not happen again because I don't have plans to come into contact with any more magically charged items any time soon." I turned towards Agent Cunningham. "Tomorrow morning at nine, right? I've got a lot to discuss."

He raised an eyebrow. "You discovered something?"

I felt my eyes slip sideways as the memories threatened to emerge, but I firmly slammed them back into their requisite compartment for later examination. "I can't go there right now. Sorry. I'm a little tired, and I need time to sort things out." I avoided saying I needed 'time to recover' because I didn't want to argue about going to the hospital again.

Not waiting for permission, I hopped off the gurney. I picked up my purse and lunch bag from the ground, where I assumed Vince had dropped them, and then said my goodbyes. Unhindered, I stalked toward the parking lot, half expecting the EMT to stop me. My legs were rubber, but I resolved to back up my words by making it totally obvious I didn't need medical attention.

The personnel standing around the scene gave me a wide berth, as if I were contaminated with some highly contagious disease. I had an irreverent impulse to shout, "Boo!" at the next person who stared at me, but I refrained.

Vince had no choice but to follow me after sparing a few words for Cunningham and Jensen. He caught up, just as I reached the edge of the parking lot.

"You're the most infuriating woman I've ever met, you know that?"

I looked behind him, saw that we were unobserved, and leaned closer to whisper near his ear. "I know." I resisted the wild desire to kiss his cheek.

He smiled and shook his head. "You know, if there weren't three news vans sitting in plain view that way, you'd be in big trouble right now."

"Yeah? And what kind of trouble would that be?" I narrowed my eyes and planted my left hand on my hip.

He propelled me toward the car and grinned. "The kind that's not okay for prime time viewing."

"You wish," I said, but wondered whether his response implied violence or romance.

In the car, after several stern words from Red and a few more for good measure from Vince, I fell asleep without divulging anything about my encounter with Trinity. I knew Vince was eager to hear about it, but I was more than a little tired, and he let me sleep. When we arrived at my apartment building, Vince had to shake me awake. I felt groggy, hungry, and stiff. There were drool marks on my coat, but bleary as I was, I hardly cared.

FOURTEEN

Vince escorted me up to my apartment with his arm around me for most of the way. This time, I wasn't shy about leaning my head on his shoulder in the elevator. I asked him if he wanted to come inside for some of Julie's lasagna, and he accepted.

We stepped inside and hung up our coats on the rack. I leaned my handbag against the wall so Red could climb out. It felt really good to be back home and even better to have some company. Although, I suspected the main reason Vince decided to come in was because he wanted to hear the details about Trinity's death.

Boy, sometimes it's nice to be wrong.

I turned to walk toward the kitchen when Vince unexpectedly grabbed my left hand and pulled me off-balance into his embrace. A surprised squeak slipped out of my mouth, and my hands went to his chest for support. The wheels in my head had to spin for a few moments before I figured things out.

As he leaned down to kiss me, I slid my hands up his chest, around the back of his neck, and pulled him close. His lips were warm and moist, and all those butterflies that never seemed to leave my stomach tried to exit with one dizzying swoop, catching my breath. Our initial tentative kiss became deliciously passionate as the seconds ticked by. When our tongues finally met, the warmth that had blossomed down low in my body increased to four-alarms almost instantly. Patty's magic couldn't hold a candle to this blaze. I moaned into his open mouth, relishing the feel of his deft tongue and the heat of our mingled breaths. When the kiss finally ended, I held him close and tried recover some semblance of composure.

Careful not to let my bare cheek touch his shirt, I snuggled against the swell of his chest, letting my hair act as a barrier. "Uh ... wow. I seriously need to catch my breath."

He stroked my head and chuckled. "Yeah." Vince's nearly breathless voice rumbled beneath my ear. "I'm finding I have that same problem."

I laughed against his chest.

Oh. My. God. My mind raced with images of Vince's smooth skin rubbing strategically against mine, but at the same time, a small voice whispered not to take things too fast. Co-worker, remember? Or, what about the old adage, 'Why buy the cow when you can get the milk for free?' Or all the countless advice columnists who always tell their readers to not jump into bed with a guy on the first date? Vince and I hadn't even had a first date! On the other hand, most of those advice columnists weren't skin-touch deprived individuals. It had been over ten years since I'd last felt the touch of a man's warm lips plainly against mine. Let's face it—kissing through the fabric of a skin suit just doesn't cut it.

After a moment, I pulled away and gazed into his eyes. Now that some of the heat had dissipated, I managed to step away from his body.

I tilted my head, regarding him with a small smile. "Do you realize it's only been two weeks since we first met down at your station? It seems like ages ago, doesn't it?"

Vince laughed when I admitted I'd been tempted to give his ear a hard flick on more than one occasion, especially when he gave me a hard time about reading the blouse.

He gave me a look that sent a direct message to a very specific location in my body. "I know. I was terrible to you. Please, feel free to take it out on me now."

I laughed and yanked him toward the family room couch where we enjoyed another round of heated kissing, but I resolved to not get carried away. When things began to get a little too intense, I put my bandaged hand on his chest and pulled away with a delighted gasp.

I mumbled, "I'm sorry. It's been such a long time for me. This is all happening a little fast."

"No worries. I can do slow." Vince's quiet, intimate tone gave me a thrill.

I buried my face into the crook of his neck. "You're not helping."

Vince chuckled and apologized, but his roaming hands didn't reinforce his repentance.

I sat up to peer at him and stroked his cheek. "I just want to make sure this is right, for the both of us. And I don't want to screw things up by plunging ahead without thinking." I made a sound of exasperation and looked down so my hair fell across my eyes, masking them. "God! I don't know. My head is saying one thing and my body is saying another."

Vince laughed his deep, sexy laugh. "I know what you mean. It's okay. I can do things slow, remember?"

I stared at him from under my long bangs. His expression denoted something to the contrary, and I shivered. "That is definitely going to require some serious willpower."

Vince continued to stare at me intently.

"Again—you're not helping." I tossed my head to get the hair out of my face.

Vince stood up, chuckling, and held out his hand to me. "Come on. Let's have some lasagna."

Per Vince's orders, I sat at the table and waited while he heated two portions of Julie's lasagna in the microwave. I was glad for his help because, without the flush of hormones running through my body, fatigue dogged me.

"So, um, what about work. I mean ... I don't know. Is this considered bad form? Should we, you know, keep things quiet?" I added hastily, "Not that I plan on hanging all over you, or anything."

Deadly Remains - Chapter Fourteen

"I'd say that making out in front of the guys is probably a bad idea." He gave me a wry grin and then shook his head. "Yeah. Keeping things discrete will be in our best interest, at least until the case is solved." He put a plate of steaming lasagna in front of me. "I don't think it'll be much of a surprise to Jensen, though."

I looked up from my plate. "Why do you say that?"

"Let's just say I've seen a couple of raised eyebrows."

"Oh." I looked down at my plate, trying not to frown. "You know, that's something you should consider. Not everybody's going to be happy about us dating. I'm not saying Jensen will object. He's a good guy. But, other people ... people who don't understand my magic." I met his eyes. "I've had years to become accustomed to the discrimination. Even now, it can be difficult for me. For someone who isn't accustomed to it, it can be pretty shocking." I shrugged. "It's something you should think about."

Vince nodded, looking regretful. "I suppose I leaned that way before we met. I never did anything on the conscious level, but I'm sure it was there. My upbringing, I guess."

I sat up straight. "God. Your parents. They won't like me one bit."

"It doesn't matter what they think. It wouldn't be the first time they've objected to something I've done, so I'm not going to worry about it and neither should you."

Our relationship was just budding, so I didn't comment further, but the potential issue with his parents worried me. I did my best to put it out of my mind.

As I struggled to eat with my left hand, I asked him what had happened after I touched Trinity's bone.

"If you never touch a bone again, it won't be too soon. I thought you were dead." Underneath his casual tone, I could tell he was still upset.

I reached across the table and touched his hand. "I'm sorry."

"I know you are." He smiled and gave my fingers a squeeze. After a moment of heartfelt eye searching that got my blood to the boiling point, he broke the moment with a casual shrug and let go of my hand. "I already gave you the high points, but if you want the blow-by-blow ..." At my nod, he continued, "As far as I could tell, you went down right after touching the bone. For once, I caught you before you hit the ground."

"It's about time. You've had enough practice."

He snorted. "I'm going to start wearing a catcher's mitt around you from now on."

"I don't blame you." I laughed. "Okay. Sorry. Go on."

He finished chewing. "Right away, I noticed you felt cold. Unusually cold. Frosty air started streaming out of your mouth, thick with ice crystals, like it was minus twenty or something. Freaked the hell out of me. Your lips and eyelids turned blue, your fingertips too. If it weren't for the frosty breath coming from your mouth, I'd have sworn you were dead. Believe me—I've seen enough dead bodies to know." He shrugged. "That's about it. I yelled for the paramedics, Cunningham and Jensen ran back and grabbed the foil blankets, and by the time the medics got you on the gurney, your coloring started coming back."

I wiped my mouth and pushed my nearly empty plate to the side. "Things weren't as bad this time because Trinity's soul prevented me from getting totally blasted."

Vince looked thoughtful as he finished the last bit of lasagna on his plate. After he swallowed, he asked, "If that's the case, then why didn't anything like this happen after you touched Jason's bones? I mean, you passed out, but you didn't turn into an ice cube or end up in the hospital."

I laughed. "I told you, my temperature issues from the last two readings were because Patty and Trinity were energy manipulators. And the reason Patty's remains put me in the hospital is because her soul wasn't bound to her bones, like the others." I leaned forward. "I wondered the same thing about Jason's reading and then I remembered. Something *did* happen; it just wasn't as dramatic as what happened with Patty or Trinity. At least, I think something happened. Right after I touched Jason's bone, I was airborne for a moment. At the time, I chalked it up to the power of the warlock's spell knocking me backward, but I think it was actually some of Jason's leftover psychic energy."

He frowned. "So, this magic that seems to stay inside the bones ... it only affects clairvoyants? Because I know other people handled the remains and nothing bad happened to them."

I mulled it over and considered my dream conversation with Jason. Not only did I acquire part of Jason's soul, for lack of a better description, but also got pummeled by his magic in the process. It was important, I knew, but I couldn't figure out how.

I shifted in my chair. "Maybe everyone else has worn gloves?"

Vince nodded. "Possible."

I sighed. "I don't know. Most clairvoyants know better than to go around touching people's remains, so there's not a lot of precedence, but I can't believe it's never happened. Clairvoyants have been around since the beginning of time. Even if getting blasted by reading another paranormal's remains had only come up a few times, you'd think word of it would have been noted and passed down through the generations as a major risk."

Vince shrugged. "If the FBI's clairvoyant reads the bones and gets zapped, then I suppose we'll have our answer."

I doubted their clairvoyant would do it, but I shrugged. "True."

"Did your experience with Trinity shed any new light on things?"

I checked my watch. "Are you sure you don't want to wait until tomorrow to hear this? It's getting pretty late." I smiled. "You're welcome to stay here, but I assume you need to go home for a change of clothes."

"I have an overnight bag down in my car." After a moment, he noticed my expression and said, "Hey. I didn't think I'd be staying *here* necessarily."

"Uh-huh." I folded my arms and studied him.

He laughed. "I wasn't sure how up-and-around you were going to be. I wanted to be prepared, in case you needed some help."

"Right." I laughed at his boyish smile and relented. "Okay, but if we're going to talk about Trinity, I at least need some coffee."

His smile faded. "Is this going to be difficult?" No doubt he remembered my vomiting episode from earlier in the day. Beauty.

"It's always difficult, but it won't be as bad as dealing with Patty. No, Trinity was good people. It makes things easier." I smiled and got up to clear the table. "I'll put some coffee on."

He stood up. "I'll get this. You go ahead and make the coffee."

The brownie points kept adding up. Pretty soon, I might think he was too good to be true. God, how did that happen? Magi-phobic jerk one week, perfect boyfriend material the next. Of course, given my recent luck, something was bound to come along and screw things up.

Fifteen minutes later, dishes in the dishwasher, leftovers refrigerated, and coffee made, we settled into the cozy chenille couch with our brimming coffee cups and cookies. Even Pepperidge Farm had jumped onto the psi-free bandwagon. I relished every bite of two chocolate Milano cookies, which given my recent lack of exercise were surely destined for my hips. Sadly, if Vince hadn't been there, I probably would have eaten at least two more. Damn them.

While we were still sipping, Vince asked where Red had gone.

"He's either outside or in the office. He tries to make himself scarce whenever he thinks I need privacy." I smothered a smile by drinking from my cup.

"Ah. Outside? He can open the door by himself?"

"Not the big door. When I had the loft renovated, I added a tiny *Alice In Wonderland* door over there." I pointed toward the patio doors.

He leaned over the end of the couch and looked down. "Cool."

I shrugged. "I do what I can to make his life as comfortable as possible."

After finishing every drop of my coffee, I placed the empty mug on top of the depleted cookie plate and deposited the stack next to me on the lamp table. I turned to the side, with my legs folded under me and my arm over the back of the couch, propped my head against my hand, and admired Vince as he finished his coffee. Almost immediately, my mind took Track Seventeen to Gutter Central. I had to reign in my thoughts or I knew we'd never get around to talking about Trinity's memories. Vince eyed me for a moment but must have figured out my line of thought because a sly grin emerged from behind his coffee mug.

"What's on your mind?" he asked. His gaze smoldered from under his slightly canted brow. His voice was nonchalant, but his look was pure testosterone.

The expression sent a wave of warmth directly to the region nice girls don't discuss in public, and my temperature spiked. It was embarrassing what he could do to me with just one look.

I wagged my finger at him. "Uh-uh. Don't even go there, or we'll never get around to Trinity."

His eyebrow went up. "Go where? I'm just sitting here, drinking my coffee. Minding my own business." He bent forward to put his empty cup on the coffee table.

"I see. Well, my mistake." I folded my arms and matched his raised eyebrow with one of my own.

He smirked. "You know, you never did tell me what you were thinking before we left to meet the FBI."

I smiled and bit my lower lip. "I thought you were minding your own business over there."

"You know, helping you stick to this willpower thing is not going to be easy."

I resisted the urge to move toward him on all fours and run my tongue over his sensuous lips. Instead, I closed my eyes and inhaled deeply. "Who said life was easy? I need a Coke. Want one?" I jumped up.

He chuckled. "Sure."

I cleared the coffee cups and returned with two cans of psi-free Diet Coke. I handed one to Vince, and he thanked me before popping the tab and drinking. After a few sips, he traded the can for his pen and dog-eared notepad. He looked every bit the detective, which helped clear the air of excess hormones.

"Okay, gimme me a sec." I put my can on the coffee table before closing my eyes.

I relaxed my shield, and Trinity's memories rushed to the fore. I didn't bother to control them. It wasn't possible to keep them locked away forever. But, since Trinity's stream wasn't corrupt like Patty's, I knew I didn't have too much to worry about. Of course, every time I took in another person's memories, a small voice in the back of my mind wondered whether my magic and my psyche could handle it. How many memories could I store without going insane? Was there an upper limit? Did I have the capacity for more, or would the next memory turn me into a gibbering idiot, destined for a clean-room? It was a disturbing line of thought, one that wouldn't be answered until it was too late, so I did my best to put it out of my mind.

All at once, I remembered a great many new things. Some of them were distant and near forgotten, others more clear but little more than snippets, and many more, especially recollections of family and lovers, were bright and clear. There wasn't a glut of memories, like what I experienced with Patty, because Trinity's soul had blocked most of it. Even so, there were more than enough to cause me distress. I fought with emotions ranging from apathy to absolute terror.

I remembered ...

... my powers surfacing at the age of five ... skating for the first time and delighting in the feel of the ice slipping beneath the blades ... people I didn't know calling me a natural ... the

neighbor cat going poop in my sandbox and Mom angrily rubbing his face in it ... my amazement at being able to alter the ice to better my skating performance ... my first crush in fifth grade ... my utter despair at learning the US Figure Skating Association had suspended me from competition after becoming aware of my powers ... pancake breakfasts on Sunday with Dad ... enjoying a life outside of skating practice ... my first French kiss on the darkened floor of a high school dance ... the college frat party where I met Tom ... my first apartment ... losing my virginity ... working my ass off at Microsoft ... breaking up with Tom ... my abduction and waking up face to face with a demon ... the realization I was about to die ...

"I suspect you're still with me, Lire. Not one to turn down a challenge, are you? Even when presented with a reading that no other clairvoyant with any sense would perform." He makes a sound of disapproval and shakes his head. "It boggles the mind." He blows out a dramatic sigh. "I suppose I should give you some kind of reward for your persistence."

He folds his arms and regards me for a moment.

"You probably want to know why I am doing this. What is my motive? I'm sure the police would love to know. Well, I'll tell you. It's one of the big three. You know, money, power, love, or some combination thereof." He chuckles. "Hey, that's pretty catchy. Let's see. Which one is it? Is it financial gain? Or love maybe? Or, what's the third one again? Oh yes, power. Is it perhaps power? Hmmm. Let me think."

He drums his long fingers against his cheek in an overly dramatic gesture. The ring on his finger glints sharply with the movement. I notice the ring is a square shaped signet on the middle finger of his left hand.

"Mmmm, yes. Power. That fits. But why power? Why do I need power?"

He drops his arms and stares at me.

"One simple clue will answer that question for you, and it's a clue that will all too soon be at your back door. You'll see. Continue to help the police and they will come for you, and *then maybe you'll understand." He sighs. "Of course, by then it will be too late, but don't say I didn't warn you."*

He reaches into a pocket in his dark robe and withdraws something white before walking toward me. Upon closer inspection, I see it's a white handkerchief. I flash back on the memory of my abduction. I scream for help and struggle against my bonds, knowing the effort is futile. I am effectively staked down. The cloth nears my face and I throw my head back to keep it from covering my nose and mouth. Once again, I try to call my power to no avail. His hand moves almost as quickly as I can fling my head about, and it gets in close enough that I begin to feel woozy. The cloth presses down over my mouth and nose. I try not to breathe while I stick my tongue against the hankie, trying to dislodge it. My taste buds vaguely register a sweet, chemical taste. After a few more seconds, everything seems to slow down and my eyes droop downward, even though I fight against it. I relax, and my world goes black.

I glanced at Vince's surprised eyes before diving into his arms. "No more. No more bones." I overruled my threatening tears and frantic breathing with slow, steady breaths.

Vince rubbed my back while I gathered my wits. I nestled against his chest and enjoyed the scent of his body. Under the fragrance of what I guessed was his deodorant or aftershave, he smelled warm, pleasantly musky, and slightly of sweat. It was a purely masculine scent, uniquely Vince, and it made me feel warm and tingly inside.

After I had calmed down enough to tell him about Trinity's memories, Vince wondered aloud. "Who is this mysterious 'they' he keeps blabbing about?"

"No clue. Presumably he thinks a group of individuals are out to get him, but he also claimed they don't want him to be caught by the authorities. So they must want him for some other reason, not just because he's murdering people." I rolled my eyes. "As if that's not enough of a reason. But why? Why don't they want the police to catch him?"

I mumbled the question mostly to myself, but Vince answered, "He must have information this group doesn't want made public."

I shrugged. "Could be. Or maybe he has a major paranoia complex. Anyone who can take out four innocent people without remorse and work with a demon has got to have some sort of screw loose."

He grunted. "I'm not so sure. He also implied they, whoever *they* are, will go out of their way to stop you. You specifically. Not the police necessarily, but you. I find that interesting. And disturbing."

"Yeah. But look on the bright side. At least he's not the one threatening me."

"He also implied they are worse than he is."

I glared at him. "You're a glass-half-empty kind of guy, aren't you?"

"Only when it's alcohol, babe."

I rolled my eyes and hauled myself to my feet. "God, I'm tired. I definitely need to pull a Rip Van Winkle. Or is it Wrinkle?" I shook my head. "Whatever. I need some sleep."

I went to the patio to check for Red. "Red? You out here?"

"Yes."

"Didn't mean to drive you outside. You okay?"

"I am quite content, thank you. I was gazing at the stars. We actually have a clear night tonight and no moon."

"Huh. That doesn't happen often this time of year." I considered the sky for a moment before looking for him amid the shadows of the patio. His small black form didn't offer much contrast against the darkness. He perched on one of the wooden benches near the left side of the large balcony.

A cold breeze swirled past my body, making me shiver. "Okay then. Vince is staying over again tonight since we both have to go to the FBI office in the morning."

"Thank you for telling me. And, Lire?" He lowered his voice. "I am very glad for you."

I smiled. "Me too. Night, Red."

"Good night. Sleep well."

When I turned back inside, Vince headed out of the kitchen. Holy crap, he was sexy. I smiled as I walked toward him, trying not to feel self-conscious.

"Are you sure it's okay to stay over?" He rubbed my arms.

I met his eyes while my insides smoldered. "It's a bit of a temptation, but I think I can handle it." I groaned and then rammed the top of my head into his chest. "God, I hate this awkward stage."

He laughed and smoothed my hair. "I know where the blankets are. Go on up. I bet you're tired."

When I looked up, he pulled me close and kissed me. It wasn't long before our heavy breathing had heated the air between us, and our bodies grated together, making me wish I had two functional hands so I could easily unbutton his shirt. Somehow I managed to pull away and rest my head against his chest again.

"Oh, man." I groaned.

Vince chuckled, and I heard it as well as felt it vibrate through his chest. "I know. Maybe it's not such a good idea that I stay over." His voice sounded thick.

As if to prove his point, his hands pressed a flaming path along the curve of my back, over my posterior, and then back up again.

I gasped, barely keeping myself from grinding my pelvis against him. "No. It's okay, at least for tonight," I panted and stepped backward. I could hold it together for one night, I assured myself. Being dog-tired helped.

Vince laughed. "Okay. I'll be right back. I have to get my bag from the car."

"You remember the pass code?"

He repeated it.

"Yes, you do. Here." I walked to the front door and my handbag. "Take my keys. I'm sorry, but I need to go collapse. I'm wiped out. Don't forget to lock up when you get back."

He told me to sleep tight and then wiggled his eyebrows up and down at me. I laughed and was still smiling when I staggered into my room.

Sleep came upon me quickly even though I couldn't stop thinking about Vince and his warm, firm body.

I must have been more tired than I thought.

FIFTEEN

I woke up feeling happier than I had in years, and it did-n't take long to remember why. The previous evening's more heated memories occupied my thoughts for a couple of drowsy minutes. I opened my eyes fully and looked to-ward the door of my bedroom. My nose told me coffee had been brewed, and if I listened carefully, I could hear Vince and Red talking downstairs. I marveled at the turn of events. Wow. Vince. *Boyfriend*. A grin of satisfaction gave my lips a workout. My life was as close to normal as it had ever been, and it felt amazing.

And then I remembered the murderer's ominous mes-sages. Talk about an instant downer.

My bedside clock said 7:25. If I wanted get down to the FBI's office by 9:00, like I'd promised, I needed to get into the shower right away. Since my bandaged hand required the plastic bag treatment, things would take a little longer. Under normal circumstances, I needed at least an hour to get going in the morning. Maximizing my shower time eased me into the daytime routine almost as well as my first cup of coffee. Besides, I wasn't ready to let Vince see my morn-ing face, which was completely ridiculous since he had al-ready seen me look like death warmed over. I shook my head in disgust. I was definitely on vanity's payroll.

When I was almost ready, a light knock came at the bath-room door. I opened it to find Vince on the other side with his devious smile.

"Hi there. I came up to wake you. I guess you already did that, huh?"

"Figured that out, did you? You must be a detective."

He laughed. "Yeah. I'm pretty handy too." He looked down at my belted silk robe. "Need any help getting that knot untied? Looks pretty tight."

I just laughed and shooed him back toward the stairs, but the encounter tantalized my thoughts and I hurried to finish getting ready.

After his own turn in the shower, Vince left for the FBI office while I was still cleaning up from breakfast. It probably wouldn't be viewed as unusual for us to arrive together, as if Vince had picked me up on his way, but we decided it was better to promote the illusion that we weren't overly cozy with each other. I hated the need for the deception, but Vince worked with many of these people on a regular basis and knew the clubhouse rules. Besides, the ruse was only necessary until my job was done. After that, we were free to act normally.

I sighed. As if I needed another reason to want the murderer caught.

On my way to turn off the coffee machine, I passed my telephone and noticed the furiously blinking light. Vince mentioned the messages earlier, but I had neglected to notice just how many waited to be played. The digital number read 23. I blinked and refocused. I don't think I'd ever seen it read higher than five or six. Jeez. I was torn between taking the time to play them and ignoring them for a bit longer. It was already 8:35 and the FBI office was a ten-minute drive. That didn't count the time to and from the car and trying to find parking. I decided to skip the secretary thing. I'd deal with the messages later. I wondered absently how many messages my machine could hold before it ran out of room and who all was calling me. I hoped they weren't all from reporters.

With Red in tow, I hurried out of the apartment. I contemplated squeezing in time for a cappuccino from Peabody's. I dithered and then finally caved when Red pointed out that the FBI probably didn't offer psi-free coffee. Bless his heart. Guess I was going to be a tad late.

It seemed 8:48 on a Saturday morning was a popular time for Peabody's because the only parking to be had was two blocks away. I resented every extra second it took for me to reach Julie's shop. As I walked, I silently cursed all the caffeine-addicted patrons all to Hell. Myself excluded, of course.

Maybe that's why I was slow to notice the car.

I heard the roaring engine and turned just as the sedan charged up the curb. My eyes clicked to their maximum aperture as I simultaneously drew in a shrieking breath and pushed out my hands in front of me in a ridiculous gesture to ward off the blow. It's not every day that a speeding hulk of metal comes barreling toward me, but I knew intuitively there was no hope of getting out of the way. I wasn't close to being fast enough. Everything slowed down, and it seemed like I had minutes to consider how much this was going to hurt and what the *hell* this person was doing driving on the sidewalk. Fleetingly, I wondered whether it was possible to jump or throw myself onto the hood. Maybe I could roll off without it hurting too much. Just as the hood ornament came within touching distance, a strange sensation came over me, like I had just crested the first big precipice of a monstrous roller coaster—a fluttery, excited, scared shitless feeling.

And then suddenly I was in the air, twirling, instinctively trying to stand, my toes flirting with the metal surface. One second I was on the hood, the next second on the roof. Turning around, not quite falling, and then finally losing my balance, rolling off of the trunk, and landing in a heap on the sidewalk.

Relatively, miraculously, unscathed.

I looked up the sidewalk to see the car careen away, bounce back down the curb, narrowly miss two newspaper dispensers and a parked car, speed pell-mell down the wrong side of the street, and then screech around the corner. By the time I gained enough of my senses to look for the license plate, the car had turned the corner.

I had a moment to assess my body for signs of injury before pedestrians from every direction rushed over shouting in excitement and asking me whether I was okay, although, not surprisingly, most people kept their distance. As far as I could tell, I just had a scrape on my left elbow. I must have fallen onto my left side because my bandaged right hand wasn't sore in the least and the white wrappings were unblemished.

An ambulance arrived on the scene in a surprisingly short time, about when I decided to experiment with standing. My entire body shook like I had been left outside in the rain, so one of the paramedics sat me down just inside the open door of the ambulance. He checked me for injuries while explaining I was in shock and then covered me with a thermal blanket. His partner proceeded to clean my scraped elbow.

I don't know about shock. All I know is everything felt really fuzzy, almost surreal, but I was sure it was nothing a really big espresso couldn't cure. Besides, I decided I couldn't be that far gone because my revved up libido definitely noticed both paramedics were really cute.

While the tall Latino EMT patched up my scrape, I spotted a gray-haired patrolman with a paunch belly and clipboard, hovering nearby. He introduced himself and wanted to ask me some questions about the accident. Before I could say a word, Julie appeared at my side shouting my name in dismay. I assured her I was fine, cast an apologetic look at the officer, and let her gush about how she had no idea all the hoopla was centered on me or she'd have been out sooner. The accident happened at the beginning of Peabody's block, but with the flock of customers waiting to order coffee, it wasn't possible for her or Steven to take the time to gawk. She told me it was only after Steven stepped outside, some ten minutes later, that he noticed me.

After articulating her alarm, Julie took notice of the policeman standing across from me and apologized for interrupting. It was probably a good thing to make her feel useful, so I asked her to telephone Vince's cell and tell him I was going to be late for our appointment with the FBI. I also had enough sense to beg a double cappuccino as I dug in my purse for Vince's business card. She hurried back to the shop twittering with purpose.

When I turned my attention back to the officer, his gaze had sharpened. "You're the one helping with the Circle Murders, aren't you?"

"Uh, yeah, I am."

"Thought so. Did I hear you have an appointment this morning with the Feds? They getting involved, huh?"

"Yeah. I was supposed to be at their office at nine. I wanted to get a quick cappuccino at Peabody's before heading that way." I shrugged as if to say 'what a mess this turned out to be.'

He grunted. "Then let's get moving on this, so you can go. Full name, please." He glanced at me over the top of his clipboard.

"Lire Devon." I spelled it for him.

He jotted it down. He asked my address and telephone number and I gave it to him.

"Now. Can you tell me what happened, Ms. Devon?"

"I was crossing the street, just there." I motioned around the ambulance at the intersection where I had crossed between blocks. "I got maybe ten or fifteen feet up the sidewalk when I heard the roar of a car engine. Now that I think about it, I might have heard some people yelling, but it didn't register at the time. I didn't turn around until I heard the car engine right behind me. I don't really know how I managed to avoid getting clobbered. I mean, one minute I was standing right in the way, and the next I was up on top of the roof." I shook my head. "I must have jumped up at the last minute."

His eyebrows raised in surprise. "You sure the car didn't hit your legs and flip you up there?" He peered behind me at the paramedics.

I rubbed the tops of my legs. "No. No bumps or bruises. I'm pretty sure I'd be able to tell if the car actually hit me."

"Yeah, I imagine you would at that," he said with the barest of a smile. "Did you happen to get a look at the driver at all? I know you were concerned with other things, but I have to ask."

"I understand. No. I was mostly fixated on the front end of the car as you can imagine. I didn't get a look at anything else."

"What can you tell me about the car?"

I thought back to the incident. "I want to say it was yellow. A light-yellow, or cream color. I remember the front had a large chrome grille and a rectangular hood ornament. I think it might have been an American car. I remember it being sort of rectangular looking. Maybe mid-nineties vintage. I don't know. I'm afraid that's the best I can do. By the time I thought about getting the license plate, the car was going around the corner."

He nodded. "That's okay. We're pretty sure the vehicle was abandoned a few blocks away. I just wanted to check it out with you to be sure." He paused and gave me a half nod. "It was a yellow Chrysler, by the way. Your memory didn't play you false."

I frowned. "So, it was a car jacking or joyride or something?"

"Probably. The car was reported stolen, late last night." He nodded toward me. "Glad you're okay. Luck was definitely on your side this morning. Here's my card. If you think of anything else, gimme a call."

I nodded, taking it, and thanked him, just as Julie returned with my cappuccino. Before taking the cup, I stood up, removed the foil blankets draped around my shoulders, and slipped the policeman's card into my purse. The major trembling had subsided, although I still felt shaky. I held the cup with my left hand, but had to brace it with my bandaged one to take a sip without spilling. *Ahhh. Heaven.*

"You sure we can't persuade you to let us take you in?" the swarthy, young paramedic asked one last time.

"Nah. I'm fine. Just a scrape, remember?" I returned his smile and noticed again how cute he was. Very nice dimples. Awesome smile. Not as attractive as Vince, but it almost made having my bloody elbow cleaned and bandaged a pleasure. He was also considerably less pushy than the last paramedic who tried to persuade me to go to emergency.

I almost rolled my eyes. How pathetic. At the rate I was going, pretty soon I'd be familiar with the relative merits of all the paramedics in the major metropolitan area.

I thanked them for their treatment and Julie walked with me slowly back toward her shop. On the way, she grilled me for all the details of my accident. After she had heard everything forward and back, she mentioned the telephone call to Vince.

"I called Vince, like you asked, although why you wanted to go out of your way to be courteous is beyond me."

Oops. I hadn't told Julie about the change in our relationship.

She continued, sounding puzzled and slightly miffed, "He sounded really concerned though when I told him the reason you were running late. He practically bit my head off. Said he was coming right over."

"Didn't you tell him I was all right?"

"Yeah. I think I did." She sounded unsure.

"Jeez, Julie. No wonder he was upset." I looked up and down the length of the street, expecting him at any moment to come screeching up. "Uh, I haven't had a chance to tell you. Things have sort of changed about Vince." I looked back at her and couldn't suppress a shy, satisfied smile from taking over my face.

Julie's eyes got big. "What's this? O-M-G! You're kidding?"

I shook my head.

"Hon, are you sure about this?" She looked at me with concern until she registered my expression. "Well. Okay. But he better be good to you, or I'm going to have something to say about it." She jumped up and down like a schoolgirl. "Oh my God!" After a moment of mutual chatter and delighted giggles, Julie lowered her voice to a conspiratorial level. "He is so hot! You deserve it, girlfriend."

While we continued to talk giddily, Vince came jogging up the sidewalk from the same direction where the accident took place. I heard the running footfalls and turned to see his grim expression. My heart skipped a beat as I admired his muscular form. I think Julie muttered, "Holy cow," under her breath.

He was breathing hard when he got to us. Julie quickly excused herself, giving me back Vince's business card and squeezing my arm as a way of goodbye.

Vince cupped my chin with one hand and gripped my shoulder with the other. "Are you okay? What happened? Julie told me a car hit you. I saw the ambulance." His face was filled with apprehension and he looked me up and down.

I was overwhelmed by gushy, warm, romantic feelings for this man—this gorgeous, sweet, utterly kissable man—who ran God knows how many blocks to make sure I wasn't hurt. It took all of my willpower to not wrap myself around him like a koala and kiss him senseless.

I peered into his eyes. "I'm sorry Julie worried you. Yes, I'm fine. Just a scrape."

Once Vince was satisfied I hadn't been horribly injured, he released his tender hold, but didn't take a step back. He continued to watch me with a concerned expression.

I lifted my arm, careful not to spill my coffee, so he could see the evidence of my injury. "See?"

"What the hell happened?"

"Someone taking a joyride across the sidewalk almost turned me into a pancake." I gulped my now lukewarm cappuccino.

"What? Where? You were stopping for coffee?"

"Yeah. I had to park way down the street and walk up about two blocks. The car drove up onto the sidewalk back there, at the corner." I pointed in the direction of the now departing ambulance. "A police officer said the car was found a few blocks away, abandoned." I shook my head. "I still don't know how I avoided getting hit."

"What do you mean?"

I shrugged. "Somehow I ended up practically standing on the roof of the car. I must have jumped, but I don't remember doing it. Adrenaline, I guess." I shook myself. "I even managed to hold onto my purse."

I threw my empty cup in the trash so I could open my purse and look in on Red. "Some excitement, huh, Red?"

"Yes. Thank God you are okay. Just hearing it was bad enough. You must have been terrified."

"That's an understatement." I tilted my head. "But it was surreal too. Everything just sort of slowed down to a stop, just before the car was going to hit. It was strange." I smiled and shrugged. "We'll talk later, 'kay?"

I slipped the business card into my purse before closing it and then looked up at Vince. "Did you run all the way here, or is your car parked down that way?"

"I ran. I knew Peabody's was only a few blocks away. I figured it would get me here faster." He touched my cheek with the back of his hand. "I'm glad you're okay."

I leaned up and kissed him, just a quick brush of my lips. Before I could pull back, he wrapped me inside his arms and kissed me harder. Afterward, I hugged him, resting my head on his chest. His heart was beating quickly, but whether it was elevated from our kiss or from running, I could only imagine. After a moment, we pulled apart. All I could think about was how it wouldn't be too soon until I had him alone in my apartment again. By the look on his face, I was fairly certain he was thinking the same thing.

He took my hand. "Come on. We can drive over in your car. They'll be happy to hear you're okay. Agent Cunningham is anxious to hear what you have to say."

I snorted. After hearing that a car hit me, he was probably worried as hell he'd have to start from square one with a new clairvoyant.

Since it was Saturday, the FBI building was officially closed to the public, but following a quick call from Vince, Cunningham appeared to escort us inside. In contrast to the sparsely lit, deserted lobby, it was a relief to find our third floor destination bright and surprisingly busy. I wondered whether most of the agents had much of a home life. It occurred to me that Vince must work some pretty long hours too, although, maybe it was only when there was a really pressing case. I'd have to ask him about it. Of course, we probably weren't going to have a traditional relationship anyway, since we lived almost an hour drive away from each other—and that was without traffic.

The three of us walked through a maze of gold fabric covered cubicles toward the back of the building, where several hard walled offices were located. The carpets were industrial gray, the walls stark white. The premises looked like any other company I'd had occasion to visit, except for the majority of employees wearing business attire. This being the Pacific Northwest (the home of grunge, remember?), many office workers dressed casually—especially those in the software industry. Apparently that relaxed attitude didn't extend to the FBI, even on a Saturday.

Agent Cunningham opened one of the closed wood doors to reveal a large conference room dominated by an impressive oval mahogany table that probably sat at least twenty. Sitting at the forward half of the table were Jensen and two other gentlemen who I didn't recognize. They each had a white coffee mug and some kind of notebook in front of them. Cunningham invited me inside as he proceeded to the position immediately adjacent to the head of the table.

"Come on in. We don't have any psi-free coffee to offer you, but I dug up some bottled water." Cunningham motioned to the empty seat at the head of the table, next to his spot.

Clearly, this was where I was supposed to sit, with Cunningham to my right and Jensen to my left. A small laptop was open in front of Cunningham's place, trailing black cables that snaked across the center of the table to connect with a device placed on a small black tripod down at the other end. Another stand in the center of the table appeared to be a microphone.

I sat down where Cunningham directed, trying not to appear as nervous as I felt.

As I settled in my chair, Jensen asked, "What happened? Vanelli said you were in some kind of accident. He went zipping out of here pretty quick when he got the news. You okay?"

"Barely." I shook my head. "Those Saturday drivers. They just don't know how to drive on the sidewalk."

They all laughed, a short concert of guffaws and chuckles, and then Cunningham questioned me about the accident. My story seemed far too short, especially since the accident almost rearranged some important body parts, but I resisted the temptation to embellish. I didn't want to come off like a drama queen. My hands still trembled, so I kept them clasped together in my lap. When I made the offhanded comment of being at the wrong place at the wrong time, I noticed Cunningham shoot a meaningful look toward Vince. Apparently, Agent Cunningham didn't buy into the coincidence. Until that moment, I hadn't considered anything else. Now that the possibility of foul play had been set loose in my mind, it nagged at the outer edges of my thoughts like a terrier worrying the fringe on a rug.

The boys, being detectives and all, peppered me with questions that extracted the few details I had left out in my attempt to keep the story concise. After their curiosity had been sated, they all wished me well, the most notable exception being the man sitting next to Cunningham, who had not involved himself in the discussion and continued to regard me with a reserved expression.

Finally, Cunningham got around to introductions. The silent man sitting to his right, who wore a Coventry County

Sheriff uniform, was Sheriff Bruce Lancer, and the term 'good ol' boy' seemed an understatement as far as he was concerned. He looked middle aged and was stout, with slicked back, auburn hair, a substantial mustache, and penetrating, closely set gray eyes. Instead of a twang, he was surprisingly soft spoken. Even so, I got the distinct impression Sheriff Lancer could be a hard-ass whenever it suited him.

The other man, who sat further down the table next to the Sheriff, was Agent Cheung, an extremely thin man of Asian decent, although, calling him a man pushed the limits of the definition. He hardly looked old enough to drive without a learner's permit. The fit of his navy blue suit was comical and only served to further accentuate his youthful (and skinny) appearance. It looked as if he was playing daddy dress-up. His voice pitched deeper than I expected, but still remained firmly in the tenor section of the choir. I'll give him credit though, he may have looked young and inexperienced, but he conducted himself with the professional aplomb worthy of an agent.

You know what they say: 'Never judge a book by its cover.' I was betting there was more to these two men than what I inferred by their appearance.

Agent Cunningham made a comment about getting started. I pressed my lips together. I knew the tripod at the other end of the table held a camera and Cunningham's computer was digitally recording the whole session.

"Ms. Devon, I'm sure we all have our own questions we'd like to ask, but I thought we'd start by having you tell us what you learned from the remains yesterday. Detective Vanelli explained your unconscious episode at the crime scene was the result of coming into contact with one of the victim's bones. Is that true?"

"Yes." I tried not to squirm under Cunningham's intense gaze, but it was a challenge. I refused to feel sorry about my action, other than for the stress I caused Vince.

"And you did this in order to obtain a reading?"

"Yes."

He made a slow twirling gesture with his hand, signaling it was time to elaborate. "Will you please provide us with as much detail as possible regarding the remains? Gentlemen, please feel free to ask questions if you need clarification."

"Okay. Uh, first of all, the victim's name is Trinity Wilson. She was a cryokinetic. She lived in Seattle, but her family is from Monroe. She was twenty-three years old, worked at Microsoft. And she too was involved in Nick's study, just like the other victims I've read."

Sheriff Lancer spoke up. "Ms. Devon, I'd like to spend a moment discussing this study. How did Trinity come to be involved with Mr. Coulter?"

It was odd hearing Nick referred to as 'Mr. Coulter,' and I felt a tug on my heart at the mention of his name.

I searched my memory. "Trinity heard about the study from her doctor. As I'm sure you know, Coventry Hospital specializes in treating the common and not so common ills of psychics and magic users, in addition to individuals who have been injured by magical means. They have one of the best psi-wards in the country. Nick's study was partially funded by the hospital. Since Trinity's doctor was on staff there, she knew about it and recommended Trinity for the study. Her doctor's name is Jane Brier."

"What about the other victims? Jason," he consulted his notes, "Warner and Patty Schaeffer."

"The same was true for Jason, but not Patty. Patty came into the study because she answered an advertisement in the paper. Jason's doctor was Patrick Neidelmeyer."

I pushed some errant strands of hair behind my ear. Movement in the air from the overhead heating and cooling vent caused them to brush against my face. There were times when the floating wisps made me feel sexy, womanly somehow, but now wasn't one of those times. Right now they tickled the sides of my face and it was just annoying.

Lancer nodded and made notes in the pages of his leather-bound notebook. "What was Trinity's understanding of the study?"

"She knew they were studying her brainwaves and physical responses when she used her magic. But that's about all. The same was true for Jason and Patty. They were all told they'd be contacted with the details and results of the study after it was over."

I wanted to ask the Sheriff whether he had already spoken with Nick's partner in the study, Dr. Ford, but resisted. My business didn't lie on that path, and I had a feeling the Sheriff would be more than willing to point that out. Although Sheriff Lancer was professional in his questioning, something told me he wasn't thrilled with me. I assumed it was because of my gift, but I was only partially right.

"Ms. Devon, did you know you are the sole beneficiary to Nick Coulter's estate?"

I blinked at the sudden change of subject and stared at him. My forehead knitted down to a frown as unwelcome tears burned my eyes. I glanced at Vince. He looked just as surprised as I felt.

Returning my attention to the Sheriff, I stammered, "No. No, I didn't."

"He was estranged from his family, was he not?"

"Yes."

"You knew he had no plans to leave his estate to them." He made the statement a question.

"Yes. Long time ago he told me he had written them out of his will. He and I had, at that time, similar problems with family members." I added, "Although, I didn't know he had plans to leave everything to me. That surprises me."

The conversation Vince and I shared at my apartment came to mind. For a fleeting moment, I wondered if Vince had reported the details of our conversation to his superiors, but quickly put it out of my mind. Even if he had told them, it was before we established any kind of romantic relationship. At least, that's what I told myself.

"I see. So who else did you think he was going to leave everything to?" The Sheriff kept his voice controlled and sounding reasonable, but his eyes had narrowed and he looked less than friendly.

I answered honestly. "I don't know. I guess I just supposed he intended to leave his money to charity—to Coventry Hospital—but we never discussed it."

"Would you have known if there was someone else in his life who he might have provided for in his will?"

One minute I thought he was going to accuse me of something and the next I wasn't so sure. "Yeah, I think so, we were good friends. The last month or so we were both really busy, so we hadn't talked for a while, but yeah, if there was someone else in his life who meant that much to him, I know he would have told me about them."

"So, why claim surprise at being named in his will? I mean, you would have known about anyone else, right?"

I frowned and then cast my eyes over to Agent Cunningham who regarded me with a neutral expression. I had hoped Cunningham would quash this ridiculous line of questioning, but he apparently wanted to see where it all netted out.

I gritted my teeth and looked back to the Sheriff. "I never gave it any thought, Sheriff Lancer. Nick and I are the same— " I took a steadying mouthful of air and tried not to cry. My emotions still bubbled right under the surface where Nick was concerned, and the Sheriff's inference that I had something to do with his murder sickened me. I continued with a little more calm, trying to keep any disdain from coming through in my voice. "Nick and I were the same age—thirty. Dying was not something we discussed. Our wills were not something we talked about either, except for the brief conversation we had about disinheriting his family. And that was in the context of our screwed up relations with family and not about our estates."

"I see. And you're not the least bit curious as to what he left you?"

I had the distinct feeling the Sheriff wanted to get a rise out of me, so I didn't bite back. I narrowed my eyes and shook my head. "You obviously haven't checked my financial records. I have absolutely no interest in Nick's money. Or is that not what you're trying to imply?"

Deadly Remains - Chapter Fifteen

Jensen finally demanded, "Cunningham, what the hell is this?"

To my relief, both Jensen and Vince had displeased looks for both Agent Cunningham and Sheriff Lancer.

The Sheriff remained silent, ignoring Jensen and Vince's disapproving expressions, and continued to glare at me.

I was about to shoot my mouth off when Agent Cunningham said, "Agent Cheung?"

The youthful agent answered directly, his hands steepled together on the table. "She is telling the truth."

I looked at him, not bothering to cover my surprise. Cheung returned my gaze with an air of confidence. No wonder. He was a truthsayer, and it explained a lot. It explained his youth, for one. These days, the FBI hire MBAs. They don't recruit at the high school level, unless, of course, you happen to have an extremely useful magic ability. Like truthsaying. It also explained his assured disposition, in spite of his geeky, youthful appearance. The FBI was probably sending him to college in exchange for use of his talent. Lucky kid. In the mean time, Agent Cheung was there to tell Cunningham whether I was telling the truth, and it pissed me off.

I glanced across the table at Vince, angry that he didn't at least warn me about Agent Cheung, but the expression on his face told me he had no idea what was going on. He looked from Cunningham to Agent Cheung with a demanding look. Jensen appeared to be just as mystified.

My angry glare centered back on Agent Cunningham, but I kept my voice level. "You know, I can understand including a truthsayer in order to provide further credibility to my testimony, but to do it in such an underhanded way—to lay a trap and then ask such inflammatory questions—it's insulting."

Cunningham sighed. "I hoped this would help get us all on the same page."

He didn't come all the way out and say it, but I figured he had arranged this to appease Sheriff Lancer. The Sheriff suspected I was responsible for Nick's death—that much was obvious—and Agent Cunningham had provided him with a means of dispelling (or proving) the theory.

I sighed. "You people are so used to dealing with criminals I think you've forgotten how to treat others with respect." I glared at Sheriff Lancer. "Okay, get this: I did not kill Nick. I did not kill Jason. I did not kill Patty. I did not kill Trinity. In fact, I can safely say I have never in my life murdered anyone." I looked around the room. "*Okay*? Can we move on now?"

Agent Cheung looked at me with considerable amusement. "She is telling the truth. That last statement was a little murky, but I believe this is due to her acquisition of memories from other individuals who have indeed been guilty of murder."

Once again, Agent Cheung surprised me. I had never considered that my other memories might affect the results of a lie detector, or, in this case, a truthsayer. This realization made me uncomfortable because it suggested the memories weren't as tightly confined as I might have hoped. I thought of Patty and suppressed a shudder.

The Sheriff stared at me all steely eyed and then shifted his attention to Cunningham. "How do we know this murkiness doesn't account for anything?"

Agent Cheung spoke before Cunningham had time to respond. "It is safe to say I know my business, Sheriff Lancer. She is not the murderer."

Lancer grumbled something about all psychics sticking together and then sat back in his chair with his arms folded across his chest, looking more resolved than ever. Unfortunately, he seemed to be one of those people who resisted believing in magic, no matter how incontrovertible. Magic was 'mumbo jumbo,' so I must be guilty because I told them things only the murderer could know. Short of irrefutable hard evidence proving someone else guilty, I was going to remain at the top of Lancer's suspect list. I realized trying to gain access to Nick's remains was going to be next to impossible as long as Sheriff Lancer held the keys. All I could hope

was that after the killer was found, the bones would be released to me for burial. I might be able to push for them now,
since it sounded like I was the executor of Nick's estate, but
I was pretty certain the Sheriff could easily get a local judge
to deny the request, in light of his steadfast belief that I was
a suspect.

Agent Cunningham wasted no time in getting my testimony back on track. I tried to put all thoughts concerning
Nick and his soul out of my mind.

"Where and how was the latest victim abducted?" Cunningham asked.

I put myself back into Trinity's shoes, not without difficulty, and answered, "From the Safeway parking lot. She
had plans to stay with her parents for the weekend, so she
made the drive up after traffic had died down. She left work
around eight o'clock. It was an easy drive. She stopped at
Safeway to pick up some pastries at around nine or nine-
fifteen."

I couldn't help thinking about her dad and his partiality
to apple turnovers, but I quashed that line of thought before
it got me wondering about how her parents must be handling the news of her death. I was already a wreck. I didn't
need to step on any further heart-rending emotional land
mines.

I stared at the far wall without seeing it. "She hit the ATM
at the front of the store for forty bucks, picked up some apple turnovers before getting a latte from the in-store Star-
bucks, and then headed back to her car around nine-thirty."
I shrugged. "Her abduction was a lot like Jason's. When she
came out of the store, there was a white van parked next to
her car. As she went between her car and the van, the sliding
van door opened and she was grabbed from behind. A cloth
was put over her nose and mouth. I assume it was chloroform. She blacked out quickly."

Jensen, Vince, and Cunningham proceeded to question
me about every possible detail, which extracted everything
from the weather to the exact time, where she had parked,
other cars in the parking lot, people she encountered in the

store, how she paid for the turnovers, what she was wearing, and on and on and on. Every time the questions appeared to wind down, I dared to hope we were nearly finished, but then someone would come up with yet another seemingly trivial inquiry. It was exhausting.

After about forty-five minutes, Cunningham told me he wanted to hear about Trinity's final encounter with the murderer. Once again, I related word-for-word the murderer's last conversation. As with Vince the night before, the discussion quickly turned toward speculating about the mysterious 'they.'

Sheriff Lancer, who had surprised me by remaining silent for the past hour, made sure we were all well aware of his disgruntled feelings about this latest turn in the questioning. He huffed and grumbled under his breath more than once. When I looked over, he sat straight in his chair, arms folded tightly. Finally, Agent Cunningham called him on it, but first he clicked something on his computer.

"Lancer, if you have nothing better to offer than grumbles and eye rolling, then get the hell out. Otherwise, pipe down and try to do something more constructive than distract the rest of us from the discussion."

Lancer closed his notebook with a slap and stood up. "There is no 'they.' This is just another ruse to distract us from the crime. I don't believe any of this shit. If you need anything from me, you can damn well ask for it by going through official channels. I'm done with this."

I drilled holes into Lancer's head with my eyes as he stormed toward the door.

Cunningham leaned back in his seat. "Lancer, just make sure you don't stand in the FBI's way. You may find the government taking an extreme interest in your department."

In spite of his collegial tone, the implied threat hung in the air, and Sheriff Lancer turned his narrowed eyes toward Cunningham. "Is that a threat?"

Agent Cunningham regarded him coolly. "Not at all. Just call it professional advice."

Lancer cast one last dirty look at the rest of us and then slammed the door behind him.

After a moment or two of silence, I piped up, "I guess I better not plan any vacation travel to Coventry County any time soon." I was only half-joking and worried my nervous trembling would be obvious to everyone around the table.

Cunningham snorted and shook his head. "Did my best to get him to work with us. Even got another clairvoyant to confirm the reading of the rock. But some people refuse to have anything to do with magic, no matter how useful it might be."

"They don't see it as useful," I replied.

He sighed. "No. No they don't." He leaned an elbow on the table. "Now, myself, I'll take leads wherever I can get them. I'm not picky as long as they help me solve the case." He drilled his fingers on the tabletop and looked over at Vince and Jensen. "That reminds me. In light of these two readings, I have to express a certain level of concern regarding Lire's recent accident."

"I'd say it was just a coincidence if the driver had been a little old lady or a drunk. But the car was stolen, which makes it suspicious," Vince pointed out.

Jensen grunted. "I agree. I have my own doubts about whether this is a new individual or individuals, and not just the murderer trying to scare her off of the case, but either way, it's something to take seriously."

Cunningham nodded. "My thinking too." He considered me for a moment, maybe pondering all the recent facts and the likelihood of further problems. Finally, his expression changed from being contemplative to one of resolve. "Ms. Devon, I'd like you to give us your exact schedule for the next couple of weeks. I don't know if this is anything to get worried about, but we should play things safe."

I nodded, squeezing my hands together in my lap. I couldn't help wondering what my life would be like, flitting to and fro from my apartment, to work, to grocery shopping, to Sotheby's ... all the while being scared to death someone was out to get me.

Agent Cunningham raised his eyebrows, waiting.

"You want to know my schedule, right now?" I asked, trying not to sound like a mouse.

"Please." His pen was readied.

I forced my mind on track. "Uh, I usually leave for work around eight thirty. Unless I have a meeting with clients or something, like I did a couple weeks ago when I went up to Chiliquitham." I nodded toward Jensen and Vince. "Every week or so, sometimes twice a week, I go over to Sotheby's in the morning. On those days, I don't usually leave until nine." I thought about the location of the accident, suddenly awash with panic. "Oh, and I usually stop at Peabody's for a coffee, almost every morning."

"That's where you were earlier, isn't it? Where the car almost hit you?" Cunningham looked up briefly from his notes to see me nod. "From now on, I think it would be best to avoid going anywhere that isn't absolutely necessary."

Agent Cunningham was too busy writing to notice my apprehension. I raised an unsteady hand to push some stray hairs behind my ear and struggled to keep from imagining a hit man out there, right now, lying in wait for me.

He continued without a glance, "Also, until I say otherwise, please don't make any appointments with unknown clients."

My terrified expression must have jumped in magnitude because Vince said, "Lire, we just want you to play it safe for a while. It could very well be nothing, but it's better to be safe than sorry. Okay?"

"Yeah. I get it." I tried to sound calm, but my voice quavered. "But I need to go out on appointment. I often get called to perform readings on items from an estate."

I was scared, but I had to live my life. I had my business to think about. Besides, it was probably just a car jacking. "What if someone comes with me? So far, the murderer has only struck when his victims have been alone."

They looked thoughtful. After a tick, Cunningham replied, "I'd rather you found someone else to go instead, but if that's not feasible, then check with one of us first. We can at least do a background check on your new clients."

I nodded.

We established the rest of my daily schedule, including when I usually went grocery shopping, to yoga class, and whether I had a nightlife—Sunday mornings, not lately, and, pathetically, no. Agent Cunningham also asked me whether I lived alone or had a boyfriend. If Agent Cheung hadn't been in the room, I would have just said I lived alone with no boyfriend, but he was, so I ended up fumbling around for a response. I finally mumbled something about dating someone but wasn't sure whether he qualified as my boyfriend. It sounded lame, and Jensen looked at me with a raised eyebrow. I avoided looking at Vince and felt my cheeks grow hot.

I glanced down at Cunningham's notepad. He had reduced my life to text on a page. It was especially depressing because it took less than a small paragraph. I really needed to get a life.

I opened my water bottle instead and proceeded to defend myself to myself. How many people can say they've helped the FBI solve a murder case? That was pretty cool, if not a bit creepy, but still pretty big on the coolness scale. And, wasn't I almost dating a really foxy guy? If it weren't for the runaway cars, touching deadly remains, and losing consciousness every five minutes, life would actually be pretty good.

I'd hardly call it boring, anyway.

Agent Cunningham cut short any further self-indulgent ego building when he clicked his computer and asked me to describe Trinity's last interaction with the murderer.

Hands clamped together in my lap, I recounted the murderer's behavior and dialog. Cunningham interrupted twice to ask questions about the murderer's appearance and whether Trinity had been in the same location where she held the rock.

I explained, "Other than her actual kidnapping, everything happened at the same location, in the woods behind

Safeway. Of course, Trinity didn't realize she was behind Safeway. She just saw the surrounding trees."

"Then how do you know it was the place behind Safeway?" Jensen asked.

I thought about it. "I guess I don't know for sure. It just feels right. Trinity was inside a magical circle while the murderer spoke to her. I don't think the warlock would go through the trouble of setting up the circle and calling Paimon, only to clean everything up and then move Trinity to the Safeway site just to finish the ritual. Setting up a magic circle takes a lot of effort and power. Not to mention the significant risks involved in summoning a demon. I don't think he'd do that twice, unless he absolutely had to."

"After being kidnapped, did she wake up prior to her experience in the woods?" Vince asked.

I thought back. "No, she didn't."

Vince continued, "After the warlock had finished talking to her, she was chloroformed again and never regained consciousness?"

"Correct. She didn't wake up again. Her psychic essence ends soon after."

Agent Cunningham redirected. "So she was grabbed next to her car and then woke up in the woods. What happened right after she woke up?"

I had hoped to avoid discussing her encounter with the demon. I hesitated before answering, "She woke up near the demon, although, she didn't know it was the demon at the time."

Unable to stop myself, I rubbed my left hand across my lower jaw. Although this was my third encounter with Paimon's evil presence, I was by no means accustomed to reliving the experience. I forced my hand back into my lap. "Many demons have the ability to cloak themselves in human form. Paimon attempted to trick Trinity by appearing to be a fellow prisoner. At first, she was comforted by his presence. The prisoner appeared to be her age and was really good looking. He encouraged her to believe they might have a chance at escape. But she soon realized something wasn't right. The prisoner wanted her to join him in calling up a demon to help them. The chant required her to renounce her faith in God. When she refused, he grew angry." My voice threatened to break and I had to stop.

Cunningham clicked a key on his laptop before looking at me. "I can see this is difficult. If it weren't so important, I wouldn't be asking you to talk about it. Take a moment. Let me know if there's anything I can do to make you more comfortable. We can continue when you're ready."

I nodded. "Thanks. This is the worst part, but I can get through it."

Cunningham hadn't meant to offend me. I'm sure his concern was genuine, but it made me feel like a little kid, scared of the monster in the closet. I straightened my back, took a sip of my water, and then told him I was ready.

After he switched the video recording back on, I resumed where I left off. "After Trinity refused to recite the evil chant, the demon ripped away its magic veil, revealing its true form. The effect on Trinity was devastating." I tightened my jaw. "I will not describe the demon. Just know that its presence is worse than anything you can possibly imagine. Even if I tried, there just aren't enough evil words in human language to describe it."

I didn't wait for approval. "After the demon revealed itself, the warlock came out of hiding. I'm pretty sure he had concealed himself behind a tree or something, while the demon tried to trick Trinity into renouncing her faith. When the warlock appeared, he scolded the demon, saying, 'You've had your chance.'"

I tucked my hair behind my ear. I'm sure it looked like a nervous gesture, but I couldn't help myself. "The demon was infuriated. It started spitting and growling at the edge of its circle, but the warlock stared it down until the demon stopped its tantrum. I'm pretty sure they had a battle of wills. If the demon had won, it would have been very bad for the warlock." I shrugged. "After getting the demon under control, the warlock instructed Trinity to listen carefully to his words. He said her complete focus was mandatory. Her continued well-being depended on it. That's when he gave her the stone and started talking directly to me. Afterward, he removed the stone from her hands and then proceeded to deliver the second message. When he was done, he chloroformed her and that's it."

Cunningham leaned forward and peered at me. "You told Detective Vanelli the reason you felt compelled to touch the remains is because you thought you might know the warlock. Now that you've read them, do you suspect anyone?"

I gritted my teeth and shook my head. "No. I'm sure it's a man though." I threw up my hands in frustration. "I can't imagine how he learned all those personal details about me. I've been wracking my brain, but I can't figure it out."

Jensen asked, "Who would have been aware of those facts?"

Some of the warlock's words came back to me …

… it all started when you asked your mother why she had been naked … Red talked you out of suicide … dearest Nick … your first love … your first kiss … your first …

"I've confided in very few people. The things he mentioned …" I shrugged and looked down. "I tend not to talk about them."

Jensen ruffled through his notebook. "I can see why this might be upsetting. But we need to go through them. Find out who would know. If they're so closely guarded, then we need to know who might have had a slip of the tongue and to whom they might have talked. It might help lead us to the killer."

I nodded but I'm sure I didn't look happy.

Jensen read from his notes. "He spoke of your mother and how you discovered she'd had an affair with your Uncle. It sounds like something that occurred when you were a child—the warlock spoke of you holding your mother's hand at the park. I know this happened a while ago, but can you tell me who may have known about this event?"

I tried to avoid hunching my shoulders forward like a turtle and probably ended up looking like I had a board strapped to my back. "The warlock was talking about how my mother first discovered my psychic ability. As you might imagine, it was a deeply unsettling experience—for the both of us. My mother never really recovered from the shock, and her reaction so traumatized me that I didn't tell anyone about the encounter for years. Nick was the first person I ever told. Until then, I hadn't spoken of that day to anyone." I paused in thought for a moment and tried to ignore the bead of sweat dripping down my side. "After that, I've told only my best friend Julie and Detective Vanelli."

Jensen nodded, apparently unmoved by my mention of Vince. He probably thought I had told him about my mother after the reading of the rock, and not a blurted comment on the first day of our meeting.

"Your friend Julie—what is her full name? How long have you known her?" Agent Cunningham asked.

"Julie Peabody. She and her husband own Peabody's Beans. I started going to their store, around the time Jack and I started ST&C. The shop is across the street from Sotheby's, but I'm in there almost every day for my cappuccino fix. Julie's around my age and her brother is a pyrokinetic, so that drew us together. I've known her for about eight years, I guess."

Cunningham nodded and jotted down notes about Julie in his notebook. I felt bad dragging her into this mess. Maybe I could warn her and apologize about it before the FBI showed up in her shop. But then I reconsidered. It might look suspicious. I waffled back and forth about what to do and got so irritated with myself that I came right out and asked Cunningham.

"I'd prefer you not say anything. It will be best to let us call Mrs. Peabody. Please do not discuss the case with anyone who is not officially involved. If someone presses you for information, please refer them to either myself or Lieutenant Jensen. Is that clear?"

"Yes. I understand." I crossed my arms, hunching in my chair. "I just feel bad about bringing Julie into this. I don't want her to think I've implied she's a blabbermouth."

Cunningham looked sympathetic. "We'll be sure to explain that. Don't worry."

I nodded stiffly and hoped Agent Miller wasn't the representative Cunningham chose to send over to speak with Julie. If the session wasn't being recorded, I might have said as much.

Jensen continued to consult his notes. "Okay, next, I believe the murderer talked about someone named," he squinted at his notebook, "Red, and then something about him being a guilt gift and stopping you from suicide when you were a teenager." Jensen peered at me. "Is this the same Red who provided information about the demon at Jason's crime scene?"

I crossed my legs, surreptitiously rubbing my sweaty palms on the fabric of my jeans. "Yeah. Red's not exactly a secret, but I don't go out of my way to introduce him to everyone I meet either. He's a bit unusual. Detective Vanelli can tell you. On the day we went out to Jason's crime scene, I inadvertently introduced them."

Vince snorted. "Yeah. Damn near crashed my car when I first saw him."

When Vince didn't elaborate, I explained, "Red is very unique and I didn't exactly plan for Detective Vanelli to see him while we were driving down the highway. Red isn't human, per se. He's a seventeenth-century necromancer whose soul has been bound to a psi-free black teddy bear. He was a gift from my dad and has been my companion since I was five."

Agent Cunningham's eyebrows went up. "How many people would you say know about Red?"

"I minimize his visibility, but don't keep him a secret, so dozens and dozens of people, at least. Who knows how many people then talked about him to others?" I shrugged. "When I was at Coventry Academy, many of my classmates knew about him. All my close friends know him and, of course, my coworkers know him too. But, the thing almost no one knows is the other detail—the one about him saving my life. The only people who know that detail are Julie and

Nick. That's why I was so determined to read Trinity's bones." I sighed. "That fact, out of all the things the warlock said, is so private, I just *had* to hear the murderer's voice again. I figured it was someone I knew from school."

Jensen frowned. "Red stopped you from committing suicide?"

I bit my lip and nodded. "One of my closest friends in high school, a boy named Daniel, was transferred to another school when I was thirteen. We'd been friends since the first grade, and ... well, I guess he was my first love. At the time, he was the only person, besides Red, who I really trusted and connected with. When he transferred, without any warning at all, it was a huge shock. I literally wanted to throw myself off a cliff. If Red hadn't been there, I probably would have jumped."

I didn't actually set out to jump off a cliff. The chance just sort of presented itself to me. I realized Daniel was gone and never coming back. I started running. I had no clear destination in mind. I just needed to run. I ran with tears blotting my vision and desperation dogging every step. The cliff happened to fall across my path. I almost blindly ran off the edge, but stopped myself in time. But, as I stood there crying, mist in the trees and no ground in sight, I began to think about how lonely I was going to be for the rest of my life and how much pain I had already endured in thirteen short years. And when I was just about to take that one, final step, Red's voice permeated the emotional fog that had overwhelmed my judgment.

"No, Lire! This is not how it is meant to be! You are here for a reason, just as I died, and my soul was cast about for over three hundred years—for a reason. You were that reason! Your father was meant to find me, just as I was meant to be here with you. We are both on this earth for a purpose, and God did not grant you life, just so you could throw it away. Dearest, we will get through this difficult time. Please trust me. You will see. I am here for you always. Please, do not do this. I love you, Lire. Step back. Please."

I remember turning and staggering away from the precipice. I fell to my knees and let the rain wash away my tears as Red stroked my cheek. No one, except Red, knew just how close I came to ending it that day. Later, the only people who I told were Julie and Nick. Either someone had been watching me, someone I did not see up on the plateau, or one of my dearest friends had betrayed my confidence. How else could the murderer know this intimate detail?

Cunningham echoed my thoughts. "Except for Julie Peabody and Nick Coulter, you're certain no one else knew of this event? Where did this happen? Maybe someone saw you."

I took a shaky breath. "I was out on the Redridge Plateau—about a half mile from the school. Not exactly a heavy traffic area, plus it was raining. I don't think anyone saw me, but I suppose anything is possible." I shrugged. "Believe me, I've been thinking about this a lot since yesterday. Nick was an honorable guy. He wasn't the type of person who would have blabbed that to other people. I suppose it's possible Julie told her husband, but she wouldn't tell anyone else. I'm sure."

Vince asked. "Is it possible another clairvoyant touched you at some point? Just like you've touched the remains? Could someone have learned these details that way?"

The question took me aback. It was something I'd never considered. "That wouldn't be possible without my knowledge. If someone touches me, I'm well aware of it. Even if I'm sleeping or unconscious, my powers are still active." I pressed my lips together in thought. "There are mind readers, they're called telepaths, but that psychic ability is very rare." I considered. "The boy I told you about earlier, Daniel, he was a telepath. We often goofed around with our powers when we were kids. And whenever he tried to read my mind, I was aware of it."

This was why we'd been so close. We knew many intimate details about one another because our inhibitions as children allowed us to read each other without worrying about adult issues. I have Daniel to thank for my strong psychic shield. He taught me how to better use my power, and we frequently played shield battles with each other. The object was to see how long we were able to block the other's psychic intrusion.

Both Vince and Cunningham regarded me with surprised expressions.

I nodded at them. "That's made me think: Daniel is another person who was aware of how my mother discovered my magic ability. When we were kids, Daniel and I frequently tested each other psychically. He read my mind on more than one occasion. I'm sure he knows of that memory. But he wouldn't have known about my suicide attempt since that happened after he left Coventry Academy."

Cunningham looked thoughtful. "Telepath, huh? Then I suppose he would have also known about Red, right?" I nodded, and he continued, "Can you tell me Daniel's last name? Did you remain in contact with him after he left your school?"

"No. I could never get a straight answer about where he went. It was probably because the adults at the school didn't feel it was appropriate to discuss a student's personal matters with another student. At one point, when I was in college, I tried to track him down. I didn't get much further than checking with the Academy secretary and doing some on-line research, neither of which got me anywhere."

"What did the school say?" Cunningham asked.

I thought back to my telephone conversation with the secretary at the school. "Gosh, I don't remember. That was years ago. The secretary just shut me down pretty quick, you know? I think she told me she wasn't allowed to give out that type of information. I didn't bother pursuing it with the Dean." I remembered Cunningham's other question. "Oh, and his last name was Stockard."

I realized, since I was now personally acquainted with the Assistant Dean, I might be able to pursue the information with greater success. Of course, with a police investigation going on, I should probably leave it alone. After the investigation, I could think about trying to make contact with Daniel again.

"What about another clairvoyant touching something you touched? Could a clairvoyant get these types of memories by touching your used Peabody's paper cup, let's say?" Jensen asked.

I tilted my head, considering. "Maybe. But, most of the time, I don't take off my gloves when I'm outside my apartment." I shrugged and thought about the last time I had touched a disposable cup with my bare hands. I might have done it at Sotheby's last week—the time Vince was with me—but I couldn't remember for sure.

And then I mentally rolled my eyes. My hands weren't the only body part that touched a coffee cup. *Duh.*

I felt like smacking myself in the head. "I'm obviously not thinking clearly. My lips touch the cup. So it's definitely a possibility. Of course, I'd have to be thinking about a particular thing, at the time I'm drinking or eating, for that memory to be imprinted clearly—or at all, since my shield is always in place."

It was interesting having the tables turned, so to speak. Until now, it was always other people who were concerned, even terrified, by how I might be able to probe unwanted into their personal lives. Now, I was on the receiving end. It never occurred to me that someone might want to learn my intimate details by touching something I had touched. Honestly, it was a little unnerving.

"What about the items you read? Like the rock or the blouse. You touch those with your bare hands," Jensen observed.

"True, but when I do a reading, I compartmentalize my memories. My shield is strongly in place, so I don't leave a psychic imprint on the item. At the most, if I'm not careful, I might leave a small psychic tail that another clairvoyant could identify as belonging to me. But, they would only know I had read the object and not much more than that."

After a moment of attention to his notebook, Jensen nodded at me. "Okay then. That leaves us with Nick. So, judging by what the murderer said, you and Nick were romantically involved. He's referring to Nick Coulter, is that right?"

I felt my cheeks flush and tears sting my eyes before I firmly told myself to get a grip. "Yeah. He was my first real boyfriend—my first adult relationship. We met in college, but the things the warlock said aren't exactly earth-shattering secrets. All of my friends and acquaintances at school knew Nick and I were together. We dated for over a year. Anyone who knows anything about touch sensitive individuals is fully aware that finding someone who can block direct skin contact is extremely rare." I fought the desire to look at Vince and kept my voice matter of fact. "We didn't run around saying, 'oh yeah, we had sex last night,' but I think most people could have guessed we were intimate."

Jensen snorted, looking amused. "So, maybe he just brought those facts up because he knew they'd upset you."

I simultaneously shrugged and nodded.

"What about Red? I'd like to speak with him too. He lives with you?" Cunningham asked.

"Yes, he does. But he's never shared any of my secrets with anyone."

"That may be your belief, but I'd like to speak with him, just the same."

I wanted to say no, but couldn't find a justifiable reason to refuse, other than my concern for Red's safety. If I couldn't trust the FBI to keep their hands off him, then just whom could I trust?

"You want to speak with him right now?" I asked.

Agent Cunningham raised his eyebrows at me, but nodded. "That would be acceptable."

I frowned, feeling all four men's attention transfixed on my every move. I brought my purse into my lap and pulled it open. "Red? Agent Cunningham wants to ask you some questions. Are you up for that?"

Red looked up from his opened magazine, which was illuminated by a tiny book light, and cocked his head at me. "If that is his wish, then I am at his service."

I split my gaze between the men around the table. "Please, don't attempt to get any closer to Red and don't try to touch him. Red has several spells that will protect him if you aren't careful. Trust me, you don't want to be on the receiving end of either one." I shook my head. "I'm not trying to scare anyone. I just want to avoid any unpleasantness."

I brought Red to the tabletop, on the palm of my hand. He stepped off to take a seat next to my water bottle. Everyone, except Vince and I, regarded Red with wide eyes, and Agent Cheung looked both surprised and pleased.

"Red, this is Agent Cunningham, Agent Cheung, Lieutenant Jensen, and you already know Detective Vanelli." I motioned toward each person around the table.

"Pleased to make your acquaintances," Red said in his usual polite manner, with a curt nod of his cuddly head.

Agent Cunningham regarded Red with a mixed expression of disbelief and awe. After a moment of shocked silence, he said, "Red. Excuse me, do you mind if I call you Red?"

"A casual tone to these proceedings is acceptable. You may address me as Red if you wish."

"Thank you. Please call me Mark or just Cunningham—whatever makes you comfortable." He shifted in his chair. "Have you been following our discussion? Are you aware the murderer has mentioned several private facts involving Ms. Devon's personal life?"

"Yes. My hearing is excellent and my memory is impeccable. I have been at Lire's side for most of her life and witness to most of her conversations. I have nothing to add to your discussion. She has mentioned all the individuals with whom she has discussed the facts in question. Of course, I cannot comment on conversations that took place when I was absent. During her desperate flight through the Redridge woods, where she nearly ended her life, I was aware of no other individuals on the plateau that afternoon. It is my continued belief we were unobserved that day."

Cunningham made a short entry in his notebook and spoke again before he had totally finished writing. "I understand you provided information about the magic at Jason Warner's crime scene. Would you please discuss your findings with us and how you know about such things?"

"Certainly. My past history will explain somewhat, I do imagine. I was born to my mortal life, in the year 1665, in London, and was trained in necromancy by my reclusive uncle, from the age of six until I was twenty. I came to America in the spring of 1691, where I met my fiancée, who was also a magic user. In August of the next year, I was imprisoned, tried, condemned, and hung to my death, during what most Americans now call the Salem witch trials. At the time of my death, however, I allowed my soul to be captured because I didn't want to abandon my fiancée and was afraid to die.

"Although I can no longer practice sorcery, I am able to detect magic. At both crime scenes, I determined the warlock summoned Paimon because that demon is known for utilizing a particular spell that suppresses most forms of magic. The remnants of that spell were still present when we visited those sites. I also felt the after-effects of a forced confinement spell, which is an extremely powerful spell only beings like Paimon are able to produce." Red hesitated. "There was one other spell cast before the circle was broken, and it was one with which I am unfamiliar. I can tell you, however, it was not a spell used in necromancy."

"Interesting," Cunningham muttered as he wrote in his notebook. "And this forced confinement spell—it is used for what, exactly?"

Red put his paws together on his lap and explained, "A confinement spell is what was used when I was executed in 1692. It is a spell both necromancers and witches or warlocks are able to perform, but it cannot be forced upon an individual. More specifically, the person being targeted by the spell has free will and cannot be forced into committing their soul to someone else. If they refuse, then their soul makes its way to its intended destination, depending upon how they lived their life. As you might imagine, most of the people who allow their souls to be captured either have unfinished business in the world of the living, are afraid to die, or know their soul is destined for Hell and want to avoid going there.

"Now, in the case of a forced confinement spell, the targeted individual has no free will. At the time of their death, if the spell is cast, their soul is captured and confined to the intended storage medium. In the case of Jason Warner and Trinity Wilson, Lire discovered their souls were confined to their bones."

Agent Cunningham shook his head in amazement as he committed the important details to paper.

"I don't believe it." Jensen frowned. "This Paimon ... it can just pop up and snatch someone's soul anytime it wants?"

"No. Certainly not. There are strict rules that govern the spirit world. Any demon, not just Paimon, can *only* cross over to this world when specific magic allows it. Once they are here, they have a limited range. Unfortunately, the murderer is a warlock with great skill. He is utilizing the evil power of Paimon to further his plans. Paimon has its own agenda, to be sure, but it must operate within the boundaries of its covenant. Each of the victims was tempted by Paimon because the warlock has allowed it."

Cunningham grunted. "This third spell, you say it isn't a necromancy spell. Why?"

Red paused before answering, "I am loath to speculate. My general feelings about the spell may or may not prove to be helpful. I can only say I am unfamiliar with it. Although, I felt as though it was an evocation I *should* be familiar with, almost as if it was on the tip of my tongue." He shook his head. "I am sorry I cannot be of more help. If I may ask, what did your own magic expert say about the spells?"

Cunningham sighed and made an off-handed motion with his pen. "We had two experts visit the site and both of them said basically the same thing you have. One was a necromancer and the other was a Rowan witch. Neither of them could determine the third spell, but they both said it felt familiar."

Agent Cunningham looked at me. "Ms. Devon, I was hoping to hear about your experience with reading Jason Warner and Patty Schaeffer's remains. We have Detective Vanelli's report, of course, but I was hoping to discuss it with you here, in person."

I couldn't help but issue an audible sigh in response to his request. "Okay. Do you just want to ask me questions, or do I have to start from the beginning and retell each individual encounter?"

"We can review the report and then go from there," Cunningham suggested.

We spent the next ninety minutes reviewing my statements and answering various questions. I didn't feel as though the additional information provided anything significant toward identifying the murderer, but maybe I was just grumpy after being confined to the conference room for nearly four hours without a break.

It pushed one o'clock, and I was tired of wracking my brain for details. My stomach growled incessantly, which furthered my crabby mood.

When the questions died down and I figured we had gone around in circles enough, I complained to Cunningham. "I'm tired and hungry, and I'd like to enjoy what's left of my weekend. Do you mind if we adjourn for now? I think we've covered just about every detail possible." I widened my eyes in exasperation.

Cunningham chuckled and turned off the video recording. "That's fine. Thank you for coming down and speaking with us, Ms. Devon. Red, thank you." He removed a card from a small leather case and put it on the table. "Here is my card. Please don't hesitate to call me if you think of anything else that may be of interest to us. You can also, of course, continue to communicate with Lieutenant Jensen and Detective Vanelli. Don't forget to let one of us know if you need to meet with a new client outside of your office. Your accident earlier today may have been a coincidence, but it doesn't hurt to be cautious."

I nodded and held my purse open for Red as everyone gathered their items and stood up to leave. Before wandering toward the lobby, I thanked Agent Cheung, which seemed to entertain him. Since I didn't want to reveal our personal relationship, I said goodbye to Vince and Jensen and then headed toward the front door on my own. As I neared the lobby, however, I heard Vince call my name from behind me. I turned around and saw him talking with Jensen, just outside of the conference room. He held up his index finger in a gesture that told me to wait.

I lingered at the other end of the hall, trying not to feel self-conscious, while Vince finished his conversation. When he finally walked toward me, his lingering gaze made me feel awkward and I'm sure I smiled like a goof. It sure wasn't easy trying to play things cool.

"Jensen wanted me to walk you to your car." He winked mischievously.

While my stomach lurched, I folded my arms and looked down. I fought to school my expression. "Okay."

Before turning to leave, I glanced down the hall and caught Jensen's eye. He was talking with Agent Cunningham, but waved at me. I returned his goodbye gesture and followed Vince out the door.

"How are you feeling?" he asked when we were in the hallway outside.

I gave him a wan smile. "Pretty stressed about, well, *everything*." I shook my head and tried not to sound whiny. "There's so much going on right now—this case, Nick's death, the incident with the car, Sheriff Lancer, my mom. Ugh! It's overwhelming."

Vince was sympathetic. "You've had a lot to deal with. I'm impressed with how well you're doing."

The elevator opened almost immediately. As soon as we were inside with the doors closed, Vince stepped closer and hugged me. I sighed with contentment. It felt amazingly good to be comforted in this way. Contrary to Dad's old adage, sometimes good things did indeed come from wishing.

Vince walked me to my car and told me he'd meet me back at my apartment. On the short drive home, I debated with myself about whether or not to take him into my bed. I had to decide now, or I'd end up going with the flow when we got back to my apartment. And I was willing to bet the flow would be hot and heavy, unless I made sure to keep things under control. It was the classic push-and-pull debate between my head and my hormones. My head told me I should take things slow, get to know Vince, and make sure the relationship was right for the both of us. My hormones made sure to flood my body with sparks of desire at the mere thought of Vince's naked pectorals. And I was thinking about those (and some of his other well-formed body parts) a whole heck of a lot.

After warning Chet that Vince was somewhere behind me, I pulled into the parking garage and parked in my designated slot. I walked toward the guest parking stalls, just as Vince drove into the garage. My hormones spiked as I watched him climb out of his Jeep and saunter toward me. I paid particular attention to the way his leather coat and snug blue jeans accentuated the contours of his body. When his roguish smile hit me, I knew nothing short of a miracle was going to keep me on the right side of the sheets, puritanical decision or not.

"I'm just going to walk you up," Vince told me as he held my hand and walked with me toward the elevator. "I have to get back home and take care of a few things."

I'm sure my face displayed an amusing array of contradictory emotions—chiefly disappointment and relief. Vince must have noticed because he tugged my hand. "I wish I could stay longer though."

"I do too ... and then I don't." I laughed and leaned into him while we walked. "If you stay, I know my willpower will be tested to the extreme."

Once inside the elevator, we kissed. Armed with the knowledge that Vince wasn't staying, I was a little more on the uninhibited side. When the elevator bell rang at my floor, we reluctantly pulled apart.

Vince muttered, "Wow."

I couldn't help but laugh.

At my door, I was pleased to note that Vince looked breathless. So was I, for that matter.

Vince pulled me closer. His expression was ardent. "Now I wish I hadn't said that I had to go."

I leaned against him in a very strategic way. "Mmmm. I'm afraid I let you have it because I knew I was safe. Terrible of me, don't you think?"

"You're a rascal." His husky voice sent a delicious tremor throughout my body.

After several heated kisses and two aborted goodbyes, we finally parted. I went inside, giddy that Vince seemed just as reluctant to leave as I was to let him go.

My good mood lasted for the rest of the weekend, in spite of the fact that most of my telephone messages were from reporters and one was from Nick's attorney, who told me I was indeed Nick's sole beneficiary and the executor of his will. I was going to have to take some additional time away from work to deal with Nick's estate. The process was likely to take several days if not more. Because I had already missed so much work, I hoped to postpone the trip to Coventry for at least a week or two.

I didn't see Vince for the rest of the weekend, but he made up for it by calling several times, and it was his voice I always heard just before I went to bed.

Surprisingly, I did not dream of Vince but went flying with Jason and Trinity.

SIXTEEN

When I left for work on Monday morning, I decided to skip stopping at Peabody's, my recent brush with a speeding hood ornament foremost on my mind. The night before, Vince admonished me to be careful on my way to and from work, as if I needed reminding. By the time I reached ST&C, I saw assassins lurking around every corner, my nerves were totally shot, and I practically bolted for the front door.

When an unfamiliar man called my name from his nearby car and strode toward me, my heart dove into my stomach. Panicked, I stood with my body wedged halfway inside the office doorway.

"Yes?" I checked his appearance thoroughly and looked for any sign of a weapon.

From another direction, I noticed several other people walking quickly in my direction, some of them with cameras. It finally dawned on me that these people were probably reporters.

In no time, there were at least six people in front of me, all asking questions at once, mostly about the Circle Murders. I had to shout above them to make myself heard. "Please, stop. I can't answer any questions about the case. You'll have to talk with the Chiliquitham Police Department or the FBI." When they still persisted in asking questions, I just held up my hand and shook my head. "I'm sorry. I can't comment."

Two of the reporters made a move to follow me inside and I admonished them. "Don't even think about it!"

Looking over my shoulder for intruders, I walked inside and probably gave Monica a really distracted greeting.

Monica was enthusiastic. "Lire! How are you doing? It's so good to see you." Before I could answer, she added with a sympathetic frown, "I'm really sorry to hear about your mom and now your friend Nick."

"Thanks, Monica," I mumbled. I stopped in front of her desk, but kept the front door within sight. "I'm doing okay. It's been one thing after another, but I'm hanging in there. How's it been here?"

A combination of relief and excitement flooded her expression. "Everyone's going to be so glad to see you're okay." She took a big gulp of air and gushed, "Things here have been insane! You wouldn't believe all the calls we've gotten in the last week. And the reporters. Well, you can see for yourself. They've been calling and coming in—all wanting to talk to you or hear about you."

I slapped a hand to my face. "I didn't think about how this whole mess would affect you guys." I sighed. "I guess we'll have to see how it goes, now that I'm here. I'll give you the number of the Chiliquitham Police Department and the name of the person the reporters can contact for information." I pulled out Jensen's business card and wrote down the main number for the station, along with his full name.

I continued, "Just tell them I'm not allowed to comment on the case and they should speak with Lieutenant Jensen. Not that they don't already know this, but if they ask you for the number, at least you have it. Or, you can just hang up on them if you want." I looked again toward the front door. "If they try to come in and it becomes a problem, I'm sure we can call the police for help."

Monica nodded at me. "Don't worry. I'll drive 'em off!" She slapped her fist into the palm of her hand with a hard expression on her face and then laughed. "Jack really let them have it, last week. You should have seen him." We both giggled, and then I took the opportunity to walk back toward my office.

Jake's office was two doors down from mine. The lights were on and the door was open. I peered inside and saw him typing away at his keyboard. He was tall, thin, and had dark-brown, almost black, hair. His face was narrow, dominated by high cheekbones and a slightly upturned nose. I noticed he had attained a bronze tan while on vacation. He and his girlfriend had gone to a resort in Mexico, I recalled.

When I said hello, Jake jumped up to greet me. He looked me over, as if to verify I had indeed recovered from my recent hospital stay. I had to assure him I was fine. After we chatted for a few minutes about his vacation, I filled him in on everything he missed while he had been gone, which turned out to be a lengthy discussion. Not soon after, Nathan, John, and Samantha also arrived at work and joined us in Jake's office. They all seemed excited to see me. After the initial queries regarding the status of my health, they barraged me with questions about my recent experiences with the police and FBI. I gave them answers that didn't compromise the confidential nature of the case, and they were good natured about my evasions, much to my relief. Finally, the conversation turned to the reporters outside and all the publicity. There was considerable speculation about what the media attention would do for our business. After nearly thirty minutes, we finally broke up to meet with clients or push papers or make with the magic.

By the time I walked into my office, I was more than ready to sit down, put my feet up, and spend some time catching up on paperwork. I fully expected e-mail and voicemail messages up the wazoo. A tad daunting, but it felt good to be back at work.

So, I was a little distracted when I entered my darkened office and threw my coat on the spare guest chair next to the door.

A deep, unfamiliar voice came from inside the room. "Hello, Lire."

I gasped and clutched my chest with surprise. My head snapped up, and I zeroed-in on a figure sitting on my bench in front of the window.

An amiable laugh resonated from the shadowed figure. I had a vague sense of broad shoulders and closely cropped hair before I flicked on the lights. The illumination revealed a man, probably in his early thirties, with golden brown hair tied back in a ponytail; large brown, or maybe hazel, eyes; and a swooping, refined nose. All in all, it was an attractive face and it struck me as familiar.

He stood. "I'm sorry I startled you." Although he was smiling, he sounded apologetic.

Put at ease by his amused disposition, I gave him a light scolding. "Jeez! You scared the hell out of me. Who are you? What are you doing in my office? Monica didn't tell me I had a client waiting."

He had a charming smile, revealing teeth straight enough to make an orthodontist proud. "No, she wouldn't. She doesn't remember that I'm here."

I cocked an eyebrow at the strange statement. "Come again?"

He laughed. "You don't remember me either, do you?"

"Uh ..." I shook my head as if to clear it, walked closer to the stranger, and peered at him. "Now that you mention it, you do seem a bit familiar."

The sudden realization sent chills spiraling down my spine.

He tilted his head, examining me. "We were friends at Coventry Academy until I left in the eighth grade. I'm Daniel Stockard."

Without thinking, my hands flew to cover my mouth. I stared at him, focusing on his face, examining his features. It was simply too much of a coincidence. *God.* What would Cunningham think, now?

I forced my hands to my sides. "This is just too weird." I staggered over to my desk chair. Daniel moved out of my way, so I had room to sit. I landed heavily before putting my purse down on the window bench so Red could climb out.

Normally, if Red heard an unfamiliar voice, he'd stay out of sight. Since he knew Daniel, he climbed out.

Daniel looked down. "Hello again, Red."

"Good morning, Daniel. It has certainly been a long time."

I gazed at Daniel and shook my head. "I'm stunned." I laughed. "I don't know what to say."

Then don't say anything, he thought at me.

Already reeling from the shock of seeing him, the intimacy of Daniel's thoughts in my mind was too much. My hand flew up in a blocking gesture as my shield shot to full strength, forcing him from my mind. I gasped and it sounded both surprised and pained.

He stepped closer, hands up. "I'm sorry. I didn't mean to upset you."

I inhaled deeply and nodded at him, waving away his need to apologize. "It's not you. I've had a trying few weeks. This just adds to the list of shocks I've experienced, lately." I straightened my back and gestured for him to sit in the guest chair across from my desk.

He said, "You've grown a lot stronger since I knew you. You never used to be able to push me out like that. I'm impressed."

"You weren't even trying," I chastised, even though I knew it was the truth. "God, Daniel! It's been a while."

He settled into the chair. "I know, and I bet you're wondering why I'm here."

"It doesn't take a mind reader to know that."

He smiled but looked a little sad too. He leaned forward and clasped his hands between his opened knees, resting his elbows on his thighs. It was a friendly, casual pose, but it also conveyed the impression he had something important to say.

"It isn't a coincidence that I'm here at this time in your life." He cocked his head to the side. "Did you ever wonder what happened to me after I left so suddenly from school? For years, I wondered how you were doing and what you were up to."

"Then why didn't you contact me? You could have written me a letter. I was at Coventry for another four-and-a-half years after you left." I peered at him. "No one would tell me what happened to you. At first the staff was nice about it, but after a while they told me to mind my own business or I'd be in trouble. After I graduated and went on to college, I tried a little digging, but the school still wouldn't tell me anything. I gave up. I figured you'd forgotten about me."

"I didn't forget." He sighed and leaned back in the chair. "I wasn't allowed to contact anyone from my past for a very long time. If it weren't for recent events and the fact that I knew you in my past life, I wouldn't even be here now."

I frowned at him. "Why? I don't understand."

He crossed leg over knee to get comfortable and considered me. "Do you remember the day I gave you a false memory about running naked in a field of tulips?"

I blushed. Even after so much time, I still felt the embarrassment associated with our budding sexuality and the progressive change in our relationship from childlike adoration to more adult themes. It was a confusing time, made even more perplexing by the unique way in which we shared the totality of our thoughts with each other.

I replied, "I remember."

"That was the first time I realized I could insert or alter someone else's memories or thoughts."

"Yeah, I remember. We were both surprised." It was thrilling too. I recalled kissing him for the first time in the stairwell behind the library, just before the incident with the tulips.

"Well, that act didn't go unnoticed by certain individuals."

I frowned. "Someone was spying on us?"

He tipped his head in thought. "Sort of, yes. I didn't know it, but representatives from another school had been scanning me. They were keeping an eye out for any indication that I could alter thoughts as well as just read them."

"Oh. So, when they discovered it, they asked you and your parents if you wanted to go to their school instead?"

"No. It wasn't that simple. Or nice. I wasn't given an option." He sighed. "That day, two men showed up and told me they were taking me to their school. When I refused, they said I didn't have a choice. My parents had already agreed to send me, and that was the end of it. The Dean was there and told me the same thing. They forced me to pack all of my things and then escorted me out. I wasn't allowed to say goodbye to anyone, and they arranged it so no one saw me leave. It was one of the worst days of my life."

"But why didn't you write me?"

"I wasn't allowed to contact anyone. Lire, you don't understand. This school ... it's more than just a school. It's a secret organization too. They don't want anyone knowing about them. In fact, they go out of their way to prevent that from happening."

I opened my eyes wide. "You mean they kill them?"

He barked with laughter. "No," he said, quickly turning serious. "Think about it. All they have to do is go and alter someone's memories."

I gazed at him as the murderer's words jumped to mind.

... sooner or later they'll come calling and, believe me, you're no match for them. They don't want the police to catch me, you see. They'll work their deceptions, their subtle magic, and then catching me suddenly won't seem so important ...

They. Could this be the mysterious 'they' the murderer couldn't shut up about? Daniel said it wasn't a coincidence he was here.

I regarded my childhood sweetheart and put all of my energy into creating an impenetrable shield around my thoughts.

"Daniel ..." I made a gesture with my hand, but didn't know what to say.

"Listen, I'm not here to hurt you or mess with your head ... but there are others." He put both feet on the floor and again leaned toward me. "I came here to warn you and to talk to you because you have no idea what a precarious situation you're in."

I decided to play dumb for the time being. "I don't understand. What am I doing that's so terrible? Until now, I didn't know anything about this secret organization. It seems to me you've just put me into danger by coming here to tell me all this."

"You've been told about them, and they know it. Don't deceive yourself. You know what I'm talking about."

I frowned. "The Circle Murders."

"Yes."

"But what do the murders have to do with this secret organization? You said yourself they don't have to go around murdering people." I glared at him. "Dammit! This warlock killed someone I loved! I want him caught, and I'm going to do everything in my power to help that happen. Are you saying this secret group doesn't want him stopped? Do the victim's lives mean so little to them?"

Daniel turned his head to the side and closed his eyes. After a moment, I thought I heard steps in the hallway receding toward the direction of the lobby.

I narrowed my eyes. "You altered Monica's memory, didn't you? That's what you meant about her not remembering you were here." I glanced at my open office door. "And just now, you redirected someone who was coming to check on me, didn't you?"

"Yes. No one can know I'm here."

I groaned with frustration and massaged my temples. Just this morning, I was able to remove the cumbersome bandage on my right hand and it felt good to be rid of it.

I slapped my hands down into my lap and glared at him. "If I stop helping the police, this secret organization will leave me alone. Is that it?"

"Yes."

"And if I don't?"

He sighed. "If you don't, then things will go badly for you. You will inexplicably lose clients. Your friends and family will turn against you. The government will take an interest in your tax returns. Your neighbors will shun you, or the police will decide you're involved in a criminal activity. Or, worse."

I felt sick. I shook my head progressively faster and faster. "No, no ... they can't. They can't."

Daniel looked stricken. "I'm sorry. There's nothing I can do. My superiors asked me to come here. They hope hearing the message from me will make you more inclined to cooperate."

"Daniel, why? I don't understand! Why don't they want the murderer stopped? He's killing psychics for God's sake!"

"They have their reasons." He didn't sound reassuring.

"What reason is there for letting this warlock kill people? He's a warlock! He's not even a telepath!"

Daniel looked at me with a strange expression—a combination of surprise and fear, I decided.

I sat up straight. "Holy crap! He's a telepath *and* a warlock, isn't he?" Thoughts raced around in my head and I couldn't help thinking out loud. "That's why they don't want him caught. He knows about them, doesn't he? Maybe he even went to school with you. He knows about this secret organization, and they don't want him caught because he might reveal things about them." I frowned. "But, that doesn't make any sense. Your group ... they can just alter everyone's memory—pull out any mention of their secret club. When the murderer is first caught, not that many people will have access to him. Why can't they just change everyone's memories, even the killer's?"

Daniel snorted. "We're not gods, Lire. Something of that magnitude is uncontrollable. The spread of thought is a bit like the spread of a virus. Once it gets loose among a group of people, it's virtually unstoppable. It must be contained as much as possible. To do this, it's necessary for the murderer to remain at large until we can catch up to him. It isn't as if we condone his activities. We are using all of our powers to look for him and pursuing every lead possible, just like the police. In fact, we are monitoring the police and the FBI closely. He *is* being pursued. You don't have to worry about that. We want him stopped as much as you do."

I wondered how I was meant to remove myself from the case. The police and FBI expected my help. Was I supposed to just tell them no, without any explanation? I thought about Vince and our budding relationship. How could I say no to him?

"I really don't see how my continued help will change things very much. I mean, if you guys are closely monitoring the situation, can't you just swoop in before he's about to be caught? It's not like I'm going to lead the charge in his capture. I'm just a consultant, not a detective. So far, I haven't told them much more than the connection between all the victims and Nick's study."

Daniel considered me for a moment, clearly considering what to say. "There are other things at work here. Things you don't know. Things even I don't know, although, I've heard a few rumors." He paused in silent thought. "I've been told you're currently one of the individuals centered at a crossroads of timelines. These timelines, or prophecies, concern the murderer and our organization."

I must have looked confused because he shifted to a different subject. "Look, didn't you notice I wasn't the only student at Coventry who left suddenly?"

My thoughts shot back to memories of school and the friends and acquaintances from that time in my life. I tried to recall if anyone else had left in similar circumstances. Vaguely, I remembered a girl a couple of years younger who left suddenly in the middle of the year. I didn't know her personally, but I thought I remembered some hoopla over the incident. And there were several other students who left unexpectedly, but the reason had been attributed to poor grades or just the normal comings and goings that happen when families move to other parts of the country.

He nodded when he noticed my expression. "I can see you do. I'm guessing most of those students were probably either telepaths or diviners."

I examined him as I tried to remember. One of them, the girl that was a few years younger, was indeed a diviner.

"So you're saying this school you went to, this secret organization, they were recruiting diviners *and* telepaths from Coventry?"

"Yes."

If he was going to add anything further, I didn't let him. I plunged ahead. "And Coventry just let them stroll on in and evaluate to their heart's content? And then snap up anyone they thought was a good addition to their secret school?"

This sounded way too farfetched. Coventry had tight security. Any strangers roaming the school, observing students, would have stood out like a goblin at a Tupperware party.

Daniel was unflappable. "Yes. That's exactly what they do."

"Come on, Danny! I would have remembered strangers coming into the school to watch us. It was a closed campus. Remember all the magic we had to use, just to get outside unobserved? And more than half the time we got caught."

He nodded. "I know. I think some of the spies were security guards. And, think about it. Think about how I just got into your office." He raised an eyebrow at me.

I flopped back into my chair. "This sounds completely crazy, you know that?"

Daniel pressed his lips together and shrugged. "I know. But the murderer told you some things that lend credence to what I'm telling you. And, I think you also know I wouldn't lie to you."

"The Daniel I knew, way back when, wouldn't lie to me, but this Daniel," I pointed my finger at him, "I don't know. A lot of years have gone by."

I shook my head and tried to remember why we deviated to the subject of diviners. How did they figure into the conversation? While I was in mid-thought, I heard the sound of footsteps approaching from the direction of Jack's office. Once again, Daniel turned his head and narrowed his eyes in concentration. The footsteps stopped. After a brief moment, I heard them retreat. I imagined Jack walking back to his office, totally unaware he'd been looking for me in the first place. The image was disturbing. I detested him for mucking about in my friend's brains and altering their thoughts.

In spite of my worries, I tried to collect myself. I'd been thinking about diviners. They had the power to see into the future—a small part of the future—but the further they attempted to foresee, the more uncertain their prophecies became.

"You said the people you work for think if I involve myself significantly in the murder investigation, somehow I will ... what? Cause them harm? Diviners in your organization have foreseen this. Is that it?"

"Yes. That's what I've heard. They believe unless you remove yourself from the case, you'll be entangled in the timeline and become part of the future they've foreseen." Daniel gave me a pleading look. "Lire, we are not evil people, but it is paramount that our organization remain secret. Can you imagine what the government would do, not to mention the population at large, if they realize there's a large group of psychics who have the ability to alter their thoughts?"

I sighed. "So, I guess telepathy is not as rare as we've been led to believe?"

Daniel just stared at me with raised eyebrows.

"Right. So, this whole thing is about your secret organization's desire to stay under the radar? And, this warlock, if he's caught, they think he'll blab secrets to so many people that it will compromise their organization?" I laughed. "Give me a break. It's like I've been teleported into some deranged science fiction spy movie."

"I can assure you, this is serious. There are those who will stop at nothing to protect our secrecy. I had to call in several favors just to get permission to speak with you. It's not in their nature to be trusting, but I am one of a growing number who feel strong-arm tactics are not always the best choice of action; especially when another psychic is concerned."

"What? So, the deal is: I stay out of the way or things get nasty?" My anger was growing, despite his placating words. "That sure sounds like strong-arm tactics to me."

"No, Lire. Strong-arming is sending in a group of tele-paths to wipe your mind." He frowned. "Please. I don't want to see that happen to you."

I felt the blood rush out of my face. I didn't know pre-cisely what a mind wipe entailed, but he said it in such a chilling way that I knew it wasn't pleasant.

... let's just say you won't be in your right mind for long ...

I shivered. "God! This is absurd. It's like some twisted nightmare." I slapped both hands to my forehead in frustra-tion and covered my eyes for a moment.

Red spoke from his perch on the window seat. "It's not as though the FBI are solely relying on your help to capture the murderer—you said so yourself. You have been through enough on this case already. I think Cunningham will be more than understanding if you tell him you don't want any further involvement."

I sighed in resignation, although, a part of me railed against being blackmailed into the decision. "Fine." I glared at Daniel. "Go tell your associates your mission was accom-plished."

Daniel stood up, looking regretful. "I will. I'm sorry this had to be the subject of our first meeting after so many years."

"So am I."

He walked to the doorway of my office and turned to me. "Please watch yourself. I've tried to protect you as best I can, but there are others who will be watching you closely. Don't give them reason to ... confront you, okay?"

I snorted. "You mean like confronting me with the front end of a Chrysler, like the other day? Don't worry, I got the message."

He walked partway back into my office, puzzlement plain on his face. "What are you talking about?"

I rolled my eyes. "I guess your secret pals haven't kept you totally informed. Somehow, that doesn't leave me feeling reassured." In fact, the thought terrified me. Maybe this conversation was totally meaningless and a telepathic hit squad was gunning for me regardless of my agreement to stay out of the investigation.

"Tell me."

I sighed. "There's not much to tell. A stolen car attempted to rearrange my internal organs on Saturday—the morning of my scheduled appointment with the FBI." I raised my eyebrow to underline the significance of the last part of the statement.

He shook his head. "No. We don't work that way."

"Uh-huh. Right. Well, be sure to tell your friends not to jump to any conclusions when they see the police or FBI offering me some type of protection. They asked me for my complete schedule. They don't think the hit-and-run was a coincidence. I'm supposed to call them if I need to go out on an appointment with any new clients."

Daniel looked concerned and then closed his eyes in concentration. After nearly thirty seconds, he asked me, "Do you give me your word that you will not participate any further in the murder investigation?"

He hadn't really asked me for a commitment earlier. Now he, or rather, *they*, demanded a promise. Just a guess, but I had a feeling they weren't going to let me go home and think about it.

A dreadful thought came to mind and started to percolate. What if Daniel was somehow involved with the murderer? What if this was just an elaborate ruse to get me to stop helping the police? What if there was no clandestine organization of telepaths and the man in front of me was a stranger in league with the murderer, or even the murderer himself? Terror crept over me like a slow moving wave.

At that moment, I noticed the gold ring on the middle finger of his left hand.

My vision narrowed as a hot flush of adrenaline surged through my veins. Without thinking, I jumped up and backed toward the window seat where Red was sitting. The sudden movement caused my office chair to topple over sideways with a resounding crash. I focused intently on Daniel's behavior. For the moment, he remained near the doorway.

"Stay away from me," I shouted.

Daniel hadn't yet made a move, but he watched me through narrowed eyes. I tried to picture what he would look like with a cape and mask.

"What's wrong?" He took a few steps toward me and raised his palms in a placating manner. The flash of his gold ring taunted me. He asked, "Did you sense my sending?"

He put on a good act, but I remained on guard and redoubled the power of my shield, in case he decided to launch a telepathic attack.

"I don't know you. You could be anyone! How do I know you're really Daniel? How do I know you're not— " I shut my mouth with an audible *clack*.

I should have gone along with him. God, I was an idiot. Now that he knew I was on to him, there was no telling what he would do. I scanned the room for some kind of weapon. I remembered my silver letter opener stashed inside my desk drawer. Before I knew it, I had the sharp implement in my hand and brandished it in Daniel's direction.

He hadn't moved, but the look on his face was not what I expected. He didn't look aggressive or violent in the least. He looked horrified.

"Oh my God! The prophecy," he exclaimed and glanced toward the door.

The sound of many footsteps and concerned voices came from the hall. Clearly, my shouting had been heard by most of my coworkers. Daniel, or whoever he was, clenched his fists and closed his eyes with obvious concentration.

The hallway fell silent.

My terror ran up another notch. I was alone and without help. The impersonator, now blocking the doorway, had the power to send away anyone wanting to help me. What was I going to do? While I waited for inspiration to strike, I stared wide-eyed at the faux Daniel, letter opener still clutched in my hand. I watched as he opened his eyes and slowly sat down in the guest chair he had occupied earlier. He put his head in his hands.

This strange behavior had the effect of bringing me down from my adrenaline high, although, my heart still raced.

I regained enough sense to ask, although not as politely as I might have otherwise, "You're still gong on about that freaking prophecy? Are you kidding?"

Here I was, brandishing a knife at him, and he starts babbling about the supposed prophecy. What the hell?

He glared at me. "How long have you been able to do that?"

"Do what? What the hell are you talking about?" I had serious doubts about the sanity of the man sitting in front of me, and that thought alone almost sent me into adrenaline orbit all over again.

Daniel looked at me as though I was completely bonkers. "*Levitate*! What do you mean, 'Do what?' You just telekinetically grabbed the knife from your desk!"

I looked at the knife in my hand, like it might suddenly sprout wings, and then at my opened desk drawer. "You're out of your mind! I grabbed it myself, just now ... because you're the damn murderer! Get the hell out of my office!"

"You're the one who's out of her mind. Jesus, Lire. What the hell is wrong with you? One minute you're talking calmly and the next minute you're threatening me with a knife and calling me a murderer. What set you off?"

I looked at him and didn't know what to say. If he was the murderer, or in league with the murderer, then this innocent routine was sure convincing.

"Red? What should I do? I don't know what to do." I felt like collapsing on the floor and curling into a ball. Everything was spinning out of control.

Red spoke in his usual calm manner. "Follow your instincts. I believe this to be Daniel, just as you do. At the moment, he is not offering you harm. Keep on your guard, but talk to him. One thing is certain, however. Daniel is correct. You did not physically grab the knife from your desk. You did it with your mind, not your body."

I gasped and dropped the knife. I at least had the sense to jump back, so it didn't spear my foot. It landed with a *clank* and skittered under my desk.

"But, but th-that's not puh-possible!"

No psychic *ever* had more than one power.

It had something to do with the different energies involved. The powers didn't mix. Well, that was one theory. Others claimed more than one power diluted a person's ability to wield magic, which was why witches and warlocks needed rituals and runes to focus their power. Truthfully, nobody really understood it. It's just the way things were. It's what made psychics different from the other spell casters. A psychic never had more than one gift. Period. End of story.

The idea that I somehow had acquired more than one psychic talent was unfathomable. One power was what defined me as a psychic. Having more than one power made me something … else.

I backed up against the window seat and sat down hard.

"So you're saying you didn't know you had this ability?" Daniel looked at me with narrowed, disbelieving eyes.

"No! I mean yes. I didn't know. I still don't know." I shook my head. "But Red says I did it, so I guess it's true. How can that be? It's impossible."

"God! What are we going to do?" He quickly amended, "What am *I* going to do?" Daniel's face contorted into an expression of grave worry.

"What are you talking about?"

"The prophecy! This is part of it." He stood. "I have to go. Shit! I wish I hadn't seen you do that. They're going to find out and God help you when they do."

His grim demeanor frightened me. I practically screeched, "What? Daniel, what's going on? What do you mean?"

"There's not much else I can do for you now. I'm sorry. I've done what I could, and I'll see what else I can do, but ..." He shook his head and moved toward the door.

I jumped up. "Wait! Daniel, don't go. Please. I don't understand. What is going on? Why have things changed? I told you I'd stop with the investigation."

"I don't think that matters now. They were hoping to stop you before the crossroads. Now, I'm afraid it's too late."

"*Dammit*! I don't understand! Please, stay and talk to me. Tell me what's going on."

"I'm sorry. Truly I am, but there's nothing more I can do. If I say anything else, I put the both of us at risk. I have to go."

I protested, but Daniel strode from my office. He was through my office door and into the hallway before I had even come around my desk. In the hallway, Jake, Jack, and Samantha headed toward me, totally oblivious to the man who had just run past. Jack asked whether I wanted to go with them for a coffee, and it took me precious moments to skirt around them. By the time the lobby came into view, Daniel was gone. I rushed to the front door, but the reporters were there, blocking my way. I knew Daniel had telepathically alerted them so I couldn't follow.

Stymied, I turned to Monica. She regarded me with a confused but amiable expression. "What's up? You expecting someone?"

Before I could respond, Jack and the gang walked into the lobby and asked where I was going in an all fired hurry.

I don't think I've ever felt so completely lost and confused. What the hell was going on? What was I supposed to believe? I didn't bother asking the others whether they had seen Daniel or felt his presence in their minds. It was obvious they had no recollection of the heated exchange in my office, the redirection of their actions, or Daniel's rapid exit.

Red. I needed to talk to Red. He'd help me figure out what to do.

Quickly covering my distress, I apologized, made an excuse about having a client to deal with, and managed to get back to my office without company. I closed the door behind me. It was meager protection against a possible telepath attack, but the secured door felt reassuring nevertheless. Red stood next to my desk.

"Jesus fucking Christ! What the hell is going on?" I didn't swear often, but Red was hardly a prude and the profanity helped to exorcise some of my pent up fear.

"I do not know, but we will discuss it. You need to calm down so we can consider all the facts, meager as they are, and then we can contrive a course of action." He paused and tilted his head. "Lire, you are not without power. You are not helpless. We will be all right."

I walked over to my overturned office chair and struggled to get it upright. Red climbed into his usual position on the bench.

Pacing back and forth in front of the window, I fretted, "That was Daniel, wasn't it?"

"What do *you* think?"

I sighed and plopped down into my chair. "I thought so. He tried to think to me, just like we used to, but I shut him out. It was too overwhelming." I leaned my head back and thought back to my impression of Daniel. "But then I started to worry maybe he wasn't really Daniel—that he was actually the murderer." I cringed. "Now it seems stupid, but right then I saw his ring, looking just like the murderer's. And it was on the same finger."

"And then you panicked?"

I nodded. "I couldn't help it. I mean, all the crazy stuff he was saying, it sounded just like the murderer. It seemed like something the murderer would do, just to get me off the case. And the ring was glinting, just like in Jason and Trinity's memories." I threw up my hands. "I don't know. Things just spiraled from there. His voice didn't sound the same as the one I heard in my readings, but maybe the murderer has an accomplice. God! It's all so confusing."

Red perched against his basket of books and brought his paws together over his tummy. "I believe the main problem is you were being asked to take Daniel's word about this secret organization and that he was their messenger. If you don't trust the messenger, then the message will be in doubt too. Is that not the case?"

"Yeah, I suppose so. I haven't spoken to him for years. I can hardly say I know him any more. He's practically a stranger. And then I started to consider the possibility he was a fake. He could be a telepath who stole Daniel's memories."

Red nodded. "There are three main possibilities. One—there is a secret organization and Daniel was here to deliver their message; two—there is no secret organization and Daniel, or an impostor, is in league with the murderer; or three—someone within the FBI, or knowledgeable about the case, wants you removed so badly they'd risk hiring a telepath to impersonate Daniel. Those are the only three scenarios that explain the messenger's knowledge of what you recently told the FBI."

I thought things over. "Yes, I guess, but was it really Daniel?"

"Presumably not many people know about your past history with him, especially the incident with the tulips."

"That's true. Until this visit, I assumed only Daniel and I knew of that particular event. And you, of course, since I told you about it after it happened."

Red sat next to the basket, crossing his legs, and gestured with his paw. "So that, in addition to the similarity in appearance and voice pattern, strongly indicates to me the man here today was, in all probability, Daniel."

"Yeah. I suppose." I shrugged. "Even though I think the notion of a secret society of telepaths with a mind-wiping hit squad is completely outlandish, there are just too many similarities. He did mention the thing with the tulips and he thought to me telepathically. I suppose it's possible another telepath acquired this information from Daniel, but there's the strong resemblance and his voice to consider too. It was so long ago, but the way he talked was the same, don't you think? His voice was just deeper?" I groaned in frustration and banged the back of my head against the chair. "I keep doubting myself just a little, but you're right. It was Daniel."

Red nodded. "So, we agree. The man here today was indeed Daniel. That eliminates the third scenario then, unless you think he works for the FBI and wants you off the case? Or that someone inside the FBI asked him to come and threaten you in order to remove you from the investigation?"

"Both of those scenarios seem pretty unlikely. And, besides, the Daniel I knew and loved wouldn't do something like that to me."

"Then we are left with scenario one or two." When I nodded, he said, "If you don't think Daniel would threaten you to get you off the case for personal reasons or because someone from the FBI asked him to, then you cannot honestly believe he is in league with the murderer."

I sighed. "No. I wouldn't think so."

"Lire, there are two circumstances to consider—either you believe Daniel is capable of murder, or at least accessory to murder, or he was telling the truth about being a member of a secret telepath and diviner organization." He tilted his head. "Which is the more plausible?"

I slouched to the side, resting my uninjured elbow on the arm of my chair. "When you put that way, I guess we're back to believing what he said about the secret organization. And I suppose that's why he and the murderer have the same ring. It's probably some secret *club* ring." I know that last bit sounded sarcastic and bitter, but I couldn't help it. I was angry at being manipulated by some secret, nefarious organization that sent old friends to threaten me into doing their bidding.

"Yes."

"Hell. Now what do I do? Presumably some fanatical telepathic hit squad could come after me at any time, as farfetched as that sounds."

"Get back home. You will be safe there. Then we can think about what to do."

The wards. Yes. The wards of my building would keep any telepathic attack at bay. The djinn and security guards would protect me from any other physical attack. But what about my friends? My family? My coworkers?

I sat up straight. "Red. What about all the other things Daniel said? What about all his other threats? They can turn everyone against me."

He stood and stepped as close as the bench would allow. "You can't worry about that right now. First things first. We need to get back home and then we can think about what to do. But you should call Vince immediately. Tell him to meet you at your apartment."

"But won't that just drag him into this? I don't want him to get hurt."

He put a paw on my knee. "I don't know, but you need help. At least when Vince is in your building, he will be safe."

"Yeah, but he'll have to leave at some point."

Red sighed. "We will deal with that later."

Still doubtful, I punched up Vince's cell number. He answered on the second ring. "Lire? Hey, what's up?"

Tears threatened to taint my voice. "Hi, um, I've got a problem. There's been an incident at my office."

"What? What happened? Are you okay?" Over his concerned voice, I heard traffic noises in the background.

"Yes, I'm fine, just a bit shook up. Can you meet me at my apartment? I need to get home where I know I'll be safe."

"Don't move. You're at your office? I'm on my way. I was in the area anyway. I can be there in ten minutes." I heard the sound of wind buffeting the telephone and Vince's elevated breathing. After a moment, a car door slammed. He spoke above the noise. "What happened? You sound upset."

"Someone came to see me a few minutes ago. Remember the guy I mentioned in my interview with the FBI? Daniel. The one who left Coventry when I was in eighth grade?"

"The one you nearly killed yourself over. He came to see you?"

"Yes." I hesitated, trying to figure out how much to say. "And he said some pretty frightening things."

"Like what? Did he threaten you? Did he try to hurt you?"

"No, but he said a group he's involved with isn't happy with me. He implied they might try and hurt me. It made me think of what the murderer said. God, I don't know! He said a lot of things that seem ludicrous, but it scared me. I don't know what to do. Red told me I should get home where I'll be safe."

"Okay, but I'd like you to wait for me. I don't want you going out by yourself. You're safer in the building. What else did this guy say to you? Start at the beginning."

I blew out an anxious breath and tried to calm down, think about things rationally. In detail, I relayed what Daniel told me about his involvement with the telepathic organization and how they forcibly recruited him from Coventry.

Vince asked, "And he said this group isn't happy with you and they want to hurt you? What do they want?"

I tightened my grip on the telephone. "To stop involving myself with the Circle Murder investigation."

"What? Did he threaten you?"

My eyes roamed around the office and then settled on the door. I could feel panic leaking into my system again as I considered Daniel's warnings. I remembered how he easily redirected everyone in the office.

"Vince ... telepaths are powerful. I mean, think about it. Really, really think about it."

He didn't say anything for a few seconds. "You said this friend from school ... he could alter your memory?"

"Yes."

"And they can insert false memories?"

Even though he couldn't see me, I nodded. "Yes."

After another brief silence, he said, "They can control you."

"Yes. And they can destroy your mind. He called it a mind wipe." I shuddered.

Vince was quiet, but the sound of road noise came through in the background. He muttered, "Jesus Christ."

Once again, I hovered on the verge of tears.

"Why do they want you to stay out of the investigation?" he asked.

"That's where things get a little weird. To be honest, I'm not too clear on that. He said it was because of some kind of prophecy."

I told Vince about the power of divination and Daniel's comments about the supposed prophecy. "If I stay involved in the investigation, they believe I'll become tangled up in an event that will ... gosh, I don't know, compromise the secrecy of their organization or something like that." I grunted. "It's completely insane. And then, to make matters worse, I did something that totally freaked him out. He ran out! He said there was nothing else he could do to help me and they were going to come after me."

"He ran away? Did anyone else see him?"

I choked out a laugh. "He's a telepath, remember? He altered their memories. Jake, Samantha, and Jack were all standing in the hall when he bolted out of my office. He pushed right past them. They were in the hallway and said nothing! They don't even remember hearing us argue and me screaming at him." I hesitated before continuing, my voice grim. "Vince, if they really want to get me, there's absolutely nothing that will stop them. Daniel's visit here proved that."

"But you said you'd be safe in your apartment."

"True. But I can't stay inside forever and I can't control what they might do to my friends, my family. He even suggested they could enthrall the police into thinking I'm a criminal. My apartment is safe, but there are still ways to get to me."

"That's crazy. An entire police force? Look, don't worry. I'm almost to your office. He's probably just some lunatic who saw you on the news and remembered you from school. You knew him a long time ago. Anything could have happened to him. There's no telling what he's like now."

"I wish you're right, but he sure didn't come off like he's crazy. And how does he know about the murderer's comments about some group coming after me? That's not in the news."

"We'll sort it out," he told me. "I just pulled into the lot. I'll be right in."

I hung up and then hurried out of my office to the lobby. Vince was just walking up to the glass door as I neared Monica's desk.

Monica looked up at Vince when the door opened. She sat up especially straight in her chair, just to show off her assets. "Can I help you?"

"He's here to see me, Monica," I said from behind her.

She turned around to see me standing just outside of her field of vision. "Hey. I didn't see you there. So I guess this is who you were looking for earlier." She smiled brightly, directing much of the radiance in Vince's direction.

I replied, "Uh, yeah."

Vince looked puzzled, but before he could say anything, I introduced him to Monica. They said hello, and I cut short any chitchat by suggesting he follow me to my office, but Vince paused for a moment at her desk.

He looked down at her with an amiable but serious expression. "Monica, have you seen anyone you didn't know come in or leave since Lire arrived at work this morning?"

She looked pleased to have Vince's attention. "Nope. Just the usual crowd."

"Did you leave the lobby at any time?" he asked.

She shook her head, and it seemed to me she made sure her hair slithered over a slightly raised shoulder. It wasn't anything I hadn't seen a hundred times before, but given my current state of agitation, all the provocative gestures made me want to smack her upside the head.

"Um, no, I've been here the whole time. Is everything okay? Did a reporter sneak in or something?" She looked back and forth between Vince and me with a worried expression and wide eyes.

Vince smiled, projecting calm. "That's what I'm checking out. Thanks."

Monica beamed at Vince again, watching us as we headed to my office. When we got there, Vince stopped me from closing the door.

"Wait. Did he touch the door when he came in or when he left?"

I thought about it. "No. I don't think so. The door was open when I got here, but that's not unusual." I told him about how I discovered Daniel in my office.

Vince nodded and then closed the door behind us. When he turned toward me, I dove into his arms. He embraced me, rubbed my back, and said he was glad I was okay.

I acknowledged his words with a small nod of my head, inhaling his scent. After a moment, he squeezed my shoulders, pushing me away to look into my eyes. "I need you to tell me everything, but first, do you remember if he touched anything in here?"

Reluctantly, I stepped out of his arms and looked around the room. "There's the chair of course." I motioned at the guest chair. "But I don't know if he touched it when he sat down. I wasn't really paying attention." I shook my head, trying not to feel helpless. "We didn't close the door, so there won't be anything on the inside knob, but he did run out of here through the lobby's front door. I didn't think to tell people not to use it, so who knows whether any prints are still there."

"Since it's a door you push, we probably wouldn't get anything useful there anyway." He turned to the guest chair. "He sat here? Did he have anything to drink or touch anything else you can think of?"

"I don't think so." I looked toward the window seat. "Red?"

"He sat in the chair, like you said. He did not touch anything else."

Vince got out his notepad and pen. "Tell me what he looked like. I'm going to put out an all points. How tall is he?"

"I don't know, about five-eleven? You agree, Red?"

"Yes, he was several inches taller than you."

"He has a medium build, not bulky but not skinny either." I shrugged. I never realized just how difficult it was to describe someone in detail, especially someone who had been in my office for only ten or fifteen minutes.

"Caucasian?" Vince asked.

"Yes."

"What color hair, eyes?"

I frowned. "Light brown hair, straight, tied back in a pony tail, so I guess it's probably shoulder length. Nice hairline, not thinning or receding. Hazel eyes." I tried to think of anything else to add. "Uh, clean shaven, good complexion." I shrugged again.

"Any unique facial markings, moles, scars, that kind of thing? Was he wearing glasses?"

"No glasses and no facial markings that I can remember."

Vince gestured with the hand holding his pen. "And you're certain this was your friend from school? Daniel Stockard?"

"Yes. As certain as I can be after not seeing him for seventeen years."

Vince seemed surprised. "How can you be certain at all?"

"He mentioned several things that aren't common knowledge. And he spoke to me telepathically." I peered at him. "I'm ninety-nine percent sure, and Red agrees."

He nodded. "I want to know what he said to you, but first, do you remember what he was wearing?"

I closed my eyes, trying to visualize Daniel in my mind. "He was wearing a dark-brown leather jacket and khakis, I think. He might have had on a button down shirt under the jacket. I'm sorry. I should have been paying more attention to stuff like that."

"It's okay. That happens. What about you, Red? Anything to add?"

"His shirt was a plaid of some type and mostly red, I believe. And he wore brown leather boots."

I gasped. "The ring! I almost forgot. He had a ring that reminded me of the murderer's, on the middle finger of his left hand." I shook my head. "That's when things really got crazy—when I noticed the ring. It scared the crap out of me."

Vince studied me. "You think he was the murderer?"

"No, no. I freaked out when I saw the ring and started jumping to conclusions, but now that I've had time to think about it, I'm sure Daniel isn't the murderer. For one thing, their voices don't match. I think they have the same ring because they're both members of this secret society." I shrugged. "That's my theory, anyway. It could also be total coincidence that they both wear a similar looking signet ring on the same finger of the same hand." I cocked an eyebrow at him.

He grunted and jotted down some more notes before pulling out his cell phone. "I'm going to call this in."

"Okay."

"Don't touch the chair. I'll need to dust it for prints."

I picked up my coat, which was draped across my second guest chair—the slightly wobbly one I kept next to the door—and tossed the garment aside. It ended up in a heap on the floor, but I didn't care. I sat and listened to Vince's telephone calls.

Not only did Vince telephone Jensen but also Agent Cunningham. He didn't mention any speculation about a telepathic hit team, only saying I had been threatened with physical harm. Even though I heard just one side of the conversation, I got the gist Cunningham wanted us to meet down at the FBI offices. I worried about what the secret organization was going to think about me tromping down to the FBI offices again, but knew it was useless to protest.

After Vince dusted both arms of the chair for fingerprints, we took his Jeep to the FBI office. I told him my car was certainly safer with its armor plating, but Vince's car had the police radio and emergency lights with siren, and that was the end of the discussion. He wouldn't hear of me following behind in my car.

SEVENTEEN

The FBI office was little changed from when I had seen it on Saturday, other than a well-lit lobby with receptionist and the general feeling that more people were working in the sea of soft-walled cubicles. Once again, Agent Cunningham escorted Vince and me to the large conference room.

I greeted Agent Cheung, and then Cunningham told us to take a seat. We ended up, more or less, in our previous positions. With Jensen absent, Vince sat in the chair immediately to my left. The microphone and camera tripod were set up and a psi-wrapped water bottle waited for me at the head of the table. The guys spent time fixing coffee for themselves while I invited Red to join us.

As soon as everyone had settled, Cunningham clicked his computer to start the video recording and then asked me to recount my encounter with Daniel. I started at the beginning, explained how Daniel was waiting for me when I first entered my office, and slowly described our meeting.

Agent Cunningham stopped me almost immediately to ask for a complete description of Daniel, which was easy since it was fresh in my mind from my discussion with Vince. After I told him everything I could remember about his appearance, I continued my account, stopping to answer frequent questions from Vince and Cunningham and allowing Red's occasional comment.

When I had finished, Cunningham sat back in his chair, gesturing at me with his pen. "And what do you think of all this, Ms. Devon? Do you really believe there's a secret tele-path society capable of doing all the things Mr. Stockard threatened? To be honest, I'd always thought telepathy was a myth. I've heard rumors of the existence of mind readers, but not the ability to alter someone's thoughts."

I pressed my lips together and shrugged. "I don't know what to think. All I know is the possibility terrifies me. I re-member what Daniel did to me back in eighth grade. He im-planted an absurd memory into my mind." I shook my head, frowning. "If he hadn't warned me ahead of time about what he planned to do, I never would have been able to distin-guish it from a real memory." I leaned forward in my chair. "And I saw what he did to my coworkers. I heard them com-ing to help me—their footsteps, their worried voices—and then Daniel closed his eyes and everything went silent."

Red held up his pudgy paw. "Agent Cunningham, I can attest there have been many secret organizations through-out history. Some of them still around to this day, for both magic users and normal people alike. In fact, back in my hu-man days, I belonged to a secret society of necromancers. At that time, the use of magic had been driven underground because anyone suspected of having such a skill was at risk of being executed. I do not find it difficult to believe a secret society of telepaths and diviners exists in our midst. It is not uncommon for outcasts to band together for strength and protection."

"So you believe Ms. Devon is in danger and the rest of us are helpless subjects of possible mind control?" Cunning-ham asked.

"Yes. Although whether or not they will choose to esca-late the situation remains to be seen," Red answered. "Until now, they have kept to the shadows. If this group is working to apprehend the murderer prior to the authorities, then they are doing so carefully. They are aware any obvious moves against Lire could potentially draw even more atten-tion to their existence."

Vince grunted. "Although they may not all be on the same page about that. There's the hit-and-run to think about, unless we all think it was just a coincidence."

After a moment of silence, Cunningham asked, "Is there anything we can do to protect ourselves against a telepath?"

I replied, "No. Not for a normal anyway. Not without the help of magic. That's why my apartment is safe. Powerful wards were put into place during construction and they restrict any hostile magical incursion. But, outside the wards, only a skilled magic user who is practiced with shielding techniques would be able to fight one off. It would be a battle of wills. And if there were more than one telepath ..." I shook my head.

Cunningham narrowed his eyes. "This all sounds completely improbable. If this group exists, why aren't we living in a world run by psychics right now?"

Red answered, "What makes you think we aren't? They may be manipulating things behind the scenes. But, that said, Daniel acknowledged they don't have God-like power. There are billions more normal people than there are telepaths. A telepath can control only so many at a time. This is why they keep their society secret. They fear possible retribution from the government or from society in general. I believe they have stayed a secret for so long because they have used their skills with restraint and avoided overusing their magic."

Cunningham looked thoughtful and then gestured toward me. "We've deviated from your account, Ms. Devon. Please continue."

I thought back to my encounter with Daniel and told them how I had agreed to back off of the case. "When Daniel turned to leave, he warned me about not giving them any reason to come after me. That's when I mentioned the hit-and-run, but Daniel seemed certain his group had nothing to do with it."

When I told them how I practically jumped out of my skin upon noticing Daniel's ring, Cunningham perked up. "What did the ring look like, exactly?"

I tried to visualize it. "It was a signet ring of some kind, gold, with a square bezel, just like the murderer's. I think it had a design on the face of it, but I didn't notice the detail." I sighed and shook my head. "Once I saw the ring, on the same finger of the same hand, not to mention the same shape, I lost it. He hadn't done anything to indicate he intended to physically harm me, but I flipped out anyway." I hesitated, unable to stop myself from tucking nonexistent stray hairs behind my ear. I forced out, "That's when I remembered the letter opener inside my desk."

Their gazes sharpened. Had I done something illegal?

Vince coaxed me, "It's okay. You were scared. Tell us what happened next."

I tried not to squirm in my chair. I told them about brandishing the knife and Daniel's strange reaction. When it came time to tell them about the levitation, I stopped. Agent Cunningham regarded me with a friendly expression and encouraged me to continue.

I stammered, "Uh, instead of attacking me or something, Daniel told me, well, he told me I'd just levitated the knife into my hand." I frowned and sank down into my chair. "I just couldn't believe it. I didn't remember doing anything of the sort. But then Red told me I had levitated the knife ..."

I wrapped my arms around myself, averting my eyes to avoid their penetrating gazes. "That scared me too. Daniel was really upset—not violent, just really, really freaked out—which is understandable since I had just done something totally *effing abnormal*." I couldn't suppress a shudder. "Then he said there was nothing else he could do to help me. It was part of the prophecy, or something." I threw up my hands and grunted. "He basically said I was screwed and then took off."

Cunningham asked, "And this thing with the letter opener, this levitation, you weren't aware you had done it?"

I shook my head, keeping my gaze firmly fixed to the table in front of me.

"And you believe that act caused him to flee? You're both psychics. Why would that upset him?"

Agent Cheung spoke up for the first time, his voice forceful in spite of his slight appearance. "Psychics never have more than one talent. It would be like you suddenly waking up with an extra arm."

When I looked up, Cunningham regarded the agent with a perplexed expression. "Okay, so what Ms. Devon did was extremely unusual— "

"Sir, not just unusual but completely unprecedented. My analogy is not an exaggeration." His demeanor remained impassive, but I sensed an undercurrent of unease in his voice.

Cunningham sighed, nodding at Cheung. "Okay, unprecedented." He returned his gaze to me and said, "But you implied his reaction was not just to the levitation. You said he mentioned the prophecy again?"

I nodded while struggling with my emotions. Agent Cheung's response, although controlled, was unsettling. I replied, "He said something about a crossroad in the time-lines. They wanted to reach me before that point. I assume to redirect the prophecy. My ability to levitate had something to do with that. He said he wished he hadn't seen me do it, they would find out about it. And he said something like, 'God help you when they do.'" I bit my lip and clasped my trembling hands in my lap.

"And he ran out of your office after that?" Vince asked.

"Yes."

Cunningham shifted in his chair and tapped the end of his pen on the notepad in front of him. "You said he did something to your coworkers. Did they see Daniel, either coming or going?"

"No, and he ran right past them. If he hadn't altered their thoughts, there is no possible way they could have missed him."

Vince told him about questioning Monica and dusting my guest chair for fingerprints.

Cunningham nodded at the new information and wrote something down in his notebook. "Ms. Devon, after this incident, did you ask any of your coworkers whether they had seen Daniel or heard your argument?"

I shook my head and snorted. "No. I didn't bother. It was clear Daniel had altered their minds. So I knew it was useless to even ask."

"After Daniel ran out, that's when you telephoned Detective Vanelli?"

"Yes."

He paused and then discreetly looked at Cheung, who nodded subtly in return. I knew without asking that Agent Cheung had just verified the truth of my words.

Cunningham considered Red. "Red, do you have anything to add?"

"No. She has covered all the important points. It happened exactly as she described."

Cunningham shifted his gaze to my face. "Then I'd say the chance of apprehending Mr. Stockard would likely be slim to none." He sighed. "I'll put out the all points for his detention anyway. I wouldn't mind speaking with Mr. Stockard about this incident myself. Who knows, maybe we'll get lucky." He sounded doubtful.

"What about Lire?" Vince asked after a moment.

"I don't suppose there's any way you can work from home for the time being?" Cunningham ventured. "I'll speak with our resident magic users. Maybe we can come up with something that will offer some protection. But it seems to me, out of all of us, Ms. Devon and possibly Agent Cheung are the only ones capable of protecting themselves from a telepath, if I understood correctly."

I nodded. "I can check with my own contacts as well, but I can tell you a talisman won't come cheaply. A ward of this nature will take quite a bit of time and energy to create, and it has to be imprinted on the person it's supposed to shield. You can't just buy a box of them and then hand them out to all your employees like pocket protectors."

For the first time, I heard Agent Cheung chuckle. Cunningham grunted with amusement.

"It can never be simple, can it?" Vince muttered.

Agent Cunningham clicked something on his computer and then looked over at Vince and me. "I'll send someone to Ms. Devon's office to check things out. Detective, go ahead and take Ms. Devon back to her apartment. Find out what you can about possible wards and check back with me later."

I tried not to mope. I was happy to spend more time around Vince, but the circumstances left a lot to be desired.

After saying goodbye to the agents, Vince led the way to the building's elevators. A few people from higher floors were already in the car. While we traveled downward, I wondered what their jobs were. Two of them didn't seem like agent types. Maybe they were administrators or executive assistants. I noticed Vince surreptitiously scrutinize all of them, even though we had agreed an escalation of the situation was unlikely.

The elevator made several stops before we finally emerged into the parking garage, unaccompanied. The chill in the air made me shiver as we began walking down the aisle toward Vince's Jeep.

"You okay?" he asked while fumbling in his coat pocket for his keys.

Lost in thought, I shook myself and glanced over at him. "Yeah. It was just so warm in there, so it feels chilly down here."

Ahead of us, a car door closed, and we both looked down the aisle to see a person walking in our direction. After a moment, we both recognized Jensen.

"Hey, Rich," Vince called.

Jensen appeared distracted and didn't immediately respond to Vince's hail. I smiled when I heard him whistling *Zip-A-Dee-Doo-Dah*.

"You meeting with Cunningham?" Vince's voice echoed inside the enclosed space.

I wondered whether Jensen was wearing earbuds. He still hadn't acknowledged us or focused on our approach, even though we were close enough to see one another readily.

Vince chuckled and mumbled something about him zoning out. "Hello! Jensen!" He waved his hand to get his attention.

I finally understood the cause of Jensen's inattention. I threw all of my strength into my shield, just as a powerful force tried to hammer its way into my mind. With a cry, I fell to my knees and channeled everything I had into maintaining the force of my shield.

"Jen—" Vince stopped, obviously taken aback by my sudden collapse and cry of agony. "Lire!"

I sensed Vince next to me. "What's wrong? Rich, where are you *going*?"

I felt Red force his way out of my purse.

I clasped my hands to the sides of my head and shrieked, "*No!*"

It took all of my concentration to keep the intruder out of my head. I couldn't spare the effort to tell Vince to run away. There was safety in numbers. It was imperative he retreat to the FBI office as quickly as possible. But I could do little except grunt from the physical exertion and mental pain of the telepath's attack.

"She is being assailed by a telepath," Red exclaimed. "We need to get her out of here."

Red, no! I tried to yell at Vince to run, but every time I made the attempt, my concentration slipped and I had to fight to regain the strength of my shield. I could only leave a small part of my consciousness aware of my surroundings, but that was all.

Red shouted, "Get her back to the elevator. Follow Lieutenant Jensen. Our only option is to find safety upstairs. Do it!"

I felt Vince grab me under the arms and drag me backwards. I could do nothing to help him and forced myself to remain limp. There was no way I could devote the energy to standing and walking.

"Lire, help me," Vince scolded.

"She cannot! Don't disturb her concentration. She needs all of her focus and energy to keep them out of her mind," Red said.

Vince struggled with my body and, over his exertions, forced out, "Where are they? Are they down here?"

"Yes, almost certainly."

"Then as soon as I get Lire to the elevator, I'm going after them."

What was the matter with him? Wasn't he paying attention earlier? There was no way he had any hope of going up against a telepath, never mind more than one. And I knew there were at least two telepaths in the vicinity because one was attacking me and the other had attacked Jensen.

I was about to risk ordering Vince to leave them alone when the psychic attack redoubled. Now I battled two telepaths, probably because the second telepath no longer needed to redirect Jensen. The tentative grasp I held on my surroundings vanished, and all my strength went into protecting my mind.

If I hadn't already been on the ground, the pain would have dropped me in an instant. I'd never realized a forceful psychic entry could be so debilitating. When Daniel and I had played the power game as kids, his attempted incursions never caused me pain, presumably because I knew it was safe to let him break through. I always cried uncle when his probes got too strong for my shield. But this was no game. These telepaths were malicious. Their incursion not only threatened my memories and thoughts, but my life as well. And I'd be damned if I let them inside!

The attack weakened as one of the telepaths withdrew from my mind. I took the opportunity to thrust a spike of energy into the remaining intruder's presence. My shield pushed him away, giving me some breathing room. I became aware of my surroundings but didn't risk opening my eyes.

"Were you trying to go back upstairs?" A malignant voice came from somewhere to my right.

Vince no longer supported my weight. I sprawled on my side on the cold ground. The way the voice echoed, I assumed we were still in the garage.

"What are you going to do, Detective? Shoot an unarmed man?"

Vince's voice was steadfast. "No witnesses. I might just do that. Thanks for the suggestion."

The man snorted. "My. You are a cocky one. You obviously have no idea who you're dealing with. Maybe we'll *tell* you all about it." He chuckled. "Lire could tell you, but she doesn't look like she's feeling up to it right now."

Oooh! I quelled the reckless impulse to launch myself at that voice and kick him in the nuts. If my concentration wavered, I knew they'd waste no time before penetrating my defenses. My anger smoldered while I continued to focus on keeping the remaining telepath out of my mind.

An unsettling silence ensued, mostly because my eyes were closed and I couldn't see what was going on. After a few moments, Vince replied, "Yes. I'm waiting. You were going to tell me about just who I'm dealing with?"

Something was wrong. The probe into my mind withdrew. After a moment, I opened my eyes and saw a man with mousy brown hair standing about ten feet away. He wore a tightly belted black raincoat, black gloves, and gray slacks. His furtive scowl was directed at something to my right and it made his already narrow face look even more rodent-like.

I remained motionless as I considered my available options. I was determined to help Vince, but I had no weapons at my disposal. Even if I did, I'd never handled a gun in my life. My first weapon-wielding experience had been the letter opener, hardly a stellar encounter. Anyway, Vince had a gun and it was useless, unless he wanted to shoot an unarmed man.

With no other option, I decided to risk sitting up while continuing to channel all of my energy into the strength of my shield.

Vince stood over me. Currently, the gun was trained on a man nearest the elevator, who looked back at Vince with a strained and fierce expression. He was fat and completely bald with thick lips and blunt features. His thick, camel-colored wool coat only added to his sausage-like appearance.

Not feeling terribly predisposed toward liking either telepath, I decided to call the fat one 'Sausage-Man' and the one in the trench coat 'Rat-Face.' At least, in my head.

Rat-Face glanced down at me momentarily before returning his attention to Sausage-Man. They both looked perplexed and perhaps a little worried.

Vince said, "Okay. I've had enough of this. You both are under arrest. Put your hands on your head. Now!"

Instead of complying with Vince's command, Sausage-Man chuckled. "Why? We simply inquired as to whether you were trying to go upstairs. You plan on arresting us for that? I think your friends at the FBI will be wondering what has gotten into you, Detective." As I expected, his was the menacing voice I had heard moments earlier, when I had been occupied by the other telepath.

"I guess we'll find out when we get there, won't we?" Vince retorted.

I glanced up at him. "Vince. Don't go there. You have to trust me."

I knew if we all trooped back upstairs with the two telepaths in tow, things would not go well. In fact, the telepaths were bound to alter the situation to their advantage and discredit anything Vince or I could possibly say. Or worse. All the agents carrying weapons sprang to mind. It wouldn't take much prodding of minds to have an accidental sidearm discharge in my general direction, especially if the telepaths were feeling forced into a corner.

"What? You want me to let them go?"

I touched his leg. "Yes. I'll explain later."

Sausage-Man turned his gaze on me. "You have won this round, but don't let it go to you head. You won't always have the protection of your daoine friend."

Shocked by that parting comment, I watched from the ground as the two men turned and walked toward the doorway leading to the stairs. When I was sure they had gone, I stood up, but continued to vigilantly maintain my shield just in case.

"Why did you tell me to let them go?" Vince kept his eye on the exit to the stairs but spared a glance to glare at me.

I scooped up Red and headed toward Vince's Jeep. "Hurry." Over my shoulder, I asked, "Didn't you notice what they had done to Jensen? If you had hauled them up to Agent Cunningham, they would have used the situation to their advantage. They would have looked all the innocent and we would have looked like the criminals." I couldn't help glancing behind us. "We need to get to my apartment. Then we can figure out what to do."

Halfway to my apartment building, I relaxed my shield, but I was still too wound up to do anything except keep a watchful eye out the car's windows.

Vince broke the silence. "What did he call me? Your deenie friend? What does that mean?"

I frowned. "Daoine." I spelled the word for him. "It's a Gaelic word. Directly translated, it means people, I think. Although, that's not how he meant it." I stared at the passing scenery, my mind awash with the implications.

He asked, "Then what did he mean?"

I sighed. "I think he meant daoine sidhe."

"Deenie shee? What's that?"

His pronunciation wasn't exactly right, but it was close enough. I let my gaze slide to Red.

From his perch on the dashboard, Red answered, "People of the mound. They are the most ancient of the races and rarely seen. Our world became uninhabitable to them not long after humans began to populate the Earth. At least, that's the story I was told. Our worlds are closely linked, however. On certain days and at certain locations, they have the ability to visit, so sightings aren't completely unknown. In my three hundred plus years, I have only seen two." Red sounded almost wistful. "Perhaps you will better know them by their colloquial English name: *Elves*. Some people call them the fae, but that word actually encompasses several races, including the daoine sidhe."

"*Okay*. Then why did he call me that? I'm certainly no elf."

He wouldn't want to hear what I had to say, so I remained silent. My eyes stayed glued to the road ahead while my mind whirled over this most recent revelation and the rest of the day's extraordinary events.

Vince, never one for a mystery, pursued the issue. "Do I look like an elf or something? I don't have pointy ears—that's for sure."

Red scoffed. "One famous example and the entire human population thinks all the sidhe have pointy ears." He sighed. "True, they have a striking appearance, but it is more to do with their stature and luminous complexion. However, it is possible to be part elven and not display any outward indication of such bloodline."

"What? You think I'm an elf. Or part elf! That's a laugh."

Red replied, "I know nothing of your bloodline, Detective, although, it does offer a possible explanation as to why you are not affected by Lire's magic. The daoine sidhe are rumored to possess a variety of magical abilities. Being able to block some forms of magic may be one of them."

Vince laughed heartily. "You're serious? You seriously think I'm part elf?"

"I merely said it was a possibility. The telepath obviously believes you are at least part elven. I can think of no other reason for his remark."

"Ridiculous!"

Red continued, resolute, "Ridiculous or not, it saved Lire's life or, at the very least, her mind. They were not able to alter your thoughts, so their plans to subvert the two of you failed. Instead of risk their anonymity, they decided to try again when Lire is less protected."

Vince shook his head and snorted, but refrained from arguing further. There was no denying I had weathered the encounter unharmed, and Vince's intervention was solely responsible. Despite the powerful assault, I survived only because their attack had not been sustained. If the telepaths had been able to subvert him, I would have been at their mercy. My shield would not have held up indefinitely. Eventually they would have broken through and raped my mind.

He glanced at me. "So, the reason Jensen totally ignored us and got into the elevator is because the telepaths removed us from his thoughts?"

I nodded. "Yes, and thank *God* he happened to show up right when we were leaving. If I didn't have that early warning, then they may have been able to enter my mind. When I realized why Jensen was ignoring us, I put all of my energy into my shield just before one of them attacked."

He sighed. "Whatever the reason, I'm glad you're okay."

We waved at Chet, who was warmly ensconced inside his heated security booth, and Vince pulled into my parking stall. Relieved at making it to safety, I blurted, "Thank God."

"You're certain about the safety measures? Even in the garage?" Vince's eyes scoured our surroundings.

"Yes. The wards encompass the perimeter of the building. They were built into the foundation. No magical attack can penetrate them. Anything else is handled by our house djinn or the armed guards."

"Gin? What's that?"

"Djinn. You know, genie?"

"No way. You mean like *Aladdin* or *I Dream of Jeannie*?"

I snorted. "Hardly. That would be like comparing a housefly to a fire-breathing dragon. But that's a topic for another time. Let's get inside."

I got out of the car and strode to the elevator. I noticed Vince walked so that his body blocked my view to the outside. I smiled inwardly at his protectiveness.

While we waited for the elevator doors to open, Vince scanned the garage. "How do you know the wards and these djinn really work?"

I shrugged. "It's what I was told when I bought my place. The impregnable security was a key selling point, and we all paid a premium for it. We still do—there are monthly fees. Anyway, when I moved into my apartment, I was introduced to the djinn. Trust me. They're, uh ... impressive."

I omitted telling Vince about how I am blood-bound to the two djinn and, along with the rest of the building's owners, their master. Djinn are not of our world. In order for them to stay on earth they must bind themselves to a mortal human in servitude. Of course, that doesn't mean they'll do anything they're told. Just because they're bound servants, doesn't mean they're slaves. Strict rules govern the compact to prevent any misuse of their abilities for evil or material gain.

Vince examined me. "What's so impressive about them? Are you certain the telepaths can't alter their thoughts?"

The elevator finally dinged and I got ready for the doors to open. I knew we were totally safe from the telepaths, but I liked the idea of being inside my apartment better than being out in the open. I wasn't absolutely sure the djinn could save me from a well-placed bullet, and I didn't really want to test the theory.

I answered, "Well, for one, the djinn would have to be outside the perimeter wards for that to be a possibility, and, two, they're not susceptible to magical influences anyway, so it doesn't matter."

"Uh-huh." Vince sounded doubtful but remained silent.

Once inside the empty elevator car, Vince pressed the top button.

Red spoke from his perch on my shoulder. "You should alert the djinn. If they are aware of the situation, they will be better able to serve you."

I grimaced. Red knew darn well I wasn't comfortable interacting with the djinn. They scared me, to be honest. I had only summoned them once since the day of the binding ritual. Most of my neighbors enjoyed a friendly relationship with the two otherworldly entities and frequently called on them for help around their apartments. Maybe they had more experience dealing with magical entities, but I just couldn't see asking a powerful being like a djinn to change a light bulb. The one occasion I did call for their help was when my washing machine overflowed. I was frantic. I didn't want the water to damage my hardwood floors or downstairs neighbor's ceiling.

Red patted my head, persistent as usual. "It is also possible they will have some useful information pertaining to your current dilemma."

"Okay, Red, I get the message." I didn't relish the thought of contacting either one of the djinn, not to mention both at the same time, but he was right.

When we got inside my apartment, all I wanted to do was crawl under my down comforter, but there were things that had to be addressed, like contacting the djinn and calling a neighbor or two to find out about ward possibilities.

I procrastinated by making a fresh pot of coffee. After Vince used the bathroom, I listened while he telephoned Cunningham to tell him about our encounter with the two telepaths. Vince looked relieved after hearing Cunningham's mindset hadn't changed since our departure. Jensen had indeed met with Cunningham and was shocked by Vince's story. If I hadn't remembered the tune Jensen whistled down in the parking garage, I'm not sure Vince would have convinced him that his mind had been altered. It was the only proof I could think of that offered some credibility to our story.

After Vince hung up, I gave him an arch look. "So, I guess the understatement of the year is Jensen was pretty surprised by that one, huh?"

"Yeah." Vince shrugged. "But knowing how much I used to discount this magic stuff, I think he was more inclined to believe me."

I smiled. "So your previous magi-phobia was actually an advantage to us."

He snorted and gave a curt nod.

"Speaking of phobias," Red interjected. "You need to call upon the djinn."

I rolled my eyes. "I do not have a phobia. They just make me uncomfortable."

Red continued to stare at me.

"Oh, all right!"

I put down my half finished mug of coffee and strode to the middle of the family room. It didn't seem right to call on the two immortal beings from sitting at my kitchen table, although, the family room didn't seem quite right either. I wondered at what possible location such a calling would feel appropriate—a medieval temple? A desolate, wind-swept hilltop? No, no. Stonehenge. Yeah, Stonehenge. I was about to say as much to Red, but stopped myself. He'd just say I was stalling, and he'd be right.

I sighed and focused on my task. My voice rang out, "Maya and Tanu come to my side. Maya and Tanu come to my aid. Maya and Tanu come to me of your own free will."

I don't know what possessed me to call the two beings in such a manner. The words just tumbled out of my mouth. Actually, it was only necessary to say their names three times in close succession, but just as it didn't seem right to call them from my kitchen table, somehow it didn't seem right to call out their names multiple times as though I was hailing a taxi.

A mist began to swirl in the open space near the patio doors. As it grew in size, it was accompanied by a clear voice. "Could it be the blood-bound Lire does not believe the djinn have free will?"

A second voice, equally precise in its diction, said, "Is it because of this belief she feels it is necessary to grant the djinn free will upon her calling?"

Two nebulous balls of vapor gradually coalesced into two roughly humanoid forms possessed with disturbing eyes. Their bright eyes swirled counter-clockwise, like the Great Red Spot on Jupiter; except these miniature storms churned not with red but silver, gleaming like molten metal.

The djinn had the ability to transform their appearance into whatever form they chose. Whenever their duties took them down into the public spaces of the building, they appeared indistinguishable from the other human guards. Why they did not present themselves in human forms at the moment, I didn't know.

"Does the Lire speak?" the first voice asked.

Befuddled by their strange habit of addressing me as though I weren't in the room, I gathered my wits and answered, "Of course, I can speak."

"If it were up to the Lire, would she grant the djinn free will in all things?" the second one asked as it swirled around its counterpart.

I hesitated, thinking, before I replied, "Within certain parameters, yes."

"That the djinn do not have free will ... this bothers the Lire?" the first djinn asked.

Was that Maya or Tanu? I wondered. There was no way to attribute a name to the voice. In this form, they looked the same and had nearly identical voices.

"It bothers me, yes."

"The other blood-bound have no such problem. Why does it bother the Lire and not the others?"

They had swirled around each other several times, so now I didn't know whether this was the first voice or the second voice. I sighed as I resigned myself to the perpetual confusion of dealing with the alien entities.

I replied to both, "I don't know why I'm in the minority. I guess I don't feel comfortable calling upon you to do whatever menial task comes to mind. You are not slaves. You have the job of protecting us from harm, not to serve our every whim, unless, of course, that aid is freely given."

"Does the Lire feel the other blood-bound take advantage?"

I considered the question. "If they treat you like another neighbor, then probably not. With neighbors there is give and take, and we can say no if we're not comfortable with whatever request is made of us. But there is always that relationship of give and take. I know when I ask a favor of a neighbor, they may ask me for something in return. Most people won't take advantage because of this notion." I shook my head. "Am I making sense? I'm sorry, it's not something I've ever had to explain."

"The djinn understand the Lire's words. It is not a notion the djinn share. The Lire does not know the djinn world. If the Lire knew that world, then maybe she will understand why the notion of free will is misplaced."

One of the forms moved closer to me. "Will the Lire take a brief journey with the djinn?"

I looked surprised. "What? You mean travel to your world? Right now?"

"Yes," they said at once.

Their eyes regarded me, seething disks of liquid silver, but I detected no malice in spite of their alien appearance. They were blood-bound to protect me from all harm, so what they proposed was probably safe.

I nodded, finally. "I will go with you. We won't be too long, will we?"

"No. For those entities in the room, the Lire's essence will be gone only moments."

I wondered how Vince felt about being called an entity before considering the djinn's other words. "My essence? You mean my body will stay here? How does this work?" My unease ramped up a notch.

"Yes, the Lire body will be safe here. Her inside self will travel. The djinn will keep both safe. The Lire need not worry."

I frowned but nodded toward the djinn. At my acknowledgment, the two strange beings floated toward me. I'd never been this close to them, even at the binding ceremony, and my stomach clenched with apprehension. I forced myself to stay still, watching as they positioned themselves, one on each side of me. Nebulous arms formed and separated from their bodies to link around me, like they were about to play an otherworldly game of ring-around-the-rosy. Their forms drew closer as they tightened the ring. Where they came into contact with my body, I felt a cool but not unpleasant sensation.

Before I had the chance to ask what they were doing, the earth shifted beneath my feet and a wave of nausea replaced the knot of nervous jitters in my stomach. My brightly lit living room blinked out of existence and was replaced by something … *other*.

I could still see, so I had eyes. When I looked down, I saw my body and my feet seemingly planted on a firm surface, although, the ground had a strange aspect to it. When I looked up, I saw nothing that could be described as a place. The atmosphere had a shimmery quality to it, as if my eyes were blurred by water or sleep. I waited for the place to resolve into something definable, but nothing immediately materialized. The place was empty and hollow.

I felt the djinn's pull upon my body, followed immediately by another bout of nausea. The movement wasn't natural—I hadn't physically moved—and the unnatural sensation was compounded by the way the insubstantial surroundings didn't promote any visual explanation for the feeling.

"Is this your world?" I forced out. I half expected the sound of my voice to be swallowed by the strange nothingness.

"No. This is what the Lire's kind calls the Between. Limbo, if the Lire likes. Others call it Purgatory. There are many human names for this place but few return to the Lire's world to describe it."

The djinn's misty forms had merged together and were less substantial than how they appeared in my living room, but I felt both of their presences distinctly and they never lost contact with me.

"Why am I still in my body? I thought you said only my essence was traveling with you."

"The Lire's essence brings with it many things. The human body is how the Lire perceives her essence. For now."

I nodded, rubbernecking at my surroundings. There was a familiarity, a sense of déjà vu, but before I could unravel the mystery, everything changed. Thrust into a world absent of light, I lost sense of my body. It was a frigid environment, although, the constant cold didn't adversely affect me. Along with Maya and Tanu, I sensed many other entities with me in the darkness, and we moved effortlessly through each other's awareness, like feathers or clouds floating on a breeze. It was a peaceful world, totally devoid of the boisterousness of life. My essence drifted among the strange population, and I felt delight in each contact, but it wasn't enough to distract my mind from the complete absence of sights, sounds, and warmth. The more I tried to ignore the lack of stimulus, the more I seemed to crave the cacophony of life. I yearned to return to my own world.

Without a body, I had no way to communicate my wish. I panicked at the thought of being trapped. The two djinn must have sensed my distress because their essences drew close. After a moment, we were back in the place they had called the Between, and my body felt entirely too small to fit the incredible volume of emotions, thoughts, and questions spinning through my mind. The strangeness of the Between didn't help. Again, I felt nauseous.

"Stop, please. I need to catch my breath."

"The djinn cannot, for the safety of the Lire. The Between is not the place to linger without training. It is too easy for the Lire to get lost."

With one last surge of invisible momentum, the world shifted back into place. When I opened my eyes, I was lying on the wood floor. Light stung my eyes and warmth scalded my skin, but I relished the sensations. I sat up to look for the djinn.

"You okay?" Vince kneeled next to me, looking concerned.

I stood up with his help and was hardly able to contain my elation. "Yes. More than okay. That was absolutely incredible!"

Energized by my new understanding, I moved toward the two djinn and held out my hands. In a moment, their insubstantial bodies surrounded me. I laughed while they swirled around me faster and faster and squeaked with surprise when they lifted me high into the air. They carried me twenty feet up, to the cross-braces of the ceiling, and we twirled through the air as though it were water. My stomach fluttered like crazy. The sensation was familiar but, at the same time, completely foreign. It was the most amazing experience of my life and one I'll never forget.

After a few moments of sheer pleasure, I remembered my current dilemma and reluctantly urged the djinn back down to earth.

"Does the Lire now understand?" the right-hand djinn asked.

I panted happily between words. "I do. This world is such amazing pleasure, no matter what you are asked to do. Everything is life and light and warmth and delight! You do have free will. You choose to be here—with us."

"Yes," they responded in unison, sounding pleased.

The right-hand djinn floated close. "The Lire's essence has changed. Does the Lire know this?"

I touched my face. "My essence? It has? Because of our trip? What do you mean?"

"No. The visit does not change the essence. The Lire's essence was different before the visit. The djinn see all the human essences. The Lire is not the same human that was blood-bound. The blood is the same, but the essence is different. Does the Lire understand?"

I frowned. "I'm not sure."

"The Lire is one in body, but four in essence. Is the Lire not aware of these other energies flowing inside? It is most unusual."

My thoughts flickered to the memory of talking with Jason on the porch swing.

The other djinn floated next to the first. "One of memory, one of movement, one of ice, and one of fire. We see them all."

I looked back and forth between them. "Yes. Jason, Patty, and Trinity. Their memories have altered my essence? What does that mean?"

"The Lire's essence shows the djinn her powers."

"My powers." I shook my head, emphatic. "No. You don't mean ... all three of them? I have more than just their memories?" I gasped. "Are you saying I have their powers too? All of them—all *three*?"

"Did the Lire not just fly with with the djinn?"

My mind rebelled at the notion. I couldn't seem to catch my breath. "But ... I thought you did that!"

Finally, it dawned on me—the bizarre fluttery feeling—it was familiar. I remembered that same feeling when the car nearly plowed into me and in my dreams with Jason. The strange fluttering feeling was how it felt to be levitated.

Oh God! I might have figured it out sooner, but that possibility was so incredible it wasn't something I remotely considered.

"The djinn did not. Why does this bother the Lire?" The nearest djinn seemed puzzled.

I was too busy hyperventilating to answer. "I ... I ... ugh ..." I dropped to my knees.

Vince crouched down at my side in a heartbeat. "Calm down. You're going to pass out. Come on. Deep breaths."

As I struggled, a tendril of vapor from the closest djinn slid toward my mouth. In too much distress to consider avoiding it, the cool mist entered my lungs, calming them almost immediately. I recovered in moments and the djinn drew back its tenuous appendage. Because it seemed appropriate, I murmured a raspy thank you.

"The Lire is a puzzle to us," the farthest djinn commented. "The djinn have learned to be human is to crave power. Yet the Lire is troubled by such acquired power. Why is this so?"

Red asked, "Have you not also found it is human nature to desire acceptance?"

The djinn seemed to pause in thought. "Yes, the djinn know this about humans, but always power brings acceptance. Is this not so?"

"Generally speaking, this is true, but when it comes to humans who are in the minority, most of the time that power is met with resistance and hatred by the majority," Red replied.

"Yes, the djinn have witnessed this," the nearest djinn said, and then the second added, "But, overall, it is better to have power than not."

"Sometimes," Red bobbed his head in agreement, "But because of this power, Lire is in danger."

"Yes. This is why the Lire called upon the djinn, is it not?"

I looked up at the two misty forms. "A group of telepaths believe I'm a threat to their organization. About an hour ago, two of them attacked me. They meant to destroy my mind, even though I've offered them no harm. If what you've told me about my new powers is true, then this must be why they want to wipe my mind or destroy me all together."

"What is it the Lire desires the djinn to do?" the nearest one asked.

I sighed. It all seemed so futile. The djinn could only offer me their protection while I was inside the building. There was nothing they could do once I ventured out of their confines.

"I thought it was important to let you know of my predicament. Be on your guard, not just for me, but for my friends and neighbors as well. Other than that I guess there's not much more you can do."

The second djinn floated closer so it was next to the first. "The djinn already protect the blood-bound Lire, as do this structure's wards. Nothing will harm the Lire or her friends while they dwell with the djinn."

Before I could think of it, Red asked, "If you please, do you know of any wards for the body Lire might use for protection from telepathic attack when she is on the outside?"

"Wards of this type are possible. Speak with the blood-bound Claude. The Claude has this skill. The Claude may tell you much, but there is one closer still who may provide such help. Is the Lire not aware?" the left-hand djinn inquired.

I stood up as Vince offered his hand for support. "Closer than Claude? You mean another neighbor? I'm sorry. I don't know who you mean."

The right-most djinn swirled around and insinuated itself between Vince and me. A vaporous tendril swept over Vince. "This is the one. This one has ancient blood. This one has the power to help. Did the Lire not know?"

Vince grumbled, fanning his hand in front of him as though to clear the air, "Not this again. Now *you're* telling me I'm an elf?"

The djinn swirled around Vince, leaving a trail of fog that dissipated quickly. It circled once and then floated back to its companion. "Ah. The djinn understand. This one denies the truth. This one locks away the power. The Lire must go to the Claude."

Vince folded his arms across his chest and glowered. I wanted to ask the djinn more about his suppressed power, but restrained my curiosity for later. He wasn't ready to deal with it. I sympathized and swallowed the question, leaving the mystery to simmer.

I forced a smile. "I will speak with Claude. Thank you, Maya and Tanu. I will keep you here no longer. And I won't hesitate to call on you again."

"The djinn will help the Lire with her new powers if she desires. Call on the djinn soon. The djinn will come with free will."

The entity on the right floated toward me and touched my face with a trail of mist. Cold pierced the skin of my forehead, and just as I was about to cry out, the sensation ceased.

"The djinn give the Lire a binding to strengthen the blood bond."

They disappeared before I could thank them.

I felt the spot between my eyebrows. The smoothness of my skin was unbroken, but cold shocked my fingertips whenever they brushed over the small area.

When I turned to Vince, he frowned but stepped closer. He brushed my hair away from my face and touched my forehead.

"There's a silver mark there. It's cold." He rubbed his fingers together and then placed his hands on my shoulders. "You okay?"

I wrapped my arms around him and nestled my head in the crook of his neck, sighing when he returned my embrace.

"I guess so." After a moment, I pulled back to see his face. "How about you?"

A fleeting expression of anxiety and something else crossed his face before he covered it and shrugged. "Confused. Worried about you, but otherwise okay."

I didn't believe him. Not completely. He seemed ill at ease, and his eyes, which were normally warm and alert, regarded me with a strained expression. I wondered whether he regretted our fledgling romance. The unwelcome ache in my chest cautioned me. No, it couldn't be. I was not falling for him.

The urge to pull back and protect my heart was irresistible.

Vince examined me. "What's wrong?"

I stepped away, testing the cold spot on my forehead with the tip of my index finger. "Nothing. I'm fine."

I tried to prove it, but it was an act. I wanted Vince to pull me back into his arms. Wanted him to show me how much he cared. But he didn't. He overlooked my unconvincing testament, acknowledging me with a slight nod of his head.

Even though I had just done the very same thing to him, I couldn't help being disappointed. I mumbled something about calling Claude and walked stiffly into the kitchen.

EIGHTEEN

Claude opened his front door almost before I had finished pressing the doorbell.

He beamed, "*Bonjour ma chère Lire!* I have been tormented by not seeing you of late." My name rolled off of his tongue the way it was intended, smooth with a delicate ring, even though his voice was quite deep.

Before I could answer, he waved us into his entryway. "Please, come in."

To describe Claude as 'a character' was an understatement. He was a womanizing scoundrel and an outrageous flirt, but was so charming that he got away with it. Probably because he managed to make every woman of his acquaintance feel special, even though it was totally obvious he flirted with all of us equally, sometimes at the same time, and intended to remain a bachelor indefinitely. Plus, he was French, unquestionably attractive, and had that wonderful accent that made most women forget about playing hard-to-get.

I wasn't necessarily immune to his charms, but my clairvoyance thwarted any escalation beyond mutual egregious flirtation. Besides, sleeping with men without any type of commitment was not my normal practice, which probably came across loud and clear. Because of that, Claude and I ended up forming a close friendship that wasn't completely platonic, yet never crossed the line into romance.

Deadly Remains - Chapter Eighteen

As usual, Claude had dressed impeccably, although, he could probably wear anything and still look like he had just posed for *GQ Magazine*. His stature and physique were undeniably eye-catching. Today, he wore black trousers and a trendy midnight-blue button down shirt, tails out for a more casual look. The color contrasted with his dark-blonde, shoulder length hair, which was parted neatly down the middle and tucked behind each ear. No wonder women practically swooned at his feet—the French accent combined with his overall appearance was bound to lead to a 'little black book' the size of an encyclopedia.

I introduced Vince. After their polite greeting, Claude gazed at me. "Powerful things are moving within you, *chérie*."

He stood close and peered at the djinn's mark. I tried to tamp down the childish feeling of triumph at Claude's focused attention while Vince watched. Claude's piercing hazel eyes examined my face thoroughly and the set of his eyebrows somehow managed to convey the fact that he enjoyed our close proximity.

"Yes, very powerful. That I can see. But I am being rude. Come sit." Claude led the way into his living room. "I've been seeing you on the news, *mon amie*. You are having a interesting time of late, I think."

"Yeah, you could say that." I glanced at all the striking paintings, gleaming glass block walls, and bright chrome accents that seemed to oppose the brown leather and dark wood furnishings.

"Can I get you something? Coffee, tea, mineral water? I have psi-free." Claude waited as Vince and I sat next to each other on the dark-brown leather sofa.

"No, thank you, Claude," I said.

"Detective?"

"I'd love some mineral water if it's not too much trouble."

"No trouble. *Un instant, s'il te plait.*"

When Claude left the room, Vince surprised me by running his finger along the side of my neck. I shivered. When I turned to look at him, he kissed me lightly on the lips. He leaned back into the cushion and placed his arm casually along the back of the couch while I sat, blinking and wondering at the motivation behind his impulse. While my emotions vaulted to Cloud Nine, my inner voice scolded me for getting carried away. I looked away, trying not to frown. The emotional ups and downs of our budding romance exhausted me.

A moment later, Claude emerged from the kitchen and handed Vince a glass with ice, sparkling water, and a wedge of lime. The lime was a nice touch.

Claude sat adjacent to me. "So, I think you said on the telephone you are in need of some magical assistance?"

I nodded. "Yes. I wonder whether you, or someone you know, might be able to craft a talisman of some kind to repel a telepathic attack."

Claude considered me. "Yes, such a thing is possible. I am wondering, is this for you, or someone else?" He glanced at Vince.

"For me and possibly for others, depending upon how easy they are to construct. To be honest, I have no idea how difficult it might be. Maybe I am asking for the moon." I laughed.

He smiled. "Yes, it is quite difficult. I will tell you, such a thing might take several days to create. For a coven, perhaps only some hours, but of course, a coven is very expensive. You fear such an attack?"

When I glanced at Vince, he said, "She's already been attacked. Earlier today."

Claude's eyes widened and then immediately narrowed. "I will do this for you, *chérie*. Anything for you. You know this. I can have it ready in a couple days. But, for more than one, I will talk with my coven. Maybe they will help. Maybe only for a price. I do not know." He tilted his head and studied me. "The charm will only work from a distance, *tu sais*? Bah, of course you do." He cocked an eyebrow suggestively. "If not, then a charm could be made to block your magic as we both know. But this is not possible. No?"

I nodded and covered my amused smile. Claude was clearly on his best behavior with the detective sitting next to me, but his salacious nature peeked out occasionally.

Vince leaned forward. "So, what does that mean? If one of the telepaths touches Lire, this talisman won't work?"

"*Oui*. Detective, think of the charm as something that gives the wearer a ... how do you say? Shield, er, no. Armor? Yes? Just over the skin." Claude moved his hand an inch over the surface of his clothing. "But this armor—it is of magic. Not metal. If the psychic touches the skin, like so, he will break through the ward. You see?"

I nodded my agreement and turned to Vince. "If it was possible to ward the skin, I'd already have one. Believe me."

"Yes, exactly so." Claude turned a serious eye toward me. "Now, Lire, you know ... to create the charm I will need something of you. Hair or fingernail, *peut-être*? I will protect it with my life. That is my promise."

I bit my lip and nodded. Freely giving something from the body was extremely dangerous, especially if the item fell into the wrong hands. A warlock or sorcerer in possession of such a thing could perform any number of spells, many of which had the potential to affect the donor to the extreme. I had known Claude for several years and trusted him. Still, this particular act of faith was never arbitrarily given.

Vince returned his drink to the coaster and looked back and forth from Claude to me. "What's up? Is there a problem?"

Claude tilted his head at me and then regarded Vince. "Detective, you know of course about magic that uses something from the body? Like the voodoo doll? That is the one most people know."

"Yes, but I thought voodoo dolls were an urban legend, a joke, something some Caribbean religious fanatics tout to the tourists."

"That is what many believe because most of the time the, ah, connect? No, sorry, the ... connection is not freely given. That is why most people, they don't believe in the voodoo." Claude sighed. "How do I explain? Without a connection, freely given, the magic cannot flow. Freely giving, like the hair, or fingernail, or even blood, something of the body, gives a magic user much more power—power over the giver. You see?"

Vince frowned. "I think so. And you need something from Lire, in order to make this ward?"

"*Oui*. Just so. It is a grave request and one that requires a great deal of trust."

I turned to Vince. "Exactly. Which is why we won't be able to get a talisman for everyone working on the case. Some people will be unwilling to take such a risk."

I tipped my head forward, carefully culled out a single strand of hair and yanked it out.

"Ah, *attend*." Claude jumped up. "Let me get something for it."

Less than a minute later he returned with a white envelope. While he held it open, I placed my single strand of hair inside, and then Claude sealed the envelope.

He rested it flat against his chest, over his heart. "I promise to keep this safe and use it in total for the making of a telepathic charm. *C'est promis.*"

Standing up, I thanked him and said that I trusted him completely. "*Merci beaucoup*, Claude. *Je sais que je peux te faire confiance. J'apprécie ton aide énormément.*"

Vince looked surprised, and I winked at him.

"Ah, *chérie. Ton français est impeccable.* As always, you speak like a fellow Parisian."

"Hardly," I said with an embarrassed laugh.

"I only speak the truth." He chuckled. "I will call you, of course, when the talisman is complete. Do not worry."

"*C'est parfait. Merci.*"

We said our goodbyes, and then Vince and I headed back to my apartment.

While we were waiting for the elevator, Vince turned to me. "You speak French, I gather. Do you know any other languages?"

I nodded. "Yeah. Over time, from my various readings, I've picked up a few. Some I know better than others."

"How many do you know?"

"Not sure. Five, six, maybe. Like I said, I'm not fluent in all of them." I shrugged. "I suppose it's one of the few benefits of being a clairvoyant."

We stepped into the empty elevator, and I pressed the button for my floor.

"Wow." He looked at me wolfishly. "Say something to me in Spanish."

I laughed and after a moment of thought, leaned toward his ear to whisper, "*Quisiera sentir tu piel contra la mía.*"

He pulled me toward him. "What did you say?"

I just laughed and decided to refrain from saying anything I didn't actually want to reveal. Telling him I wanted to feel his skin next to mine probably wasn't one of my better ideas.

Vince jostled me. "Tell me."

"*Il se peut que je le fasse, mais on verra.*" Maybe ... I'd have to wait and see.

"You are so asking for trouble." Vince pushed my back against the wall of the elevator and kissed me thoroughly. My hormones soared. It was all I could do to walk in a straight path toward my apartment when the elevator doors opened on my floor.

Vince provided me with an interesting distraction, pulling my hair aside to do wonderful things to my neck, while I attempted to insert my house key into the deadbolt. It only took me three or four tries. By the time the door opened, I was breathless and we more or less stumbled into my apartment. I turned around in his arms, blindly struggling to close the door. Vince solved the dilemma by pushing me against the inside so that it closed with a slam. Freed of their previous task, my hands roamed freely over Vince's chest. I delighted in every ripple as we kissed and pressed our bodies together. I fumbled with his shirt, determined to run my fingertips over his bare skin. Of course, the gloves still needed to come off.

"Lire?" Red's voice came from the direction of the family room. "I am sorry to interrupt, but something important has come up."

I let my head fall toward Vince's chest with a frustrated moan. "Be with you in a second, Red," I called. I think I kept the aggravation out of my voice.

Slowly, we pulled back. Vince smiled, gazing at me with an expression of amused disappointment. He leaned forward. "I guess you'll have to be in trouble later."

I rolled my eyes. "Only if our luck changes."

Vince laughed. With one final kiss, he grasped my hand and led the way to the kitchen.

"I am sorry, Lire, but Darren called about five minutes ago. I told him to call for you at Claude's." He hesitated, as if carefully choosing his words. "Your behavior just now seemed to indicate Darren did not manage to reach you."

I glanced at Vince. "Uh, no. He didn't. What's up? What does Darren want?"

"Daniel is in the lobby. He is asking to see you, and he is not alone."

I glanced at the telephone and then back at Red. "Daniel's in the lobby?"

"Who is he with?" Vince asked.

"He didn't say. He only told me Daniel Stockard and an associate are waiting in the lobby."

The telephone started ringing just before I reached it. Caller ID told me it was the lobby desk.

"Darren?"

"Yes. Hello, Lire. There are two gentlemen here asking to see you—a Daniel Stockard and his associate, Michael Thompson. I can transfer you to the guest telephone if you'd like to speak with one of them."

What did I want? I knew they couldn't offer me harm as long as the building's wards protected me, but my instincts told me to be cautious.

"Darren, please ask Tanu to escort them to a conference room and wait there for me. I'll be right down."

"That I can do. If there's anything else, just let me know."

I thanked Darren and hung up while silently cursing my luck. There was no way I'd convince Vince to stay out of the meeting. I could only hope Daniel would still want to talk to me with a detective in the room.

I regarded Vince. "I guess we should go find out what they want."

"First I have to notify Agent Cunningham." Vince had his cell in hand.

"Wait." I stepped toward him. "I don't want them involved yet. Daniel is here to speak with me, not the FBI. I'm already in this mess because of my involvement with you guys. I don't want to blow things out of proportion or screw things up by charging in with the cavalry. You'll be with me—that's enough."

Vince's jaw tightened. "I can't do that. There's an all points out on this guy. It will be my ass if I don't report it."

I glared at him. "And it will be mine if you do."

Vince hesitated, but his eyes radiated determination. My demand for secrecy was bound to put a strain on our relationship, or even break it completely, but my situation was dire.

I covered my face with my hands and turned my back. What was I going to do? Calling in the FBI to detain Daniel was absolutely the worst thing to do. Why didn't Vince see that? My life versus his career. It seemed to me that my life was way more important than his career. And the petty side of me was upset he didn't see it that way.

I sighed. "Vince, do what you have to do, but I'm telling you it's a mistake to call. Daniel is possibly here to make me some kind of deal." I faced him, arms crossed. "I don't want to spend the foreseeable future waiting for a telepathic attack. If he has some kind of truce in mind, I'd like to hear it. If you call Cunningham, I can probably kiss that goodbye."

Vince stalked to the couch. "Goddammit." He kept his back to me for several moments before turning to glare at me. "Fine. But if either of them steps out of line, I'm hauling both their asses over to Cunningham before you can say magi-phobe."

I frowned. I hated asking him to go against his professional ethics, but what else was I supposed to do? I moved toward him while peering into his eyes, trying to gauge his mood. His expression softened when I drew near.

I wrapped my arms around his neck and whispered into his ear, "I'm sorry. I don't want you to get into trouble, but I don't know what else to do."

He sighed and returned my embrace. "I know. I just hope Cunningham doesn't blow a gasket when he hears about this."

I pulled away and placed my hand against the side of his cheek. His eyes were warm and brown, and I wondered sappily whether I would ever tire of looking into them.

He cocked an eyebrow at me. "Come on. Let's go meet the mysterious Mr. Stockard."

We were silent in the elevator. Lana, a neighbor one floor down, accompanied us for most of the way. I greeted her, but didn't say much more than a simple hello. Lana was relatively new to the complex, so I didn't know her well. Fortunately, the elevator didn't make any further stops, so the trip was a quick one.

The building's entire second floor was dedicated to social spaces for all the tenants. There was a kitchen with great room for parties, a video arcade, basketball court, fitness area, and a couple of meeting rooms. I led Vince to the right, past the empty great room, and down the hall toward the conference rooms.

In the hallway, a barrel-chested, silver-haired security guard stood next to a closed door. He regarded Vince and me as we approached, turning his body toward us.

"Hello, Tanu. Is everything okay?" I didn't expect any problems, but I asked anyway.

He—it nodded. "The Lire's two telepathic guests are inside. They offered no conversation and followed without incident. Does the Lire wish the djinn to remain on guard here?"

I bit my lip. "No. I don't think that's necessary. Thank you, Tanu. I'll call you if I need anything."

"That will be a pleasure, as the Lire knows." Tanu sauntered past us in the direction of the elevator.

Vince watched the gray-haired guard walk out of hearing distance. He shook his head. "I see the strangest things when I'm with you."

"I told you the djinn were impressive." I turned to the closed conference room door. "Ready?"

Vince nodded and we entered the well-appointed conference room. Seated at the rectangular table, kitty-corner to each other, were Daniel and his dark haired associate. They both stood up as Vince and I entered. Daniel appeared a little nonplussed, and I assumed it was because of Vince's presence.

"Hello, Daniel. I'm glad to see you again." I motioned toward Vince, who stopped to close the door behind us. "This is Vince Vanelli." I narrowed my eyes at Daniel. "He was with me not long ago when I was attacked by two telepaths in the parking garage of the FBI offices. He is a detective with the Chiliquitham Police Department ... and a good friend."

"Hi." Daniel glanced at his companion. "This is Michael Thompson. He's a like-minded associate."

Thompson, who was not much taller than me and probably around my age, had dark-brown eyes, a nose that looked as if it had been broken sometime in the distant past, and hair so close to black I hesitated to think of it as brown. Although his complexion was fair, I wondered whether he shared some Native American or possibly Asian ancestry— it was something about the shape of his eyes, wide forehead, and high cheekbones. His closely cropped, dark hair showed off a striking widow's peak.

"Nice to meet you, Miss Devon. I'm sorry some members of our organization decided to escalate the situation. Not all of us feel it was the best course of action. I'm glad you're okay."

I relaxed at hearing him speak. His voice sounded nothing like the murderer. Of course, his height didn't qualify him either.

I dipped my chin in acknowledgment. "Uh, thanks. Nice to meet you too."

Thompson turned to regard Vince and leaned across the table to offer his hand. "Detective," he said with a nod. "I must tell you, your involvement with Miss Devon has caused quite a stir. If you don't mind me asking, why is an elder descendant involved in these human matters?"

Vince tensed, his eyes narrowing. "I don't know what you mean. I am involved because it is my job, Mr. Thompson. I apprehend criminals."

Thompson looked uncertain. "I see."

Daniel stepped in to offer Vince his hand. "Detective Vanelli. So, you are not a sidhe representative?"

"No. I am not." Vince clipped each word, but he was polite enough to shake Daniel's hand. "I'm a detective with the Chiliquitham Police Department. I am currently involved in the apprehension of the person or persons responsible for what are being called the Circle Murders."

Daniel glanced at his associate before turning his attention to me. "Then perhaps we cannot speak as freely as we had hoped."

Vince replied, "Maybe a trip to the station will help."

Daniel ignored the implied threat and continued to look at me. "Unfortunately, your visit with the FBI has caused considerable uproar within our organization. Mike and I were hoping to speak about possible ... options, but I have to be honest, the Detective's presence here complicates things."

"It's only complicated if— "

With an extended hand, I cut Vince off before things escalated. "Please. Just hold on a second. Okay?" My expression pleaded with him to zip it.

Gritting my teeth, I contemplated throttling Daniel until he turned blue, or alternatively pinching Vince's ear. I pulled out a chair instead.

I glared at Daniel. "You and your damned organization are flipping infuriating, you know that? If it weren't for your interference—coming to my office and scaring the bejeezus out of me—I wouldn't be in this situation. When you ran off, I panicked. What did you expect? I called Vince because I didn't know what else to do." I narrowed my eyes at him. "And, just so you know, I've put my relationship with Vince on the line by asking him not to call in the cavalry. Since this is mostly your fault, the least you can do is tell me what the *hell* is going on."

The two men remained standing, clearly deliberating. I sat down in the chair closest to Daniel and folded my arms across my chest.

"Oh, for heaven's sake!" I lowered my shield a crack and pointed at Daniel. "You have permission to enter, but not him. Do you understand? If I get any whiff of his intrusion, I'll cut things short but quick."

Daniel looked surprised for a moment and then acquiesced with a nod. He retook his chair at the head of the table. Thompson sat across the table from me.

Vince remained standing. "Lire? What are you doing?"

I swiveled in my seat, so I could give him an imploring look. "Trust me again, okay? I'm just going to have a private conversation with Daniel. Sit here." I motioned to the empty chair to my left. "If anything happens, you have my permission to arrest them, okay?" I smiled and cocked an eyebrow at Thompson.

Vince looked angry, but sat down on my left, like I asked. I decided to reward him profusely, later, for going along with my lead. That is—if we ever had more than thirty minutes of private, uninterrupted world-not-falling-apart time together. I suppressed a sigh.

Daniel glanced at Vince and thought to me, *So, you and the Detective have something going?*

I replied, *Uh, yeah. Maybe. Just barely, and with all this crap happening, I'll be lucky if he still wants to keep it that way.*

His eyebrows went up. *Ah, well, I'm sorry about that. I guess him being part sidhe makes him a good candidate.*

I snorted. *Candidate? Yeah, right. As if I have an endless line of guys auditioning for a starring role in my life. Until the telepathic psychos in the parking garage tried to attack us, I had no idea why he was unreadable to me. I had hoped he was one of many possible normal humans who could stand up to my gift.* I shrugged.

Not everyone needs to stand up to your gift, Lire.

I wondered whether he was alluding to our childhood relationship, but deliberately chose to ignore the possibility. *Obviously you haven't had to resort to dating normals.* I wanted to get away from any further discussion of my love life, so I redirected the conversation. *So, I guess you guys have experience with the sidhe? You know for certain Vince is part elven?*

Yes. Our organization has some contact with the Otherworld. Sidhe emissaries have sought our influence at times. Daniel frowned. *He is truly not aware of his ancestry?*

I replied, *No. In fact, he was pretty repressed when we first met, typical magi-phobe, and had almost no experience with our world.*

He tilted his head. *Interesting. If you want, I can ask around about him. Maybe I can find out about his connection to the sidhe.*

I thought about it. *I don't know if that's such a good idea. I don't want to draw any undue attention to him. I'm sure you've noticed. Vince is in major denial mode right now. I don't think he'd be terribly receptive to any overtures. I'm the one who's curious, and it would probably behoove me to stay out of it.* I shrugged. *Um, I guess we should probably start talking about the issue at hand. Don't you think?*

His laughter tickled my mind. *Of course, but I have to confess talking with you again brings back a lot of memories.* His face took on a sympathetic expression. *I'm sorry to hear my departure from school was so difficult for you.*

I stared at him, aghast. It took me a moment, but I figured he had probably gleaned the information about my suicide attempt from the police and not from probing my memories. My shield faltered, and thoughts of that dismal day entered the fore of my mind. I pushed them back and strengthened the wall around our conversation. *Yeah, well ... not your fault. Red saved me from my near misstep, thank goodness.*

He regarded me steadily, and I tried not to consider his good looks. He suppressed a smile and I knew my thoughts had betrayed me. I didn't hide my face in embarrassment, but it was close.

If it makes it any easier, I also had a tough time, especially the first several months away from you and my other friends at Coventry. I missed you horribly, and my new school wasn't nearly as carefree as Coventry. We both suffered. He paused and then added, *And I too think you've grown into a very attractive woman, just as I knew you would. So, now you don't have to feel I've invaded your privacy. We are both of the same mind, if you'll excuse the pun.*

He smiled with just a hint of mischievousness, and I couldn't help but shake my head and laugh out loud.

I thought, *Okay. Now that we're on the same page, will you tell me what this is all about? I'm feeling okay right now because you're here in my head, taking my mind off things. But, we need to talk about what's going on with the murderer and why my life is being threatened by your organization. Those two bozos in the parking garage ... if Vince hadn't been there ...* I shuddered as some of the memories of the terrifying event leaked into my mind.

Daniel looked troubled. *Yes. I heard. I can't tell you how relieved I was when I heard they had failed.* He paused for a moment, and I sensed that he was carefully choosing his words. *To be honest, Mike and I are here because we represent a growing number of people in our organization who want to see some changes in the hierarchy. As I mentioned earlier, not all of us are happy with the methods frequently employed by our leadership. Your arrival onto the scene has only served to widen that rift.*

He sighed and explained, *To be completely candid, Mike and I risk much in coming to you. The reason we're here is because we believe the prophecy foretells you will be instrumental in the reordering of our organization.*

I felt my eyes widen. *What? Danny! I don't have the first clue about your secret club, and I don't want to. Three days ago, I didn't know them from a hole in the ground, and now you're telling me I'll be instrumental in ... what? Some major changing of the guard? What's with you guys? I can't believe you place so much faith in these divinations. Haven't any of you stopped to think it's your influence that's responsible for bringing about this supposed shake-up?*

Daniel nodded. *Yes, that is one of the main arguments behind our cause. We, and our fellow dissenters, believe our leaders have been relying too heavily on divinations. By interfering with the timeline, we quite possibly end up causing the very thing predicted.* He sighed. *And, there are other disagreements as well, but it isn't necessary to go into all of them right now.*

I looked at him intently. *Uh-huh. To be honest, I couldn't care less about the details, I simply want my life back—free and clear from any worries of a visit from the brain wiping squad of doom. And I want the murderer stopped—now—before he kills anyone else. If we can come to some sort of arrangement that will get all of us what we want, then that's fine with me.*

I heard Vince move slightly in his seat and felt his fingers caress the back of my neck. As I turned to give him a reassuring smile, I became aware of a feather-light touch in my mind. It was ever so slight, just a whisper in the din, but I knew instantly that while I shared thoughts with Daniel, his cohort took the opportunity to peruse my memories undetected. Just how he was able to do that, considering the strength of my shield, I didn't know. But I felt him now as he moved through my mind, sifted through my memories, and violated me beyond measure.

I gasped.

My reaction was immediate and automatic. I directed all of my power into ejecting both of them from my mind. I stood up with such force that my chair flew backwards with a crash, but that was nothing compared to the sound

Thompson's body made as it sailed through the air and collided with the nearest wall. A burning anger I'd never felt before ignited within me and its accompanying power quickly overwhelmed my mind.

I gestured with my hand, and Daniel joined Thompson, pinned to the wall like a fly on paper.

I screamed at them, "How dare you!"

Unbidden, the fiery force driven by Patty's malevolence surged through my core and coursed down my arms all the way to my fingertips. No longer internal, the energy burned bright, causing my arms to flare like a pair of incandescent gloves. I held out my hands to regard their hypnotic power and watched the plasma dance between my fingers. I leveled a piercing gaze toward my two captives and contemplated the urge to set the fire to consume those who caused me pain.

Vince uttered an expletive, and out of the corner of my eye I saw him stagger back from his chair. "My God! Your hands. What are you doing?"

I ignored him and leveled a fire-encased finger at Thompson. "You were not invited. You violated me. The both of you are no better than the two from the parking garage!"

Through my blazing anger, I heard Daniel struggle to speak. "No! Listen, Lire. I told Mike to test you. Please. Don't do something you'll regret later. Let me explain. I swear, there'll be no more mind probes. I give you my word."

Contemptuous laughter bubbled within me, like molten magma straining to reach the surface, to explode from my lips. But, just as the burning potential brought me to the brink of my sanity, my forehead flared with a blinding, familiar pain. The frigid sting cleared my head of the pernicious anger, along with my intense desire to extract retribution.

I sensed Tanu's invisible presence in my mind. The djinn reminded me the wards of the building had not interfered with Thompson's incursion, which meant he truly offered me no harm. This knowledge didn't make me any less upset about his violation, but it helped me deal with my feelings more constructively.

With renewed control, I stepped back from the brink. Through our shared conduit, Tanu encouraged me to open myself up to my newfound powers. I closed my eyes as the energies mingled within my body and throughout my mind. I freed myself of Patty's fury and, although I was still spitting mad at the two men, I discovered the burning power was something I didn't have to regard with fear or keep locked away behind my shield. The force was well within my control, as Trinity's memories confirmed. This knowledge soothed me, and it was from this new calm that I found the power to control the flames.

Daniel and Thompson regarded me with wild eyes as I drew on my power. However, instead of lashing them with fire, I smothered my burning arms with a thick layer of ice and then smashed them down on the table with a final grunt of anger. Pieces of ice flew about in all directions.

I brought the two men down from their unwilling aerial perches and made sure they were standing before releasing my grasp.

Totally spent, my legs collapsed beneath me and I crumpled to the floor. I buried my face in my hands. At that point, I almost didn't care if the two telepaths had their way with my mind.

"What is happening to me?"

I felt like a monster—like the Incredible Hulk whose powers are unleashed at the mere spark of anger—a freak of nature. My body, still recovering from the barely controlled power and flood of intense emotions, started shaking. Hugging my thighs to my chest, I pressed my forehead against the top of my bent knees. It wasn't easy, but I didn't fall apart.

For a long moment, no one moved or made a sound, and the person who finally came to comfort me wasn't who I expected or hoped it would be.

"I'm sorry. I had a feeling you'd be angry if you were able to detect Mike, but I never ... *never* wanted to hurt you or cause you pain." Daniel paused, giving my shoulder a squeeze. "In hindsight, it probably wasn't the best plan. We just needed to know the extent of your power—your shield, I mean—and your ability to detect and repel a mind probe. I'm sorry. I didn't expect the rest. I knew you had the ability to levitate, but the rest ..." He sighed again.

Can you ever forgive me? He asked.

As I loosened the grip on my folded legs, I ordered myself to get the useless emotions under control. I had faced difficulties before—things that seemed insurmountable at the time—and I had always managed to come out on top. I would do it again. I had to, for Jason and Trinity and Nick.

I looked into his eyes. Sorrow and regret permeated his expression.

I frowned at him. "I don't understand what you were hoping to achieve, but there was no way for you to anticipate my reaction."

I glanced at Vince, who stood at the edge of the conference table. He stared at me with an expression of shock and disbelief. At that moment, I knew I could kiss goodbye any hope of a lasting relationship. In his mind, I was an aberration.

I'm sure the pain was evident on my face. I closed my eyes against the threatening tears.

He's just in shock. Give him time, he thought.

I opened my eyes and shook my head. *No amount of time is going to cure this. He thinks I'm a freak. And, the sad thing is, he's not wrong.*

Daniel reached out and placed his palm against my cheek. As my magic flared and drew his psychic essence into my mind, he thought back, *No, you're not. You are a power to be reckoned with, yes, but you are definitely not a freak.*

I tried to pull away from his touch to avoid the burden of his memories, but Daniel maintained the contact. He wanted me to accept his essence.

What are you doing? I used my shield to control the flow of his psychic energy, unsure whether I should cast it out and try harder to pull myself away from his touch.

I want you to know a few things. Don't worry, I'm not allowing you every detail. I do have some control over that, you know. I've learned a thing or two since we were kids.

The panic on my face must have been comical because Daniel laughed and said out loud, "Don't worry. I wouldn't do this unless I was confident in my abilities. The sidhe aren't the only ones who can resist your gift."

At Daniel's comment, Vince finally spoke up. "Do what?"

Daniel glanced at Vince. "I'm sharing some important memories with Lire. Things that will explain much about what is going on and give her the answers to many of her questions."

Even before Daniel finished answering Vince, I knew why he and Thompson had come to see me, why the murderer was killing psychics, and, most importantly, how I'd acquired Jason, Patty, and Trinity's powers. But, instead of making me feel better and more in control, the information weighed me down.

Things were never going to be the same again.

Daniel withdrew his hand and I stared at him, shaking my head. "Oh God! I don't want any of this. I wish this all never happened."

"Nevertheless, they are the facts. And you and the traitor are at the center of it." His smile was wistful. "And as a certain someone liked to tell me—quite often, as a matter of fact—no good ever came from just wishing."

I sighed. "Yeah, I know, but it never stopped me from doing it anyway."

Daniel looked at me sympathetically before he stood to help me up. "So. Now you know everything I could tell you. Use the information as you will. I'm sorry, but we have to go." He glanced toward Thompson. "Good luck, Lire. I hope we will meet again soon."

And under better circumstances, he added.

Vince remained silent as Daniel and Thompson said goodbye and closed the door behind them. When they were gone, Vince regarded me with an unreadable, far-away expression. I felt my eyebrows and mouth draw down into a sad frown. Again, I fought back the urge to cry. Unsure what to do or say, I picked up my overturned chair and returned it to the conference table.

Small puddles of water covered the surface of the table, along with larger pieces of ice that hadn't completely melted. The desire to collapse into tears was overpowering, but I determined not to make any more of a fool of myself. Instead, I got some paper towels from the nearby wet bar and began soaking up the water. The pieces of ice went into the small sink. As I endured the uncomfortable silence and busied myself with the cleanup, I reminded myself I was strong, I had power, and I would not fall apart.

When the table was dry, I tossed the towels into the trash and then sat down in my previous spot. I did my best to hold it together while I waited for Vince to do or say *something*. After what seemed like an eternity, but was probably only a minute, I heard Vince move. I turned to watch him take the chair across the table from me.

"I guess you're not so sure about ordering that freaky surprise sundae, now, are you?" My tone was flippant, but my expression probably conveyed otherwise.

Vince ran his fingers through his hair without comment. Confronted with his silence, I wondered whether he remembered our conversation, in which he implied that my life, ripe with magic, was more interesting than his pure vanilla world.

My bottom lip trembled, and I bit it hard to keep myself from crying. I didn't need him in my life anyway, I told myself. All the emotional ups and downs were annoying, and I had more important things to worry about than the meager, pathetic status of my love life.

There's nothing like anger to head off a bad case of heartbreak.

I made a hurry-up gesture with my hand. "Let's just get this over with then. Get out your notebook. You're going to want to write this down, I'm sure."

Vince blew out an exasperated sigh. "Look, I'm sorry I can't roll with the magical punches like your friend Daniel. I wish I could, but it's not that easy for me." He paused and rubbed his hand over his mouth and chin. "There's a lot going on right now and, well, I just need some time to get my head around things."

Ponying up a detachment I didn't feel, I thanked my wretched luck we never made it past second base. "Yep. Gotcha loud and clear."

I ignored the fact that Vince hadn't yet transitioned into detective mode (he still looked slightly lost for words), quashed my urge to feel sorry for him, and launched into my brain dump.

"The man you're looking for is Brian Stalzing. Not that it will help you much, of course, since all memory of his identity has been eradicated. But you guys seem to place so much interest in a criminal's identity that I feel compelled to tell you anyway."

I pressed my lips together and watched as Vince got out his notebook. When he was ready, I continued. Instead of looking at his face, I allowed my focus to wander between his moving pen and the window behind him. "He was indoctrinated into Invisius Verso when he was thirteen, a year before Daniel. Invisius Verso is the name of their little secret club. It's Latin. It basically means 'unseen influence,' which says a lot about their mode of operation. Their organization goes back hundreds of years."

I slumped further back into my chair and crossed my arms. "Daniel thinks Brian is a sociopath. He cares very little for other people, unless it serves him in some way. Brian is on a one-man crusade to take over control of Invisius Verso. He knows the only way to achieve this is by becoming so powerful that no one can possibly stand up to him. That's why he's killing psychics. He found a way to gain their power with an ancient shaman spell.

"This spell was originally used to pass down a shaman's abilities to a younger apprentice. It was indispensable for our prehistoric ancestors because it more or less guaranteed the clan would always have a powerful shaman, who not only was skilled in magic, but also carried all the memories of past generations. This was incredibly important in a time when there was no written language. So, when the elder shaman felt he was nearing the end of his life, the ritual was performed and all of his memories and power flowed to the chosen novice. The old shaman died in the process and a new, young shaman took his place."

I paused to ease the tension in my neck before continuing. Vince regarded his notes silently.

"Anyway, that's how Brian knows all those intimate details about me. He has many of Nick's memories. And it also explains why I ended up with some of the victim's powers. The residual magic must have been strong enough to affect me, perhaps because I'm a clairvoyant. I don't know. It seems like an unlikely scenario, but then again, everything that's happened so far sounds farfetched."

I waited for Vince to finish writing before telling him the part I knew he wasn't going to like. "So, now you know the murderer's name and his motive and his method, but it's not going to help you much."

Vince examined me. "Why? You think his identity has been erased that thoroughly?"

I shook my head. "That won't help things, but no, that's not it." I frowned. "Invisius Verso is going to apply their influence at the highest level. They're going to make sure our most recent theories are discredited and we're removed from the case."

In fact, Daniel and his associates had to exercise much of their own influence to prevent those in charge of Invisius from going even further. There were some who wanted to make sure our reputations and personal lives were so completely trashed that there was no possibility our claims could be reexamined in the future.

The muscles along Vince's jaw twitched and his neck went rigid. "How? What are they going to do, exactly?"

I suppressed a shiver as I recalled Daniel's memories of the voting process. Not only had my life been at stake, but Daniel's too. Because of our relationship, he had to keep his feelings and memories heavily shielded and remain out-wardly dispassionate at all times. Any chink in Daniel's ar-mor could lead to the discovery of his revolutionary thoughts and doom him, along with his compatriots, to a mind wipe—or worse.

Daniel was a powerful telepath. If he was worried about being discovered, then I surely had reason to be terrified.

I answered Vince truthfully. "Daniel didn't know the spe-cifics. He was only involved in the vote regarding whether or not influence should be applied and to what extent. There were several on the committee who wanted to make sure our reputations and personal lives were completely ruined, but Daniel and his associates managed to convince the ma-jority that a heavy handed approach was too dangerous. They reasoned it's always possible to apply more pressure, but not as easy to undo what is already set into motion." I slapped my palms on the table to underscore the finality of the situation. "They will start with a small nudge. If—for whatever reason—that initial nudge is not enough to derail the current direction of the case, then they will apply addi-tional pressure. If we resist and continue to pursue either the murderer or Invisius Verso, then it will get ugly. It's as simple as that."

Vince's eyes bored into mine. "So that's it? We're done? We just walk away and forget about all of this? And, mean-while, the murderer is free to kill someone else. Is that it?"

I sighed. "Vince. If you refuse to ... go with the flow, you will be ruined. And not only you." I leaned forward to stress my point. "Don't you understand? You are special—no mat-ter how much you try and deny it. They can't get inside your head. They can't break your mind. So, they will do the next best thing. They will destroy your life. They will manipulate those around you and possibly destroy the minds of those people closest to you." I leaned back into my chair. "It's your choice. Don't be fooled into thinking otherwise. It's a choice you have to make—let others pursue the murderer or don't. If you decide to persist, then you and your loved ones will pay the consequences."

He looked angry and accusing. "So you're going to walk away. They win. End of story?"

"Yes." I resisted the urge to look away. "I have some of Daniel's memories. I know what they can do. But, I also know they'll pursue Brian Stalzing relentlessly. They won't stop until he's apprehended or killed, of that I have no doubt."

Vince regarded me coolly. I studied him, wondering what he was thinking, whether he would lay off the case, whether he believed me. The jarring ringtone of Vince's cell broke the silence and caused me to jump. It rang several times before Vince reached down to answer it.

"Yeah?" he said as he stood up.

I wished I could hear the person talking on the other end. Vince glanced briefly at me and then said, "I'm here with Lire. We checked with one of the warlocks in her building about the wards and— "

He turned and moved away from me while listening intently to the person on the other end. I watched him pace at the back of the room and then stop near the window that faced the office building next door.

He stood, body rigid, left hand in a fist at his side. "What? What the hell are you talking about? What did he come up with?"

Vince listened for a moment before saying, "Jensen, all the facts checked out. The victim's names. Everything. Don't you think it's odd just when we find out about a telepathic group, Cunningham's mind suddenly changes?"

After listening to a lengthy response, he pulled the phone away from his ear and jabbed a button. He stayed facing the window for a long moment without speaking to me. I stood and walked around the conference table, but I didn't join him at the window. Instead, I leaned back and perched myself on the edge of the table where he had been sitting previously.

I spoke to his back. "It's starting. Just like I said. Isn't it?"

He didn't have to tell me what happened. I knew from his side of the conversation my skills had been discredited and he had probably been ordered to leave. My stomach lurched. The thing I didn't know was how much damage had been wrought against me personally. Was I going to be publicly humiliated? Or just blackballed from working with the FBI? Were all police organizations going to shun me now? Or just the Chiliquitham station? I tried not to agonize over the extent of the damage, but it wasn't easy. I had enough money to live comfortably for the rest of my life if I was frugal. However, my coworkers probably didn't have an inheritance to fall back on, like I did. I hoped the collateral damage wouldn't adversely affect their lives, but only time would tell.

He replied without turning. "Jensen told me Cunningham suspects you faked some of your readings in order to have a key role in the investigation." He slid his cell into the holder at his belt. "Jensen and I are off the case and I've been ordered back to the department."

When Vince turned toward me, his face was set in a harsh expression. He looked ready to beat someone to a pulp. Unfortunately, his gaze was leveled at me. I tried not to squirm and failed to contain a wave of anguish that nearly undid me.

I kept things short, not trusting my composure to hold. "Then I guess that's it. I'm sure everyone will be relieved to no longer require my services."

From between clenched teeth, I scarcely told Vince to have a good life and then fled the conference room. I compelled myself to leave without looking back, and it was one of the most difficult things I've ever done.

After I made it out the door, I broke into a run toward the stairwell because it was only a matter of time before I lost it. Pathetically, I longed for Vince to chase after me.

Goddamned baby! I scolded myself.

I threw open the steel door ahead of me with Jason's gift and it crashed loudly against the wall. The excessive use of force was somehow satisfying. I plowed through the opening and down a short hallway that ended at the secured stairwell door. A repressed sob echoed in the enclosed space, but I slapped a hand over my mouth and swallowed further tears. With trembling fingers, I fumbled in my pocket for the security fob and held it against the lock. With the answering click, I slammed the door open, stormed through and vaulted my body straight over the railing.

Forty feet of empty space loomed below my feet, framed by the corkscrew path of the individual flights of stairs. I briefly let myself fall toward the bottom before taking control of my body. The freedom of weightlessness thrilled me. As the landing of each floor flew past, I blinked against the force of air hitting my eyes. I hurled upward until abruptly stalling just inches from the ceiling. Breathing hard from the exertion, I coasted down to the penthouse landing.

When I entered my apartment, Red waited for me near the front door. I dropped to my knees and scooped him up into my arms. My vision blurred, but I held on to my composure by a tenuous thread. There was much we had to discuss, and tears would only interfere.

"Oh, Red."

Before I was able to elaborate, a loud pounding rattled my front door. Sparks of alarm zapped clear down to my toes.

Vince demanded, "Lire, open up."

I stared at the deadbolt and blinked back the tears. "No. You need to go."

"I'm not leaving until I talk to you. Now open this door before I break it down."

Even though I didn't believe he'd actually resort to a battering ram, I didn't want to alarm my neighbors. I released my grip on Red, so he could sit on my shoulder, and stood. I opened my door just enough to look out.

Vince's expression was hard, but he tipped his head forward, which made him look more earnest than angry. "We need to talk. Please, let me in."

"Vince," I quavered, despising the way my voice betrayed my emotions, "you should go. I don't want you to ruin your career or put your family in danger."

He stepped closer. "Let. Me. In." His expression softened, and he added, "Please."

When he pushed against the mostly closed door, I didn't fight him. I stepped back to let him come inside and then watched in silence as he closed the door behind him. It was impossible to look confident and steadfast when my eyes were moist with unshed tears. I crossed my arms and forced myself to meet his gaze.

He shook his head. "You honestly think you could get rid of me that easily? Or that I'd leave like a dog with a tail between my legs?"

I frowned. After witnessing my freak show and hearing what Jensen had to say about me, I figured he'd be relieved to have nothing more to do with me. I had tortured myself with thoughts of him walking away with a pat on his back and a thank you heavenward for the near miss of being involved with a weirdo like me. He had the perfect excuse to leave and I'd fully expected him to take it.

I took a trembling breath and stuck out my chin. "I figured you'd do the smart thing and go back home."

"I need to know you'll be okay, first."

My heart wrenched at the sight of him. He looked strong and determined. It was all I could do to meet his smoldering stare and keep from throwing myself into his arms. Again, I reminded myself that he thought I was deviant.

"I'll be fine." I straightened my back and tried to reassure him, so he'd leave. "I'll get the ward from Claude. Things will work out. I'll be okay."

My conversation was decidedly clipped. I didn't trust myself to say too much. Any stray word had the potential to cause a crack in my unstable façade of self-control. I had let Vince witness too many of my emotional breakdowns. I didn't need to give him further confirmation that not only was I a psychic freak but also a complete emotional wreck.

"Somehow I don't think *I'll* be okay." He threw up his hands. "Not after all this."

I nodded stiffly, and bit the inside of my cheek. I would not cry. I would not cry.

"Lire ..." he began but stopped. He looked uncertain.

Not wanting to hear him tell me again how he needed some space, I didn't give him the chance to fumble for words. "Look, I'll survive. I have before. My life was always complicated, and now, well, now it's worse than a freak show, but I'll live. Things will die down. They'll catch the murderer and then life will go back to normal."

My life hadn't been normal to begin with, and I knew things would never be the same again, but I had to get Vince to leave. The longer he stayed, the more likely the Invisius Verso fixers would make things worse for us.

He dropped his arms and almost looked like he might step closer, but he stayed put. "Promise you'll call me if things get dicey."

I nodded. "I promise." *Not.*

His dark brows drew down, and he regarded me for a moment before turning toward to the door. Over his shoulder, he said, "When I figure out what's going on, I'll call you."

With those words ringing hollow in my ears, he finally left.

My composure crumbled soon after.

NINETEEN

For the next two days, I waited for the other shoe to drop. Every time the telephone rang or I had to call someone, I expected to receive bad news in the form of altered memories and ruined relationships. Each uneventful hour that went by only raised my stress level higher. A sense of impending doom threatened my every thought and my imagination whittled incessantly at my sanity. I was convinced any minute the police were going to show up to arrest me on some trumped up charge, or I'd hear from the IRS that I owed my entire fortune to the government, or some other horrible, life-changing fabrication. Red did his best to ease my mind, but he could only do so much to staunch my creative imagination.

Finally, on the afternoon of the second day, Claude called with word my bracelet was done. I hurried down to his apartment, worrying that despite the djinn and the building's wards an assassin might be lurking along the way.

When Claude opened the door, I greeted him, and he shook his head with a pitying expression. "*Ma chérie.*" Without another word, he ushered me into his apartment and sat me down on his couch. While I made myself comfortable, he opened a package of psi-free gloves and slipped them on, being careful to use the plastic to avoid touching the outside of the fabric.

"You are most distressed. I can see. You have the look of a caught mouse." He touched my cheek gently with a gloved finger to soften his words. Although he excelled at the role of playboy and irrepressible flirt, it was apparent he cared about me too.

With a reassuring wink, he said, "This will help."

He picked up a small black pouch from the coffee table. Opening it revealed a fine, delicate looking bracelet made from a braided material. It shimmered slightly, as if woven from silver thread. He draped the bracelet over my wrist, deftly manipulating the clasp in spite of the gloves.

"It was not easy, but the challenge I do enjoy." He glanced at me with one rakishly raised eyebrow.

As soon as the clasp caught, the bracelet seemed to shrink to fit my wrist and I felt a tremor of magic cascade over my skin. The feeling wasn't unpleasant, but it sent a tingling sensation along the surface of my entire body, like an extreme case of goose bumps.

My eyes must have gotten big because he laughed and reassured me that what I felt was normal. "Do not worry, *chérie*. This feeling of strangeness will not last. Soon it will not be noticed, you will see. But while it does, it will make you think of my loving embrace, no?" He smiled devilishly.

I laughed and bit my lip. "I would think of no other, Claude." I smiled at him before considering the bracelet. "Is there anything I shouldn't do? Can anything break the spell? It looks so delicate."

He chuckled, holding up my hand so the strand dangled from my wrist, and tapped it with his finger. "No, *chérie*. It has the look of, uh, how do you say? Spun glass? But, no, it is tough as the nail. My spell is *très puissant. Oui*. Very powerful. It cannot be broken, nor can one remove it without your permission. But, *mon amie*, this is *très important* ... if you choose to remove it, the spell will break. *Tu comprends*?"

"I am the only one who can remove it. But if I do, the spell will break," I repeated.

Claude nodded and his thick hair moved smoothly with the motion. "*Oui*." He lowered my hand, but continued to hold it and gave it a squeeze. "Now, is there anything else I can do for you? I have the feeling you are the lady in distress."

He expressed his concern without any leering, which was unusual. Occasionally, I got a peek beyond his hedonistic facade, and it was always a treat. Although he had hinted that I knew him better than anyone else outside of his family, I suspected the true Claude had yet to be completely revealed to me.

I considered his offer of help. For a moment, I indulged in wishing he had a bracelet for every one of my friends, coworkers, and family, but I knew it was impossible. It had taken Claude two full days to make the talisman and required God knows how much of his energy and special ingredients. A ward this powerful was a rare and generous gift. Besides, it would only protect someone from a distance. Most of my friends and family had no way to stop a telepath from physically touching them. I, on the other hand, had considerable deterrent options at my disposal thanks to my new powers.

I tried to smile and shrugged. "Maybe just a little distress. But no, you've done more than enough already. I worry about the people who help me too much."

He snorted, dismissing my concern with a wave of his hand. "I am not powerless, you know." He pulled back the sleeve of his right arm. "See? I too take the precautions." A twin to my bracelet encircled his wrist. "And if this does not, ah, take care of business, then there are other things." Claude's eyes narrowed.

I gave him a grim nod of understanding. My eyes dropped again to the bracelet. "It is not only a work of impressive magic but a work of art." He had undoubtedly saved me, and I told him so. "*Tu m'as sauvé la vie.*"

He assured me that it was a pleasure. "*C'est toujours un plaisir pour moi.* If you need anything else, you have but to ask." He fixed my eyes with a direct stare. "Any time. You know this."

"Thank you, Claude, I am in your debt. Truly."

"Indeed, *mon amie*. You have much to offer. Things are at their darkest for you now, I can see. But you are *très puissante*. You will triumph. I have no doubt." He said this with such conviction I almost believed it.

Under other circumstances, I might have hung around to gossip and flirt, but with my mind weighed down by recent developments, I wasn't in the mood. We said our goodbyes, and I left his apartment feeling more confident than I had in days.

When I got back upstairs, I commented to Red, "It still feels funny. I didn't want to ask Claude, but you don't think this will interfere with my, uh, other abilities? Do you?"

Red cocked his head. "I think not, but there is only one way to be sure. You need the practice anyway. Your new powers will save you if you are attacked again."

I blew out a frustrated breath. "And just how am I supposed to practice? This isn't exactly a firing range, you know."

"Call on the djinn. They did offer their help. I thought of suggesting it yesterday, but you were too distraught. I decided it was best to wait until you were in more control of your emotions."

I wanted to argue but gave him a stiff nod instead. He was right. I closed my eyes and focused on the mark between my eyebrows. After my experience in the conference room, I knew it was a psychic conduit. I could use it to call on the djinn with my mind.

"Could it be the Lire requires the services of the djinn?"

I opened my eyes to see both entities coalescing in the center of my living room.

"Uh, yes. Hello Tanu. Maya. I was hoping you might help me hone my new powers. If you have the time, that is." My feelings had changed considerably toward the two djinn, but I was still a little daunted by their presence.

They swirled around each other with what I took to be excitement. Their corpulent, nebulous forms trailed wisps of heather gray mist along the floor as they surrounded me with their churning dance. The vapor briefly stymied my vision before clearing to reveal a misty rectangular enclosure approximately the same size as my living room and dining room put together.

I turned around to inspect the large, empty area. I could see the vague outline of my loft through the spectral walls of the enclosure, but my furniture had disappeared.

"Whoa." I laughed, nervously. "What did you just do? Where's all my furniture? Are we in my loft or not?"

One of the djinn appeared inside the space. "The Lire's belongings are still here, only set aside. The Lire should not worry. The djinn keep her things safe."

I nodded, but wished for a better understanding of how the djinn manipulated our world. I wondered at the extent of their powers.

"This will do nicely." Red appeared from the kitchen side of the enclosure. His body seemed to push through the cloudy wall without difficulty.

"I guess. But, what should I do?" I turned toward the djinn in time to see it suddenly pop out of existence.

At almost the same moment, a dark shape broke through the misty wall from the direction of my front door. I gasped when I realized it was the cloaked figure of the murderer.

The fight or flight instincts fought for control of my brain. I lost precious seconds before I staggered backwards, fighting to get control of myself. *How did he get into the building? Why aren't the djinn doing anything? Did the building's wards fail? Maybe Paimon wiped out the wards and neutralized the djinn.*

The figure laughed, an evil, spiteful sound that grated my ears. He reached into his pocket and withdrew a white handkerchief as he strode toward me.

"No!" I bellowed. Without thinking, I lashed out with Trinity's cold power.

Frigid air exploded into the area between us with a resounding *crack*. Instantly, a thick wall of ice towered all the way to the ceiling and as far past the misty walls as I could manage. After sparing a moment to search the floor for Red, I levitated him to my shoulder.

I shifted my focus back to the murderer in time to watch a blast of fire coat the opposite side of the wall. Deep fissures snaked through the ice with ear piercing pops and cracks. Before the barrier broke apart, I thrust my hands toward it, using Jason's power to grapple with it. I pushed against the ice, forcing it to lurch and then smash into the dark figure. The impact drove the warlock backwards, disrupting his concentration. The fire went out. I directed additional force to the top of the wall, in an effort to topple the whole massive edifice on top of him. The wall tipped over, but instead of crushing the murderer as I had hoped, it broke into hundreds of ice shards that flew out in all directions.

I shielded my head with my arms and bent over as the chunks of ice pelted me and crashed to the floor around me. A chunk the size of a baseball glanced off my shoulder and drove me to my knees before I remembered to use Jason's power to repel the deadly missiles. When I concentrated, I could sense the objects flying toward me and redirect them to the side.

The cloaked figure had regained his stature and used his mind to levitate ice chunk after ice chunk toward my head. The lethal pieces of ice smashed the floor around me as I deflected them. After a few moments, instead of simply deflecting the missiles, I redirected them toward the murderer's head. His progression slowed, but I noticed he hadn't dropped the damn handkerchief. I regained my feet and madly tried to think of a way to incapacitate him. We shared the same powers. How was I supposed to beat him?

I wondered whether it was possible to use two or more of my powers at the same time. While I continued to repel the catapulting ice chunks, I sought Patty's power, this time without the driving anger. It nearly made me giddy. Both Patty's and Trinity's powers coursed through my body in a dizzying combination. Both of their gifts were just two sides of the same coin—the yin and yang of temperature manipulation—and did not cancel each other out, like I had imagined. Using both powers in tandem was definitely possible, and it gave me an idea.

First, I set about fashioning a weapon. Feeling rushed and awkward, yet empowered by the confluence of the two powers, I quickly formed the ice chunks into something that resembled a large icicle. It wasn't the javelin I had envisioned, but it was better than nothing. I didn't waste time lamenting my pathetic skill. The murderer had closed the distance between us, now that my ice barrage had stopped.

I cried out, leveling a jet of blue, hot flame at my cloaked assailant, and immediately following it with the sharpened javelin of ice. Jason's power was key in launching both the jet of fire and the icy arrow with deadly speed.

I almost laughed at how perfectly the three psychic phenomenon complemented each other. Unfortunately, my performance wasn't terribly effective. The javelin broke apart before impaling the warlock. I did notice, however, that the deadly combination forced him to retreat several paces. Feeling more confident, I repeated the same process, using chunks of ice from the floor.

My skill improved. This time I created a sturdy javelin. The heat I pulled from the air when I created it was easily transformed into the jet of fire. It was a two-for-one deal. I had the ability to supplement both powers with almost unlimited energy. And Jason's power magnified the speed at which I could transmit the super-heated air, not to mention the javelin. All three powers working together provided me with a staggering arsenal of magic weaponry.

I blasted the warlock with wave after wave of fire and ice, improving my performance each time. With the murderer in full retreat, I spared some thought about how he made it past the building's wards.

Duh. The djinn hadn't been neutralized.

I grunted with recognition and halted the psychic barrage. "Okay. It took me a while to finally figure it out, but I got it. Thank you, Maya and Tanu."

The assailant dissolved into the familiar gray form, and the remaining ice vaporized in an instant.

"You scared the crap out of me, but it served its purpose. I couldn't have asked for a better test." I dropped to my knees. My body trembled from the intoxicating mix of terror, excitement, and power.

The misty room dissolved and I found myself next to the coffee table in the middle of my living room. Again, I marveled at the extent of the djinn's powers.

"The djinn are here to serve the Lire. The Lire can control the powers." Both djinn swirled near the patio doors and the light coming through the panes cast interesting shadows through their churning forms. "Could it be that she is no longer afraid?"

"Not of wielding the fire, at least." I sighed. "The murderer ... well, that's a different story."

"The blood-bound Lire has the power," the left djinn declared.

"The human Lire is capable," said the one on the right.

"The Lire will call on the djinn again," they said together.

"Yes." I smiled and stood, using the tabletop for leverage. "And the djinn may call on Lire."

The two entities appeared to shiver with excitement and then quickly spun around me before disappearing from view.

I staggered to the family room couch with Red still perched on my shoulder. He sprang down and toddled to the arm of the couch where he sat and considered me.

I relaxed against the cozy chenille. "The bracelet is still making my skin tingle, so I guess the other powers didn't mess it up."

"Was there really any doubt?"

I snorted. "I suppose not. Claude knows his stuff, but I didn't exactly announce that I've gained three new abilities either. It's not something I'll be advertising, you know." I couldn't help but think of Vince's reaction after he witnessed my powers. I cringed at the memory. "You should have seen the expression on Vince's face."

After a moment of feeling horrible, I slammed my fists down on the cushions. "Dammit! I am not a freak! I did not choose for this to happen! And I am sick of feeling like I need to bury my head in the sand!"

Red regarded me silently. I crossed my arms and pushed myself deeper into the couch cushions. Sulking didn't accomplish anything, but it felt good.

"Have you stopped to consider that perhaps Vince also feels like a freak?" He paused, giving me time for his words to sink in. "Two weeks ago, Vince was a magi-phobic detective in a repressed police department. Now multiple sources have told him he has sidhe blood and possibly several unknown magical abilities. That knowledge, combined with witnessing your own struggle to assimilate and control your new magical talents, has undoubtedly given him much to consider."

I grunted, determined to feel wretched. "Yeah. And if it weren't for me he wouldn't be considering any of this stuff at all."

"No. If it weren't for the *murderer*, Vince would not have these things to consider. He would still be repressed and you would be shy three new, tremendously useful talents." Red padded over and looked up at me. "Are you through feeling sorry for yourself?"

"Probably not." I sighed. "But I'll get over it. Eventually."

After a moment, I sat up and rested my elbows on my thighs. "It's time to get back to work. I've had enough of hiding out."

"I agree."

I regarded my fuzzy companion. "Even with my powers and this bracelet, I'm still afraid. Daniel knew some of the details of the prophecy. It evolved over time, but the diviners all agreed the murderer and I would meet in conflict, face to face. Daniel didn't know where or under what circumstances or even when—only that we'll eventually meet and only one of us will survive." My voice cracked. "Red, I don't want to end up like the others. There are so many things I haven't done or seen ..."

He held up his paw. "You are well aware of the limitations of divinations. Just one minor change to the timeline, something as simple as tripping on your way out the front door, can have a profound effect later in time. There is no way to know whether the newest prophecy will hold true. Even if you and the murderer do meet, there is no guarantee the end result will mean your death or even the murderer's death. The statement 'only one will survive' can be interpreted in different ways. It may indeed mean one of you will die, or it may mean only one of you will survive to live life freely, or only one of you will survive intact and the other may be forever changed, either mentally, physically, or spiritually. Until it comes to pass, there is no way to know for certain what the future will bring."

"I know these things. But it doesn't make me feel any better. I'm still scared."

He touched my arm. His soft fur triggered an involuntary shiver, followed by a healthy case of goose bumps. I looked down at him and placed my hand on top of his paw.

He stared up at me. "No matter what happens, Lire, I will be with you. We will get through this together."

With moist eyes, I nodded and scooped him up in my arms.

TWENTY

Red and I agreed it was best to take a taxi to work, instead of asking one of my friends or coworkers to pick me up. My car was still parked in front of ST&C where it had sat ever since Daniel stopped by to screw up my world. Until I knew things were okay and my friends and family were safe, I planned to keep to myself as much as possible.

At 9:15, I stepped into the elevator, grousing, "Freaking Daniel. Not only did he bring me bad news and embroil me in the politics of his stupid club, but it's his fault my car is stuck at work."

Red didn't respond to my gripe. In the shiny doors of the elevator, I could see the reflection of his head just peeking out of my black shoulder bag. We set up the perch earlier in the morning—so he might warn me of anything approaching us from behind—and I wore a black coat and sweater to keep his head from standing out. This was the meager extent of our preparations. I felt like a hermit crab without its shell, and we hadn't even left the building.

The ride downstairs was uninterrupted. I sighed and steeled myself for the unprotected world beyond the lobby. Fear churned the inside of my stomach and fretted my already frazzled nerves.

The taxi waited at the curb out front. I think I looked calm, making my way from the building's glass doors to the interior of the taxicab. At least, I didn't break into a panicked run. As I pulled the car door closed and settled into the back seat, I told the driver my destination in a breathless voice. His heavy-lidded, brown eyes briefly regarded me in the rear view mirror before he pulled into traffic. I pressed my lips together and focused on taking easy breaths.

Every time the taxi stopped in traffic, I scanned both sides of the street while glancing furtively out the front windshield every few seconds. I tried to see everywhere at once. If only I had the protection of my armored car. Although Daniel felt certain the physical attempt on my life wasn't the act of his organization, I didn't understand how he could be so sure. I didn't see the distinction between a physical hit and a mental one. Once they made the decision to harm me, what difference did it make how it was done? How could Daniel be so sure the telepathic hit squad wouldn't resort to whatever means at their disposal? Who was to say they hadn't brainwashed some petty thug to steal the car and run me over? Of course there was the possibility the hit and run wasn't deliberate and I just happened to be in the wrong place at the wrong time. If that was the case, then maybe I didn't have as much to worry about.

I continued to speculate about the hit and run as the taxi wove through morning traffic. By the time we arrived at ST&C my thoughts were spinning like a whirligig on a windy day.

The parking lot was less than half-full with a majority of the cars clustered in front of the coffee shop three doors down. My car was still out front with Jack's red Audi parked next to it. Seeing his car alongside mine comforted me. God knows why. Jack certainly wasn't a martial arts master, much less magically inclined, but it made me feel better anyway.

The driver pulled the taxi into the empty spot next to Jack's car while I removed my seat belt. I heard him shift into park while I rummaged in my purse for my wallet.

"That's $9.50." His voice was gruff. Mr. Congeniality.

"Uh, okay." I tried to get my brain to calculate the total with a decent tip.

I collected the necessary bills into a neat stack and thrust my hand between the front seats toward the driver. He had turned toward me but didn't immediately make a move to retrieve the money. Instead, his head bobbed forward, as if fighting the urge to sleep.

Whoa, I thought to myself. *Is he drunk? Thank God I'm getting out.*

"Uh, sir." I waved the money to get his attention. "Here you go."

The driver seemed to struggle with lifting his head. When I finally got a look at his face, his eyes had rolled upward—the whites contrasting alarmingly against his dark-olive skin.

I froze, the money dangling from my clenched fingers. "Sir! Are you okay?"

Stupid question. He clearly wasn't okay, but my adrenalin-addled brain wasn't offering any sensible suggestions.

I closed my hand around the money to keep it from flying around the front of the car and used the side of my clenched fist to firmly nudge the driver's arm. "Sir, do you need help?"

The driver grunted and raised his head toward my voice, but his eyes were half closed and he still didn't look normal.

He wasn't simply sleep-deprived, and I didn't think he was drunk either. Maybe he was having a seizure. I didn't know anything about epilepsy or seizures and had no clue how long a seizure could last, or even whether they were physically harmful. I knew it was possible for seizure victims to bite off their own tongue. Just where I learned this grisly detail, I had no idea, but I think it was common knowledge. Thankfully, I didn't see the driver's tongue sticking out of his mouth or any blood. Even so, the time for dithering was over.

"Okay, uh, I'm calling 9-1-1!"

I threw the now wadded money at my feet, so I could retrieve my cell phone, but the driver's grunt, derailed me. His eyes opened wide and he blinked slowly.

"Oh my gosh! Are you okay? I can still call an ambulance. Sir?"

The driver emitted a rough sound that might have been a chuckle. He regarded me with a distant expression. "Sit back and calm yourself." Even though his voice was raspy and his modulation irregular, he managed to sound haughty, almost condescending.

Appalled, I stared at the smirk on his lips and resolved to telephone his cab company with a sternly worded complaint. It was pure luck he hadn't been driving when all this happened, the jerk.

"I'll calm down when I'm the hell out of this taxi." I bent down to gather the bills scattered on the dirty floor mat.

He laughed. "Undoubtedly. But we have a few things to discuss, first. Unfortunately, my preferred way of getting your attention was not available to me."

The hairs on the back of my neck immediately stood at attention. I played dumb, hoping to buy time to escape the car. "You know, whatever seizure you're having knocked a few screws loose. I suggest you see a doctor immediately." I threw the fare onto the front passenger seat, grabbed my purse, and reached for the door handle.

"If you don't want me to send this car crashing into your office, possibly killing people in the process, I suggest you sit back and *listen*." The driver bit off each syllable of the last word, so there was no misunderstanding.

God, no. I wasn't ready for this. I paused with my hand clamped to the door handle and swallowed my panic. My gaze slid to the driver, and I couldn't help imagining Sausage-Man from the parking garage, pulling his strings like a maniacal puppeteer.

"You are wearing protection. Someone in your building made you a ward of some kind, I gather." He sighed and waved away the thought with a flick of his fingers. "So, I was not able to discuss things with you in a more intimate manner. Mind to mind, as it were."

I narrowed my eyes at him. "You know, this is such utter crap. I did what you guys wanted. I stopped helping the police. So now you need to hold up your side of the bargain and leave me the hell alone!"

Magic stirred inside my core, fed by my fluctuating emotions. I tamped it down. Definitely a bad idea to show the Invisius twerps the extent of my new powers, especially since they seemed to think it factored so keenly into their damned prophecy.

The swarthy driver laughed. The demented cackle sent unpleasant shivers along my skin.

He replied, "They got to you, did they? I knew they would. I told you so, didn't I? I told you we would end up on the same side." The man laughed. "No, Lire. Invisius wouldn't use a fat middle-aged taxi driver to speak with you. No. They'd just walk up to the car, open the door, and get things done—physically, now that you have that trinket. All they'd have to do is hold you down and touch you. Really. It's not much of a deterrent for them, but I suppose it makes you feel better. Doesn't it?"

He laughed again. I didn't know whether to be relieved or even more terrified knowing the taxi driver was controlled not by an Invisus telepath but by the murderer. Was this the portended confrontation? Was I about to die?

"What do you want, *Brian*?" I tried to control the whirling emotions and jolts of magic that threatened to overcome my rational thoughts. I needed to calm down and be at the top of my game. *Stay cool and think!*

"Ah. Down to the nitty-gritty, is it? No more small talk?" He sighed. "Have it your way."

The driver examined his fingernails for a moment. It gave me the creeps to think this poor guy's personality had been shoved aside to make room for Brian's corrosive thoughts. I wondered if the driver was in there, helpless, forced to watch as the murderer spoke to me and unable to do anything to stop his body from obeying the will of his attacker.

Deadly Remains - Chapter Twenty

The driver's vacant brown eyes regarded me again. "What I want is to break the prophecy. You know as well as I do that visions of the future are fragile. The smallest change in the present can drastically alter them, which is why diviners have to constantly revise their predictions. The Invisius diviners do so continuously!" The muscles of his jaw tensed and he tipped his head toward me, looking contemptuous. "Not an hour goes by without an announcement from their inner sanctum. At critical moments, there is a literal frenzy of corrections—minute by minute, blow by blow accounts of the future."

He paused, seemed to gather himself, and continued in a less agitated manner. "We can choose to go against the prophecy, you and I. Let us join forces against Invisius. Their evil needs to end. You know this as well as I. Daniel feels the same way. I know. We're friends."

I must have looked doubtful because the puppeteer forced the driver to nod his head. "Yes. Good friends. He told me about how he was taken from you, from everything he held dear, against his will, just as I was taken from my own home."

What could I do except tip my chin in acknowledgment? Until I knew what cards were being dealt, I had no idea how to play my hand. Certainly, I couldn't allow Brian to crash the car into the building. So, I sat still and acted like I cared about the garbage he was spewing.

The driver inclined his head. "Did you know Invisius makes it a practice to alter the minds of every student's family? They implant the memory of the student's death into their minds. It's true. Every Invisius student is an orphan. My parents, my sisters, and all my friends were strategically altered to believe I had been killed in a random car crash. There's even a gravestone with my name on it that my parents visit on holidays. Every student has a gravestone somewhere. Hundreds of families suffered." His eyes narrowed. "It is unforgiveable!"

Brian closed the driver's eyes briefly and took a deep breath. Subdued, he continued, "From the moment I was forced into their ranks, I hated them. Most of the other students couldn't stand up to the indoctrination. The weaker ones all forgot about their families. The instructors' mind probes were strong and relentless, but I was stronger. I was able to keep my feelings secret, as was Daniel and a few others. But," he sighed loudly, "I was the only one who had the guts to take them on."

Before I could think better of it, I retorted, "And what? You think I'm just going to forget that you murdered someone I loved?"

"History has proven that sacrifices must be made for the greater good. Do you think the parents who lost their children to Invisius grieve any less than you? Hundreds of loving parents believe their children are dead. And there have been hundreds more before them. It's been going on for centuries. I'm trying to stop this needless cruelty." The driver's expression showed considerable disgust, and he peered at me with harsh eyes. "The leaders of Invisius are arrogant. They believe they are untouchable. Until now, they have been. They've been operating with impunity. You've seen for yourself the damage they cause. God help you if you happen to get in their way. For someone with no means of protection, there is no hope. You yourself are under their scrutiny. They have altered your life more than you know, and I don't just mean their attempt to run you over with a car."

The driver raised an eyebrow at my confused expression. "Didn't it strike you as strange that your mother had such a big change of heart before she died? Or your sister? You didn't find it strange that after scorning you and your ability for nearly thirty years, she'd suddenly go to work for one of the most renowned attorneys for paranormal rights?" He made a condescending clucking sound with his tongue. "No, Lire. Invisius has been playing you, ever since you came to their attention. They've been orchestrating and manipulating the minds of your friends and family to prevent your involvement in their business." The driver gave me a pointed look, daring me to disagree.

Deadly Remains - Chapter Twenty

I gaped at him. "That's ludicrous. For what possible reason would they alter my mother's and my sister's minds? What did it get them?"

The driver shook his head pityingly. "You left town, did you not? It got you out of the way for three days. Remember, even minute changes in the present can radically alter the future. Not only were you out of the way, but your mind was occupied with other things."

I slumped back into the taxi seat, as though the wind had been knocked out of me. Thoughts of my mother and sister whirled through my mind. I covered my face with my hands and screamed something senseless. "Dammit! I don't want to know this. I just want to be left alone."

"That won't happen, Lire. No matter how many times you might wish it. The die has been cast. Do you think you aren't being followed and watched, even as we speak? They've been watching you for weeks."

I pulled my face out of my hands and sat up straight, scolding myself for appearing so pathetic. Of course, it might be to my advantage to appear powerless and weak.

Brian rotated the driver's body to face the windshield and nodded in the direction of the coffee shop. "They are there, inside, watching us. Biding their time." His eyes caught mine in the rear view mirror. "The prophecy tells them only one of us will survive and the survivor will cause significant changes to their leadership. They will watch and wait to see who comes out on top. They will not draw undue attention to themselves before that time." He laughed. "They are fools."

I slapped my hand on my thigh in frustration. "This is ridiculous! What could I possibly do to them? Or to you for that matter? I'm a clairvoyant, not a superhero. How can they possibly think I'm any threat to them?" I hoped Brian was ignorant of my additional abilities.

Through the driver's eyes, I felt Brian's penetrating gaze. He regarded me for a moment before replying, "There is a reason for your involvement. Their relentless pursuit of you makes that clear. Which is why I want to combine forces. It will send a powerful message to their leadership. Can you imagine the uproar it will cause in their ranks when they hear we have joined together?" He laughed uproariously.

His maniacal laughter drove me to the end of my patience. I wanted nothing to do with this crazy scumbag. No matter how deserving his crusade might be, I just couldn't justify fighting evil with evil means. Sacrifices must be made! Spare me. He might be pitching teamwork and spouting righteousness, but there was no doubt in my mind this battle was all about Brian and his sociopathic quest for power.

I clenched my fists and glared at him. "I'll take no part in this absurdity. I'm not teaming up with you and I'm not having anything to do with them either. Go have your palace revolution without me. If you think you can kill me, fine, take your shot. If the Invisius jerk-offs want to bring it on, fine. But until they make a move against me, I'm ignoring all of this shit." I shot him a scathing look. "But listen closely, Brian. If you take any steps toward me or my friends, you *will* regret it." I allowed Patty's fire to flit at the end of my index finger and then leveled it at him. "Stay away from me and mine, and I'll stay away from you. That's the deal."

The driver sighed, apparently unimpressed with my small display of power. "Don't say I didn't try to do things the nice way."

Before he could put the taxi into gear, I used Jason's power to turn off the ignition and remove the keys from the steering column. The keys flew into my hand with a satisfying *clack* as I shouldered open the car door and jumped out.

"Son of a bitch!" I slammed it shut and quickly backed away from the car. "This is just freaking great! What the hell am I supposed to do now? He's not going to take no for an answer, is he?"

"Judging by his past and present behavior, I would say no," Red answered.

"Dammit! What should I do?" I moved around the back of Jack's car in the direction of my own car.

The sound of a door opening brought my attention to the taxi. I watched as the driver got out and stalked toward my office. He carried a crowbar.

"Oh, God! He has a weapon. He's heading toward the office!"

What now? I couldn't hurt the driver; he was just an innocent bystander. But I had to stop him. How could I do it without hurting him?

The only thing going in my favor was that Brian probably couldn't use his mind control and all of his newly acquired powers at the same time. If he wanted to bring his other powers to bear, he'd have to dump the driver.

First things first—I had to get the crowbar away from him. I ran through the list of methods at my disposal. I could heat the crowbar, but I was certain Brian could distance himself from the pain. I'd end up burning the driver's hand to a crisp and still not get him to drop the crowbar. Ice would only cause the driver's hand to freeze shut and cause the opposite of what I wanted.

Desperate, I used my mind to turn the deadbolt on the glass door. It was a futile gesture, but I needed to stall for time. Then, I focused my entire attention on the crowbar and attempted to pull it out of the driver's grasp. As soon as Brian felt my power yank the crowbar, he made the driver grip it tightly with both hands. I redoubled my efforts, which whipped the driver around in different directions as he fought like hell to hold on. After half a minute of intense flailing, my method had only succeeded in burning a bunch of energy. I changed tactics. Instead of focusing on the crowbar, I turned my power to each of the driver's fingers and tried to pry them loose. When I heard a finger go *crunch*, I gasped and stopped.

The driver's head swung robotically toward my direction, Brian's calculating smile playing across his lips. The expression was purely for my benefit and it churned my stomach. Brian cared nothing for the driver's welfare, and his answering smile told me he intended to use it against me.

With my power no longer hampering his movement, the driver turned toward the office and yanked on the door. Immediately realizing it was locked, he leveled the crowbar at the door's center and followed through with a solid strike. The dull *thwack* of the rod hitting the glass echoed through the parking lot. Hundreds of small, vein like cracks instantly turned the pane opaque. Inside the office, I heard Monica scream, accompanied by the crackling sound of dozens of small, blunted shards of glass falling to the pavement. The glass panel still held, but one more hit, maybe two, and there'd be a hole large enough for the driver to reach through and unlock the door's deadbolt.

Brian had his puppet wind up for another blow. It wouldn't be long before someone noticed all the commotion and added more fuel to the fire by trying to intervene. I had to think of some way to stop Brian! But how?

As the crowbar hit the glass for a second time, I focused on the driver's shoelaces and used my powers to tie them together as tightly as possible. I know! Lame! But give me a break, I was grasping at straws.

Red yelled from my purse, "Lire, just pick him up! What are you doing?"

I didn't take the time to chastise myself for being so stupid. I used my power to pick up the taxi driver and move him away from the front door. Red's suggested tactic was effective and timely. As soon as I yanked the driver and his deadly weapon away, Jack appeared at the battered, cracked door with an alarmed expression and, I swear, a fire extinguisher readied for battle.

"Jack!" I ran to close the distance while keeping the struggling driver under control. "Jack, it's the murderer! You need to get out of there! Get everyone in the office and run out the back door. Run!"

I reached the sidewalk just in time to see the driver's body go slack, still under my firm control, and hoped my restraint hadn't caused him permanent damage. My stomach clenched with foreboding as I looked up at Jack and realized why the driver had suddenly collapsed.

Jack laughed and it made my skin crawl because it wasn't his laugh. He unlocked the door and stepped outside, the scattered glass grinding against the sidewalk under his rubber soled loafers. "I have a question for you, Lire. What do you think will happen to Jack's future if I just take this handy item and use it to bash this man's head in?"

The murderer, now controlling Jack's body, gestured with the fire extinguisher canister. "He's so immobile. How do you think the police will feel about that? Or, maybe I could find another innocent bystander to brutalize. What do you think?"

I thought he was a crazy son of a bitch, but I restrained myself from saying so. Instead, I gently lowered the driver to the sidewalk and then faced Jack, keeping a watchful eye on the fire extinguisher. I readied myself, in case Brian decided to use it on me or anyone else. Over Jack's shoulder, I glanced into the lobby and was relieved to see it empty. So far, nobody else had noticed our battle by proxies, and I hoped it stayed that way. With the entrance to a crowded cafe within line's sight, the lack of public interest surprised me. This inattention probably wasn't a coincidence, but I didn't spare the time to think about it. I focused my attention on Jack and how I might protect him from Brian.

It occurred to me that all of my efforts so far had been to treat the symptoms and not the disease. If I wanted things to go back to normal, I needed to deal directly with Brian. I didn't relish the thought of killing him and certainly didn't want to die, but if I didn't face him down, people were going to get hurt.

I looked toward the driver and tried to deflect the conversation. "Why is he unconscious? Does controlling someone do permanent damage?"

Jack regarded the prone man briefly. "No. He'll come to in a while, no worse for wear. Except for that broken finger, I suppose. Of course, whether his own psyche is able to handle what just happened, I couldn't tell you."

I shook my head and sighed. "Okay, Brian. You win. Let Jack go and I'll do whatever you want."

420

He smiled broadly. "That's more like it. You just needed proper motivation." He gestured toward my car. "Get in. You're driving."

"First, let Jack go. I want to see that he's okay. Use the driver if you have to." It felt horribly wrong telling Brian to invade the driver's mind again, but I didn't want Jack to get hurt. Brian's power over me was absolute as long as Jack remained under his control.

"I think not. Not yet, anyway. When you get in the car, then I will consider releasing him."

Damn! What now? I had nothing to bargain with. If I refused to get into my car, Brian was going to escalate the situation and Jack would suffer. On the other hand, bringing Jack with me would place him at risk too.

"Fine!" I spat.

Remembering the taxi keys still clutched in my hand, I pitched them next to the driver's inert body, too angry and scared to feel bad about leaving him unconscious. As I stomped to my car, unassailable dread nestled into my thoughts. I unlocked all the doors and eased inside, keeping a close eye on Jack. Turning in my seat, I followed Jack's progression along the passenger side.

Where was the murderer parked? Was Jack going to get into the murderer's car and continue his role as a hostage? Or was he going to ride with me? Through the windows, I monitored Jack's slow, mechanical walk. As he opened the back passenger door, my breath caught abruptly when I finally took notice of a dark figure lurking in the back of my car—sitting directly behind me!

My gaze snapped between Jack's movements and the person shrouded in the darkness of the back seat. I jumped when the car door slammed shut, but my mind felt frozen, all my thoughts and actions choked by fear.

Still speaking through Jack, the murderer said, "Yes. I've been waiting for you. It is remarkably easy to go unnoticed when people's minds are so malleable."

Jack's eyes rolled up to show their whites and his body went completely slack. I heard the extinguisher thump to the floor as he slumped against the car door. When I heard his head hit the base of the window, a small, pitiful cry came out of my mouth. My dear friend was being brutalized and I was powerless to do anything about it. Anger and frustration rose into my throat, but I swallowed hard and refrained from throwing myself on top of the murderer and beating him senseless. I knew it wouldn't get me far and Jack would likely end up dead.

As if responding to my thoughts, Brian brandished a wicked looking knife. "You are a smart girl, so I know it's not necessary for me to go into great detail about how inadvisable it would be to use any of your powers against me. Jack here is going to ensure we arrive at our destination without incident. If I get any sense you are using your powers against me, I will not hesitate to deploy the knife, along with any other power at my disposal. With just a thought, I can kill Jack quite easily. The knife simply serves as a deadly reminder."

While Brian spoke, in his nerve-grating, arrogant manner, the double-edged, ceremonial dagger floated up from his hand and coasted toward Jack. It came to a stop with the sharp tip just an inch away from Jack's neck.

I gritted my teeth against the scream building in my lungs, which threatened to burst out along with my unrestrained power. It wasn't easy. I reminded myself that Brian needed Jack alive; otherwise, he no longer had a bargaining tool. If I could hold it together, Jack would be fine.

"Now. Start the car and head east on I-90," Brian instructed.

Although this was my first in the flesh meeting with Brian, I was so furious and anxious I hardly paid attention to picking out any details regarding his appearance. I was too busy imagining myself beating his masked face into mulch.

I whipped my body back to face the windshield, still fighting for calm. I gripped the wheel and counted to ten, but by the time I hit five it was obvious the effort was a waste of time. Still seething, I hammered the steering wheel with the sides of my fists before thrusting my car key into the ignition.

"Calm down. It won't do any of us any good to get into an accident. Besides, dearest Jack isn't wearing his seat-belt."

In my head, I uttered several expletives, but resigned myself to playing out the game of cat and mouse to its completion. I put on my seatbelt before exiting the parking lot and heading toward the freeway.

Out of the corner of my eye I saw Red emerge from the opening of my purse, which was lying in the footwell of the front passenger seat. My mind toyed with the possibility of levitating Red on top of Brian. Red's knock-back spell might zap him insensible, but I quickly realized the process would take too long to prevent injury to Jack. It could easily take a full second before Red made contact with Brian, plenty of time for him to drive the dagger into Jack's neck or use his power to rip Red apart. Alternatively, I could attempt to freeze Brian's brain or squeeze shut the carotid artery, but I wasn't absolutely sure it was possible to incapacitate Brain before he had time to kill Jack. The odds weren't good, and Jack's life was at stake. I had to wait.

Red hesitated before moving toward the driver side footwell. I hoped he had come to the same conclusion as me regarding our chances at launching an attack. It took supreme effort, but I avoided watching Red's movement and hoped he wouldn't do anything aggressive. After a few moments, I felt his paws rub against my left ankle as he concealed himself up my pant leg. His fuzzy presence so close to me gave me some much needed confidence and comfort. I thanked God numerous times for wide leg jeans. Believe me.

Twenty One

Throughout the forty-five minute drive up Interstate 90, my mind battled against the uneasy, ominous silence emanating from the back seat. I played through every horror filled scenario that came to mind a dozen times over, and the dire anticipation of the upcoming conflict only added to my anxiety. To make matters worse, I noticed strange behavior from the drivers around us.

I had assumed the first driver was lost and slowed down to look for an address. But, as our trip progressed, it became clear Brian was using his telepathy to keep all the nearby cars away from us. On the interstate, every car I approached changed to the farthest lane and slowed down. It was like traveling inside an invisible bubble the size of an empty football field. I bet Brian had altered their memories too, so no one would take note of our passing.

My morale reached a new low when we passed the exit for Chiliquitham. I pictured Vince back at his desk and wondered what he was thinking, how he was feeling, what he was doing. What kind of cases did he work on when murdering telepathic psychopaths weren't causing mayhem in his town? Would he miss me if I died? I gripped the steering wheel and scolded myself. No. I would not go there. I was determined to survive, even if it meant killing Brian. When this was over, I'd go back to fretting about my relationship with Vince, but until then, I had to put it out of my mind. Red must have sensed my mood because he gave my leg a firm squeeze.

In spite of my preoccupation, I did my best to keep track of the towns we passed. As we continued east, the terrain went from lush evergreen foliage interspersed with large numbers of newly budding deciduous trees to windswept, sparse hills punctuated by scraggy junipers and woody brush. The landscape looked bleak and harsh. It didn't help that it was yet another dismal, overcast day, although, fortunately it wasn't raining. The digital thermometer read 48 degrees.

When Brian instructed me to leave the interstate, I knew we were east of Kittitas by at least five miles, maybe more. A sign for the Ginkgo Petrified Forest State Park marked the exit. Heading away from the park, we drove another fifteen or so minutes along a desolate two-lane road. The landscape didn't improve. Dismally, I noted we hadn't passed more than a couple cars since exiting the interstate.

I followed Brian's directions until the road came to a dead end, blocked by a concrete and metal barrier. When Brian instructed me to park on the side of the road near the barricade, I drove onto the gravel shoulder and turned off the ignition. No sooner had I palmed my keys did they whip out of my hand and fly into the back of the car. There was an answering metallic clink as they smacked into Brian's outstretched hand. The smug squint of his eyes in the rear view mirror made me want to vomit. Never in my life had I loathed anyone so much, but all I could do was grit my teeth. I held my anger in check ... for later.

The enclosed space became intolerable. Before I knew it, I had exited the car, levitated myself over the roof, and landed five feet from Jack's closed door. I stopped short of ripping the door off its hinges since I didn't want to provoke Brian. A brisk breeze buffeted my back and blew hair around my face. I inhaled the cool, dusty wind.

The car door flew open and Jack's limp body tumbled out. I wasn't surprised by Brian's callous behavior and caught Jack with my power before he hit the ground. Brian's knife immediately followed Jack's trajectory and hovered in the air near his throat. I held Jack very still, levitated just inches from the ground, and kept my eye on the sharp dagger. The knife looked old but obviously deadly. It had a black handle carved with deep, decorative engravings and a wicked looking carbon colored blade. Under other circumstances, I might have appreciated its beautiful craftsmanship.

I considered my options. Could I prevent the knife from cutting Jack if I yanked his body out of the way? Yes, but even if I did pull his body away from the knife, Brian only had to send his power into Jack's brain to kill him. The knife was simply a reminder that Brian had the ability to kill Jack with a thought.

"Very nice. You will carry him. Down that trail. He will remain unconscious until I decide otherwise." Brian floated effortlessly from the car's interior and landed next to Jack's body. The knife never wavered as he commanded his body through the air.

He gestured at the trailhead, which was hidden by the guardrail marking the end of the paved roadway. A weathered metal sign read 'IRON HORSE STATE PARK—JOHN WAYNE PIONEER TRAIL.' The name sounded familiar. I seemed to remember reading about it at some point, but there wasn't time to dredge up the memory. Before Brian got any more impatient, I turned my mind toward using my power to keep Jack with me while I walked.

Jack's body dipped and lurched, but I eventually figured out how to split my attention between walking and keeping his limp form alongside without plowing him into the ground or slicing his throat against the ever-present dagger. It was disheartening and frustrating to have such feeble command of my inherited powers. I wished I had taken more time to experiment before leaving the safety of my apartment.

The trail was approximately twelve to fifteen feet wide, well maintained, and level. It consisted mostly of gravel and hard-packed dirt, pushing through a barren landscape of undulating, brush covered hills. Only the occasional out-cropping of craggy red rock interrupted the sparse scenery. Not a single man-made structure was visible in any direction, aside from the sporadic 'NO MOTORIZED VEHICLES ALLOWED' sign. The wind continued to claw its way into the openings of my coat, and I shivered.

For the most part, the path was elevated above the terrain by a couple of feet, providing a good view of the surroundings. Where the trail encountered the occasional hillock, the earth had been physically carved out to make room for the pathway. I wondered whether the trail had once been an old railroad bed. It seemed to go on ahead, straight and level, as far as I could see.

Brian followed behind me, but I didn't spare a glance. When I shifted my attention too far, Jack's body tended to bob toward the ground. I didn't hear his footsteps, so he either levitated himself or followed at a fair distance. The knife never strayed from the vicinity of Jack's throat.

When we happened upon a large rock outcrop to the right of the path, some fifteen or twenty minutes later, Brian came in close to my ear and told me to move toward it. I visibly startled at his silent, sudden closeness and he laughed in response.

"Go around to the backside. Head to the right." Brian paused to watch me step off the path.

My gait faltered at the thought of being close to our final destination. I knew Brian had no intention of teaming up with me. That was just a ploy to get me to accompany him without turning my office parking lot into a war zone. But why was he leading us out into the hills? Why didn't he just shoot Jack and me back at the side of the road? There wasn't a living soul around for miles. In fact, now that I thought about it, Brian had passed up several opportunities to escalate the situation. In the car, he could have easily touched my skin and tried to invade my mind. It was almost as if he was afraid to get close to me.

I walked toward the oblong formation of rust-colored rocks. The jagged outcrop was easily four times my height, one hundred feet wide, and half again as deep. A vague, narrow path appeared to lead around the escarpment. I followed it to the right, carefully pushing Jack along in front of me. When we rounded the back side, I spied a natural inlet into the rocks and headed toward it. Without being told, I knew it was our destination. Sure enough, nestled inside, protected from the incessant wind, was a partially completed magic circle. My heart skipped a beat, even though it was hardly surprising.

At the moment, I didn't sense any active magic. The circle was incomplete, but the rune stones were in place, along with a thin, braided rope that delineated its circumference.

When I stopped to face Brian, he remained several body lengths away and eyed me malevolently. "Get inside the circle. Jack too. And don't think about tripping over the rope. I might get so upset that the dagger slips."

His condescending demeanor made me want to spit in his face, but I clenched my teeth together and followed his instructions. I steered Jack a few feet into the circle and placed his body gently on the dirt. I withdrew my power and then stepped over the rope.

As Brian's little drama played out, my list of options grew smaller, but I wasn't completely despondent. He continued to keep his distance, which meant he still viewed me as a threat. Spell casting was exacting—even more so when dealing with demons. If Brian planned to raise Paimon, any number of things could go wrong, giving me an opportunity to move against him. There were also many ways to mess with his spells if I could provide a distraction. Of course, a botched summoning was just as likely to be hazardous to me as well as anyone else, but I was resolved. The most important thing was ridding the world of Brian's evil, no matter what. I would not allow him to take over Invisius Verso. Power like that at his disposal would be catastrophic. Even if it meant sacrificing my own life along with Jack's, he had to be stopped.

Deadly Remains - Chapter Twenty One

At Brian's brief, unintelligible murmur, my body vibrated with the snap of the circle closing around us. However, instead of driving me to panic, which I'm sure Brian would have enjoyed, the feel of magic strengthened my determination. I folded my arms and stared at him with projected calm. My insides roiled, but years of schooling my expression served me well.

Maybe Brian expected me to be hysterical or, at the very least, trembling with fear because his eyes narrowed. "You cannot hope to win, so don't even try. I will only release Jack if you cooperate."

Liar. "I'm listening."

"Sit down and submit to me. If you refuse, I will kill dearest Jack and then strike you down in the most painful way possible. But I won't kill you. I'll save that pleasure for Paimon."

I almost rolled my eyes. "Fine."

There was no point in arguing, so I kept things short. I sat down cross-legged on the dirt. While I watched from the ground, two lengths of rope emerged from Brian's cloak and darted toward me.

He commanded, "Turn around. Now! Put your wrists together, behind your back."

I complied and felt the rope wrap tightly around my wrists.

"Back around. Put your legs out straight. Put them together."

Again, I did as he instructed, and the second piece of rope snaked its way around my ankles. It secured itself with a complicated knot. The bonds squeezed painfully tight, but I tried not to wince. They would be off soon enough. Red gave my leg a comforting squeeze from inside my pant leg, and I willed myself to remain confident.

With the ropes fastened, Brian seemed to lose interest in me. He turned his back and began constructing another magic circle, probably for summoning Paimon. I glanced at Jack and watched as the dagger backed off, floating lazily toward the warlock. I frowned. Did he think I was just going to sit and wait for him to kill us? While I watched, I tested the bonds behind my back by twisting my wrists from side to side.

Immediately, the ropes tightened exponentially and the resulting pain took my breath.

Frantically, I called on my power to pull the rope apart. The pain was unbearable, but my efforts only seemed to succeed in winding them tighter. I imagined the rope pulling tight enough to sever my hands at the wrists. I fell to my side, thrashing on the ground, unintentionally causing the bonds of my legs to contract as well. *Dear God!* I had to get free! I writhed in agony. No matter how hard I struggled, nothing I did worked to ease the rope's tension. The bonds ground my skin and bones. The excruciating pain engulfed my mind and came out of my mouth in the form of shrill, aggrieved screams. I could hardly think of anything constructive, other than the stark desire to loosen the bonds.

When I thought my bones were seconds from breaking, Red squeezed my face firmly between his paws, shaking me. "Lire, the ropes are spelled! They will tighten at any hint of escape. You must calm your mind. You must not resist. Relax. Stop fighting!"

Red stroked my face as I focused on keeping my body still. Although I was far from relaxed and the bonds remained viciously tight, the magic ropes stopped their constriction. I turned my mind to expunging any thoughts of breaking free. It didn't matter. Escape wasn't my prime concern. I was here to defeat Brian, not run away. Yes, use of my hands and feet would be nice, but they weren't absolutely necessary. My powers were not dependent on my appendages. There were other ways to deal with the challenges ahead. Dwelling on escape was not one of them.

After several minutes of deliberate focus and meditation with Red whispering his encouragements in my ear, the ropes had loosened to a bearable level. They were still painfully taut, but had relaxed enough that I could pay attention to my surroundings. A lot had happened while I was fighting the bonds.

Deadly Remains - Chapter Twenty One

I pushed myself up to a sitting position. Because I wasn't focused on escape, the spelled ropes didn't react to my movement.

"Ahhh. I see you have figured out my ropes. Pity. Your ridiculous display was quite amusing." Brian's voice grated my already frayed nerves.

"I'm glad you were entertained."

I steadied my expression and fought to remain poised as I came face to face with the creature standing next to Brian. Red squeezed my arm and I avoided looking down. I didn't want to draw any more attention to him than necessary.

Although the demon stood over ten feet away, confined to a smaller magic circle, my stomach churned with fear and it was a fierce struggle to keep my thoughts from spiraling out of control.

The creature was cloaked in a human form, and ... oh, wowzers! He, I mean *it*, was a showstopper, not to mention stark naked and unbelievably gorgeous. I had to remind myself to breathe. It exhibited easily six feet of smooth, defined muscles. Dark blonde hair, chiseled features, glorious arched brow—if there was a list of Lire's top ten eye catching traits, the demon exhibited every one. And then some. If it weren't for the foul magic emanating from its direction, I probably would have appreciated the show much more readily. Still, its drool-worthy appearance gave me pause.

The demon was, of course, all about temptation. It strutted around as far as its circle allowed and demonstrated, both physically and verbally, how much potential pleasure was involved with an oath of allegiance. With a silver tongue, it spouted virtuously about how all my dreams were about to come true. Apparently, my chance at eternal bliss was well within my reach. No skin suits to worry about. No errant thoughts to overwhelm my senses. It offered absolute dedication to my every whim, my deepest desires. It reminded me of the pathetic state of my love life, my trials and tribulations, my near suicide, men spurning me because of my gift. It regarded me as a truly special individual. My gift should be held in awe, not derided or feared.

I'll be honest, it was very persuasive. Its chosen form was sexy as hell. It was intelligent and witty, captivating and entertaining. The display of concern and attention it paid me flattered me. I wondered whether the human conception of Hell was really true. Perhaps it was just an old wives' tale, like the demon described—stories passed down over the millennia to scare children into behaving like well-mannered adults. After all, the djinn also came from an alien otherworld. They too could present themselves in human form. I wondered whether—*ouch*!

A jab of icy pain between my eyebrows derailed the thought. I shook myself, trying to clear my head. What was I just thinking? I gasped. *Oh my God!* My bowels tightened. I pulled my hands to my chest, tried to curl up into a ball. The demon had almost hooked me. It had taken advantage of my weakness. If it weren't for the pain sent by Maya and Tanu … I shuddered and tried to focus on them. I could just sense their thoughts through the psychic conduit. It was a fleeting connection and the demon was relentless in its distraction.

"Lire," the demon whispered, its voice husky and appealing, "I will dedicate myself to you. I desire only to make your every dream come true. I ask you, truly, will you join me?"

I struggled to avoid meeting its eyes, flailing mentally for the means to fight off its seduction. Red grasped my arm with his paws. My insides melted at the sight of him, cute certainly, but the cuddly body also contained the personality of a being I truly adored. The love I felt for him warmed my spirit and restored my composure. It strengthened my resolve. Even so, love alone wasn't enough to fight such an unassailable creature directly. More powerful tools were necessary to pit oneself against a Prince of Hell—tools I simply didn't possess. If I couldn't defeat the demon, I hoped, at the very least, my meager efforts would be enough to foil Brian's plans.

"Lire. You have not given me an answer, I think because part of you knows the truth I speak. Come to me, Lire. You are a goddess among puny beings who will never appreciate you. I will make you my equal, my partner, my queen. Again, I ask you, truly. Will you join me?"

Finally, I had the strength to look the demon in the eye. It regarded me with a serene, understanding expression, but I was not fooled. "No. I will not."

The demon looked disappointed. "I am sorry for you, Lire. You have chosen a difficult path and one that puts you at odds with my plans. Can we not discuss this, first? I do not wish to see you suffer." It spoke with the voice of a loving boyfriend or husband, but I knew it was a lie.

I ignored the demon's appeal and answered truthfully. "I will do whatever it takes to see Brian is brought to justice and my friends and family are left alone to live their lives freely. If I can do that without suffering, you can bet I'll try."

The demon folded its toned arms across its flat abdomen, and I fought a losing battle to resist admiring its well-toned physique. I reminded myself this gorgeous façade hid a monumental horror. I had Jason and Trinity's memories. I knew the truth.

Brian retorted, "You've failed on that score. Just one spell. I get your powers and you die. The prophecy will come to pass. Only one will survive, and we both know who that's going to be." Looking smug, he glanced at the demon.

I rolled my eyes and forced myself to remain calm. "Uh-huh. That being the case and all, don't you think it's time to remove that ridiculous mask? Daniel gave me his memories. I've seen what you look like, so there's no reason to keep up the disguise."

Since I had zero options at my disposal, I figured stalling for time was as good a tactic as any. Maybe I'd figure out a way to fight Brian directly, on more even footing. Red's comforting presence at my side kept me hopeful.

Brian glared and then shrugged. "Why not? I don't suppose anyone else will be stupid enough to read your bones. Besides, I might just take them with me, as a memento." He laughed and removed the mask with a flourish, revealing the man familiar from Daniel's memory—brown hair, brown eyes, and a face more cute than handsome.

I tilted my head. "So, are you planning on putting me under with the chloroform so your spell continues to be a mystery? You know, I think I've figured out why you didn't want any of your victims to witness that spell. You don't want everyone to know Paimon is actually the one casting it. In fact, I'm guessing Paimon is the mastermind behind all of your actions, not the other way around as you've wanted everyone believe."

Brian snorted and stared down at me. "Paimon takes orders from me, as you will soon see."

The demon shifted in its circular prison and struck another enticing pose, casually running a hand through its thick, wavy hair. "Lire, join me and I will free you from your miseries and guarantee Jack's complete recovery. I will even spare Red. Nothing is served by your death. If you continue on this path, Brian will gain from you the remaining power of his earlier victims, Jack will die, and Red will be cast into oblivion. I can change things, however, if you agree to join me."

I laughed. "Nice try. You don't have that power. Brian is calling the shots, the last I checked. Somehow, I don't think he will allow for such a bargain."

Brian regarded me with a righteous smile and narrowed eyes. He glared at the demon. "Enough! She will not agree, no matter what persuasions you spout. Chloroforming her isn't necessary. Let her feel the full wrath of your spell, demon. It is time to end her meddling and get on with my plan. With the full power of Invisius at my disposal, I will be unstoppable."

Paimon's mouth turned up at the corners to form a wicked smile. "I think not, warlock. Lire is entirely too important to waste on your petty ambitions."

Brian pulled himself up taller. "Your opinion is irrelevant. Demon, I command you to strip the powers from her and give them to me. You will cast your spell now!"

The demon ignored Brian and gave me a conspiratorial smile. After a moment, it slid its eyes to the side without moving its head and regarded Brian. I got the distinct impression the demon was playing things up for my benefit.

Red tugged my arm. When I glanced down and saw him, my stomach clenched with foreboding. His furry face managed to look frantic. I wasn't sure, but I guessed his anxiety was due to Paimon's marked lack of obedience.

I shifted my attention back toward the demon just in time to see it casually step out of its summoning circle and face Brian.

Looking suitably shocked, Brian backed up several paces. His eyes were wide with surprise and confusion as he sputtered a nearly unpronounceable, multi-syllable name. "You are mine to command! Stop! Now!"

The demon laughed, the sexy human sound quickly morphing into a deep, vibrating guffaw. Something fleeting and unsettling shifted under its beautifully tanned skin. When I looked past the demon's muscular body, I saw Brian's confused expression had been replaced by one of abject terror.

"I think not, stupid human. You did well, bringing Lire to me unharmed, but your time of usefulness has come to an end. Now it is you who will serve me, in your next plane of existence."

Brian turned and launched himself away from the demon and, for a moment, I wasn't absolutely sure Paimon intended to chase him. With the demon's gloriously naked backside toward me, I had a perfect view of every toned muscle, and not a single one tensed up for pursuit.

Brian's frantic run carried him to the edge of the circle before I noticed something dark coalesce in front of the demon. The undefined shadow lashed out, preternaturally quick. It moved in an organic, spreading fashion, as ink might when squirted into a tub of clear water. The black appendage easily wrapped around Brian's waist, lifted him clear off the ground, and whisked him back to face the demon—all in the space of about five seconds. His body dangled helplessly and he twisted in a futile effort to escape.

Every nerve ending in my body screamed at me to flee. If it weren't for the magic bindings and Jack's unconscious body, I might have done just that.

Brian screamed piteously, and although I wanted to see him pay for his crimes, his slow, brutal death at the hands of Paimon was too much for me to watch.

I won't describe the details of his suffering and eventual death. Suffice it to say, when I saw the black shadow rip a strip of skin from Brian's midsection, I firmly clamped shut my eyes. I wanted more than anything to stuff my fingers into my ears, in order to block out Brian's horrendous screams and the disgusting wet sounds of the demon's methods. Several times, I felt the splatter of blood hit my face and heard it hit the dirt around me. I leaned to the side to vomit and wretched more times than I can count. As I teetered on the brink of madness, Red climbed to my shoulder, firmly placed a paw on each side of my face, and sternly told me to listen to his instructions.

When I didn't immediately respond, he squeezed my face painfully. "Lire! Listen to me! Focus!"

Numbly, I nodded my head and Red released me from his grip. He jumped to the ground, but before I turned away from the nearby horror, I couldn't stop myself from peeking. Blood was everywhere. The demon continued to grasp Brian, and I averted my eyes before I could process the exact details of his condition. Brian's loud, chilling screams and the demon's frequent promises of more pain told me his ordeal was far from over.

As I focused my attention on Red, I made the mistake of breathing through my nose. All at once, the putrid smell of excrement mixed with the coppery odor of blood assailed me. I nearly lost it, but with tenuous control I swallowed hard and bent down to better hear what Red had to say.

Red placed a paw on my leg. "Lire, I will not lie. You may die here, but my knowledge may help you preserve your soul if not your life. I will be by your side. We will face this together. Please, whatever happens, do not despair. God will not abandon you if you have faith."

I closed my eyes tightly before acknowledging Red with a stiff nod.

"Even full fledged Warriors of the Holy Cross are hard pressed to do anything except guard the perimeter of a high demon's range." Red rubbed my knee. "Even so, I believe there is hope. Clearly, Paimon wants you spared; otherwise, it would have allowed Brian to have his way with you. It must have a reason. Perhaps you can use this to your advantage."

I shuddered at the prospect of being bent to the demon's will. Whatever it had in mind, it surely wasn't good. It took supreme effort, but I pushed my thoughts away from the frightful speculation and tried to think instead about how to survive. I thought about the demon's circle and hoped Red had been able to pay some attention to the summoning.

"How did Brian lose control? Did I miss something while I was occupied with the bonds?" I asked.

"I believe Brian had only part of Paimon's true name." Red scoffed, "Clearly, Brian has little understanding or training in necromancy. Otherwise, he would have known this is a common demonic ploy."

"So, if you call a demon with one of these partially true names, then they're not bound to the circle at all? They can wander the world freely?"

Red shook his head. "No. The circle is elemental. It is their source of power and portal to our world. Paimon is irrefutably bound to it, although, without a true covenant, the demon has retained all of its power and freewill. Even so, Paimon cannot wander far from the circle without sacrificing power. If it wanders too far, the demon will cease to exist in this world."

"Like the djinn? I was told the building's foundation is their portal. But they can't wander outside the periphery of the building."

"Yes. Maya and Tanu were summoned in much the same way, but they are bound with a true covenant and they are neither demons nor angels. They are neutral."

I risked a glance over my shoulder. Brian was still alive, but his head lolled to the side, and his screams of pain were infrequent and pitifully weak. I closed my eyes before my brain had time to ponder all the red globs and glistening bits of gore surrounding the demon.

I looked back to Red. "How far can Paimon wander from the portal before reaching the limit of its tether?"

"The most powerful demons can wander several fur-longs, perhaps half a mile."

"Can I close the portal?" A ragged scream almost made me glance away again, but I kept my focus on Red.

Red paused significantly. "I don't know."

I once saw a documentary about the famous oil well fire-fighter Red Adair. The name stuck in my head for obvious reasons, but his story came to mind because the portal made me think of an oil well. It seemed to me the dangers associated with putting out a hazardous, high pressure col-umn of fire while it consumed an unlimited fuel supply was-n't all that different from attempting to close off a high demon's power source. I wondered whether physically damaging the summoning circle might cut off the power long enough to cause the portal to disintegrate.

"Can the circle be blown up? You know, like fire fighters sometimes do to cut off the supply of oxygen to a fire?"

"The portal is not subject to physical assault—it is not entirely of our world. Only magic can affect the demon and its power source. And not just any magic. Only magic wielded selflessly by a soldier of God will have any hope for success."

I sighed. "I suppose it doesn't matter. I'm fresh out of dy-namite anyway."

Red clutched my arm with both paws. "I love you, Lire. I know it isn't much consolation, but your presence here saw to the end of Brian's evil. Even if we both meet our death, you have succeeded in saving countless lives and brought peace to Nick's, Jason's, and Trinity's souls. For that you should be very proud. I am honored to be at your side."

I sobbed before managing to reply, "I love you too, with all my soul."

Red looked past me toward the demon and nodded. "Brian is finally dead. Keep your faith, Lire. It will protect you."

I felt the demon's dreadful approach. It stood, resplendently covered in unspeakable, blood-soaked gore and ran its tongue seductively across its lips. Fresh blood ran down the rippling muscles of its abdomen. I closed my eyes before I was tempted to follow the trail of blood to lower regions. Waves of dread combined poorly with my unwanted feelings of attraction to the demon's human form. I felt light headed and breathed deeply through my mouth to avoid getting sick.

Before the demon could speak, gunfire erupted from outside the circle. I flinched so suddenly from surprise I lost my balance and fell onto my side. With bullets zinging overhead, I decided it was just as well to be down low. Absurdly, I wondered when Jack had started carrying a gun.

The demon uttered a hideous laugh as it stood tall against the barrage of bullets. After countless rounds were fired, the noise finally stopped, and I turned my head to see the demon, unscathed. Its smooth, tanned skin and taut muscles remained perfectly intact, albeit coated haphazardly with Brian's blood. I was briefly discomfited by the view of my low vantage point before the naked demon turned away to face the gun-wielding assailant.

Red spoke urgently into my ear. "Lire! It's Vince!"

My breath caught. If my hands had been free, I probably would have smacked my forehead. "Dammit! I just can't get a break!"

The demon chortled. "Very good. Never have I succeeded so thoroughly."

Before I had righted myself, Paimon strode toward the source of the gunshots. I looked over just in time to get a view of it lashing out with its dark tentacle. It grabbed Vince just as easily as it had snatched up Brian, and the fresh memory was my undoing. I jumped up, wavering on my still tightly bound feet. My ankles flared with intense pain, and I came a hair's breadth away from falling on my face.

I bellowed, "Demon, stop! Hear me! If you harm him, I will pit myself against you and *never* agree to your terms. I will fight you to the bitter end and never give you what you desire. But if you do not harm him or any of the others and leave this place now ... I will go with you. I will pledge myself to you ... before God, I swear."

Red grabbed my leg. "Lire, no! You must not forsake your soul. Not for anything!"

I looked down at him. "Not even for love?" I shook my head in astonishment. "Red, what else can I do? I love you. I love the both of you."

The demon tilted its head back and laughed victoriously, pitching Vince's limp body to the side. Vince moaned and rolled over as he tried to orient himself. He appeared to be shaken but not badly hurt.

The demon sauntered toward me, halting just inches from my body. I stared defiantly up into its cold blue eyes and demanded, "Are we agreed?"

The demon chuckled and its gaze lingered on my face. Its voice pitched low and resonated with desire. "Yes. One soul such as yours is worth dozens of lesser mortals. I agree."

I shivered and closed my eyes. "We will swear it with blood. I will accept nothing less."

"Done." The demon's voice vibrated down the length of my body, but I was past fear. My chosen course felt right and that knowledge calmed me.

Vince stumbled toward us. "Lire, what are you doing?"

With my arms and legs still tied, I wasn't able to interpose myself between him and the demon, so I tried to warn him with the tone of my voice. "Stay out of this! There is too much you don't understand."

The demon's arm shot out with blinding speed and knocked Vince clear across the circle. I cringed at the sound of impact.

Deadly Remains - Chapter Twenty One

"Dammit! That wasn't necessary!" I glared at the demon before recovering my composure and setting my sights on our agreement. "Release my hands for the oath."

A sense of urgency supplanted all other concerns. I had to press forward before Vince interfered any further. Verbal agreement or no, I wasn't absolutely sure the demon could resist hurting Vince, especially if he interposed himself again.

Without any physical effort, the rope around my wrists fell to the ground, along with the one at my ankles. The demon knew full well I wasn't going to run.

I gasped as my arms flopped down to my sides, setting my shoulders ablaze by the sudden movement. My arms were numb and unwieldy. It was a monumental struggle just to clasp my hands together in front of me. Frustratingly slow, I managed to remove my gloves, mostly with my teeth.

I held out the palm of my right hand. My body tensed with anticipation, but I attempted to be brave. "Cut me."

The demon's previously human eyes turned black and alien, and its mouth opened wide to reveal an inhuman tongue. So this was the source of the disturbing, darkly fluid tentacle. I fought to suppress a scream as the unnatural appendage disgorged from the demon's mouth and moved with the same bizarre, organic-like fluidity I had witnessed earlier. Instead of cutting my palm, however, the extremity boiled down to the ground and undulated quickly across the circle. After only a moment, it contracted, returning with Brian's blade and a gold chalice, which the tentacle placed into the demon's human hands. The tentacle disappeared back into Paimon's mouth and its eyes returned to normal.

Before I had time to cringe, the demon slashed my palm with the knife.

I gasped. The pain of the cut was immediate, and blood welled up along the length of the two-inch incision. I held my dripping wound over the proffered chalice where my blood slowly collected into a small puddle at the bottom of the gleaming vessel.

I felt the djinn's mark sting with cold, as a stream of careful words trickled into my mind through the weakened conduit. Without hesitating, I repeated them. "To this demon the human Lire commits her eternal soul, provided said demon leaves alive and unhurt all mortals within its current purview, immediately escorts the human Lire directly to its exclusive domain through the portal whence it came, and thereby closes such portal forever."

Paimon regarded me steadily. After only a moment, it slowly drew the knife in a line just below the nipple of its human body. Dark, viscous blood oozed slowly from the egregious wound. Paimon moved the bloodied chalice to catch the inhuman fluid. "I accept Lire's terms and take her proffered soul as payment in full."

The demon's quick acceptance worried me. I had expected some negotiation at the very least. In a slow, dramatic gulp, the demon consumed the contents of the chalice. As he drank, a disquieting tremor of magic pressed against me.

It licked it's lips slowly with a pink, human-looking tongue and then grinned victoriously. "It is done. You are mine. Move!" It shoved me hard, with the now empty chalice, toward the summoning circle.

Pain and dread dogged my every step, but I somehow forced my legs to move toward the summoning circle. Behind me, the demon cackled in triumph, every so often giving my back the occasional savage push. When I reached the edge of the summoning circle, I had a brief moment to turn back and observe what I was leaving behind. Vince, who was cradling an injured arm and bleeding from a cut on his cheek, shouted my name and struggled to his feet.

Unwanted tears toppled down my cheeks. Fear had returned, but I held my head high. "Vince ... take care of Red. I— "

The demon shoved me through the portal before I could finish. I felt the hard edge of the chalice press into my back, and then the scenery shifted with a sickening lurch. My stomach clenched with nausea, but I hardly noticed, anger overriding judgment.

I lashed out at the demon as bitter tears blurred my vision. "Damn you! I wanted to say goodbye!"

The demon avoided my attack with ease and wielded the sharp knife in response. It viciously slashed down my forearm, and the resulting pain was twofold. Not only was the jagged wound agonizing, but it was accompanied by all the horror filled memories associated with the dagger's use.

Disoriented by the sudden return of my clairvoyance and the excruciating pain of my injury, I was slow to cast out the terrible memories. On top of it, the pain of the inflicted wound was not purely physical. It went deeper. The pain radiated directly into the core of my being and tortured my spirit, even as it left despair in its wake.

I screamed, and the demon growled with displeasure. "You will soon learn your desires are immaterial. I am your master and the rules are simple. You will serve me or there will be pain. Pain like you have never before experienced. This is but a small taste."

My legs buckled beneath me and I fell to the ground. The demon loomed over and threatened me with the knife.

"Get up or your education begins now."

I wiped the tears from my eyes and drew my legs under me. Only then did it dawn on me that we weren't in the fiery pit I had imagined.

"This is Hell?"

I did not move quickly enough for the demon's taste. It struck me across the face with the empty chalice. "Do not ask questions, you pathetic miscreant, or I will whittle down this sack of flesh until only your soul remains."

I grunted and fell over, overcome with the dark, hideous memories of the chalice and crippling pain of the grievous strike. I felt blood drip down the side of my face. Although I barely had room for conscious thought, my unanswered question stuck firmly in my mind. This was Hell? Really?

Wasn't Hell supposed to be dominated by fire and brimstone, or was that just legend? And why was the demon still in its human guise?

Through the haze of pain, I looked around. My surroundings were empty and, even more surprising, familiar. We were definitely not in Hell, at least, not yet. This was the Between—the place I briefly visited with Maya and Tanu on the way to their world. With a sudden rush of understanding, I realized there might still be hope for me, but the boundary to Paimon's domain was likely very close. Even now, I felt a tugging sensation as the demon pulled me closer to its world.

Dear God, don't let it be too late!

Now that I was outside the warlock's circle, my powers were no longer suppressed. Ironically, if it hadn't been for the physical contact with the knife and the chalice, I might not have figured it out. With barely a thought, I levitated myself upright, just outside the demon's immediate grasp. When I moved, the bizarre nothingness of the environment shimmered, as though I viewed the demon through the waves of a desert mirage.

Even Paimon's booming voice sounded strange. "You must enjoy pain to disobey so willingly. But you will soon learn. I will enjoy breaking you."

While I still had the time, I opened my bloodied hand and leveled it at the demon. "Demon, you have broken the terms of our covenant! You were blood-bound to escort me through the portal directly to your exclusive domain. Limbo is not your exclusive domain. By the blood of our covenant, the bargain is null and void."

Paimon roared and attempted to gut me with the knife, but I was ready. I levitated myself to the side. The djinn's words about getting lost in this place were on my mind, so I moved just enough to avoid the strike. Even so, the effect was drastic. Suddenly, Paimon stood at least fifteen feet away and the shimmering aspect of the atmosphere became more pronounced.

The demon's voice sounded distant, more so than a mere fifteen feet. "Lire, do you think me so stupid? Did you honestly think I was fooled by your flawed oath?" The demon laughed. "No. I was fully prepared for such trickery—if you can even call such an obvious ploy a trick. For just this occasion, I made sure someone special came along for the ride."

Red appeared from behind the demon.

I choked back a sob. "No!"

He sounded tiny and fragile. "Lire! I am sorry."

"If you do not wish to see the love of your life ripped to shreds and his soul cast into oblivion, I suggest you return to my side immediately."

No! It just wasn't fair. I had won free, dammit! How was this possible? Was there a way out? Could I rescue Red without going to Hell with the demon?

I dithered too long. The demon grabbed Red with its slithering appendage and used it to rip off one of his fuzzy legs. As the black tentacle coiled around it, the part simply disintegrated.

"Red," I sobbed and screamed at the same time.

The demon laughed, managing to speak in spite of the nasty tongue. "I wonder how far I can pare down this vessel before it can no longer hold his soul."

Red's voice sounded pitiful—so small and weak. "Lire! Help me!"

The demon didn't hesitate or make further demands. It merely plucked at Red's other leg and it parted from his cuddly body, as if made from clay. Tormented by the sight, I could only watch as the severed leg gradually dissolved like the last.

"Stop! Please! I'll go with you! Just release him!"

The demon regarded me with narrowed eyes. "Come to me."

God forgive me, but I was reluctant. It seemed so much easier back on Earth when I committed myself to save Jack, Vince, and Red. Now, however, I found it difficult to comply.

Red made a moaning sound and it broke my heart. I straightened my back and readied my levitation. This was a strange place. Any movement seemed to be magnified here, so I needed to be careful with the application of my power. As I set about to use my magic, it got me thinking. How was it that I had my powers, but Red didn't seem to have his? Was the demon immune to Red's magic?

Red cried out, "Lire! Please! We'll go with the demon together, just don't let my soul go into Limbo!"

The demon's vile extremity had coiled around Red's neck, but I hesitated. Something didn't feel right. Red wasn't acting in a way I expected given the nature of the situation. He'd never ask me to forsake my soul, not for anything. And, especially, not for him.

I sat back on my heels and clenched my fists. "No, demon. I see through your lie. That isn't Red. And I won't go with you. Not now, not ever."

Paimon sighed and the body of Red disappeared. "Very well. Then let me be the first to welcome you to oblivion!"

At astonishing speed, Paimon's tentacle lashed out at me. I had a split second to register the glint of the knife. Instead of attempting to grab me, like it had to both Brian and Vince, the demon resorted to striking with the dagger.

In that fleeting moment, while I readied my power to escape, I came to an improbable realization ...

Paimon was avoiding my touch.

There was only an instant to think it through. Was Paimon truly avoiding physical contact? Niggling thoughts, which I had simply ignored, now came to mind. At the time of our blood oath, I had offered Paimon my palm, but it did not strike the skin with its powerful tentacle as I had expected. Instead, it had used the dagger and chalice. When Paimon shoved me through the portal, it used the chalice. And here, in the Between, when I had expected to see Paimon's true form and its most horrible tools of pain, it elected instead to use Brian's knife and chalice as weapons. At every opportunity that came to mind, I realized Paimon had gone out of its way to use one of Brian's tools. Why, if not to avoid contact?

In a flash, I changed my plan. Rather than levitating myself away from the demon's strike, I used my power to turn aside the blade and forced myself to touch the dark, slithering appendage. Immediately, my mind was flooded with the most intimate thoughts and desires of a being so alien and malevolent I nearly lost all sense of myself. Disassociating my essence from the demon's consciousness and remaining in contact with the nasty appendage took nearly every ounce of my power.

The demon reacted with equal aversion. It bellowed indignantly and snatched back its tentacle. Grabbing the insubstantial appendage was impossible, so I launched myself toward the demon. It was completely foolhardy, but somehow I knew it was imperative to stay in contact with the demon, in spite of the danger and the utterly loathsome contact.

Although it wasn't my intention, I hit the demon in what amounted to a telekinetic flying tackle. Not exactly what I had in mind—crashing into a Prince of Hell and inviting injury—but I latched on to its body in sheer desperation. With the fast approaching dagger nearly forgotten, I submerged myself into the black abyss of Paimon's mind, even as it fought to push me off.

I knew my life was in mortal danger. Paimon was absolutely, undeniably intent on killing me before I discovered the truth. And because I was inside Paimon's mind, I knew precisely what it intended to do. Through its eyes, I saw the moment the tentacle returned with the knife and its violent strike. The demon easily drove the sharp dagger into my throat, all the way to the hilt, before savagely tearing it downward.

But the demon's attack was too late. I discovered what it did not want me to know.

The essential nature of my power is to seek and reveal truths. Once I come into contact with an item or a person, its essence enters my mind. The essence does not lie. It cannot be deceitful. The essence is the truth of the object or person, for better or worse. Paimon's power, on the other hand, is nothing but lies. It only affects those who believe in them.

Paimon had power over me simply because I believed it did.

I opened my eyes to see the demon triumph in the killing blow, but the jubilant expression faded quickly as the dagger disintegrated and my skin emerged unblemished. The knife didn't inflict injury because I knew the truth. Only a creature's essence existed in the Between; anything else was a projection, including flesh and pain and death. The demon was only able to hurt me if I believed it was possible.

There was something else I discovered—something I did not want to accept, in spite of the truth. Although Paimon was an evil, debauched creature, it was not completely irredeemable. Deep down, Paimon harbored an even more desperate secret. The secret had been denied and hidden so completely it was nearly forgotten, but I unearthed it. My magic laid it bare, and it gave me pause. Paimon's most urgent longing was to be human. It wanted to breathe the fresh, pine-scented air of the mountains, feel the rush of the ocean over its toes, know the embrace of a loved one, and touch freshly fallen snow, but most of all, it wanted freedom. It was this unfulfilled need, corrupted by ages of jealousy and hatred, which drove Paimon to its ends.

As I released my urgent grip and rolled off the demon's body, I realized one final thing. I knew Paimon's true name. It was intrinsically bound to the demon's essence. Now that I knew Paimon's truth, its name was obvious. It was not possible to learn one without knowing the other.

I sat up and called its name. In the Between, it wasn't possible to make demands, but I had no desire to command anything except the demon's attention.

I met Paimon's vengeful eyes before pointing out the obvious. "You no longer have power over me. I know your truth."

The demon snarled as it raised itself into a crouched position. "That may be, but you will end up like all the rest who learned my name. It is but a small matter."

"Oh? And how did they all end up?"

It leaned toward me and leered. "Under my dominion where they spend eternity in pain and torment."

I shrugged. "Doubtful, but believe what you will. I have no intention of repeating your name. Ever."

The demon stood up and laughed with its deep, appealing human voice. "That is exactly what they all say. But at some point, you will be desperate for help. My name will jump to your lips and you will call me. It is inevitable. It is foretold."

"You know, I've really had enough of the prophecy crap."

Paimon offered me its hand to help me up, and I didn't shy away. I already knew its essence and it could no longer hurt me. It pulled me up, but did not relinquish my hand. Instead, it tugged me closer until I stood inches away and was forced to stare into its light blue eyes. Interestingly, the demon no longer seemed to radiate evil, but I assumed it was because we were in the Between.

The demon's intimately husky voice sent shivers down my spine. "You may know my truth, but I also know yours. It is a connection you cannot deny." It placed my hand on its naked chest and held it captive. "We will meet again."

With that parting remark, Paimon released my hand and shimmered out of sight. I was left alone in the desolate emptiness of the Between, puzzled by the demon's final words, and clueless about how to get back to Earth.

TWENTY TWO

With the demon gone, I had time to consider my predicament. The djinn had mentioned something about getting lost in the Between without the proper training, so I didn't dare move for fear of going astray. I imagined my situation was similar to getting lost in the wild. Rescuers always started looking for errant hikers at their last known location. So it was smart to just sit down and wait until help eventually arrived. Great concept for the wilderness, but somehow I didn't think Vince was going to be able to call in a search and rescue team for me in the Between. In fact, Maya and Tanu might be the only ones capable of finding me.

I focused on the djinn's mark, in the hope that Maya or Tanu might hear me, but soon realized the conduit was either broken or didn't exist in the Between. My human body was probably lying inert, back in the summoning circle, but how long could I be away without negative consequences? For that matter, how long had I been in the Between with the demon? Minutes? Hours? Certainly not days! In a place that didn't offer any hint of change, I had no way to determine exactly how much time had passed.

Although my body was left behind on Earth, along with the djinn's mark, it was my essence that was bound to the djinn. Surely that meant the djinn could find me if they knew where to look, didn't it? Since the djinn had devised the flawed covenant, they clearly hoped I might figure out its loophole and escape. They probably realized I was here. Maybe.

Not sure what else to do, I surveyed my surroundings. The environment was just as barren, just as empty as it was five minutes ago. As I spun on my heel, I considered the nebulous aspect of the Between. If not for the missing balustrade, this place was identical to the dream I had when I first met Jason. Was that just a coincidence? Jason and Trinity were more than just a dream. I felt sure it was possible to see them in this place. With Jason's image in my mind, I focused intently on drawing him out.

Suddenly, Jason stood next to me with a surprised expression and a wide smile. He looked around. "It's not exactly a hot spot, but I won't complain."

I laughed and hugged him before turning my attention to Trinity. A moment later, the three of us stood in a tight group and discussed the quandary at hand.

"My instincts tell me I should wait here for the djinn, but I'm not entirely sure they know I'm here." I sighed and considered the infinite nothingness surrounding us. "And even if they suspect it, I don't know if it will be easy for them to find me."

Jason tilted his head. "Why? They escorted you here, so they obviously know the way."

"Yeah, but they were adamant about not stopping, even though I wasn't feeling well. Remember? They said something about it being too easy for me to get lost."

"Right." Jason's brows knit together in thought.

Trinity tilted her head, but remained silent.

I fought the urge to pace around. "I assume my body back home is lying comatose—waiting for me to return. You don't think it's dying without my essence do you?"

"I don't know." Trinity's expression was pinched with doubt, but her eyes remained lively. "I don't think so. After all, you went to the djinn's world and didn't die."

Jason agreed. "Yeah, Vince would have mentioned it if something had gone wrong while you were gone."

"Yeah, I suppose so." I threw up my hands and grunted. "There is so much I don't know about all this."

Jason and Trinity glanced at each other before regarding me. They both looked uncertain.

"What?" I cast my gaze back and forth between them until Jason spoke up.

"The demon knows about this place."

I nearly backed up a step. "I am not calling on that ... *thing*. Not ever."

Jason waved me off with a palming gesture. "No. No. That's not what I meant. But you do have some of the demon's memories. Maybe if you examine them more closely, you'll spot something."

I sighed and sat down on the strange surface. I wrapped my arms around my bent knees and looked up at Jason and Trinity. "I'm not super eager to do that. Its memories make Patty's look like a day at the beach."

Jason's expression was sympathetic. "I know, but you can't keep them locked away forever. Now's as good a time as any to let them loose. Don't you think?"

I bit my lip and nodded before resting my chin on my knees and closing my eyes. Jason was right. It wasn't ridiculous to assume there might be helpful information within the cesspool of Paimon's mind.

With my shield relaxed, the demon's memories vied for my attention. The influx of such unrelenting feelings of hatred and jealousy made me gasp.

I waded through the flood of corruption, mentally recoiling at each atrocious thought. After a few moments, I realized what disturbed me most weren't the detestable acts or even the demon's evil intent. Not that those weren't completely horrible, of course. What bothered me above all was the demon as a whole did not repulse me the way I expected. Yes, Paimon's methods were completely repellent and loathsome, but part of me was drawn to the creature. I felt sympathy toward it.

How could I feel anything other than complete aversion toward a being that exploited human frailties for its own benefit? A being that delighted in torture? Had I been swayed by Paimon's seductions after all? Or perhaps these feelings of sympathy and fascination were due to a connection with the demon I didn't want to acknowledge. I certainly didn't feel any such connection, but knowing the demon's true name was a perilous burden. Its parting remark came to mind, and I shuddered with foreboding.

It wasn't easy, but I deliberately set aside my tangled feelings and turned my attention toward sifting through Paimon's memories. It was a long shot at best since I had only received a small fraction of its thoughts, but I soon discovered the demon's memory of pulling me toward its domain. I focused tightly on that recollection.

Jason and Trinity were staring down at me anxiously when I opened my eyes and looked up.

I smiled. "It's not like I have an instruction manual in my head, but I think I understand how to move between worlds." My expression faltered as I reconsidered. "Maybe I should rephrase that. I think I understand how the *demon* moves between worlds. Whether it will work for me, I don't know."

Jason crouched down next to me. "It's a place to start. What did you learn?"

"It's hard to describe." My eyes drifted to the side as I considered the memories. "Paimon knows its domain intimately. It knows the way it feels, the way it tastes. As far as I can tell, in order to go there, Paimon latches on to that feeling and pulls itself toward it." I shrugged. "Maybe the same thing will work for me. If I just concentrate and think about home—how it feels and how it resonates—then maybe I'll be able to notice its pull. Maybe I can follow that feeling toward my body."

Trinity's expression was serious. "Or it could just get you lost." She shook herself and then smiled sheepishly. "Sorry. Not helping."

I snorted. "That's okay. You're hardly saying something I'm not already thinking."

Jason shifted his weight so one of his knees rested on the ground. "What do you think? You going to try it?"

I considered the surroundings. "I can at least try to feel around a bit." I turned my attention back toward Jason and then up at Trinity. "Uh. You guys don't want to stay here, do you? I mean, stay here without me?"

Jason shook his head. "Not me. I'm not sure we can stay here without you anyway, but thanks for offering."

I smirked at him. "Oh yeah, this being the hot spot and all."

"Nah, it's just off season. Come spring break, this place will be jumping."

We laughed, and then I felt Jason and Trinity pull on our connection. Their projections dissipated from view, but I knew they were still with me. Jason was right. Our essences were linked. It wasn't possible to leave either of them in the Between, whether they wanted to stay or not. Actually, it was a relief to know I couldn't lose them somehow. The demon's performance with the false Red had left me worried they could be lost to oblivion if I wasn't careful.

Thinking of home, I mentally cast about for a way back. It didn't take long to sense a staggering number of possible pathways, each with its own unique timbre. The sheer number of choices was absolutely stupefying. With sudden clarity, I realized the Between was a nexus. It was a gateway between an infinite number of universes, each with limitless possibilities. Finding the way back home suddenly seemed an insurmountable task.

After a moment of complete panic, Trinity and Jason reassured me it was more than possible to get back home. Both Paimon and the djinn deftly navigated the Between. It was simply a matter of knowing the correct path. I thought back on the demon's memories. Paimon didn't so much pick a path, as the path seemed to pick the demon. There weren't quantifiable instructions or a map with directions—it was more of a feeling. It was instinctual.

Once again, I cast out for the correct path, but this time I didn't shy away. I used my essence to make contact, as if I was playing an otherworldly instrument. Almost immediately, the timbre of dozens upon dozens of pathway strings became more pronounced.

Okay. So it wasn't going to be easy, but at least I was no longer faced with an infinite number of possibilities. With slow deliberation, I combed through each resonating string. I don't know how many pathways I tested. There were hundreds, maybe even thousands. Finally, after countless probes, I touched a string that resonated with the same vibration as my essence. I knew it was the pathway back to my body.

Once I found the string, it was deliriously easy to latch on to it and move through the Between. I felt the same pulling sensation upon my being that I felt during my previous visit with the djinn. The feeling of nausea that plagued me earlier was gone. Now that I understood the method of movement—now that I knew how to navigate—the pull on my body no longer seemed unusual. The feeling of home, its timbre and familiar resonance, filled my being with unmitigated joy.

As the edge of the Between drew near, the surroundings darkened and the nebulous horizon faded to black. Before I had time to consider how to find my body, I slid effortlessly back into familiarity.

In an instant, my senses were bombarded with the light, sound, and vibration of Earth—not to mention the unexpectedly restrictive feel of my body. While I was in the Between, I hadn't paid much attention to the absence of sensory input. Now inside my earthly vessel, the sensory overload was shocking. It took several minutes for me to acclimate to the deafening clamor of stimuli. Finally, I separated the individual sensations. I was in a helicopter, on my back, and something squeezed my neck.

The dim light of the small cabin stung my eyes and I squinted back the brightness, straining to bring my surroundings into focus. The sound of the engine and the beat of the rotor blades hammered against my ears and body. I blinked several times before my vision revealed a figure sitting near me. After a moment of deliberate focus, I realized it was Vince.

He sat on a jump seat to my immediate left and gazed distantly at something behind my head, toward what I assumed was the cockpit of the helicopter. The illumination streaming inside from a forward window bathed his face and body with diffused afternoon sunlight and made his eyes appear golden. His left arm was inside a blue canvas sling, dried blood coated parts of his forehead and left cheek, and he wore a large, black headset over his ears. Most striking, however, was his expression. In the brief time since knowing him, I had never seen Vince look so grim and despondent.

While I regarded his emotionally ravaged face, Vince's attention wandered from the front window down toward my eyes. When he met my gaze and realized I was conscious, the transformation of his expression was dizzying.

Because of the loud whine of the turbine, Vince's voice wasn't audible, but his lips were easily readable. He sat forward in his seat and mouthed, "Oh my God! Lire!"

After Vince's initial look of disbelief, several other emotions vied for control of his expression—relief, concern, and tentative happiness. At that moment, I had no doubt he cared for me deeply. I returned his gaze with an initial, fleeting smile before the emotional impact of my experience overcame my shaky self-control. Although I was safe, back in my body, and relatively unscathed, I just couldn't avoid being undone by all of my pent up emotions and the memories of my horrific experience. The restraints hampered the movement of my arms and I struggled against the straps in a frustrated attempt to cover my face. Fat, hot tears coursed down my cheeks and my view of the world blurred into a wet haze.

After a moment, I felt Vince at my side and the touch of his fingers as he smoothed my hair and gently wiped the tears from my face. My voice was swallowed by the ambient noise, but I repeated his name and tried to turn my head in his direction.

The startled paramedic insinuated himself between us. From what I gathered, Vince's careless touching without the benefit of gloves alarmed him. There wasn't much I could do, except watch the two men converse through their headsets while I tried to staunch my tears. Again I attempted to free my arms from the tightly cinched straps of the gurney, but the paramedic noticed and placed his gloved hand firmly on my shoulder.

I tried to shake my head to show my displeasure, but the brace around my neck almost completely prevented any lateral movement. The feelings of intense frustration combined with the agony of my ordeal threatened to unhinge me further. Vince leaned down and put his lips near my ear.

"Lire! It's okay! Don't move!" I could tell Vince was shouting, but his words were barely audible.

Unfortunately, there wasn't anything I could do except blink my eyes in acknowledgment. I'm sure my expression was dominated by a look of frustration. I wanted more than anything to wrap my arms around Vince's neck and bury my face against his chest, but I had to settle for the annoying experience of dealing with the medic's examination. Vince sat back in his seat while the middle-aged, mustached EMT did what he could to check my current condition. With hand signals, he told me to follow the path of his finger as he moved it around my field of view. Afterward, he checked my pupils with a small pen-sized flashlight and then shouted some basic questions into my ear.

"Do you have a headache?"

The paramedic put his ear near my mouth and I shouted, "Yes!"

"Is your vision blurred?"

"No!"

"Can he touch you?" I guessed he was talking about Vince.

"Yes!"

At my last answer, he regarded me doubtfully, but nodded and focused on writing things down on his clipboard.

The landing was softer than I expected, and my ears buzzed at the reduced noise level. In a frenzy of efficient coordination, I was maneuvered out of the helicopter, pushed into an elevator, wheeled to emergency, and then transferred to a slightly less uncomfortable hospital gurney. Finally, after answering dozens of questions and attempting to sign a couple of forms with my injured hand, the restrictive neck brace was removed and I was left alone to wait.

Throughout the hustle and bustle, I never lost track of Vince, and the staff was nice enough to put us next to each other in the emergency ward.

After a moment of silence, I heard Vince's footsteps and saw his head peek around the privacy curtain separating our two fabric cubbies. "Hey."

"Hey yourself," I replied with a weak smile. "Open it. Come sit." I patted the end of my bed and, although it was painful, scooted my legs over the side so he had room to perch.

Even though a sling secured his left arm, he held it slightly away from his body, like the straps weren't doing an adequate job. Pain lanced his expression when he shifted his weight to get comfortable.

I studied him. "How's your arm?"

"Honestly, it hurts like hell, mostly when I move, but I'll be okay. I think it's just dislocated."

I frowned and nodded. The horrid memories of my encounter plowed their way into my thoughts and pushed aside my almost peaceful state. Brian's grisly death replayed in my mind. I remembered looking at Vince, just before Paimon shoved me through the portal.

Tears welled up into my eyes and I choked out, "I thought I was never going to see you again."

Vince used his right arm to pull me into his embrace and I clung to him.

The tears were brief. He held me close and spoke into my ear. "Lire. I thought so too. Red told me ... he told me you were gone." Vince squeezed me, and there was a brief lapse before he continued, "He could feel your body was empty. He told me you were as good as dead, that you were just an empty shell. I didn't want to believe it, but he seemed so certain." He heaved a sigh, and I felt the warmth of his breath on the side of my head. "I kept him safe. He's over there, in the duffel bag."

I nodded mutely and felt the wetness of my tears against his skin, although my major waterworks had passed. I stared at the floor, my cheek against his neck. "I'm sorry. I did what I thought was right. I didn't want to see you hurt, not if I could save you." I took a shuddering breath. "Red wasn't wrong. The demon ... it nearly got me. It almost took me in, but I broke free. I found my way back, and when I opened my eyes, I saw you. The person I most wanted to see." I blundered ahead, possessed by the heartbreaking memory of my earlier unspoken goodbye. "I love you."

Now that I had lobbed the 'L' bomb, I immediately regretted it and began to doubt my earlier intuition about his feelings. With an embarrassed shrug, I loosened my urgent embrace, but Vince didn't let me go. He hugged me even tighter and said the words that kept me tingling for the remainder of the afternoon. "Babe, I love you too. But, God! Please—do me a favor. Stop scaring the crap out of me."

I chuckled into the crook of his neck. "I'll do my best."

When I pulled away, Vince took the opportunity to cup my face with his free hand and wipe away my forgotten tears. His tender expression warmed me, and I didn't wait for further encouragement to lean in for a brief kiss. His soft yielding lips sent sparks of pleasure and a wave of warmth throughout my body. As we parted, I heard the sound of approaching footsteps. I pushed away to sit up straight on the edge of the bed. Vince smirked with amusement while I attempted to look casual. The footsteps continued past our closed curtains to one of the neighboring beds.

While I attempted to ignore the doctor interview a woman about her wicked sounding cough, I said quietly, "I still haven't figured it out. How did you know what was happening? How did you find us?"

"I followed you. I wasn't about to hightail it back to the department after they pulled me off the case. I told Jensen I was taking vacation time and spent some miserable nights in my car instead." He shook his head and snorted. "Fat lot of good it did though."

Taken aback, I stared at him. "Are you kidding? You risked your life for me. If you hadn't been there, I'd probably still be lying on the ground with Jack unconscious and Red unable to call for help."

Vince waved it away, as though his efforts were nothing special.

I shook my head. "You really cased my apartment? Day and night?"

Vince looked slightly uncomfortable. "Yes."

I felt a goofy, appreciative smile spread across my face before turning serious. I touched his free arm. "I'll never forget what you did for me. *Never*. You're acting like it was nothing, but it means a lot."

Vince placed his right hand on my knee. I tried to grasp it, but my hands weren't working properly. I looked down. A distinct ridge of purple, swollen flesh encircled my wrists, forming an almost identical copy of the demonic rope. A square of white gauze had been taped over the cut on my right palm. I shuddered.

"They must hurt," Vince murmured.

I sighed and nestled my head into the crook of his neck. "Yeah, they do. My ankles too. But I'm lucky to be alive."

Vince held me, but after a moment, my thoughts turned toward all the other unanswered questions on my mind. I gasped and sat up straight. "What about Jack. Did he wake up? What happened after I went through the portal?"

Vince frowned. "Jack was alive, but out cold. I wasn't able to wake him. When we're done here, we'll find out what's going on with him, okay?" When I nodded, he said, "There's not really much to tell about what happened after you ..." Vince's jaw tightened, but his voice remained calm when he continued. "As soon as the demon disappeared, you collapsed. When I made it over to you, you were unconscious. I figured you'd be okay, like all the other times, until Red told me otherwise." He shook his head. "Jensen and several other detectives from the department got there about twenty minutes after you collapsed, and then the first emergency helicopter arrived not long after. Jack went out on the first chopper since I knew he'd been unconscious for much longer than you. The second helicopter came about ten minutes later. I told Jensen about everything I'd witnessed, and then he ordered me into the helicopter with you. That's about it."

I nodded. "Understatement of the year, but I'm just so glad it's all over. I'm almost scared to hope things will go back to normal now that Brian's dead. It's been one horrible thing after another." I closed my eyes and sighed.

Vince stroked my back and looked at me with a determined expression. "It's over. Things will definitely be better if I have anything to do with it."

I regarded him, frowning. "Yeah? You know, my powers haven't gone away. They're still there—all *four* of them. You sure you're okay with that?"

Although I could tell it was quite painful, Vince bent down to look me straight in the eyes. "All I know is how I felt when Red told me you were dead." He shook his head. "I don't care about your powers. I care about you—the incredible woman right here. I want you in my life."

I sighed and leaned in for a kiss, but we were interrupted by one of the ER doctors. Fortunately, he announced his presence before opening the curtain.

The middle-aged man at the foot of the hospital bed wore the obligatory blue medical scrubs and introduced himself as Doctor Fredericks. I liked him instantly. His friendly but direct demeanor and open smile put me at ease.

His blue eyes bounced back and forth between Vince and me. I could see the wheels turning as he observed Vince's hand cupped over mine.

He asked, "Okay. Who's up first?"

Vince and I gestured at each other.

"He is."

"She is."

He chuckled and settled on Vince.

This, of course, entailed the removal of Vince's shirt. I winced at seeing him in pain but couldn't help enjoying the view. Several times I felt my cheeks grow hot and hoped nobody noticed. After the doctor examined Vince's shoulder, he agreed it was dislocated and ordered X-rays. Chagrined, I watched as Vince put on a hospital gown before being whisked down the hall by an orderly.

The doctor interviewed me for several minutes, clearly wanting to know how and why I had lost consciousness. I hesitated before explaining I had passed out after witnessing Brian's murder, which explained how I hit my head. It was the truth. I just left out the part about the demon.

Doctor Fredericks checked the lump on my head, listened to my heart and lungs, checked my reflexes, examined my pupils, and made me perform several balance tests. He also examined the cut on my palm and the bruises on my wrists and ankles. Unfortunately, only time would tell if the bindings had caused nerve damage. He advised me to make an appointment with a specialist if the numbness and diminished fine motor response didn't improve after a couple weeks. He handed me a package of cloth psi-free gloves and told me he'd send a nurse to clean the cut on my hand.

Before I could retrieve Red from Vince's black bag, Daniel showed up. He didn't stay long. To my relief, he informed me that Invisius had voted to take a wait-and-see approach where I was concerned. He was obviously relieved and happy to see I had survived, but because he had allowed me a brief peek into his mind earlier, I knew he intended to use our relationship to further his power base within the ranks of Invisius. The prophecy was alive and well, whether I agreed with it or not. Judging by Daniel's demeanor, I guessed his clout had blossomed exponentially.

Honestly, I didn't care whether Daniel took advantage of our relationship, as long as Invisius stayed out of my life. I had no desire to have any further dealings with their stupid club, nor did I want to know details of Daniel's palace revolution, which I made abundantly clear.

He regarded me, looking amused. "I hear you. Before I go, is there anything I can do for you personally?"

I ignored his subtle inflection on the word 'personally.' "Yes, actually. Jack and the taxi driver. I want you to repair any damage from Brian's mind control. Jack is here somewhere. I'm not sure about the driver."

He nodded and handed me a card. His mobile number was written on the back. "Call me *anytime*."

I watched him leave with mixed feelings. I hoped he had enough political capital with Invisius to ensure a lifelong cease-fire. But, just in case, I planned to make Claude's bracelet a permanent accessory.

Vince wasn't pleased to hear about Daniel's visit. He made sure to tell me more than once he didn't trust 'that guy' and I'd be smart to keep my distance. The scowl on his face didn't abate until a nurse arrived to give him an IV drip and administer the muscle relaxer.

With notable anxiety, I stayed and watched the 'dislocation reduction procedure,' although, I decided the terminology made the whole thing sound worse than it actually was. The procedure required Vince to lie flat on the hospital bed while the nurse wound a bed sheet under his armpit and applied counter traction. The doctor then manipulated Vince's arm to help guide the dislocated bone back into place. Because Vince was so doped up on drugs, I don't think it fazed him all that much. My personal fringe benefit was that the whole process provided me with another glorious view of Vince's muscular torso, which didn't suck. Although, I'm sure I would have enjoyed the ogling much more if I hadn't been worried about the process being painful for him.

While we waited for Vince's medication to wear off, the nurse stayed to clean the wound on my hand. After she had applied the bandage and departed, I finally had the opportunity to speak with Red. Fortunately, Vince had recovered enough to help me with the zipper on his duffel bag. When it opened, Red practically jumped into my arms.

"Oh, Red!" It was all I could say. I sat next to the bed where Vince was recovering and hugged my beloved companion. Silent tears blurred my vision.

"Dearest Lire. When Paimon took you away, I despaired. I gave up all hope. Even now, I can hardly believe you are here."

I whispered into his soft fur, struggling to keep my voice subdued. "Red, I love you so much." I sniffled and choked back my unshed tears by taking a deep shuddering breath. "I want to tell you everything, but it'll have to wait. This isn't the place for it. Someone could walk in."

"There will be plenty of time later," he said quietly.

Red gave my face one final squeeze before sliding down my arm toward the open top of the duffel bag. When he was safely inside, Vince groggily zipped it shut and I replaced it next to the bed.

As soon as we were both officially discharged, Vince set out to locate Jack, even though I suspected his shoulder remained quite painful. When we discovered Jack was in the ICU, I worried Daniel had failed to help him.

Since I wasn't a family member, Vince spoke with an ICU nurse and used his police influence to get a meeting with the on-call doctor. (Although, I have to say, Vince hardly had to bat an eye before she acquiesced. He just seemed to have a way with women.) After waiting for nearly twenty minutes, a doctor emerged to tell us Jack was showing signs of regaining consciousness. I still didn't know whether there would be lasting damage from Brian's mind control, but I was relieved and hopeful that he'd recover fully.

Although Jensen did his best to keep my name out of the media, it didn't take long for reporters to get word that I was one of two survivors left injured by the Circle Murderer. Much was made out of the fact that the murderer had been killed in the latest attack, but the full details weren't disclosed. It was only a matter of time before the macabre truth came to light. But, for now, the officials had managed to keep a lid on the exact means of his death.

Hoping to dodge the reporters, we arranged to meet Julie down in the parking garage for a ride to my apartment. By the time we had finished hearing about Jack and made our way to the underground level, Julie waited for us. While she drove, she fished for details about my ordeal, but bless her heart, she was sincerely understanding when I told her I didn't want to talk about it just yet.

My apartment had never felt so cozy as it did that night, and I know Vince's presence had much to do with it. I doted on him, feeding him dinner and fluffing pillows, while he comforted me with his calm, understanding demeanor. In an effort to soothe my inner turmoil, he gently coaxed the entire story out of me, from start to finish, every ghastly detail, almost without distress. I knew my account was destined for his police report, but it was just as clear he wanted to help me overcome my ordeal. Talking about it was the first step.

With my reluctant permission, he took pictures of my injuries with his cell phone camera. I half hoped his police report would spare me repeating the whole horrible story to Jensen or Cunningham later—although it was probably a futile wish.

To be honest, Vince was my savior that first night at home. When I asked him in a bashful voice to sleep with me in my bed, he acquiesced without the slightest hint of a leer. It was clear he was in no shape for any funny business and just as obvious I suffered from post-traumatic stress. Later that night, when I woke from a terror filled dream with a scream choking my throat, he snuggled close and soothed me until I fell back into a fitful sleep.

I knew the coming days and weeks weren't going to be easy and my future was bound to be complicated, but the thought of sharing my life with Vince sent tingles all the way down to my toes.

I guess being a fire-starting, levitating, ice-freezing clairvoyant might not be half bad. Who knew?

AUTHOR'S NOTE

If you're anything like me, you're a rabid Scrooge when it comes to your free time. You carefully ration it and begrudge the need to spend it on ridiculous distractions like eating, sleeping, and shaving your legs. Okay, that could just be me. Even so, the fact that you spent your valuable time, reading something I created for enjoyment, means a great deal to me.

But if I don't hear from you, cherished reader, I'll have no clue whether I succeeded or failed (or maybe just left you saying 'meh') in my attempt to entertain you.

I hope you'll consider posting a review of *Deadly Remains* on the site where you purchased it. Reviews not only help other readers decide if my novels are something they might enjoy, but they also let me know where I need to improve as a storyteller. I appreciate all reviews, whether positive or negative. Let me know what worked for you and what didn't. You're also welcome to visit and correspond with me on my website at www.katherinebayless.com. I'd love to hear from you.

You've just read the first novel in the *A Clairvoyant's Complicated Life* series. The second is *Deceiver's Bond*. The third is *Reluctant Adept*. I will be writing a fourth!

If you'd like to read an excerpt from the next book in this series, *Deceiver's Bond*, please turn the page.

AN EXCERPT FROM DECEIVER'S BOND

CHAPTER ONE

Reading weird shit is the curse of a clairvoyant. But this was a new one—even for me.

That alone should have been my first clue.

I sat cross-legged on a hot, white beach across from Veronica Michaels, the acquisitions coordinator for Sotheby's, explaining there was no way I could perform a psychic reading on her wedding cake. "Look." I sighed. "This is a disaster. The icing's already melting."

A deep laugh rumbled behind me, making me jump. Veronica and the absurd cake forgotten, I whipped around on my beach towel to confront its source—a buck-naked Adonis who sunned himself, not eight feet away. Each exquisitely taut and tanned muscle gleamed in the sun, and, *holy moley*, I had a spectacular view of half of them. Stretched out on his stomach, he relaxed, head resting on folded arms. His burning gaze flicked over my body, so intent, I was surprised not to feel its caress.

This was no mere man. I recognized the creature immediately. I was riveted to the spot, my hands clawing at the sand behind me. I opened my mouth to scream, but the sound lodged impotently in my throat.

The demon blew out an imperious sigh, but other than rolling its eyes, it remained still.

I knew Paimon didn't have to twitch a muscle to be a threat. Memories of its dark appendage, which could disgorge from its mouth like some caustic worm, were still fresh as the day I'd seen it flay the skin from a man's body. And I had no doubt it could do the same to me if that's what it desired.

Making matters worse, it wasn't confined to a summoning circle. It was free to do whatever it wanted.

So, why was it sprawled on a towel catching rays?

"Really, woman. Do I have to endure this silliness every single night?" Even while irritated, its seductive voice managed to stir my insides—fear mixed with a heady dash of desire.

Night?

I blinked and risked a look around.

The beach at Seattle's Golden Gardens Park. I spotted the boathouse, maybe a hundred yards distant. And it wasn't nighttime. It was sunny and hot.

Gazing down the shore, I frowned. Except for Paimon, the beach was ... empty?

At last, the light came on.

You're dreaming, bonehead.

"I simply wish to speak with you," the demon continued. "Have I offered you any harm? Made any terrifying move against you? Why do you insist on acting this way?"

In a dream, Paimon couldn't harm me. Not physically, anyway.

Regaining some poise if not calm, I straightened up and stopped clutching at the sand behind me. Dusting off my hands, I retorted, "Because the only thing you offer is pain and torment."

It rolled to its side, facing me, right arm folded into a triangle to support its head. I had to close my eyes. My dream cheeks flamed. Its desire was plainly obvious.

Paimon laughed. "That is not all I offer, as you well know. You are lying to yourself if you believe otherwise. I have no wish to cause you pain. Quite the opposite, in fact."

"Right. That explains why you brutalized me, cut me, and tried to claim my soul."

It drew the fingers of its left hand down the center of its chest, enticing me to watch, a devilish smile playing on its very human face. "It was the most direct means to get what I wanted. Nothing more."

"Exactly. My soul for you to toy with for all eternity."

It ran the tip of its currently pink, human-looking tongue across its perfect teeth and grinned. "If that was indeed what I wanted."

I resisted following the path of its fingers, but it wasn't easy. Its continued covetous gaze made me wish I wore something more concealing than a skimpy bikini.

Why the hell hadn't I dreamed of being in the Arctic?

I laughed harshly. "The master of lies. I guess it's too embarrassing to admit I outsmarted you. Isn't it?"

"Believe what you wish. It matters not."

"If you don't want my soul, then why are you here?"

"I want to help you."

"Because you're such a caring guy."

"I care what happens to you, yes."

I rolled my eyes. "You must think I'm stupid."

"To the contrary. I assure you."

"And why should I believe you?"

"Because you have touched me and taken my measure. And you know there are other things that motivate me besides the acquisition of souls. You are a unique individual, Clotilde Devon. A worthy mate. I do not wish to see you harmed as others surely do."

"Wait just a darn minute. Mate?" I waved my hands as if to erase its words. "There are so many things wrong with what you just said, I don't even know where to begin."

"Now who is the liar?"

"What? We are so done with this. Begone! This is my dream. My head. I want you out."

It chuckled, moving gracefully to sit up, and loosely draped its arms around bent knees. I tried not to appreciate its physique and failed. Not a surprise. Everything about its human façade was crafted to seduce me, from finely slashed brows and square jaw to wide shoulders and defined muscular body. Its exterior package captivated me like no other man had or, possibly, ever would.

Paimon's lustful expression turned serious. "I will do as you ask, for now. But know this: Your life and the lives of countless humans may depend upon what I have sought to give you. I do not wish to see my efforts squandered, nor my refuge invaded. It is time you finally recognize the increase in mass slayings and demonic possessions for what they are. I will not have you defenseless.

"We will speak again."

My eyes popped open to darkness. I sucked in a shuddering breath and labored to control my trembling, which started in my center and radiated to the rest of my body until my teeth chattered.

Red stirred on the pillow next to me. "Lire? Are you okay?"

"Nightmare," I whimpered.

He patted the top of my head with his fuzzy paw.

While he soothed me back to sleep, I tried to convince myself that the demon's sole purpose was to terrorize me. That's how it got its jollies. But even with Red's reassuring touch, I couldn't shake the sense of foreboding that settled into my bones.

CHAPTER TWO

My telekinesis came in handy when it was time to empty Nick's refrigerator.

I stood across the room and juggled a moldy package of cheese, rancid tempeh, and a half-filled jar of Vlasic pickles through the air toward the open garbage bag.

"Frigging power company," I grumbled for the dozenth time, holding my nose against the putrid smell. Twelve feet away wasn't far enough. "But I'm getting better at handling several items at once."

The jar landed with the sound of breaking glass. I'd withdrawn my TK too soon, but at least, it landed inside the bag. I cringed and laughed. "Oops. A little trouble with re-entry."

Red's voice came to me from the living room. "An improvement over last time."

"With all the training you've had me do, you'd think I'd be an expert by now." I sounded crabby, even though I'd resolved to keep a positive outlook on these things. As a clairvoyant, my life had never been normal, but my three new powers had me feeling even more freakish than usual. Psychics never possessed more than one gift. And it didn't help that I had control issues.

"Expertise requires more than just practice," Red reminded me.

"Yeah, yeah. First I must accept my new self. Only then will I realize my full potential." I wrinkled my nose at the pungent blend of odors permeating the kitchen. "Why does that sound like something Yoda would say?"

He toddled into the kitchen, the soft feet of his stuffed bear body making the smallest of sounds on Nick's polished hickory floor. "Because I am wise beyond my years and you have subjected me to those movies more than once. Nevertheless, I speak the truth. The sooner you accept that you are better for your new abilities, the sooner you will master them."

"Better, huh?" *That'll take some convincing.*

I knew he was right, though. A majority of my problems were psychological. If I stopped thinking of myself as a freak, there was no telling what I could do. Of course, that was part of the problem. Some of the things I could do scared me. Like my pyrokinesis.

I sighed and immediately regretted it. Using my mind, I pressed the button for the cooktop's ventilation fan, hoping it might help with the smell.

Forsaking levitation, I walked over to the nearest window and opened it the old fashioned way. Cool springtime air wafted over the exposed skin between the top of my black formal-length gloves and the short sleeves of my t-shirt, giving me a raging case of goose bumps. Although Nick had been a clairvoyant, like me, I couldn't remove my gloves without risking exposure to the countless memories bound up in the objects around me—objects he had touched with his bare hands. Still raw from his recent death, I didn't need his intimate thoughts adding to my grief.

My nose just shy of the screen, I breathed deeply. A familiar smell in the air reminded me of fresh-cut scallions. It was comforting, but I wasn't sure why. The late morning sun had pierced the wispy clouds, hinting at the possibility of a rare sunny spring day. Vaporous tendrils of steam rose from the damp fence where the sun's haphazard rays had heated the wood.

"I know this is hard for you," Red said. "Being different is never easy."

I regarded my diminutive friend. If anyone could understand my current anxiety, it was Red. Having lived as a human necromancer in colonial times, he knew something about being an outcast. At least my abilities just made for social discomfort these days instead of a death sentence.

"You understand my feelings better than anyone." I pulled out a kitchen chair and slumped into it. "It's just ... I worked hard to be happy. I had a place in the magic community, but now ..." I shrugged, reluctant to voice my fears.

"You assume these additional talents will be met with rejection. Yes, some will be hung up on labels and alarmed by your uniqueness, but not everyone will automatically re-ject you. Take Daniel. He, for one, is not repulsed by your new gifts."

I snorted. "Daniel's motives are hardly selfless. There's the whole Invisius Verso thing. Okay, maybe he doesn't agree with everything his stupid club does, but he still thinks I'm part of that damned prophecy, just like the rest of them."

The back of my neck got clammy just thinking about the obsessively secretive group. Its telepathic members made hardened CIA operatives look like Austin Powers. Interfer-ing with an organization of telepaths was a great way to kiss your memories goodbye, along with a chunk of your person-ality.

Before I could stop myself, I skimmed my fingertips over my left wrist. The magic bracelet was the only thing that stood between my mind and any telepaths who might still have it out for me.

Red paused before saying, "There is Detective Vanelli."

My eyebrows drew down. Three weeks of struggling to come up with excuses for Vince's continued distance had worn thin. Now, instead of my heart being aflutter over his 'I love you too,' it had been crushed under the weight of re-jection.

"You sure wouldn't know it by the way he's been acting. Whenever I get him on the phone, he's distracted. I thought he was just skittish from all of those possessive ex-girl-friends, but … yeah, it's just an excuse."

"Do not be so quick to presume the worst." Red tipped his head to the side as he considered me. "The sidhe are known to possess a wide variety of powers, including the gift to glamour. It is possible the detective has this ability. Because he denies his sidhe blood, it is likely he has little or no control over it."

"You think he's using magic to make himself irresistible? You can't be serious."

Red put his paws together over his ample teddy bear belly. "I have been loath to voice my opinion because it is merely a possibility. I have no proof. However, it may explain his numerous past experiences with possessive and jealous girlfriends."

Good grief. Vince was going to love hearing this. I could see his reaction now—jaw clamped tight, running his hand through his thick hair, and growling that there was no fucking way he was part *elf.*

"You don't think—?" I frowned. "I'll admit I fell hard for him and I think he's sexy as hell, but it feels normal. I'm not acting like a crazed stalker. Am I?"

"No. But you are not completely human either. Your magic likely gives you protection."

I shot him a sour look. "Right." I considered this as I slumped further into my chair. "I guess that could explain some things. More than once I've noticed women acting, well, swoony around him. At the time, I just chalked it up to his looks. But maybe there's more to it."

I heaved myself up to close the window. It was still too cool to leave open for long. Remembering my expanding to-do list, I shook myself and turned back to the refrigerator, grateful for the distraction.

Not long after hauling the garbage out to the curb, a resounding rap echoed from the front door. I jumped, sending a wooden salad bowl spinning out of my hands. I caught the serving piece before it could topple off the counter.

I told myself my startled reaction was due to the quiet surroundings, not because of my recent traumatic experience at the hands of Brian Stalzing. "Jeez. Who could that be?"

"Perhaps your distant neighbor noticed you outside earlier," Red suggested.

As I crossed the living room, another determined knock jarred my already frazzled nerves. "Coming!"

I opened the front door and immediately recognized the thickset man wearing a Coventry County Sheriff's uniform. His gray eyes were narrowed. This was not going to be a friendly visit. Of course, judging by our first meeting, Sheriff Lancer wasn't the type to pay a hospitality call on someone like me.

"Clotilde Marie Devon? Also known as Lire Devon?" he demanded.

"Yes. We've met before, Sheriff. What are you doing here?"

He held up an official looking document. The words 'Coventry District Court' caught my eye at the top of the page. "Lire Devon, I have a warrant for your arrest for the murder of Nicholas Anthony Coulter. Turn around and put your hands behind your back."

I stood, mouth agape, before sputtering, "What? That's ridiculous. You were on the task force. Brian Stalzing killed Nick. He kidnapped me, along with my business partner Jack Beaumont. The abduction was witnessed by a Chiliquitham Police detective, for God's sake. You must have read the FBI's report."

His face twisted into a hostile sneer. "That story may have played for the FBI, but here in Coventry County, we have higher standards." Looming toward me, he said. "Hands behind your back. Or do you prefer to do things the hard way?"

"Okay, look, I'll go with you. Please, just don't touch me. I'm a clairvoyant. Do you have to use cuffs? I'm still bruised from when I was held hostage."

"I said, put your hands behind your back." Grabbing my arm, he shoved me toward the door. His fingers wrapped around my left bicep, the part not protected by my elbow length gloves.

Helpless to stop it, my magic flared, responding to his touch. In an instant, Sheriff Lancer's memories spiraled into my mind. My psychic shield held them back, but I wasn't strong enough to keep them out for more than ten seconds at most.

"Stop touching my skin," I said, trying to jerk my arm out of his grasp, "I don't want your memories."

He pressed me against the door. I just managed to keep my cheek from touching the painted wood surface. It surely harbored additional memories that I didn't need to deal with.

"Shut up. I don't care what you want." He grabbed my hand and folded my wrist, pulling it toward the center of my back. At the same time he ordered me to put my other hand on the back of my head.

Dealing with a brief touch was one thing, but Lancer maintained his painful hold. His fevered, angry thoughts overwhelmed my shield. They entered my mind, a steady barrage of corrosive memories and savage intentions. Desperate to get away from the onslaught, I let my legs go slack. I landed hard on my butt and right thigh. My arm burned where my flesh had pulled through his fingertips.

"Please! Stop touching my skin. I'll go with you." I searched the room in vain, even though I knew escape was futile.

He ignored my pleas and lunged down. I scrabbled away, like a demented crab, narrowly evading his grasp. Instead of throwing himself on top of me, he stood and drew an item from his holster. At first glance, it looked like a firearm, but I realized it wasn't. He came at me with a stun gun.

Not wanting to exacerbate the situation, I refrained from using my TK. I was ready to protect myself, if need be, but hoped he'd listen to reason.

"Hurting me is not going to bring Stewart back," I shouted.

The mention of his brother's name had the effect of throwing ice water down his collar. A shocked expression crossed his features and his gait slowed. "Despicable. Checking my background to prop up your lies. I shouldn't be surprised. Maybe nobody else sees through you, but I'm no sucker."

"Marianne Cramer may have been a phony bitch, but we are not all alike," I blurted, frantic to come up with anything that would shock him into easing up on the aggressive tactics. "I know that's what you were thinking. You're also wondering whether my interviews with the FBI are going to be enough to cast reasonable doubt. And you're pissed off there wasn't any hard evidence tying me to the crime."

When he looked ready to pounce, I all but shrieked at him, "You asked Carl Jessup's secretary to call you as soon as I showed up to deal with Nick's estate! That's how you knew I was here. You've been waiting for the call so you could come arrest me without the fuss it would raise in Seattle."

The sheriff hesitated, and I continued, "You came here alone because not everyone in your department agrees there's a case against me. You argued with Chief Deputy Collins this morning about pursuing me. I got that from your thoughts. I'm for real. I'm not trying to piss you off. I just want you to stop touching my skin. Please."

He towered over me, the menacing weapon clutched in his white-knuckled grasp. A lank of his auburn hair fell forward, no longer neatly slicked back, and obscured his left eye. Although his expression of rage didn't lessen, I could almost see the wheels spinning inside his twisted mind. To my relief he didn't attempt to use the stun gun on me. When he straightened and holstered it, I kept the surprise from showing on my face.

"Get. Up," he ordered, clipping each word from between clenched teeth.

"Sure. No problem." The trembling in my voice irritated me, but I ignored it. "I'll go with you. You don't need to cuff me. But I suppose it's a rule?" I turned to put my hands behind my back and he slammed the cuffs on. As long as he didn't touch my skin, I wasn't going to complain. It wouldn't take much to tip him over again.

Sheriff Lancer had been psychologically damaged by his youngest brother Stewart's murder. Our brief skin contact revealed that, and more. During the murder investigation, the clairvoyant on the case, Marianne Cramer, revealed Stewart's involvement in some sordid activities—sex for drugs, chiefly. Lancer was not only a magiphobe but also a homophobe. He had refused to believe the readings and accused Marianne of lying. Eight years of simmering anger had intensified his bigotry.

I wasn't stupid enough to think my words had done much more than temporarily shock Lancer. If I stayed compliant, maybe I'd make it to the police station in one piece.

Casting out my TK, I monitored the sheriff's movements behind my back. When I concentrated, I could feel everything around me, right down to the vibrations in the air, like waves in a pond. It was just a matter of extending my magic, like invisible fingers, but not using it to physically grip anything.

Telekinesis—my freak version of radar.

The handcuffs rattled behind my back. As he fastened the first bracelet around my right wrist, he began, "You have the right to remain silent ..."

Never in my wildest nightmares did I ever dream I'd hear those words first hand, much less be searched for weapons or forcibly crammed into the back of a police car in handcuffs.

You have been reading an excerpt from

DECEIVER'S BOND

by Katherine Bayless

NOW AVAILABLE at

Amazon, B&N, Kobo, and iBooks

GLOSSARY

1995 Paranormal Rights Act
The landmark civil rights legislation in the United States that outlaws major forms of discrimination against magically inclined or cursed individuals.

The Between
The vast inter-dimensional nexus where the essence of every unique life force, from any one of an infinite number of worlds, intersects. Also known as Purgatory.

Brownie
In English vernacular, refers to a diminutive, roughly humanoid race from the Otherworld. Often mistaken for a hobgoblin, they are smaller, less hairy, and do not typically indulge in practical jokes. They have been known to inhabit human homes and perform household tasks in exchange for small gifts of food. Bread (especially brioche) and honey are said to be particular favorites. They work only at night and do not like to be seen. Of all the fae, brownies have been the most eager to reside permanently on Earth.

Circle of power
A ritually defined space, usually sealed with blood, used in spellcasting to control the flow of magic (and/or physical access) within its boundaries. See *summoner*, *ward*.

Clairvoyant
A mind psychic who can read the memories associated with an object (or person) through direct physical contact.

Clean room
An enclosed space that is completely psi-free, often within the confines of a psychiatric hospital.

Coventry Academy

The private elementary, middle, and high school, located in Coventry, WA, dedicated to the education of children capable of spellcasting, possessing a psychic ability, or cursed by magic, including those affected by the strigoi curse (vampirism) and therianthropy.

Coventry Hospital

The hospital, located in Coventry, WA, that specializes in the care of those gifted with psychic or magic powers or individuals suffering from magic related injuries or curses.

Cryokinetic

An individual who is capable of siphoning ambient heat from the atmosphere or other physical objects. Also known as an icemaker.

Curse

An enchantment that, by its very nature, imparts both positive and negative effects on an individual, location, or object. When applied to an individual, a curse is often (but not always) hereditary or transmittable via body fluids. Of all curses, therianthropy and the strigoi curse are perhaps the most well-known.

Daoine Sídhe

See *sidhe*.

Dark Arts

A field of magic dealing with death and darkness. Spellcasters capable of such magic are often mistakenly labeled as evil or in league with the devil.

Department of Paranormal Affairs

United States governmental agency created to oversee all citizens possessing magical abilities. Until it was declared unconstitutional twenty-five years ago, their ID program required the registration, tattooing, and tracking of all psychics, magic users, and cursed individuals from their birth (or manifestation date). The Magic User Registration Bill, if passed, threatens to restore some of these practices.

Divinor
An individual with the gift of precognition, the ability to foresee the future. Also known as oracle, seer, or prophesier.

Djinn
A spirit-like entity that inhabits a world beyond the dimensions of Earth. Also known as jinn, genie, or jinnī. They can be physical or incorporeal in nature and are known shape-shifters. In their dealings with humankind, they are most often neutral, neither good nor bad, typically practicing noninterference in human matters unless bound by blood compact. Other than their ability to transform and hold any physical shape, it is said they have the ability to move between dimensions and travel great distances at extreme speeds. The full extent of their power is unknown.

Elder race
A class of humanoid beings that existed before modern humans.

Elf
In English vernacular, a term that refers to a sidhe, popularized by J. R. R. Tolkien in his high-fantasy books. Because 'elf' has, in the distant past, been used to describe invisible demonic beings and other unsavory (and often fictional) creatures, it isn't a term the sidhe favor.

Essence
An individual's life-force, their soul.

Fae
In English vernacular, a term that refers to the many unique beings and creatures that inhabit the Otherworld.

Faery

In English vernacular, a term for the Otherworld.

Fairy

In English vernacular, an alternate term for fae that has come to be associated with the fictionalized versions of Otherworld creatures found in European folklore.

Fairyland

In English vernacular, often used as a derogatory term for the Otherworld.

Firestarter

See *pyrokinetic*.

Flight 208

The plane crash that was caused by a terrorist wielding an object enchanted with an inferno spell.

Gateway

A magical conduit, or portal, large enough to provide physical transport from one place to another, often between dimensions or worlds.

Geas

A magically enforced prohibition (similar to a curse but without the required positive/negative interdependency), which imposes a certain behavior upon its subject. A geas is either compulsory or voluntary. If compulsory, the subject is physically incapable of violating the geas. If the geas is voluntary, violation of the designated stricture may result in dishonor, physical or mental duress, or, in extreme cases, death.

Glamours

In English vernacular, a term that refers to a class of spells innate among the sidhe, which can be used to deceive, lure, or otherwise charm humans and other creatures.

Glindarian
A member of the Glindarian witchcraft sect.

Golem
A magical being created from inanimate matter that possesses limited intelligence and typically requires the continued direction of its creator in order to function.

Hobgoblin
In English vernacular, a term that refers to a diminutive, roughly humanoid race from the Otherworld who are known to be friendly but, more often than not, troublesome. They are prone to practical jokes and fond of living in human homes, helping with small household tasks in return for food. Unlike their smaller cousin, the brownie, hobgoblins are shape-shifters and quick to take offense at any perceived slight.

Icemaker
See *cryokinetic*.

Invisius Verso
A secret organization of telepaths and divinors. Its name means 'unseen influence' in Latin.

Leprechaun
In English vernacular, a term that refers to a diminutive, humanoid race from the Otherworld who are known for their skill in shoemaking and leatherworking. They are unrivaled in their ability to evade and escape capture, often by shape-shifting, but in the event they are apprehended, will grant a favor in exchange for release. Like brownies, they are content to reside permanently on Earth.

Levitation
The act of moving objects without interacting with them physically. See *telekinesis*.

Lycanthropy

A term used to describe the human to wolf transformation curse. See *therianthropy*.

Mage, Magic User, Magus

Terms used to describe an individual with the ability to cast spells. (Generally not used to describe an individual possessing a psychic power.)

Magi-phobe

A term (often derogatory) that refers to an individual who fears, distrusts, or condemns magic and those who are capable of magic.

Magic Reservations

Government owned compounds dedicated to the care and rearing of state adopted youngsters who are spellcasters, gifted with a psychic ability, or cursed.

Magic User Registration Bill

A United States bill, which, if passed into law, would require all magic users, psychics, and cursed individuals to register with the government.

Magician

Someone who does parlor tricks. Not a true magic user.

Necromancer

A sorcerer with power over the dead.

Normal

An individual who possesses no magical ability.

Oracle

See *divinor*.

Otherworld

The world where the fae reside. Also known as Faerie.

Paranormal Help Network

A non-profit organization devoted to providing support services to families of the magically gifted.

Paranormal Regulatory Commission

An international organization of psychics that governs the conduct of the psychic community.

Peabody's Beans

Coffee shop owned by Julie and Steven Peabody specializing in psi-free coffee, beverages, pastries, etc.

Pixie

In English vernacular, refers to a diminutive, humanoid race from the Otherworld who are endearingly childlike and benign in character. They live in large clans, are tremendously fond of music and dancing, and often partake in mischievous but harmless pranks.

Portal

A magical conduit, most often forged during a summoning, that connects two different locations, providing access to another dimension or world. A portal may or may not be large enough for physical transport. See gateway.

Prophecy

A prediction of the future.

Prophesier

See *divinor*.

Psi-free

Term used to describe something that is free of life-essence contamination, untouched by humans or animals.

Psi-ward

An area within a hospital that specializes in the care of those gifted with psychic or magic powers or individuals suffering from magic related injuries or curses.

Psychic Shield

The mental shield fortified by magic that all clairvoyants and telepaths use to control the inflow of thoughts and memories into their own minds.

Psychic

An individual gifted with a mind power, either telekinesis, pyrokinesis, cryokinesis, divination, truthsaying, or clairvoyance. Sensitives are also sometimes psychic.

Puget Pacific Towers

Office building in downtown Seattle where Sotheby's is located. Across the street and a block away from Peabody's Beans.

Purgatory

See *the Between*.

Pyrokinetic

An individual who is capable of generating ambient heat. Also known as a firestarter.

Rowan

A member of the Rowan witchcraft sect.

Runestone

A stone marked with a runic inscription, often used in witchcraft to focus and enhance the magus' spellcasting.

SAM

Seattle Art Museum.

SCU

Supernatural Crime Unit.

Seer

See *divinor*.

Sensitive

An individual who can detect (and often identify) specific types of magic and/or individual spells.

Shape-shifter

A being that can change its shape and hold its new form, either by virtue of magic or a curse. A werewolf is a type of shape-shifter.

Sidhe

An elder race that is arguably the most humanoid of all the magical beings that inhabit the Otherworld. The sidhe are known by other sobriquets—aos sí, aes sídhe, daoine sídhe, daoine síth, and (perhaps least liked by the creatures themselves) fairy and elf. Humans who are reluctant to name them directly often refer to them as 'the good neighbors,' 'the fair folk,' or 'people of the mounds.' Their Earthbound gateways are typically encapsulated by a mound of earth or encircled by stones or mushrooms.

Skin-suit

A thin bodysuit crafted from psi-free, moisture-repelling fabric, used to prevent contact between a clairvoyant and other individuals or objects.

Sorcerer/Sorceress

A magus who uses gestures for casting spells, they are typically restricted to a certain field of magic.

Sorcery

Spellcasting performed by a sorcerer or sorceress.

Stake-burner

A derogatory term often applied to magi-phobic individuals, especially those in judicial or law enforcement positions.

Strigoi

An individual affected by the strigoi curse; a vampire.

Strigoi Curse

The curse that causes vampirism. An individual afflicted by this curse is granted immortality, superior strength, and, in a limited fashion, the ability to shape-shift. Countering each of these boons is an equally powerful weakness. (This duality is the hallmark of all curses.) In the case of vampirism, the cursed individual's existence is restricted to the night—during daylight hours they are helpless and virtually comatose. To satisfy their thirst for sustenance, they must drink human blood. Precious metals cause great pain and weakness. The most powerful strigoi are almost always blessed with one additional gift that may or may not be off-set by an additional weakness.

Summoner

A magic user capable of summoning a spirit being, usually from another dimension or universe, to a designated location, typically a circle of power.

Supernatural Talent and Company (ST&C)

Paranormal talent agency located in Seattle, owned by Jack Beaumont and Lire Devon.

Telekinetic

A psychic capable of levitating an object. A type one telekinetic can move only inanimate objects, a type two can move only animate objects, a type three can move both animate and inanimate objects. See *levitation*.

Telepath

A psychic capable of reading human thoughts without skin contact. Some (but not all) are capable of inserting memories into a human subject's mind. Fewer still are able to assume enough control to direct their human subject's actions.

Therianthropy

Term used to describe the curse of human to animal transformation. An individual afflicted with this curse is granted the ability to transform into a particular animal. Only rigorous training and self-discipline allows the cursed individual to retain their human consciousness during transformation. Depending upon their skill, this transformation can take place at will, however, during nights of the full moon, the transformation is compulsory. See *werewolf.*

Threefold Principal

The belief that the energy a magic user (or psychic) dispenses, whether it be positive or negative, will be returned threefold. You reap what you sow.

TK

A slang term for telekinesis. See *levitation.*

True Name

A being's intrinsic name, one which is bound so closely that it's tied to their essence. When pronounced with intimate familiarity, it can be used in a ritual to summon the being between worlds.

Truthsayer

A psychic who is capable of detecting whether a person is lying.

Ùruisg

A diminutive, roughly humanoid race from the Otherworld. Like the brownie, they are one of the few fae that thrive living on Earth, however, they are considerably less social and rarely provide their human neighbors with domestic help. On Earth, they live outdoors near streams and waterfalls.

Vampire

An alternate term for 'strigoi,' one that is viewed as somewhat coarse by those affected by the strigoi curse.

Ward

A type of ensorcellment that regulates or prohibits magic or physical interactions that take place within its area of effect. Such spells are often (but not exclusively) used in conjunction with a magic circle or within the natural boundary provided by a dwelling's foundation.

Warlock/Witch

A magus who can only employ spoken or chanted magic, they use runestones and/or other objects (such as wands) to power or strengthen their spells.

Were

Someone who is cursed with therianthropy.

Which Witch

The paranormal talent agency owned by Judith Kitchell.

Will-o'-the-Wisp

In English vernacular, refers to a diminutive spirit-like being from the Otherworld, often seen glowing like a lantern at night, that are known to lead travelers astray.

Witchcraft

Spoken or chanted magic.

Zombie

A human or animal corpse that has been raised from dead and animated by magical means.

ABOUT THE AUTHOR

Photo © 2010 Sarina Hamer

Daydreamer and committed late-sleeper, Katherine Bayless writes paranormal fantasy and romance for fun and occasional profit. When she isn't adventuring vicariously through her stories, Katherine enjoys a variety of arts and crafts, lays waste to enemies in *Diablo III* and *Path of Exile*, and indulges her addictions to cooking shows, science documentaries, and digital photography.

Katherine's writing career began when she wondered what a clairvoyant's life would be like, an idea that sparked her imagination and added 'creative writing' to her brimming list of hobbies. In her pre-author life, Katherine worked as a software engineer in the game industry, where she not only met her awesome husband but also discovered her passion for fantasy stories and role-playing games.

Over the past thirty years, she has moved eleven times, calling California, Oregon, Washington, and Illinois home states at one time or another. She currently lives happily in view of Central Oregon's ancient volcanoes with her husband, kids, two sweet and shamelessly spoiled corgis named Sunny and Luna, and Zeke, a cabinet-opening, treat-stealing commando that doesn't know his own name because everyone just calls him Cat.

Although Katherine freely admits she'd rather live inside her head and write stories instead of blog posts, she always makes the time to respond to emails and blog comments.

You can find her website at www.katherinebayless.com.

Made in the USA
Columbia, SC
26 June 2021